HARVEST

a novel

by

JEB LADOUCEUR

To Jean
Best of Luck

America Star Books
Frederick, Maryland

© 2014 by Jeb Ladouceur.
All rights reserved. No part of this book may be reproduced, stored in a retrieval system or transmitted in any form or by any means without the prior written permission of the publishers, except by a reviewer who may quote brief passages in a review to be printed in a newspaper, magazine or journal.

First printing

All characters in this book are fictitious, and any resemblance to real persons, living or dead, is coincidental.

America Star Books has allowed this work to remain exactly as the author intended, verbatim, without editorial input.

Softcover 9781634480901
PUBLISHED BY AMERICA STAR BOOKS, LLLP
www.americastarbooks.com
Frederick, Maryland

Books by Jeb Ladouceur

The Palindrome Plot
Calamity Hook
Frisco
The Banana Belt
Sparrowbush
The Oba Project
Mark if the Zodiac
The Dealer
Harvest

The Hippocratic Oath

I will prescribe regimens for the good of my patients according to my ability and my judgment and never do harm to anyone.

I will give no deadly medicine to any one if asked, nor suggest any such counsel; and similarly I will not give a woman a pessary to cause an abortion.

But I will preserve the purity of my life and my arts.

I will not cut for stone, even for patients in whom the disease is manifest; I will leave this operation to be performed by practitioners, specialists in this art.

In every house where I come I will enter only for the good of my patients, keeping myself far from all intentional ill-doing and all seduction and especially from the pleasures of love with women or men, be they free or slaves.

All that may come to my knowledge in the exercise of my profession or in daily commerce with men, which ought not to be spread abroad, I will keep secret and will never reveal.

If I keep this oath faithfully, may I enjoy my life and practice my art, respected by all humanity and in all times; but if I swerve from it or violate it, may the reverse be my life.

Dedication

To my friend, Elizabeth Ann,
a distinguished Army officer and physician,
who is the inspiration for the heroine
in the fictitious tale that follows.
Anyone fortunate enough to know this fine soldier
will recognize her instantly…and fondly.
J.L.

Acknowledgments

This is my ninth novel, and the dozens of generous supporters mentioned in previous acknowledgments know who they are. I hereby thank them all once again.

But there are several new friends who have encouraged me during the past year, purely out of kindness. Permit me to list a few of them.

Jean Gustavson, Cardiologist, is the kind of person every author needs in his corner. Her enthusiasm is absolutely contagious and (no pun intended) heartwarming.

And what shall I say about Jeffrey Sanzel, author, actor, director, and guiding light at Long Island's renowned Theatre Three. He has read all my books during the past six months, and his generous comments have made even me blush!

Felice Cantatore of *The Entrepreneur Center* has long spearheaded the annual 'Best of Long Island' competition for *The Long Island Press*, and while I have never overtaken the great Nelson DeMille as *Top Long Island Author* in the voting, I hereby thank Felice for conducting this exciting contest in which I have been nominated for four successive years.

When Cousin Chesley Ladouceur said '*The Palindrome Plot*' is the best book he's ever read, his inclusion on this page was assured. Ditto for lifelong friend and neighbor John Figari—who selected '*Sparrowbush*' for the accolade. And my earnest thanks to enthusiastic proponent of '*The Dealer*,' the lovely Jane Sharpe.

Actress of exquisite taste, Jennifer Collester Tully, has been quick to applaud my writing, though her stage skills far exceed my literary efforts. When Jen compliments you, you've been acclaimed by a true professional.

At a recent book signing (where I make it a point to introduce all authors in attendance) I failed to recognize celebrated novelist and television producer, Linda Maria Frank—I had been told she wouldn't be able to come that night. It was a most unfortunate gaffe. Ms. Frank knows I didn't ignore her intentionally, but I now scan audiences much more diligently when checking for the presence of fellow writers.

Over the years several friends have permitted me the fictitious use of their names (Jim Sentman, Nancy Darman, Debbie Lange, Steve Rosenberg, Dave Knoernschild, Bob Eckelhoff, Hank Scheinberg, JoAnn Staulcup, Mugs Zangrillo, C.B. Knadle…often in more than one book). I hope they got a kick out of their alter ego sorties into the exciting world of fiction, even if often the "equivalents" were, as the ever-articulate Jim Sentman once noted, "…*as like to me, as I to Hercules.*"

Thanks again to my literary agent, Al Hart. First, last, and always, the best there is.

Jeb Ladouceur
Labor Day, 2014

Chapter 1

Doctor Forrester leaned forward and examined Harold's abdomen.

Doctor Simeon Forrester pried his spectacles from beneath the bands that held his surgical mask in place. He lifted the glasses toward the circular overhead light, squinted, then wiped the steel-rimmed lenses with a paper towel he'd taken from the anesthesiologist's table. "What time do you leave, Lis?"

Lieutenant Colonel Lisbeth Wren eyed the large round clock on the wall—it read 7:02 AM. "About forty-eight hours," she said. "Oh-seven-thirty, Wednesday morning." She extended her right hand forward and to one side. "Number four scalpel."

O.R. Nurse Amy Longpré plucked the lancet from a row of gleaming instruments on a steel tray and slapped the handle solidly into Doctor Wren's palm.

The snoring patient on the table lay swaddled in two green paper blankets. Forrester rolled down the lower one. Now, in addition to his head, a foot-long section of '*Harold Sickpig's*' iodine-painted belly was exposed.

Lisbeth Wren paused...and frowned. "Who the hell shaved this guy?"

Doctor Forrester leaned forward and examined Harold's abdomen through the newly buffed eyeglasses. Along one side of an eight-inch, purple-painted line intended to guide the surgeon's blade, there was a series of small nicks. They had obviously been treated with either styptic pencil, or alum in some other form. Forrester glanced inquiringly at Nurse Longpré, who shook her head and shrugged almost imperceptibly.

"Somebody's got a heavy hand with the razor," Lisbeth said. "Let's swab him again, Simeon…then we'll start. I'll feel better if those scrapes are freshly cleansed." The willowy Doctor handed the long scalpel back to the nurse, peeled off her gloves, and strode toward the scrub room. She pulled down her surgical mask. "And for God's sake, sponge away that clotting agent," she called over her shoulder.

* * *

United flight 1119 from New York to the Principality of Ovosok near the European Adriatic coast, swept in a smooth southeastern arc in the sky over London, and the big Boeing 767 began its due-south descent toward the Ovosok capital of Prishta while still above dreary Belgrade…two hundred miles from the flight's destination.

Unlike its fellow European Principalities of Liechtenstein, Monaco, and Andorra to the west, Ovosok boasts its own international airport, a small but modern facility close to the landlocked country's border with Serbia. There, a single 8100-foot runway lies in a north/south configuration in the valley between the Kajlog and Shar mountain ranges. Prishta is ten miles away, practically abutting the Serbian boundary…Camp Billingham, is an equal distance from Ovosok International but in the direction of Albania and the snow-capped Kajlog range.

Billingham was where Army Lieutenant Colonel Lisbeth Wren and her three field-grade companions were to be deployed for the next four months.

From her port window seat, Major Peggy Kelvin scanned the modest panorama that was Prishta at midday. The Psychiatrist nudged Lis Wren, who awoke with a start, yawned, and peered through the window to determine where they were.

"That Prishta?" said Lis, stifling another yawn that finally unplugged her ears.

"That's it," said Peggy. "The Jewel of Ovosok. Know what's nuts, though?" she said pointing, "See that river leading in from the lake?...the thing totally disappears 'til it picks up again on the other side of town."

Lis Wren craned her neck. Indeed, there obviously was no river to be seen passing through the center of Prishta... it simply ran up to the southernmost row of buildings, vanished, and resumed at the city's northern perimeter. Yes, a river had run directly through downtown Prishta at one time. But now it flows through a series of underground tunnels and is funneled up to the surface only after undercutting the population center. The citizens of the capital had carried out the unique diversionary tactic in self-defense hundreds of years ago. Apparently, the Nosduh River became polluted when merchants along the stream's banks took to dumping their waste there. This, of course, resulted in a horrendous smell and the only viable solution was to make the open sewer inaccessible to the Ovosokan litterbugs...the alternative was to get out of Dodge altogether.

* * *

Bashkim Inasah sat sipping sweet tea outside the oblong oval of shade cast by a faded Cinzano umbrella. He was determined to take in as much of the waning November sun as possible while he watched aircraft large and small swoop downwind from the north, then turn base leg, before settling into their final, gradual approach to the Prishta airport.

At his table on the western bank of the Kumbardhi River, Bashkim removed a gold pocket watch from his vest, pressed a release button at the three o'clock position, and read the time. It was three forty-five. Six more minutes.

The 48-year-old curator of the historic 'Quilted Mosque' of Tavoto, a few miles south of the Ovosok/Madonica border, had waited months for this day, and he assumed the bright, sunny weather must be a good omen. This part of The Balkans, after all, was not necessarily noted for good weather…certainly not during the frequently unstable time preceding Christmas, at any rate. November was the month when rainfall was at its peak in Ovosok, and daily humidity averaged a bone-chilling eighty percent, rain or shine.

How great of Allah then (*peace be upon Him*) to bless the young woman's arrival with such abundant sunshine and balmy temperatures.

Bashkim noted a huge plane's landing lights, bright even in the clear afternoon sky north of where he sat. He looked at his pocket watch again. *That must be her*, he thought.

* * *

Lisbeth Wren looked across the 767's portside aisle to where the other two Army Majors in her four-woman contingent sat. Like she and Peggy Kelvin, they were dressed in Army Combat Uniforms—temperate-weather desert boots, two-piece, mottled green and white camouflaged fatigues over desert tan T-shirts, and matching camo patrol caps.

Deprived of proximity to a window in the plane's three-seat-wide center configuration, the pair watched the big jet's approach to the airport on flat-screen television monitors built into the backs of the seats in front of them. One of the women, Doctor Nanette Stufkoski, applied a dab of pale pink lip gloss as she gazed at the approaching asphalt runway 36 over the top of her small compact mirror. The officer to her right...an attractive woman of thirty-eight...busied herself re-folding a camo field jacket and inserting it once again beneath her seat. The strip on the jacket's right breast bore the name COCKBYRNE in capital letters; on the left was the designation U.S. ARMY. A combat patch was affixed to the right shoulder beneath the American flag, and the appropriate Unit emblem adorned the left. The same arrangement decked out the fatigue shirt which, in addition, held a small insignia centered approximately over the sternum. Like all the uniform's strips and patches, it was affixed with Velcro, and contained the single oak leaf symbol of the wearer's rank. Lisbeth's was black befitting her LTC status...the Majors' insignia was a dark brown.

Three of the Doctors wore their hair in snug buns at the nape of the neck. Only Colonel Wren sported a short pony tail. All four officers were blond, ranging from platinum to strawberry, as if flaxen hair were somehow required of a high-ranking female soldier. At age forty-nine, and on her fifth deployment, Lisbeth Wren was senior in age, grade, and length of service. She was also the tallest and slimmest of the uniformed group. There could be little doubt that those fetching attributes contributed greatly to dozens of turned heads and 'come hither' glances that men, especially, bestowed on her wherever she went.

Those admirers would soon include the handsome Bashkim Inasah, who up until now had relied on only a slightly out-of-focus snapshot to identify the slender Doctor…a grainy black-and-white photograph taken the previous spring in, of all places, Machu Picchu, in the Peruvian Andes. The other picture that had been sent to Bashkim earlier in the summer was a much clearer color shot of Lisbeth's dog Gigi, as she lay on the living room rug…looking intently into the camera.

Chapter 2

The man watched the four women as they strode in step across the terminal floor.

The wide-bodied Boeing came neatly to Earth a mere ten or twelve feet past the large, white numbers 3 and 6 that indicated the runway was situated on a due-north trajectory. The 767 then rolled easily for a mile and a quarter before turning sharply onto the last available westbound taxiway leading to the airport terminal.

It was six minutes after four PM, local time, when the plane carrying Colonel Lisbeth Wren and her three fellow Doctors wheeled to its assigned berth at Gate Twelve. As the huge Pratt & Whitney engines wound down, whistled, and stopped, the four American women stood up as one, retrieved their carry-on baggage, and made their way smartly to the open front cabin door.

* * *

Three Corporals and a Second Lieutenant, all ACU-clad, all men, stood waiting inside Gate Twelve's automatic, tinted glass door. No one in the welcoming quartet seemed more than nineteen, and the young officer stepped forward from among the non-com detail as soon as the Doctors entered the terminal.

Colonel Wren had led the way across the concrete ramp and was first through the door. The Lieutenant saluted her and she returned the protocol. There was no attempt to relieve any of the women of the luggage they carried, all of which was assumed to be personal and private in nature. All four field-grade officers carried large ACU toiletry bags, and the three Majors also lugged heavy-looking Sling bags. In addition to her own hygiene bag, Wren toted a padded camo attaché.

The Lieutenant looked up from a partial flight manifest. "Welcome to Ovosok Colonel…Majors…trust you had an uneventful flight."

"Great flight," said Lis Wren. "Where's the john?"

"Ahead and to your left, ma'am," said Lieutenant Forbes. "We'll meet you at carousel three."

"Guard this with your life, Lieutenant," said Colonel Wren handing Forbes her briefcase. "It's my four-month supply of Gummy Bears."

"Yes ma'am," the newly minted OCS graduate responded self-consciously, as the non-coms failed in a collective attempt to stifle their laughter. The three Majors handed the Corporals their overstuffed Sling packs and one of them, Nan Stufkoski, said. "She's not kidding, men." Major Stufkoski was a dentist. She knew a thing or two about the hazards of Gummy Bear addiction.

Over the women's room entrance was a blue and white sign that bore the international symbol of a rudimentary standing figure with a dress pinched at the waist and flaring out at knee-level in an inverted V. As the four uniformed Army Doctors entered the lavatory, three women wearing burkas came out. Visitors from another planet might logically have wondered why these people, so diametrically different in their manner of dress, were utilizing a facility identified by a symbol that looked not at all like either the women in, trousers, boots, and caps...or the mysterious females in billowing garb, sandals, and veils.

* * *

Bashkim Inasah had driven his Citroen the few miles from the riverside café where he'd been waiting. He now sat in a designated smoking area of the Ovosok air terminal holding a Murad cigarette European-style, pinched between his thumb and forefinger, palm upward, wrist bent forward at an acute angle.

He doubted Lisbeth Wren smoked. Few American Doctors did, Bashkim had heard. But that was none of his concern. The curator of Tavoto's 'Quilted Mosque' was interested only in the tall woman's surgical expertise...coupled, of course, with her inordinate love for one of the homeliest little animals that Inasah had ever seen.

Even while he inhaled the acrid smoke from his pungent Turkish cigarette, the fine-featured man watched the four women as they strode in step across the terminal's marble floor, the Lieutenant Colonel leading the way, and disappeared into the lavatory. He removed an iPhone from the handkerchief pocket of his suede jacket and glanced at the four soldiers in the welcoming detail. They had reached revolving baggage carousel #3, and were watching for eight stenciled, ACU-camouflaged duffle bags that Major Stufkoski had described.

Bashkim Inasah was confident he had not raised anyone's suspicions; however he buried the tip of his cigarette in a three-foot-tall cylinder topped with a round tray of sand, and walked to the nearest newsstand, talking and laughing into an empty phone as he went. Once at a high, free-spinning magazine rack, Bashkim walked to the far side of the wire display, turned so that he could see the women's room entrance as well as carousel #3, and selected the November copy of *Prishta Today*. He flipped casually through the first few pages and read the title and sub-head of the lead article:

A CITY HAS SURRENDERED TO MODERNITY
Prishta now wears a false face so that it may lie to the world, pretending that we live in decency, while nothing could be farther from the truth.

"Poor Prishta," the suave Madonican muttered disdainfully. "What does she know of civility?"

He glanced at the washroom door; the easily identifiable American women had not yet re-appeared. Bashkim then peered over the top of *Prishta Today* and saw that the three Army Corporals had commandeered a rolling luggage cart. They were busily loading eight large duffle bags from the moving carousel onto the transporter's flat, five-foot-long surface. The Lieutenant was halfway to the curbside door of the terminal, hauling the three smaller Sling bags by their straps. Lisbeth Wren's attaché was tucked securely under his right arm.

An olive drab Astro Van with U.S. ARMY stenciled in white on the sides and across the hood was parked in front of the center door between two black, advertising festooned 'London Cabs.' Lieutenant Forbes placed the Sling bags in the rearmost compartment of the van and locked it. With the attaché still firmly in his possession, the young junior grade officer returned to the passenger terminal door, which opened automatically. He stayed in the cone of the electric eye and the Corporal pushing the cart guided it through the wide entranceway, as the other two non-coms exited the pavilion through a narrower door.

The Lieutenant handed the van's keys to one of the unencumbered soldiers. "Pack everything as far back as possible," he instructed, "then unfold the third seat. It'll be a tight fit," he told the leering soldiers, "but you'll have to suffer through it. Prentiss, you sit up front with me."

"Maybe Corporal Manning should ride in front," said Prentiss. "He's bigger'n I am, Sir."

"Good thinking," said Forbes. "Prentiss and Rivers, you two can squeeze in with the women…Manning, you're up front." The Lieutenant took the keys from a satisfied-looking Corporal Rivers, and still clutching Colonel Wren's briefcase, the Detail Commander instructed his men to stay with the Astro Van…while he returned to Carousel #3 to wait for the Doctors.

As they stood at curbside next to the boxy vehicle, Corporal Manning looked balefully at Corporal Prentiss. "You know what Stevie?" he said darkly, "sometimes you can be a real prick."

"Prentiss can't help it," said Mike Rivers. "He gets a hard on if the wind blows."

The American women emerged from the lavatory and Bashkim Inasah replaced the copy of *Prishta Today* in the magazine rack. Majors Kelvin, Cockbyrne, and Stufkoski strode toward the waiting Lieutenant, while Lisbeth Wren spun to the right and hurried to the newsstand. She clutched a handful of euros purchased online while processing at McGuire Air Force Base in New Jersey, and she nearly collided with the dapper Bashkim as she circled the periodicals stand and brushed by him.

"*Mah FAHL-nee,*" she said in dictionary Albanian and prepared to lope in the direction of an amused cashier at the low glass counter.

"You are excused," Inasah responded in perfect English. The Madonican held the blushing Colonel's gaze with a dazzling smile that revealed perfectly even, snow white teeth beneath a slim, well-trimmed mustache.

"Oh," Lisbeth said, "you speak English."

"Not well, I fear, but perhaps I can be of help. You're in a hurry."

Wren nodded in the direction of her uniformed companions. "My associates…they're waiting for me. Do you happen to know if this place sells bookmarks?"

Bashkim Inasah frowned, squinted slightly and scanned the counter area as he stroked his square, smooth-shaven chin in contemplation. He called to the clerk by the cash register, "*El Kafrah. Sud nopthet miz lubra min?*"

The young worker answered apologetically in words equally incomprehensible to Lisbeth Wren, and the helpful man shook his head and smiled. "I'm afraid not, Miss…Miss…"

"Wren…Lisbeth Wren."

"Ah, yes," said Bashkim examining the stenciled name strip on the Lieutenant Colonel's ACU blouse. He reached in the interior breast pocket of his maroon sport jacket and removed a white calling card bearing only one line of black, embossed type.

"Lisbeth—a lovely name," he observed. "Simple and charming." He jotted some numbers on the back of the card and extended it.

"I know a place that sells the most elegant bookmarks in all of Southeast Europe. Perhaps, after you are settled, you will permit me to show it to you."

Lis took the card bearing Inasah's name and turned it over. He had written what was obviously a phone number.

"Maybe so," she said, tucking the card into her shoulder pocket…and flashing her own sparkling smile for the tall, well-dressed man's benefit.

Then she walked quickly toward her fellow Army officers, slowing only once to glance back at Bashkim Inasah.

Chapter 3

The Islamic practice best-known is the Salat—the ritual performed five times a day.

Bashkim Inasah was one of the few Muslim men working in Tavoto who could have gotten away with shaving his face, save for the thin 'Clark Gable' line of neat, black bristle that adorned his upper lip. As curator of the 'Quilted Mosque,' he'd asked Grand Imam Nazmi ben Zullah during his initial interview in 1999, whether he would be required frequently to meet with his Christian counterparts in this city where so many Roman Catholics, Protestants, and Eastern Rite adherents were employed as administrators of the area's Shrines.

The answer, of course, was that he surely would be thus called upon.

"Well, then, Imam, will I not serve Allah (*Blessings and Peace be upon Him*) to the fullest by blending in more completely with my infidel associates? Surely a man may sacrifice his beard in the name of successful Muslim enterprise."

The Grand Imam had agreed quickly and wholeheartedly… especially after Bashkim had speculated that the less hirsute his appearance, the less likely it was the 'Quilted Mosque' would be taken for an Orthodox church! Though *Salat* would likely account for that, he hastened to note.

Perhaps the Islamic practice best-known among non-Muslims is the *Salat*—the ritual prayer that is performed five times a day: At dawn, noon, mid-afternoon, sunset, and in the evening. The call to prayer is issued by a leather-lunged *Muezzin,* or a recording.

In *Salat,* the person praying always faces the holy city of Mecca, and a prayer mat is commonly knelt on. *Salat* may be performed individually when necessary, but special blessings are said to ensue when the ritual is conducted in the company of other Muslims. The major weekly prayer is the one recited in the mosque at noon on Fridays.

When performing *Salat* at the 'Quilted Mosque' or any other, Muslim believers align themselves in horizontal rows behind the Imam. He is the cleric who takes over after the *Muezzin,* sets the example for the various postures to be assumed, and leads his flock in the prayers. In that regard, the Islamic prayer sequence the world over starts with the believer standing, and he moves through a number of simple positions until the supplicant is kneeling, but never fully prostrate.

Lately, Muslim women are allowed to pray in the same general gathering as men, but they must position themselves behind the males. The rationale is that this keeps distraction to a minimum…at least, presumably, on the part of the men.

As Bashkim Inasah was keenly aware, *Salat* must always be preceded by a ceremonial cleansing of the face, hands, and feet…in that order. In some Muslim communities, of course, water is not always available for the washing, and in those locales, ordinary sand may be substituted. There is no shortage of sand in Muslim countries.

At the five appointed times, even in Tavoto's frequently toured 'Quilted Mosque,' the *Muezzin* announces the call to prayer, always from the building's minaret, and featured in the liturgical summons are the terms: *God is great… There is no god* *but God...Muhammad is God's prophet...*and the reminder that *Prayer is better than sleep.*

These days, the *Muezzin* is often heard on radio broadcasts originating in the Ovosok cities of Prishta or Jaziref, home of Bashkim Inasah. Indeed, many Muslims subscribe to a Madonican alerting service which sends a notice to the believer's phone or pocket pager that it is time to pray. The curator of Tavoto's principal tourist attraction would never have endorsed such invasive nonsense, however. In fact, as Bashkim drove south on the highway that connects Ovosok International Airport to Jaziref, he even turned off the Citroen's radio. The late afternoon sun was hanging low over the *Krahina Malore* of Central Albania. He did not need the *Muezzin* to inform him that it would soon be time for Sunset Prayer. Nor did he require prompting to know that *Prayer is better than sleep.* At eighty miles per hour, that was fairly obvious.

Twenty-four miles south of Prishta, the highway that bisects the Ovosok Valley branched east and west. Two miles to the right was Jaziref...Camp Billingham, where Lisbeth Wren was headed, was twice that distance to the east. Bashkim Inasah wondered when he would hear from the tall woman with the radiant blue eyes. It needn't be soon, he told himself. What mattered was that her trip had been safe and her arrival without incident. It was the only thing Simeon Forrester would be concerned about when Inasah e-mailed him at six o'clock—that, and of course the prompt deposit of twenty-five thousand euros in the veterinarian's discretionary bank account.

* * *

Ten minutes after Bashkim had turned for home on the westbound spur of the Ovosok Valley highway, the Army Astro Van bearing the eight American soldiers approached a slim fork in the road, veered to the left in the twilight, and began a gradual, four-mile climb into the foothills of the Shar Mountains. There, Camp Billingham, constructed on nine hundred acres of once-rolling farmland, suddenly spread out before them near the town of Civesoru.

Billingham is a huge facility by any army's standards. It is also a menacing looking place that features a seven-mile perimeter, fortified by an eight-foot-high berm and a forbidding razor-wire-topped fence.

The massive camp was established in June 1999, when it was built from the ground up by flattening two long hills and utilizing earthmovers to fill a formerly verdant valley between them. Camp Billingham was intended to be used as a staging point for the thousands of U.S. forces stationed in Ovosok in a multi-national NATO Brigade. Some 4,000 American service members were initially stationed in the leveled farm fields near Civesoru…now the number of Temporary Duty personnel is almost double that.

The camp's fortifications have been dramatically expanded as well. Today nine wooden guard towers are positioned on the installation's perimeter, and the battalion has modified the battlements by placing each on a high concrete pad. This arrangement, coupled with more-prominent tower access ladders, gives Billingham an instantly prison-like appearance no matter the direction from which the camp is approached. Be that as it may, the added tower elevation means that soldiers now view their assigned area from a strategically enhanced seventeen feet above ground as opposed to the former three yards—twice the height.

Its neo-penal facade notwithstanding, there are two well-equipped dining facilities within Camp Billingham's exterior fortifications. There, food is expertly prepared, with a wide variety of main and side dishes to choose from. There are salad and potato bars in each of the vast cafeterias, as well as a popular multiple-dessert bar. Even alcohol-free beer is available, and though full meals are served at designated times, each dining hall features a round-the-clock section where sandwiches, fruit, coffee, and continental breakfast can be obtained.

Soldiers live in what are known as Southeast Asia Huts. There are approximately 250 such semi-permanent SEA Huts set aside as living quarters and offices. Each structure consists of five living areas that accommodate as many as six soldiers per unit, and every building contains one large bathroom that, in turn, houses individual toilet and shower stalls.

Male and female SEA Huts are separate, with beds that most personnel describe as comfortable. Significantly, every room has its own heating and air conditioning units…an important feature in a climate that can feature hot summers and cold winters.

The best-equipped store in all of Ovosok is the Camp Billingham Post Exchange. Military personnel on deployment to the Principality can buy practically anything at the PX… always in stock are such appliances as reasonably priced DVD players, coffee makers, television sets, stereo systems, and the like.

In short, Billingham is hardly your grandfather's Army barracks.

The Astro Van approached the camp's main gate, and two Military Policemen with M-1 rifles held diagonally across their chests blocked the roadway. Lieutenant Forbes rolled down his driver's window and handed three stapled pages to a third MP who had drawn near the boxy vehicle with his weapon slung. The man…a Sergeant…read the typed order, looked sternly from the manifest toward the four women, walked to the back of the van where he counted the ACU bags, and finally re-approached the Lieutenant. He handed the paperwork back to Forbes and saluted crisply. The MPs holding the rifles stood aside as the Lieutenant returned the salute…and the olive drab van rolled into Camp Billingham.

"He's pretty cute," Colonel Lisbeth Wren whispered to Major Stufkoski, as she nodded toward the Sergeant in the stainless steel helmet. "Did I ever tell you I used to be a cop?"

Chapter 4

The orphaned youth would remain a Muslim in name only.

The only child of devout Albanian immigrants, at the age of fourteen Bashkim Inasah had seen his Muslim parents murdered by a contingent of Belgrade assassins in 1983. They were shot as they prayed evening *Salat* in their modest home in Jaziref…where Bashkim still lived alone almost thirty years later. The elder Inasah's only crime against the former state of Yugoslavia had been that, as a teacher of Balkan literature, he had run afoul of Tito-appointed officials determined to cleanse Ovosok schools of anything related to the despised Albanian-language educational system.

Woven into a tapestry that hangs inside the front door of the modest stone house are the dying words of Bashkim's scholarly father, Hamad. They were taken from a poem by the great nationalist leader, Pashko Vasa.

> "Awaken, Albania, wake from your slumber.
> Let us all, as brothers, swear a common oath.
> Not to look to church or mosque.
> The faith of the Albanian is Albanianism!"

On a small shelf adjacent to the framed embroidery sat a worn copy of the Koran with a handmade bookmark protruding from its dog-eared pages. Bashkim had not opened the book since the night the Serbian pillagers had descended upon the house on Ephtah Street. Nor would he ever again. The orphaned youth would remain a Muslim in name only. If *Allah* could not prevent the killing of innocents, he reasoned, what promise did He possibly hold in store for the likes of a simple, pubescent student of fifteenth century architecture?

Bashkim turned on an overhead light and locked the narrow front door. He removed his maroon suede jacket, tossed it on an upholstered chair facing the fireplace, and removed a book of coded names and phone numbers from one of two end tables flanking a leather sofa. First, he would call Jawwad, at Raiffeisen Zentralbank. When assured that the transfer of funds had been made to Citibank in Mineola, Long Island, he would call Simeon Forrester for the last time.

* * *

The 70-year-old veterinarian had just sat down to a lunch of fruit cup topped with a scoop of cottage cheese and a generous dollop of mayonnaise. Two rectangular slices of crisp Melba toast and a glass of skim milk rounded out the midday meal. The room where Simeon Forrester, DVM, sat slowly eating and studying the horse racing pages of the New York Post, was adjacent to the kennel section of the Uniondale Animal Hospital which he had founded in 1970. Over those forty years, Doctor Forrester had grown accustomed to the constant din of barking dogs, bleating goats, and grunting hogs echoing from the other side of the kitchenette's exterior cinder block wall.

An inveterate gambler, he had also become inured to leaving much of his earnings at nearby Aqueduct Racetrack from late October to early May, and Belmont Park and Saratoga Race Course the rest of the year. Fortunately, Simeon Forrester was a committed bachelor…accordingly, the dispensing of his considerable income was largely optional. There was no family adversely affected by his hopeless and expensive habit.

Nor was the locally renowned vet's lifestyle an extravagant one. No luxurious clothes, cars, or women for Simeon…he found no allure in lavish vacations to exotic places either…even the satisfaction of his most basic needs bespoke simplicity… the very food now on the Formica table before him was a barometer of the man's frugality.

And yet, since the age of thirty, the septuagenarian had thought nothing of wagering a thousand dollars on a thirty-to-one thoroughbred to win a two-minute horse race. Animals, after all, were his business, were they not? He had a wall full of diplomas testifying to it, for God's sake! If he couldn't detect the qualities that made a champion runner, who could?

Having invested four decades, and two million dollars, Simeon was still seeking a satisfactory answer to that question. Never once had it occurred to Doctor Forrester that if framed credentials like those in his austere office gave vets some sort of pari-mutuel betting advantage, all of the country's 84,000 veterinarians would likely be billionaires.

His cell phone rang. The screen contained the code name '*Musad.*' It was the Muslim word for '*Lucky.*'

"Good afternoon, *Musad*," said Forrester. "I was hoping to hear from you."

"And good evening to you, my friend."

"I assume my package arrived in good order."

"It did indeed," said Bashkim. "By air express. I have already begun a cursory examination of the contents."

The Doctor paused before continuing, and a slight frown crossed his gaunt features. "You don't let much grass grow under your feet, *Musad*."

"My people have a saying," Bashkim answered: "'*If an acquaintance sends a bag of bread, accept it readily...but weigh each loaf.*'"

"And what do your people say about making prompt compensation to the provider?"

"Ah!" said Bashkim Inasah, "they say, '*Pay the worker's wages before his sweat dries.*' "Thus I may state to you in truth...your check has arrived already.'"

The connection with Jaziref was abruptly broken and a smiling Simeon Forrester returned to his calculating of the odds in today's Fall Highweight Handicap.

It would be chilly at Aqueduct for the six furlong affair, and 'Doc,' as he was affectionately known at the track, was positive he had the seventh race exacta figured. All things being equal, the largest horses almost always won in this kind of weather 'The Doc' had estimated. With a good effort from *Yellow Team* at seventeen hands, and the big filly *Dougie's Girl* weighing in at 1050 pounds, turning *Musad's* euros into at least two hundred thousand American should be a *fait accompli*.

But the feature race would not go off until four o'clock. Simeon Forrester had much to do between now and then, not the least important of which was administering personally to the dognapped 'Gigi' in quarantine cage number seventeen. Nothing untoward must happen to Lis Wren's four-year-old Boston Terrier...and only Forrester was to attend to the unusually quiet, entertaining little captive. Those were his orders, and his six young assistants knew better than to question them.

The wiry veterinarian rinsed his dishes and flatware in the kitchen sink and gave his hands and forearms a good scrubbing.

Having graduated atop his 1965 class at Cornell University's College of Veterinary Medicine, 22-year-old Simeon had vowed always to uphold the high standards that had earned the upstate New York school its number one ranking among colleges specializing in the medical treatment of animals. That commitment included cleansing himself of all substances that might alter his patients' acute sense of smell while he was administering to them. He'd even written a thesis while at Cornell that had won him a five thousand-dollar grant—its subject: '*The need for sanitation in detecting canine allergies.*'

Forrester had always been fastidious when attending the animals under his care. He loved them all…unconditionally… great and small. Unhappily, 'The Doc' loved gambling just as much. Accordingly, every penny of his $5,000-dollar award had gone to Finger Lakes Race Track on the same day he'd won the esteemed research prize.

Chapter 5

Eric Mueller maintained the handshake a beat longer than the situation seemed to require.

Majors Kelvin, Cockbyrne, and Stufkoski had been assigned to SEA Hut 37. They'd had their NCO greeters lug the duffle bags to their three assigned rooms on the second floor, treated themselves to long, hot showers, and were decked out in clean fatigues preparatory to heading for midnight chow in the South Mess.

Meanwhile, Lisbeth Wren wasn't as comfortably squared away…in fact she was seething.

"What the fuck do you mean, '*Men's* SEA Hut?'" she demanded.

"It's only for a day or two, Colonel."

"Day or two your ass. Where's the OD?"

"He's on the way, Ma'am."

Lieutenant Forbes had left the Lieutenant Colonel's bags locked in the van, but he still kept her briefcase under his arm as he waited by the door of Men's BOQ SEA Hut 114, which also housed the Billeting Office. He was trying his best to appear nonchalant about the obvious snafu that would require the Doctor to utilize the same shower and bathroom facilities the male officers in 114 did…though not simultaneously it was devoutly to be hoped…until this muddle got straightened out.

But anyone who thought Lis Wren was going to take up residence for a single, solitary minute in a building designated for men, had another think coming. Granted, beneath her peaches and cream facade, the tall, nimble woman was as tough as they come, but her ex-Policeman's characteristics did not include immodesty.

It had been only a month since Wren had been pinned an LTC, but already she knew how to make the most of her high rank. "If the Officer of the Day isn't here in five minutes," she announced leaning on the Billeting Officer's desk, "I'm going to be pounding on the Brigade Commander's door—and don't think he won't see me!"

"Perhaps I'd better wait in the van," said Forbes. "You may need a ride to the South Mess after they've got you set up in quarters."

"What time is midnight chow served?" she barked at the Tech Sergeant who sat stiffly behind his desk, ostensibly reviewing some sort of roster.

"Twenty-two thirty, to oh one hundred, Ma'am."

Colonel Wren jerked her left sleeve up four inches, glanced at her watch, and glared at the Sergeant. It was already 9:45 PM, and she announced the fact impatiently, while folding her arms resolutely across her chest. "I assume you're aware that Lieutenant Forbes and I have been waiting since twenty-fifty. I want the OD informed of that."

"The Lieutenant can leave," said the Technical Sergeant brightly. He looked toward the young officer. "I can get a runner to fill-in if you'd like, Sir." The Sergeant lifted the receiver from his desk phone.

With a scowl that would curdle milk, Lisbeth Wren glowered at the NCO in charge of Billeting, and he quickly replaced the handset.

"My orders are to see that the Colonel is comfortably installed in her quarters," said Forbes…though that was not exactly the case…he'd been directed merely to deliver Doctor Wren and the three Majors to Officers Billeting. And as soon as Lisbeth's duffle bags were unloaded from the van, he would have fulfilled his assignment. The three Corporals had already been dismissed.

"Well, you're going to have to move the van, Sir," the Sergeant insisted. "You're parked in The Adjutant's spot."

Forbes looked uncertainly toward the Lieutenant Colonel.

"Lieutenant Forbes has no intention of moving the transporter, or in any way contributing further to this fiasco," Lis Wren growled. "He will not participate in the violation of Army regulations concerning on-post housing matters." She stood up, strode determinedly to the office door, opened it and looked out into the chill Ovosok night. "Now where the fuck is the Officer of the Day?"

* * *

Actually, the OD had entered the building through one of the South East Asia Hut's side doors, and the graying Captain approached the workplace by traversing a long hallway that led ultimately to the Billeting Office just inside the front door of the hut. The office itself was a medium-sized room with a large map of Billingham's living quarters on one wall. Its single exterior door opened onto the paved street where the dusty Astro Van was illegally parked.

Captain Mueller was a robust career soldier who was fifty-five years old, if he was a day. He swept his six-three frame through the rear door of the Billeting Office, the crown of his starched patrol cap clearing the door frame and its overhead red and white 'Exit' sign by a mere six inches.

The Sergeant leaped to his feet behind the desk and saluted the Officer of the Day neatly. Captain Eric Mueller acknowledged him with an equally smart salute. The OD approached Lisbeth Wren and extended his hand. "Welcome to Camp Billingham, Colonel." He then nodded toward Lieutenant Forbes.

Lis accepted Mueller's hand and gave it one firm downward thrust before easing her grasp. "We've got a mix-up here, Captain."

Eric Mueller maintained both the handshake and eye contact a beat longer than the situation seemed to require. Like Lisbeth's, his eyes were a deep blue, she noted, and it appeared to her that the tall man's close-cropped hair, barely visible beneath the rim of the cap he wore so well-orderedly, might have once been evenly blond...like her own. Lis could feel her tendency to blush betraying her and she involuntarily pulled her hand away a bit more abruptly than she'd really wanted to. Immediately she regretted the impulsive action and Lis rubbed her palm self-consciously on her right thigh as though attempting to erase the sensory memory of Eric Mueller's touch. *Please don't let him think that,* she said inwardly, and the color faded from her cheeks.

With a semi-smile that bespoke both experience and self-assurance in such matters, the Captain fixed Lisbeth Wren with a big brotherly wink before turning toward the Tech Sergeant, who was still standing behind his desk. "What's the problem here, Sergeant?"...his smile broadened. "In words of one syllable, Andy—as you know, I'm a simple man."

He walked behind the desk and looked over Sergeant Andy Grayson's shoulder at the Female Officers' On-Post Housing Roster.

Grayson slid his chair to one side, opened the printed fanfold flat on the desk, and gestured toward the three-foot-long document with an open hand. "We're outta' room, Cap'n. They're putting new storm windows in ten units of 111 and 112." He pointed to the long list of rooms, ten of which were underlined. "As I told the Colonel, they'll be ready for occupancy in a day or two."

Mueller unfolded the Commissioned Men's *roster* and he ran his forefinger down the list that was twice as long as the women's. "You mean to tell me that of the seven thousand billets on this Post, we have only three available?... *Three? And all Men's?*"

"Looks that way, Sir."

"Where's the Off-Post list?"

Sergeant Grayson handed the OD a thin folder containing a typed sheet with eighteen names and address.

Captain Mueller noted that two of the private homes listed showed single-room availability for year-round leasing—either short or long term. One...the residence of M. el Farfed...was located in Civesoru not ten minutes from Billingham's main gate. It was Muslim-owned. The other...the home of Frau H. Henschel...was in the Catholic section of Jaziref. A footnote revealed that the Henschel woman was a widow who lived alone...and spoke no English.

The Officer of the Day looked up from the spreadsheet and smiled. "How's your German, Colonel Wren? Your file says you *Sprechen sie Deutch*."

* * *

Bashkim Inasah set out on his regular evening walk along the Gjon Sereci, past the Jaziref-Civesoru railroad station, northwest on Ahmet Kaqiku where the low buildings of Serreqi University sit far from the street in the shape of a flat Z...and finally to the Xhamlja mosque on Daut Dauti, from whose minaret the *Muezzin* was calling the faithful to evening *Salat*. Then Bashkim re-traced his steps, stopped for a midpoint cocktail at 'Bodensee,' and arrived home at precisely 9:50. It would be nearly four o'clock on Long Island. Bashkim was certain that Simeon Forrester would have already withdrawn his finder's fee from the Mineola branch of Citibank…and soon he, Inasah, would collect his own commission.

But not until Doctor Lisbeth Wren had been vetted, tested, and favorably assessed, by the five Elders of the 'Quilted Mosque' (*Peace be upon them*), thought Bashkim. And for good measure he added mockingly, *May their blessings outnumber the stars.*

Chapter 6

An organ transplant had been indicated, and Otto was an excellent candidate.

Hanna Henschel was a stern woman of seventy-four. Like most German females her age, she carried herself with an aloof dignity that many mistook for arrogance. Hanna, however, could not have cared less, an ingrained characteristic that clearly contributed to the general misperception.

A Munich native like her deceased husband Otto, she had eloped with the young engineer when both were twenty-four. They had run off to the picturesque town of Innsbruck in Austria, were married in a brief civil ceremony, and were promptly disowned by their deeply religious parents. Christmas Eve would have been Hanna's golden wedding anniversary.

After thirty years of marriage, the Henschels had tired of a life that literally ruled out their participation in even the most informal family activities. Brothers and sisters on both sides joined the hard-nosed Henschel and Breughel parents in avoiding the childless couple. Even close family friends had forsaken them. "I've been offered a position with an American firm," Otto told his apple-cheeked wife over a meal of his favorite *Schweinekrustbraten*. "The Hallingbruen Company is building a military base in Ovosok. They want me to oversee excavation operations."

"And you want to accept?" said Hanna. "Will it make you happy?"

"If it pleases you…yes," Otto answered.

"Then you have your answer," she smiled.

Otto reached across the table and lovingly squeezed his pretty wife's hand. As always in such moments, tears formed in his eyes as he gazed at her. Soon, she was aware, embarrassment would replace her man's tenderness, and Hanna knew how to spare Otto that discomfort. She teased, "I suppose you have considered, my Darling, that henceforth you might have to refer to your beloved *Schweinekrustbraten* as plain *Krustbraten*." Hanna Henschel winked impishly. "I'm told that *Schweine* is not exactly the entree du jour in largely Islamist Ovosok."

But ironically, Otto and Hanna were more readily accepted by Jaziref's swarm of Albanian Muslims than they were by the few dozen German Catholic families living on the street where the Hallingbruen Company had provided the Henschels with a modest but sturdy home. Hanna's ever-reliable antennae had attributed the coolness to envy on the part of the other engineering professionals in the two-block-long German neighborhood. All of the men there were employed by Camp Billingham's prime contractor, and Otto held by far the most important job among them. Also, it was an open secret that the cozy little Henschel house on Ruga Dognal was the only one that had been paid for by Hallingbruen as part of Otto's compensation.

In a way, the situation reminded Hanna of life amid her hostile relatives in suburban Munich—where it seemed that practically everyone was family if you went back a few generations.

With the completion of the enormous military facility in 1999, and after Hallingbruen had won its bid to operate the Camp, Otto had been offered a position as Technical Advisor to the contractor's on-site maintenance group. Things were looking up for the Henschels...and Hanna had never been happier. Then Otto Henschel was diagnosed with Chronic Kidney Disease, the silent condition that one often cannot feel or see in its early stages. As a result, neither Hanna nor Otto realized his peril until the eleventh hour.

An immediate organ transplant had been indicated, and on paper Otto, if somewhat stubborn, was an excellent candidate: He was physically fit and temperamentally prepared for the procedure...Hallingbruen had agreed to render the required financial assistance...and no patient ever had a better built-in home support system than did Otto Henschel in the person of his capable and loving wife. Furthermore, the Camp Billingham hospital was said to be the finest in the vast stretch of Eastern Europe between Austria and Greece...a near-perfect facility for the providing of post-operative care.

But Vienna and Athens were the nearest cities with their own transplant centers...meaning, of course, their own bureaucracies and ultra-rigid, time consuming restrictions regarding organ recipient eligibility.

Thus, ten days after receiving his grim diagnosis, while Doctors voiced conflicting opinions, the newly prominent engineer died at age sixty...and so profound was the depth of Hanna Henschel's grief, that she never spoke her husband's name aloud again.

* * *

Captain Eric Mueller had dialed Frau Henschel's phone number, spoken a few brief sentences in what to Lis Wren sounded like perfect German…at least by Brooklyn standards it did…and he replaced the receiver on the land line cradle in the middle of the Billeting Office desk.

"Did you have to buy any gas for that vehicle?" asked Mueller wagging his head toward the van outside.

"No Sir," said Lieutenant Forbes. "They gassed it up at the Motor Pool before we left. It's still got more than half a tank, Captain."

Mueller stood and nodded to Sergeant Grayson. "Thanks for the use of your chair, Andy. Have a seat." He removed the OD armband and turned to the Lieutenant. "I'll take that check list…what's your first name, Forbes?"

The Lieutenant reddened, removed a quarter-folded document from his shirt pocket, and handed it to the Officer of the Day. "It's, uh, Meriwether, Sir…but most people just call me…like…Forbes."

"Too bad," said Mueller. "Meriwether's a fine name. Meriwether Lewis—one of the greatest names in the history of our country, as a matter of fact. By the way, his close friend, William Clark, was a Second Lieutenant, too." He handed the voucher and a pen to Forbes. "You can sign off on the Colonel. She's in good hands…so to speak."

The Lieutenant signed M. Forbes on the bottom line of the check list and passed it back. "You want me to help you with those two duffle bags, Cap'n?"

"Nope," said Captain Mueller. He looked at his watch. "You ready, Colonel? You've had a busy day."

Chapter 7

Salary was no object…Musad's contacts were wealthy philanthropists.

Aqueduct Racetrack was a faded green oval surrounded by two rich loam racing surfaces: A main dirt track and an inner one. Inside both of those was a manicured turf course that formed the perimeter of a brownish, grassy infield. The central area contained two freeform lakes and the grandstand-facing tote boards. These electronically operated displays listed the horses in the upcoming race by their assigned position in the starting gate…with "1" being the slot nearest the rail. Also shown on the tote board, next to each entry identifier, was another number—a long one—that changed every few seconds. It reflected the current updated odds on every horse as pari-mutuel wagering progressed.

Simeon Forrester sat confidently at his private table in the exclusive 'Cigar' Lounge. The name of the bistro had nothing to do with tobacco…'Cigar' in this case was the name of the great stallion who had won ten million dollars in purse money before being retired to stud as a six-year-old in 1996. Doctor Forrester had lost over one hundred thousand dollars betting against 'Cigar' purely out of dislike for the thoroughbred's name. Had he investigated further, however, Simeon would have learned that the horse's name derives from a navigational intersection for airplanes. Owner Allen Paulson, a major figure in American aviation, had owned the Gulfstream Aerospace Corporation, manufacturers of the famed Gulfstream business jets. He named many of the horses in his stable after the names given to intersections on aeronautical navigation charts...each of which began with a different letter and was limited to a total of five characters. Paulson also had done quite well with the speedy colt, Arazi, for instance, and the swift filly, Eliza, though 'The Doc' considered them 'too small' and never bet them.

Forrester had been waiting for this day since early June when the man who called himself *Musad* had visited his Animal Hospital in Uniondale, Long Island. He had come with a proposition that under normal circumstances would have been the answer to an inveterate gambler's prayers: *Musad's* associates in Eastern Europe, specifically in the Balkan nation of Madonica, south of Ovosok where *Musad* lived, had need for an animal surgeon. Such a person must be willing to live among the largely Algerian population for a few months and tend to the medical needs of their domesticated animals during that time. Salary was no object...*Musad's* contacts were wealthy philanthropists. Indeed, they had authorized him to offer a twenty-five thousand euro finder's fee to anyone who might recommend such a qualified person. The stipend would be wired promptly upon the surgeon's arrival.

To say that Simeon Forrester was receptive to the Ovosok man's proposal would have been a gross understatement. The idea of such a financial windfall rendered him near breathless. But the only qualified person he knew, was unfortunately unavailable for months-long periods of discretionary travel. She was a promising young Doctor...a newly pinned Lieutenant Colonel in the Army named Lisbeth Wren. Yes indeed, the 49-year-old woman was an adept (if not actually licensed) surgeon who had operated with considerable success on many of Simeon Forrester's four-legged patients. What a pity that she was committed to the military.

"Do you have her Army Serial Number, by any chance?" said *Musad*.

"I'm sure we have it on file," said Simeon skeptically, "but it's no use. Doctor Wren would not be able…"

"Why don't you show me her file?" *Musad* insisted. "My friends are very well-connected…and twenty-five thousand euros is a lot of money, is it not?"

It was true, of course, that the fee the Eastern European had mentioned…the equivalent of thirty-four thousand American dollars…was a stunning payment to be rendered for the simple service of recommending a competent medical practitioner. What harm could it do, the veterinarian rationalized, to pass along the name and minor military credentials of the woman he'd known and mentored practically since her youth? If *Musad's* friends wished to contact Lisbeth Wren, or otherwise pursue her as an attending specialist, who was he to stand in the way?

"Come with me," Forrester had said. "I'll make a copy of the Doctor's information, for what it's worth." But he'd stopped at the doorway to the personnel/patient records room and turning to his visitor, said, "It might be prudent however, if the, uh, *details* of our conversation remained…well, between us. For ethical considerations. I'm sure you understand."

The olive-skinned man returned Simeon Forrester's vague smile. "Yes. Ethical considerations. You may be sure that I understand fully…Doctor."

"Call me Simeon," the veterinarian had said, opening the office door. "Come this way…*Musad*."

* * *

The 'Doc' looked down from the bank of television monitors that occupied one complete wall of the 'Cigar' Lounge. He checked his old fashioned pocket watch—eleven minutes to post time. Then he returned his gaze to the bank of TV screens. From half a dozen different camera angles, Number 2, *Yellow Team* and Number 3, *Dougie's Girl*, could be seen along with eight other handsome thoroughbreds, proceeding slowly from the Aqueduct paddock in post-position order. As the entries were walked prancing over the rubberized surface of the grandstand tunnel and onto the main track, their mounted jockeys made last-minute adjustments to their colorful equestrian helmets and jaunty bow ties.

This year's Fall Highweight was going to be run in especially frigid weather, as 'The Doc' had assumed. The late-November sun was sinking rapidly, even at ten minutes to four, dropping the temperature ever further as a damp wind swept in from nearby Kennedy Airport and the adjacent chill Atlantic. But Simeon's selections were two large, well-muscled animals, bred to withstand such weather. He was confident that the thirty thousand dollars in hundreds that filled both inner pockets of his suit jacket would soon be replaced by a NYRA check increasing that stake tenfold when the feature race had ended, and the first and second 'exacta' horses were announced.

God, it was cold, though...even the usually comfortable 'Cigar' Lounge was nippy!

'Doc' Forrester finished the last of his brandy, signed the check that lay tucked in a brown leather folder, and made his way to the Hundred Dollar Minimum wagering window where he was well-known to the pari-mutuel betting attendants. A large uniformed security officer was stationed next to the window, thumbs hooked in his wide Sam Browne belt. He smiled thinly but said nothing.

"Thirty thousand...two—three—exacta, Tommy," said 'The Doc,' and the clerk inside made a penciled notation on a small pad. Simeon proceeded to empty his inner breast pockets and he slid six banded packets of bills through the opening in the clear Lexan. The wrapping strip on each bundle bore the handwritten inscription '$5,000' and was initialed by the issuing teller at Forrester's Citibank branch in Mineola.

Tommy the clerk, appeared unfazed by the large wager, and quietly fed the bills into a counting machine that simultaneously scanned them for authenticity. After the lightning-fast count, he bound all three hundred bills with a single adhesive strip and placed the six-inch-thick packet in his cash drawer. He punched a series of keys on the stainless steel keyboard in front of him and immediately a heavy paper slip flew from a slot on the narrow counter at Forrester's waist level. "Check it, 'Doc,'" the clerk said routinely, and Simeon picked up the receipt.

Inscribed on the four-by-five-inch beige voucher were: Aqueduct Raceway...11-17-2010...Race Seven...$30,000...Exacta...and the numbers 2—3. Simeon Forrester had just bet thirty grand that *Yellow Team* would win the Fall Highweight Handicap...and that *Dougie's Girl* would come in second.

Flanking the main tote board on the Aqueduct infield were two fifty-foot-wide displays. They listed the Seventh Race entries by number, and next to each was a slot where numbers for the other horses flashed in sequence. To the right of these pairings, in turn, was shown the increasing amount of money that was being bet on those Exacta combinations as race time drew near and the totals climbed. The Exacta Pool was the figure that professional horse players watched closest...particularly in the last five minutes before the Post. Any increase of more than five or six thousand dollars in the late wagering would be a sure indication that the 'Smart

Money' had found the likely Win and Place horses—and the rush to the betting windows would be on.

As Simeon made his way down to the spectator barricade nearest the Finish Line, he saw the betting figures for the 2—3 Exacta flash on the tote boards...and as he expected, a collective gasp emanated from the crowd. He grinned in the knowledge that his substantial wager had hiked the Exacta Pool by twenty percent. A quick calculation told him that despite the last minute action generated by his big bet, he was probably in for a two hundred thousand dollar payday.

The Track Announcer intoned, "It is now Post Time," and the tote boards flashed the odds for the last time. *Yellow Team* and *Dougie's Girl* were co-favorites at 5 to 3. The Exacta wouldn't pay much for the average bettor...but still...

"They're in the gate," said the Announcer...'The Doc' felt a familiar thrill in the pit of his stomach..."And they're off."

One minute and ten seconds later *Yellow Team* and *Dougie's Girl* had separated themselves from the ten-horse field by four lengths and flashed across the finish line at the end of the six-furlong race...but not in that order.

Once again Simeon Forrester had fallen victim to the demon over which he had no control.

Chapter 8

The 'Quilted Mosque' suggests to the western eye a cubic, jigsaw puzzle.

In the oldest section of Tavoto, on the eastern bank of the shallow Pena river, the 'Quilted Mosque' conveys to the beholder a most unusual kind of beauty...particularly for a Muslim religious edifice. Popularly referred to by those who live in its rectangular shadow as the Pasha Mosque, the sacred building was originally constructed in 1495...three years after Christopher Columbus achieved what is still considered the world's most astonishing feat of dead reckoning—the discovery of the New World.

Architecturally, the 'Quilted Mosque' is a one-room, flat-roofed building, that incorporates both Baroque and classical Ottoman components. The single most distinctive aspect of this unique structure, however, is the visual suggestion that its exterior is decorated by four stacked rows of what appear to be pastel hanging draperies. In actuality, the deceiving ranks of quadrangles are rock-solid.

The bottom, or street-level row of the painted patchwork of panels, incorporates four louvered doors, each glossy black, contributing to the impression that the forbidding portals are never opened.

The second row of twelve symmetrical rectangles, each different in some way from its neighbors, suggests that fifteenth century amateur artisans combined their talents and created one frescoed row before proceeding to the next. Apart from the matching dimensions of the contiguous panels, and the overall emphasis on green, pink, and rose coloring, the rectangles seem to have been fashioned with little or no regard for achieving a specific pattern. This, obviously, contributes to the building's mystique…and ultimately, its homespun charm.

The 'Quilted Mosque's' third tier of panels consists essentially of squares. These appear to have been decorated with an intentional continuity of design, save for the center two frescoes that are distinctly different in hue. Also, as with the dark door arrangement at ground level, this layer contains four windows, each one directly above its corresponding door two rows below.

The last level, though, is the most intriguing of all four.

Almost as if this top tier of twelve panels was designed to highlight Islamic diversity of artistic expression, each unit includes the architectural equivalent of contrapuntal themes in music. Whereas the lower three rows of colorful rectangles all consist of sections with four perfectly straight sides, the topmost level's segments are largely curved and much more ornate…intended, it would appear, to top a wedding cake…represent the pinched indentations in a pie crust…or simulate the crown of a florid Corinthian column.

The 'Quilted Mosque's' typically ornate interior, with its innumerable interlocking components, more than anything else suggests to the western eye a huge, cubic, jigsaw puzzle whose every element depends on every other for its shape and meaning. Even the intricate designs woven into the plush carpet and rich tapestries seem essential to the overall effect of a gigantic Renaissance painting where not a square inch of space is left unadorned by mysterious figures and cursive writing.

But unlike its exterior, characteristically there is not a single significant straight line painted on the suffocatingly elaborate inner walls of the 'Quilted Mosque.' What there is, is a narrow recessed stairway, hidden behind a blue curtain. The curtain hangs from a *pulpito* that is never used, and the shroud is said to have been sewn by the two sisters who financed the building from its inception in 1438. Accordingly, the relic is never touched...except, perhaps, by the Elders when they descend into their private room. Or by Bashkim Inasah when he is called upon to report his progress in arranging for competent enlistees to perform the bidding of the clerics.

* * *

Bashkim left his little house early. It was Friday (*Zhmah*), the last of his thrice-weekly commutes to Tavoto and the 'Quilted Mosque' until Monday (*Ltnahn*), and again on *Lhrba* (Wednesday). Shit, how he despised the guttural sound of even the days of the week as spoken in the bastardized language that prevails among Muslims here in the Balkan hinterlands.

The Curator's function, which he filled at the pleasure of the Elders, had been arranged by the five clerics so that Bashkim might travel—often internationally, without attracting the undue attention of Tavoton authorities. Frequent absences from his modest office near the base of the minaret went unnoticed for the most part. And the glib Inasah was more than equal to the task of explaining any foray that took him away long enough to raise suspicions.

Not that the famed mosque in the foothills of the Shar Mountains was ever totally unoccupied. Two Imams-in-training filled six-month tours at Tavoto's most renowned landmark. Both of the 22-year-old students were qualified *Muezzin* conductors, whose only other function it was to instruct a constant flow of tourists about proper conduct in and near the mosque...an adjunct role to playing the appropriate call to prayer five times daily over the state-of-the-art loudspeakers mounted on the 700-year-old building. The mosque's compact disc player and twelve all-weather speakers had been purchased online from Radio Shack (*peace be upon them*) by Bashkim himself at the instruction of the Elders. No self-respecting Madonican *Mullah*, it was assumed, would be familiar with twenty-first century electronics...while worldly Curators were surely computer literate, and fully conversant in such matters as credit card numbers, expiration dates, and currency exchange rates.

The highway south from Jaziref turned sharply west at Skopje and after a fifteen-minute drive, Bashkim Inasah exited the two-lane road on the outskirts of shabby little Tavoto. He was going to the town's oldest bookstore. There, he knew, they sold a wide variety of the most elegant Eastern European bookmarks. "First things first," he mused aloud. "One never knows when the interesting Lisbeth Wren might get around to calling."

* * *

Off the narrow, cobblestoned Karaorman Road in Old Tavoto, a block from the River Pena, Bashkim parked his Citroen in a narrow alley only slightly wider than the car itself. The surrounding buildings were all elongated structures that gave the impression that some immense fist had opened up and dropped a handful of Monopoly houses that lay random-clustered and leaning one against the other in a four-block area bounded by Ivo Ribar Road on the east, and the chilly Pena on the west. At the center of this commercial complex was a battered park that dated back to the fifteenth century. Its 'lawn' of weeds still flourishing despite centuries of pounding by the hooves of invading warhorses, exploding Nazi bombs, and the grinding iron tracks that once propelled Communist tanks.

The nattily-dressed Curator entered the quaint Lola bookstore through a side entrance that opened on the alley where a group of schoolboys, ostensibly on their way to St. Nicholas Academy, had stopped to gape and run their hands over Bashkim's futuristic-looking French automobile. The tall man barked a command over his shoulder and the five boys backed off but still pointed and whispered admiring observations to one another. "*Knezha!*" Bashkim growled again good-naturedly…and the boys scampered giggling out of the alleyway, their schoolbooks secured by single leather belts and swinging wildly as they ran.

* * *

Leaving a Camp the size of Billingham, even in late evening, was easy…getting back in was the part that involved meticulous scrutiny of orders, personal credentials, and above all…packages. The process was not unlike boarding and disembarking the world's commercial aircraft in the wake of 9/11. These days, one could spend an hour in the screening line at such airports as O'Hare and Heathrow for instance… twice that at Ben Gurion or Charles de Gaulle. But once you had landed and were off the plane, no one seemed to care who you were, where you were going, or what you were toting in that little rolling suitcase that everyone appeared to be pulling.

Thus, when Captain Mueller slowed the Army van to a stop at the installation's main gate, he and Colonel Wren were waved through with hardly a second glance from the lone M.P. manning the exit side of the gatehouse. Vehicles *entering* Billingham, however, were given the same thorough examination the olive drab van had been subjected to a few hours earlier when arriving.

"When I was a PFC in 1970," said Eric Mueller, "it always seemed to me the fences around these places were there to keep me in. When I finally realized they were really intended to keep uninvited guests out, well, that's when I took a different view of the Army and decided to try for Officer Candidate School. Never saw the inside of a college, but Fort Benning was giving equivalency exams…so…"

"You obviously passed," said Lisbeth.

"Miracles do happen," the Captain said with a wry grin and a shake of his head.

"Well, you're certainly not lacking in diplomacy," the Doctor responded. "That was a nice thing you did…making Lieutenant Forbes feel better about his name."

"You hate to see a kid walking around with that sort of hang-up, know what I mean?"

"Maybe you could give some words of encouragement to one of my new associates."

"Who's that?"

"Major Cockbyrne."

"Ouch!"

"You don't know the half of it," said Lis Wren. "Her first name's Ophelia."

* * *

Mueller and Wren turned off of the lightly traveled Civesoru-Jaziref highway, onto dead-end Ruga Dognal. After a mere two blocks the dark street terminated at a small *cul-de-sac* with a fountain in its center. Frau Henschel's tidy little house was the only one whose windows glowed with interior light, and Captain Mueller parked the van as close as he could to the narrow concrete sidewalk where it met the short, slate path leading to Hanna's front step.

After exiting the vehicle and opening Lisbeth's door, he locked the van, and preceded the Lieutenant Colonel the few steps to a blue door. Eric tapped the brass knocker twice lightly and smiled at Lis reassuringly. Almost immediately both visitors heard the rattle of a chain lock being released… and the door opened a few inches.

Hanna Henschel's pink, amazingly wrinkle-free face appeared in the opening, almost a foot lower than Lisbeth's, and instinctively the tall American Doctor estimated the woman's height at five feet; her weight, between ninety and one hundred pounds; her overall health, good.

The Captain removed his patrol cap and so did Lisbeth. Eric spoke in confident German. "Good evening, Frau Henschel. I hope we're not disturbing you."

The tiny woman dismissed the implied apology with a no-nonsense wave of her hand. "Good evening, Captain." She opened the door wide and with a crisp nod, stepped back and motioned for both Army officers to come in. They wiped their feet on a coarse 'Welcome' mat and entered, Eric closing the door behind them.

Hanna Henschel directed Lisbeth toward a neat, blue-and-white kitchen off the equally immaculate living room. There, three ladder back chairs were arranged equally spaced around a circular table. "We will sit here," she said officiously. "There are papers to be signed. And you must have tea." But before anyone could sit, Hanna Henschel seized Lisbeth Wren by both hands, looked up stiffly, and with her Teutonic blue eyes twinkling, said, "Yes, you are a pretty one…but where did you get such a silly name?"

"I know," Lis laughed. In German that was not nearly as precise as Mueller's, she said, "I would have preferred something more traditional…like, Heidi…or Gretel…but my mother's Irish. Apparently she insisted."

"Mmmm," said Hanna, appraising her guest analytically, her head bobbing slowly. "Well, at least you have your father's coloring." She walked to the stove and turned on the burner under a dented old kettle as Lis sat down. "Captain Mueller," she said, "why don't you bring in the Colonel's luggage? I think she will be staying with us."

Chapter 9

Hanna Henschel smoothed her apron. "It's so nice to have someone to talk to—and cook for."

After a long and exhausting trip, Lisbeth Wren might have been forgiven had she overslept in Hanna Henschel's warm feather bed in the upstairs guest room. As was her practice, however, she awoke promptly at six AM…today, to the aroma of baking biscuits and frying ham that wafted from the little widow's spic and span gas stove.

Like most General Practitioners, Lis had developed at an early age a high degree of discipline in the conduct of her personal life. The rigorous demands, both physical and emotional, of her early career as a New York City Police Officer, had been largely responsible for the slender young woman's acquired ability to withstand the strictures of Medical School and Residency, after the horror of 9-11 had convinced her that Medicine must be her life's work.

Now the addition of Army training to that extensive resumé had fashioned the Colonel into the dedicated sort of professional that the Military cherishes almost beyond measure.

Lisbeth made her way to the bathroom at the head of the stairs. In one hand she clutched a pair of folded fatigues and a fresh set of underwear…in the other, was her toothbrush and a miniature tube of 'Crest.' It had gotten quite chilly overnight, and Lis was thankful she'd remembered to pack the flannel pajamas she now wore. Her most recent deployment had consisted of four months in Afghanistan last summer, and the 'woolies' had sat the whole time stuffed in her duffle bag along with fleece-lined civilian gloves and a pair of pink earmuffs that Peter had surreptitiously added to her belongings on departure eve.

Peter was her significant other—a former Long Island cop who, like so many of the Boys in Blue in the suburbs, had retired to the good life on the golf course at half pay, and with two-thirds of his life still ahead of him.

"Good morning," Lis called in German down the steep stairway.

"*Guten morgen*," Frau Henschel's voice echoed from the kitchen. "*Nehmen sie ein bad. Zögere nicht mir zu sagen, wenn du etwas brauchst.*" Then she added, "*Beeile dich… zehn minuten!*" What Hanna had said was essentially, "Take a bath…tell me if you need anything…hurry…ten minutes."

Lisbeth rolled her eyes, hastened into the tiled room, and closed the door. She turned the hot water on full, draped her pajamas over an enameled chair, and snapped off a salute while standing at nude attention beside the porcelain tub. "Whatever you say, Boss."

"*Was hast du gesagt?*"

Lis opened the door a crack and sang out, "*Sagte ich, ja gnädige Frau* (I said, yes ma'am)…*zehn minuten.*"

Hanna Henschel smoothed the front of her apron with hands that were seldom if ever idle. She smiled at Otto's picture on the wall and murmured, "*Es ist schön, jemanden zum reden zu haben—und kochen*...It's so nice to have someone to talk to—and cook for."

Suddenly she sniffed the air, and frowning, looked left, then right. "*Oh mein Gott*," she shrieked, "*die kekse!*...the biscuits!"

* * *

The tin bell over the side door of Tereza Mimona's Lola bookstore clattered and she looked up from a pile of used hardcovers on the counter. "Bashi!" she exclaimed, "Where have you been?"

The Curator doffed his black fedora and leaned to kiss Tereza's cheek. "On business for the mosque...in Canada," he partially lied. "It is colder here than there."

"Surely not," the buxom woman scoffed, and she plugged in an espresso pot before guiding Bashkim Inasah to a small round table with two facing chairs.

"Regardless," said Bashkim, "it is good to be back in Tavoto...even if the Pena is frozen over."

The flirtatious 40-year-old swatted her guest brazenly on his thigh as he unbuttoned his suit jacket and prepared to sit. "I have told you a million times, Bashi Dear, 'Never exaggerate!' But tell me, my darling, is it true that there are now more Muslims in Toronto than in all of Azerbaijan?"

Bashkim leaned back and roared in laughter. "I can't say, Reza, but there certainly are more female impersonators."

"Don't be so sure, Bashi." She got up to add a substantial shot of brandy to the espresso. "If our Ayatollahs were to look beneath all those burkas, they might find more balls than breasts, I think."

"You are irreverent, Reza. Witty—but irreverent."

Tereza returned to the little table, placed a Courvoisier coaster and a steaming espresso cup in front of both of them, and sat down. "So what brings you to my humble shop, Sweetheart?" She sipped the heavily laced coffee and rolled her eyes in delight. "If you are looking for sex, I regret that I cannot accommodate you until this afternoon." Bashkim shrugged in mock resignation. "Unless, of course, I can re-schedule the two-dozen suitors who already have morning reservations."

'Bashi' returned her saccharine-sweet smile. "Reza, Reza, Reza...haven't I told you ten million times not to exaggerate?" He sipped the heady espresso and showed his approval by hiking his eyebrows and bobbing his head vigorously. "But since *you* are personally 'Sold Out' for this morning, how is your supply of those exquisite Madonican bookmarks you showed me last spring?"

Tereza Mimona frowned and looked to one side, trying to recall. Then she brightened. "You probably mean the nine-inch Byzantine pattern...red and green on gray...with the gold highlighting."

"Those are the ones—shining gold threads throughout. May I see them?"

"By all means," said Tereza. "I'm expecting a shipment this afternoon. Would you like to make an appointment?"

Bashkim Inasah slurped the remainder of his coffee while gazing at her over the china rim. He looked toward the electric espresso machine behind the counter.

Tereza sighed heavily and clapped her hands on her knees. "Help yourself then, Darling. And refill my cup like a good boy." she said. "I'll see if I have one or two of the Byzantine markers left."

They stood up and left their seats simultaneously...he, walking toward the steaming coffee pot, she, striding in the direction of a wooden flat-file whose wide drawers were thin compartments, perhaps two inches deep, that pulled out approximately two feet. By the time Bashkim returned to their table, a small, half-filled cup in each hand, his hostess had arranged three different styles of the bookmarks in the center before him.

The ornate works of art were exactly as he recalled. One consisted of flowers and vines depicted in red and yellow, the colors of the Madonican flag, with silver woven through the scarlet portions. Another was done in the not unpleasant colors of Ovosok, mostly blue, a yellow map of the Principality at its center, with white, five-pointed stars sprinkled throughout the design.

But the richest looking piece of the three was the one in the middle.

What Tereza had described as 'red and green on gray,' was actually an intricate pattern of unmistakable Eastern European icons, flowers, leaves, butterflies, and suggested Cyrillic letters, all symmetrically rendered on the nine by two-inch mosaic in microscopic threads of green, mustard, and red, with traces of violet and purple throughout. And intertwined among the decorative components was the elegant arrangement that Bashkim recognized as stitching of pure gold. As when he had first laid eyes on the tiny work of art, the bookmark's beauty virtually took his breath away. He reached and picked up the creation, holding it to catch the early morning light, which shone through the small show window that read 'LOLA.'

"The design," Bashkim asked, "is it Renaissance in concept by any chance?"

Tereza closed her eyes resolutely and shook her head from side to side. "Older," she said. "The components give it away. Look," she took the bookmark and pointed to two pairs of butterflies that flanked an almost oriental-looking ellipse. "You would never find a stylized geometric symbol like this in Renaissance art…especially at the exact center of the work."

She ran her fingertips over the embroidery. "This is definitely Byzantine."

Bashkim, the Curator of the 'Quilted Mosque,' was secure enough in his knowledge of antiquity to ask questions when he thought it appropriate to do so. "Christian or Muslim?" he said.

Tereza Mimona set the bookmark back in the center of the table and folded her arms over her substantial bosom. "It's hard to say, Bashi. Both Muslims and Orthodox Christians in the Eastern Mediterranean preserved Eastern culture long after the Byzantine Empire had collapsed." She sipped her espresso. "As you, of all people, are aware, Byzantine icons and church architecture are still maintained in Serbia, Greece, and in our own country to this day." Tereza's sassy smile returned. "I note that the Crescent Moon and Star are missing from this bookmark…so is the suggestion of a Dome. That does not mean that it isn't a Muslim *objet d'art*, however. After all, not one of those elements is included in your 'Quilted Mosque'… the most famous in Madonica!"

"Reza, some say our interior contains ceiling decorations that give the impression of a Dome," Bashkim responded with faked indignity. "As for the Star and Crescent, their adoption by Islam took place sometime after the original construction of *Sarena Jemija*."

"I must confess," said Tereza, "the last time I was there I didn't pay much attention to the ceiling." She drained the last of her brandied coffee and smacked her lips. "I was too busy looking at those two beautiful boys you have working for you."

Bashkim looked puzzled for a moment, but quickly recovered. "Ah yes, you must mean Aalil and Aamil." He flashed his broadest, most dazzling smile. "They're the two female impersonators we hired…from Istanbul."

Tereza Mimona visored her eyes and groaned. "How many of the Byzantine book markers do you need? I only have five."

"I'll take them all," said Bashkim. "How much?"

"Three euros each," she called over her shoulder as she carried the demitasse cups to a nearby washroom. "The coffee is five…twenty euros total…the best bargain in Tavoto!"

Chapter 10

This, said Colonel Wren inwardly, might not be difficult to get used to.

Actually, the biscuits had turned out exactly the way Lisbeth liked them…with a dark, firm base and a deep brown upper crust. It was the way her father had frequently baked biscuits for the family…huge mounds of steaming biscuits…made from scratch…on Sunday mornings. The aroma that had filled every room of the Wren household in New York's Staten Island on those special Sundays was one of the childhood memories that Lis would never forget. Indeed, the third in a group of five daughters, she would cherish every recollection of her beloved Franz Wren—the most loving father seven children ever had, each of them convinced that they were '*Vater's*' favorite.

Hanna Henschel's timing was nothing short of incredible. Lisbeth stepped off the bottom tread of the narrow stairway at the exact moment that the little aproned woman placed a heaping platter on the kitchen table. It contained scrambled eggs, browned sliced potatoes, and a lightly fried mixture of Black Forest ham and *schlackwurst*…a delicious German salami that Lis Wren hadn't tasted since her eldest sister's wedding. The biscuits sat in a basket, covered by a patterned, cotton dish towel. Steam rose from the wide spout of a coffee percolator whose glass knob on the lid revealed still-bubbling, dark brew inside. A small tub of whipped butter was flanked by teacup-sized crocks—one filled with honey, the other with Hanna's prize strawberry preserves.

This, said Colonel Wren inwardly, *might not be difficult to get used to at all.*

* * *

Bashkim Inasah parked his silver Citroen on *Ulica Goce Delcev* in the shadow of the 'Quilted Mosque's' tall, stone minaret. As was his practice, he'd run the car's passenger-side wheels up on the cobblestone sidewalk, causing the vehicle to lean noticeably to the left. It was the only way traffic could possibly make it around the slim import and thus negotiate the narrow *Goce Delcev* without incident.

The tower that loomed overhead had been added to the original mosque in the early eighteenth century and though when viewed from the north, south, and west it appeared to protrude from the tiled roof, the pointed spire was actually nestled alongside the eastern wall of *Sarena Jemija* (the structure's ancient name)—that is to say, it was tucked against the wall closest to Mecca.

At the base of the minaret was a low door in the façade of the eastern wall itself. It could be used for access to the tower but seldom was. The two young Imams who lived in the mosque and performed the *Salat* had no need to climb the eighty-nine steps to the minaret's circular balcony as those charged with chanting the *Muezzin* once did, the five daily *calls to prayer* having been modernized, and now announced electronically through the building's loudspeaker system.

Bashkim, of course, along with the mosque's five elders, held a key to this small portal as well as the other six doors of *Sarena Jemija*, each of which, for whatever reason, had its own seven-inch, cast iron key. It was a burdensome collection to carry around—and post-nine-eleven airline travel was obviously out of the question when thus encumbered.

But today Bashkim Inasah carried only the key to the low door at the base of the minaret—the others were locked in a briefcase, which in turn was secured in the Citroen's otherwise empty trunk. The Curator was not concerned that anyone might steal or vandalize his car. It was always parked in the same place and everyone in this small Pena River community knew very well who it belonged to…and that it was essentially 'Mosque Property.' To tamper with it in any way would be equivalent to an attack upon the mosque itself, a crime that would surely result in the most excruciating punishment. But more significantly, the stigma attached to the sentence would far outlast the physical pain of having a hand lopped off, or an eye gouged out—the penalties imposed quickly and publicly by the Elders for even a *first* offence against almighty Allah (*Peace be upon Him*).

Before entering the 'Quilted Mosque,' and assuming that the two Imams would be anticipating his arrival, Bashkim removed the tassel loafers he had purchased at the Payless shoe store on Long Island. He dropped them in a clear plastic bag he always brought with him for the purpose, and he wondered about the many American women who seemed to have taken up the habit of wearing knee-high footwear, even in summer. He'd heard that shoes in this tall, leather style were commonly known as 'Fuck Me Boots' and Bashkim made a mental note to ask Tereza Mimona at the Lola Bookstore if she owned a pair…and if she'd ever worn such things when visiting a mosque. If there was a possibility, however remote, of tourists doing that, he as Curator of one of Islam's great orthodox sites, might be required to prepare for the eventuality by having a sign made: 'PLASTIC BAGS FOR FUCK ME BOOTS—ONE EURO.

Bashkim grinned, turned the big iron key one full circle clockwise, and as prescribed by the Koran, he sang out in Farsi, "*O Allah! Open for me the doors of your Mercy.*" He locked the small portal behind him and walked in his stocking feet across the deep-piled Persian carpet to his modest office. Protecting the priceless floor covering, of course, was the real reason for the 'No Shoes' rule in this and every other mosque the world over. But the Curator of the '*Sarena Jemija*' would be damned if he was going to question the Holy Koran…not while the five Elders were around, at any rate…(*Blessings be upon them, too*).

Bashkim sat at his desk, placed the heavy key in its center drawer, and re-inserted his size twelve feet in the American-made loafers. He popped another American product into his mouth—a Pez Mint. Bashkim kept a three-inch Pez dispenser on his person at all times. Minus the oral disguise the brandy-laced espresso he'd shared with Tereza would be quickly detected on his breath by the Elders…they could identify the forbidden trace of alcohol *a mile away*, as his associate Eric Mueller was fond of saying.

Speaking of whom…he looked at his watch…where *was* Captain Mueller? The Elders would soon be convening this morning's meeting in the basement room…now that morning prayers were over and the *Sarena Jemija* had been cleared of those insufferable worshippers and their moth-eaten prayer rugs.

A gong rung by one of the young Imams sounded from just inside the main entrance to the mosque. It was the door farthest from the one through which Bashkim had entered. He pressed a button on a small console on the desk and in thirty seconds Eric Mueller, dressed in a freshly starched ACU, his boots in a paper bag, was admitted to the Curator's small workplace. Mueller acknowledged his host with an unsmiling nod, put on his combat boots, and fastened them.

"She's here," said Bashkim.

"I know," the Captain said.

"We exchanged a few words…at the airport."

"I know that too," said Mueller. "I was watching you." He stood. "Can we start? Or are those five assholes too busy counting their money?"

Chapter 11

"Doc" Forrester might be a compulsive gambler, but he was no fool.

Simeon Forrester awoke early. Last night's Powerball jackpot was over $600 million dollars for the second time in history, so though he'd retired exhausted following his afternoon at the track, and was still groggy at five-thirty AM, going back to sleep without checking the numbers on his pile of tickets was not an option. He climbed out of bed, turned on the light, and reached for his robe.

"Doc" Forrester had three expensive desktop computers strategically situated throughout the plush Marriott suite where he lived in Amityville. One was in his bedroom, another in the living/dining room, and a third was on a swivel stand in the bathroom. Each of the machines was used exclusively for a specific set of gambling functions.

The "Doc's" living room computer was on a base whose adjustable arm swung over a recliner by his picture window. It carried horse and dog races in real time from throughout the country, and in the rare hours when neither thoroughbreds, trotters, or greyhounds were running anywhere from Florida to Oregon, replays of the day's key races were shown.

The computer on the dresser next to his bed was never turned off and was set to a silent website that showed a complete analysis of lotteries nationwide. The breakdown provided every conceivable statistic on the current jackpot in each case: Federal and state withholding figures, annuity payouts, cash option amounts, annual net payments and their related tax numbers…for over one hundred U.S. sweepstakes…all, to the penny.

The machine atop a small vanity in the john focused solely on SportsView, a site whose interactive touchscreen provision permitted the viewer to watch as many as four traditional sporting events in progress simultaneously…while a crawl across the bottom of the screen provided the latest 'line' on basketball, hockey, football, soccer, boxing…and baseball when in season.

Marked above each of the monitors was the identifying number for one of three corresponding savings accounts at Citibank in Mineola. The veterinarian maintained a minimum balance of ten thousand dollars in each one. A landline telephone for calling-in bets was conveniently positioned adjacent to the computers, however "Doc" Forrester, unfailingly conscientious about documenting his perfectly legitimate wagers, preferred the accuracy that e-mail records provided.

It was a fact, after all, that of the approximately two hundred thousand dollars which the inveterate Forrester wagered annually, typically forty percent resulted in wins…while he lost sixty percent of each yearly 'investment.' With proof positive of his forty thousand dollar net losses in hand come April fifteenth, Simeon's meticulous record-keeping provided him a forty thousand dollar tax write-off.

"Doc" Forrester might be a hopelessly compulsive gambler, but he was no fool.

Neither was the brilliant computer hacker Bashkim Inasah, who had found the Uniondale veterinarian's history on

SportsView…and wondered if he might not be in the market to earn himself some extra euros.

* * *

Lisbeth Wren swore that her first meal in Ovosok was the best feast she'd dined upon since before her father took sick and was forced to stop his occasional cooking…and she told Hanna so. Frau Henschel, in turn, expressed amazement coupled with gratification that a slender woman like the 150-pound Lieutenant Colonel was blessed with such a fine appetite. "To be a German is to enjoy good food," said Hanna.

"To cook such a breakfast is a German gift," Lis responded, enjoying the necessity of expressing herself in her host's native language. Then, scanning the kitchen table, she quoted another of her Dad's, Old World expressions. "But just look… someone seems to have eaten all our food!"

"*Mein Gott*," said Hanna, "*sagte mein vater, dass!*"…"My father used to say that!"

"*Eine andere sache, die wir gemeinsam haben,*" Lisbeth laughed…"Another thing we have in common."

The tiny woman with the translucent skin rested her chin on folded hands, her half-full coffee cup between her elbows. Her eyes misted over, and Lisbeth Wren knew intuitively what she was thinking: *The daughter I never had*.

Lis jumped up from the table to break the developing spell. She carried her plates, cup, and silverware to the sink, and returned for Hanna's. "Let me help with the dishes," she said. "Shall I wash or dry…I'm as bad at one as the other."

Frau Henschel downed the rest of her tepid coffee. She removed a tissue from her apron pocket, blew her nose, and surreptitiously dabbed at the corner of one eye. "I will wash," Hanna said. "I break fewer dishes washing than drying."

After the steaming hot water had thundered into Hanna's deep sink, she held an index finger to the side of her head as if suddenly remembering something. Obviously, she continued to speak in German. "An hour ago a Jeep arrived," she said pointing to the front door. "A handsome boy is driving. I asked him to come in, but he said he'll wait."

Lis strode to the living room, parted the curtains in a front window, and looked at the greenish brown vehicle with the white star on the door. She returned to the kitchen and lifted two small plates from the drain board. She winked at Hanna. "My ride to the Camp," she said with a smile. "And yes, as you say, Frau Henschel, '*Ein hübscher Junge*,' a handsome boy indeed!"

"Do you know him, then?"

"Corporal Prentiss...Stevie Prentiss." She bent and whispered in the five-foot woman's ear, "They say he gets a hard on even if the wind blows."

Hanna frowned and looked up from the soapy water. "*Was is dat*...'hard on?'"

* * *

Tereza Mimona was almost positive that Bashkim Inasah was involved in something illicit. Maybe it was drugs... *God knows*, she thought, *there is plenty of heroin here in the Western Balkans*. But if that were the case, she assumed, surely Bashi would have been detected in the company of the unsavory pigs known to travel the infamous 'Poppy Trail' of which Madonica was said to be a key stepping stone. Every Madonican schoolchild knew the innocent sounding name given the Eastern Adriatic corridor leading ultimately to Italy, France, and even the U.K.... the three-nation destination where actual enrichment and consumption of the opium took place. Without the 'Poppy Trail' and the traffic permitted by the loosely governed new states it traversed, the source fields of Iran and Afghanistan would soon dry up, and much of the world's raw heroin supply would simply blow away on the dry, Middle Eastern winds.

Reza had finished cataloging her new shipment of hardcovers and she set them aside. Before inserting them in the stacks that covered three of the Lola Bookstore's walls, the young woman wanted to check the contents of a volume that had come in just last month, and whose provocative title had intrigued her. She slid her short, rolling ladder to the wall opposite her front door…the wall facing the imprinted show window. A hanging sign near the ceiling there read 'GEOGRAPHY.'

Tereza clambered up the ladder, reached even higher overhead, and pried free a large book on whose spine was embossed the words 'We Shall Not Sleep.'

The volume was already dusty from the rumbling traffic that bounced over the cobblestones outside on bumpy Karaorman Road. The proprietress blew on the sooty paper cover, waved the resulting cloud from in front of her face, and took the book to her chair behind the counter.

As she had recalled, the inner end-pages bore a simple relief map of Europe, Africa, and the Middle East. From Afghanistan, three curved arrows fanned westward: One arced north of the Caspian Sea toward Germany and Scandinavia; another sloped south of Suez and crossed Equatorial Africa, aimed toward the USA; and the third dart crossed Turkey and The Balkans before terminating in France.

The legend at the bottom of the map said, 'Major Drug Routes.'

A chill ran up Tereza Mimona's spine as she noted that the three arrows were rendered in yellow, orange, and bright red.

The yellow route was the one to the north and was marked 'Low Market;' the orange arrow curving southwest from Kabul was labeled 'Medium Trade;' and the red middle path...the one that bisected little Madonica and ended in Paris...was marked with the words 'Highest Traffic.'

Reza thumbed to the Index pages, then turned to page 39...**Balkan Route**

> *The Balkan Route has become the major path for transporting opiate products, in various degrees of refinement, to Europe.*
>
> *This unfortunate status has been achieved in just the past few years.*
>
> *As the Northern Route decreased in prominence, the number of opiate products (especially pure heroin) smuggled through the Balkans (Madonica, Ovosok, and Albania in particular) has grown from 50 percent to approximately 80 percent according to informed sources.*
>
> *From Istanbul, the opiates are occasionally transferred through Bulgaria, Hungary, and Romania, but more often they pass through the southwestern Balkans before proceeding to Middle Europe.*
>
> *Those deliveries from Pakistan, however, are small compared to the tons of opiates that find their way to France and Western Europe through unstable countries like Madonica and the newly formed Ovosok.*

Reza closed the thick book and nervously poured herself a generous Courvoisier. Like many in Tavoto, she was aware that the controlling political faction in nearby Skopje was corrupt, but tons of heroin passing through little Madonica? Millions in illegal drugs being transported daily on centuries old streets like her own Karaorman Road? It was almost too much to comprehend.

Perhaps, but had Tereza Mimona turned to page 40 in her copy of '*We Shall Not Sleep*,' she would have found the following entry:

Nor are opiate products the only contraband items being transported unlawfully in the Western Balkans... more and more, vital organs have been the objects of a particularly cruel harvest...and eventual sale.

Chapter 12

She reached into the shoulder pocket of her ACU blouse and extracted Bashkim Inasah's card.

Lisbeth's first full day at Billingham would be spent in Orientation. Her immunizations and medical records had been brought up to date at Fort Dix, and all that remained of her required initiation was a series of four hour-long briefings on *'Regional Weather Patterns'*...*'Foods, Persons, and Institutions to be Avoided in The Balkans'*...*'Local History Since the USSR Collapse'*...and *'Proper Conduct When Mingling with Area Civilians'*. For the most part, these advisories were to be presented in fairly straightforward films, after each of which a Q & A session would be conducted.

It was anticipated that by three o'clock Colonel Wren would have completed the Orientation Program and would be free to visit the Camp's PX. Corporal Prentiss would have the Jeep waiting at the Motor Pool adjacent to the Post Exchange from two-thirty on. He'd been instructed early this morning to assure that the Doctor was ferried back and forth in a timely manner to her quarters at the home of Frau Henschel...at least until such time as she became familiar with Billingham's half-hourly bus service to and from Jaziref. Captain Mueller, though he himself would be unavailable until tomorrow, had personally issued Prentiss's orders, the young NCO told the Colonel.

Lis Wren and her chauffeur arrived at the main gate of the Camp a full hour before the 'Weather' seminar. Perhaps she would have time to scout the huge Post Exchange for the bookmarks she had in mind. They were always the first gift she mailed home when on deployment. Bookmarks were easily mailed in a business envelope...were virtually unbreakable... required no insurance or complicated postal processing... but most importantly, they served as constant reminders of her whenever her mother, brothers, sisters, or Peter opened whatever book they happened to be reading.

Of course, there was the possibility that the Camp Billingham PX didn't stock bookmarks. Camp Jennings in Iraq hadn't, for instance. She reached into the right shoulder pocket of her ACU blouse and extracted Bashkim Inasah's calling card with the phone number written on the back. *There's always this, I guess*, she said to herself.

* * *

Ostensibly, the floor plan for Tavoto's *Sarena Jemija* is not unlike that of the Zitouna Mosque in Tunisia, though the 'Quilted Mosque' is a mere twenty-five percent the size of that great edifice three hundred miles across the Mediterranean. Both are rectangular structures that have evolved from simple, square supplication rooms. Each is walled, has multiple entrances, and contains a centuries-old recessed area known as a *mihrab*. This alcove-like niche identifies the Way to Mecca... the direction worshippers must face when kneeling for the five daily calls to prayer issued by the *Muezzin*.

Beneath the surface of Tavoto's sacred prayer room, the carpeted meeting hall where devout Muslims kneel in submission every few hours in praise of Allah, lies a subterranean complex that the faithful above have never seen, nor could they ever have imagined. The underground facility consists of a secret honeycomb of electrically lighted rooms, chambers stocked to the ceilings with medical supplies, and connecting passageways that link the granite *turbe,* or mausoleum, with a locked door immediately beneath the curtained interior *mihrab* in the mosque itself. These portals are frequently used by Tavoto's shadowy Elders—and their equally mysterious clientele—but only under the cover of darkness, and only when the faithful are engaged in prayer.

At first glance, the octagonal stone sepulcher looks like the apex of San Francisco's Coit Tower, the familiar round, concrete column that rises from the top of Telegraph Hill in the North Beach section of the City by the Bay. Like Coit Tower's octagon tip, the *turbe* crypt features eight high, arched gaps—or what at first appear as gaps—in the exterior wall, as if rendering the tomb open to the breeze. In actuality, the eight narrow arches house one-way mirrors…impenetrable Lexan reflectors that effectively conceal the almost nightly activity within. No one except the Elders, the Curator, and certain specifically invited 'guests' are permitted use of the passageway leading from the mausoleum. And to invade the fortress-like structure would be to incur a punishment unspeakable in its ferocity…and ultimate death.

Inside the graceful façade, the *turbe* is curiously stark and virtually empty at ground level. Only the sarcophagi of the two Madonican sisters are indicated by stone slabs in the earthen floor, each block inlaid with an iron ring. But oddly, it is impossible to determine visually which grave holds the remains of which sister—neither pink marble cover is marked, save for the Muslim inscription meaning: *"Purify her of sin as a white robe is cleansed of filth."*

Actually, both sisters are interred in the same vault. The 'tomb' beside it…the catacomb farther from the river… conceals a steep stairway that leads to the labyrinth where Bashkim Inasah and Captain Eric Mueller were now meeting with the 'Quilted Mosque's' impatient Elders.

* * *

In the sub-chamber nearest the hidden flight of stone steps that terminated at the *mihrab*, Grand Imam Nazmi ben Zullah sat listening with his eyes closed. His four associates… all fluent in English…had been haggling for half an hour over the expenses incurred by Inasah on his recent trip to New York.

"Why is it necessary to travel in such luxury?" said one Grand Mufti waving Bashkim's first-class airline ticket.

"I too wish to know this," said another Elder. "Five thousand Euros!"

"Even Obama would be embarrassed to buy such service," one of the Caliphs stated shaking his head. "This is criminal."

For the first time since the meeting had been convened, and the Curator called on the carpet, the Grand Imam raised his hand for quiet. "Silence!" he commanded in a voice a mere shade above a whisper. "*Criminal?* you say…I have three questions: Who engaged this man? Who dispatched this man? Who, then, is *Criminal?*"

Bashkim Inasah was off the hook…and ben Zullah turned toward Eric Mueller.

"Captain," said the Grand Imam, "Congratulations! The seed you sowed so many months ago has become a vine…and it has borne fruit at last. All that remains for us to determine is whether the grape is sweet…or sour."

Mueller looked at his watch. In less than an hour one of the young Imams would perform the duty of the *Muezzin* and electronically call the faithful to Midday prayer. If this meeting were not over in thirty minutes or so, the uniformed officer would have to wait until the sixty or seventy assembled worshippers had rolled up their rugs and left the 'Quilted Mosque.' Only then would he and the Curator be able to vacate the sub-basement…either by the *mihrab*, or the riskier *turbe* exit.

At any rate, Eric Mueller was eager to get the eighty thousand euros due him. He knew the quarterly installment was in ben Zullah's pouch at his feet, as it had been on two such previous occasions. Should he permit the Elders to procrastinate, such dawdling might become habitual, he thought. Muslims were notorious for stalling payment to contractors, their high-blown rhetoric about prompt satisfaction of debts notwithstanding.

The Captain took off his starched patrol cap…an act that in itself was a minor insult when in the presence of the Grand Imam. He placed the hat on its crown and slid it along the oval table until it was within reach of Nazmi ben Zullah. Mueller fixed the Grand Imam with a frosty stare and nodded toward the cap. The action required no explanation.

While the other clerics diverted their gaze ben Zullah lifted his soft leather bag from the floor and removed a banded wad of thousand-euro notes. He placed the one-inch stack of new bills in the patrol cap, stood, and left the room without a word.

Eric Mueller chose not to count the money, but placed the camouflaged hat containing the cash firmly on his head. Then he and Bashkim Inasah left the secret compound the same way they had come. There was time to spare before the sun would reach its zenith and the *Dhuhr Salat* would be heard throughout the old section of grubby little Tavoto.

Chapter 13

*She raised a cautionary finger.
"Take a taxi when you get to Skopje."*

Corporal Prentiss parked the Jeep in front of Frau Henschel's house just as the sun was dropping behind a row of cumulus clouds on the eastern horizon. He doubled-timed it to Lisbeth's side of the iconic vehicle that had performed so reliably in one war after another since 1940. Prentiss yanked open the small passenger door and offered the Colonel his arm in a particularly attentive manner. Lis Wren permitted herself a perfunctory glance at the Corporal's crotch to see if it might reveal the reason for his solicitude. From behind the sheer living room curtain Hanna Henschel attempted the same calculation. There was nothing especially noticeable.

"Seven-thirty tomorrow, Prentiss," Lisbeth said, returning his salute. She removed the house key from her pocket and strode to the front door in six long paces. When the uniformed woman had entered the house and closed the door behind her, Corporal Prentiss started the Jeep, U-turned in the narrow street, and rumbled back in the direction of the Camp.

Lis Wren heard activity in the kitchen. "Hanna," she called from the base of the stairs.

"*Ja,*" Hanna answered.

Lisbeth walked into the kitchen and hugged the tiny woman lightly. "I'm going to unpack and hang up my civilian clothes," she said in German, momentarily struggling over the word 'civilian,' before settling on '*Amerikaner.*'

"I have already done it," Hanna replied. "Sit…I will make tea."

"I want to take the bus down to Tavoto," said Lis. "Do you know the way to the 'Quilted Mosque' from here?"

Hanna Henschel frowned and dried her hands on her ever-present apron. "*Ja. Hij is wat moeilijk te vinden…als je vanaf de grote weg het stadje gehen sie in, moet je helemaal door het centrum…over de brug.*—It is hard to find…if you go into town from the main road, go all the way through the center… over the bridge." She raised a cautionary finger. "Take a taxi when you get to Skopje. It will soon be dark."

* * *

As she sat in the rear seat of an old Mercedes taxi she'd flagged down at the Skopje bus terminal, Lisbeth Wren shone her keychain flashlight on the careful notes she'd made during the morning's briefing on Balkan demographics. If she was going to live in this strange old place for the next four months, she'd decided, at least she wanted to arm herself with details concerning the area's antiquity.

There seems to be no figuring out the enigmatic little Municipality of Tavoto, the Orientation Director had pointed out. On the one hand, it is listed in the Army's regional demographic manuals as a key Madonican educational center…on the other, the town is plagued with the highest crime rate of any city in the Principality. The paradox is compounded by the fact that the formerly rural cluster of verdant simplicity has recently become, for whatever reason, a magnet for political splinter groups, many of which have established their headquarters in Tavoto…though Madonica's capital is but a stone's throw away.

The dusty Mercedes cab that Lis had hailed in Skopje rolled to a stop by a stone bridge. The span crossed a slate-gray stream that, judging by the direction of the sunset, ran from north to south. The octogenarian driver lit a beat-up cigarette from his shirt pocket, mumbled something unintelligible, and held up ten fingers.

"Take me to the 'Quilted' Mosque.'" Lisbeth said in English. She pointed straight ahead. "Over the bridge."

The elderly man merely closed his eyes and shrugged.

"Ahead…forward…go." She flapped her extended hand.

The driver sucked on the battered cigarette, shook his head from side to side, and held up the ten splayed fingers once again. Again he muttered something that ended in "…euro."

Lis sighed in exasperation, withdrew eleven euros from her bag, and waving away a cloud of tobacco smoke, she placed the money in the old man's gnarled hand.

She exited the dented cab, determined to walk to the 'Quilted Mosque' before the sunset sky had become completely dark. By her watch it was ten to six. Perhaps Bashkim Inasah had left for the day…if so, Lisbeth Wren would find the small nearby *Restoran VEH-cheh-rah* that Hanna had recommended…the one she'd said was so nice and clean.

* * *

In the dwindling light, Lis made her way to the bridge over the River Pena, the span that her new friend Frau Henschel had described so accurately. Then she maneuvered through the twists and turns of centuries-old Karaorman Road. This was clearly the business district of Old Tavoto. The quarter's ancient stone buildings extended practically to the cobbled streets and already, weary women in ankle-length outfits were busily shuttering and locking ground-floor windows behind which dim lights glowed faintly...then faded from view entirely as the shopkeepers disappeared inside their doorways and pulled the portals shut.

Most of the industrious proprietors wore head scarfs or babushkas and dark, one-inch heels whose drab colors matched their full-cut dresses and coarse aprons. There seemed to be no men in Tavoto at this hour...nor children, for that matter...and Lisbeth wondered where they could be. *Probably anticipating their dinner behind the drawn blinds of the second-floor windows*, she concluded—*where the next daily job waited for the all-suffering women of Tavoto.*

Dressed in fashionable flared slacks, a man-tailored shirt, and forest-green blazer, Lisbeth had drawn the censorious attention of Karaorman Road's envious female merchants, but it was the sort of disapproval to which Colonel Wren had become accustomed. The exact opposite reaction invariably was exhibited by men, of course. Predictably, they were only too quick to show their approbation for the slender Doctor's appearance...often to a degree that constituted inappropriate conduct, and worse.

It was the chief reason for the nine millimeter Beretta in her oversized Coach handbag.

Lis Wren had seen every kind of architecture in her various military and municipal deployments. Over the years she'd been assigned to areas where the natives lived in everything from makeshift huts to glass skyscrapers. As a Policewoman, she'd responded to assault complaints in the subways of New York, where thousands of the City's homeless often lived in squalor...their only shelter a cardboard box in an abandoned underground tunnel. Hours later she might be answering a backup call where a robbery was taking place in the shadow of a Park Avenue high rise.

As an Army officer, Lisbeth had lived for months among Asians whose homes were mere grass-roofed hovels…or alongside Afghans who seemed more concerned about the housing of their goats and camels than the accommodation of their wives and daughters. But never before had Lis Wren witnessed residential or commercial structures like those she saw now in Old Tavoto. Many of these slanted, crooked, pitted little buildings had been constructed, she could tell…not a generation, or a century, or a millennium ago…indeed many of Tavoto's houses and shops dated back three hundred years before the birth of Christ! And unlike the essentially temporary living quarters found in Africa, Asia, and The Orient, these sturdy edifices had been erected as if in recognition of the eternal nature…the unending needs…of Mankind itself.

* * *

Bashkim Inasah jogged the purchase orders he'd been reviewing, and he locked them away in the top, right-hand drawer of his desk. The bookmarks that he had purchased from Tereza Mimona were still spread out on the surface of the worn antique leather inlay, but they were safe there. No one would disturb such inexpensive and readily identifiable items. In fact, there was nothing of great value in the 'Quilted Mosque' that was subject to being stolen.

Granted, there were innumerable priceless artifacts within the square, thirty-foot-high chamber, but they were virtually impervious to theft by even the most enterprising thieves. The colorful paintings that adorned the *Sarena Jemija*, both inside and out, were all frescoes. As such, they formed integral parts of the ancient two-foot-thick stone and plaster walls. To make off with even a small chunk of the Fifteenth Century artwork which decorated those surfaces would require demolishing a portion of the sacred building itself. And if that task were not daunting enough, 'fencing' or disposing of a purloined mural would be a near-impossibility, given the renown attached to everything even remotely associated with the 'Quilted Mosque.'

The Persian carpet that covered the stone floor of the mosque was similarly theft-proof. Its sheer size alone rendered the massive rug impossible to remove from the prayer room in one piece. Even tightly rolled the woolen masterpiece would be twice as wide as *Sarena Jemija's* main door…and to cut it into sections would be to destroy its great value. Only the silliest souvenir hunter would have chanced the loss of a hand by defacing the Islamic treasure, at any rate.

The only other true valuables in the otherwise empty building were five dazzling chandeliers that hung to within fifteen feet of the colorfully carpeted floor—well out of unaided human reach. Each fixture contained nine rows of cut crystal elements that sparkled even in the constantly dim interior of the 700-year-old holy site.

Understandably, Tavoto's 'Quilted Mosque' had never been the target of either pilferage or vandalism.

Bashkim lifted his jacket from the back of his chair, wriggled into it, and walked in stocking feet toward the small door at the base of the minaret…not far from which Lisbeth Wren was looking curiously at the silver Citroen parked on *Ulica Goce Delcev*…with two of its wheels on the old stone sidewalk.

* * *

The charismatic Curator had planned to stop for dinner at a favorite bistro on the western outskirts of Skopje; it had been weeks since he'd treated himself to a kebob of lamb and sliced green peppers, and since today was *Zhmah*…Friday… it would probably be three days at least before he'd have a similar opportunity.

As Bashkim Inasah approached his stylish French sedan, listing to the left as always in its familiar parking spot near the minaret, a sudden sense of unease ran along his spine. Through eyes still unaccustomed to the shadowy darkness of the *Goce Delcev*, Bashkim spotted a very thin man of average height, wearing dark trousers, a white shirt open at the neck, and a blue or green sport coat. The fellow was quite young, fair-haired, and he carried an expensive-looking satchel. Furthermore, the stark-still stranger was unquestionably paying inordinate attention to the Citroen. A car thief… waiting for the owner of the silver vehicle to unlock the driver's door…and thus provide the patient culprit all the opportunity he'd need. Bashkim was sure of it.

The robust Inasah did not alter his course, but rather strengthened his grip on the handle of the briefcase, prepared to use it as a weapon if needs be, and he deliberately walked past the sedan. As he drew nearer to the lithe young man, but on the opposite side of the narrow street, Bashkim could see that he must outweigh the fellow by at least fifty pounds.

Maintaining the steady pace of an entrepreneur concerned only with the mundane business of returning home from a day at work, Bashkim Inasah consciously gauged the precise moment of his pre-emptive attack. Four more paces…three… two…then, with his attaché already flung into a vicious backswing, his black Madonican eyes grew large and round in incredulous recognition.

"Lisbeth!" he cried—while simultaneously releasing his grip on the case, thereby launching it back in the direction of the mosque.

"Bashkim!" an equally astonished Lis Wren shrieked…and she hurled her wilting body into his welcoming arms.

Chapter 14

Peter Ravens knew he was in big trouble when Gigi went missing.

Though one would never think it when observing the various breeds of modern dogs, all domesticated canines trace their origins to the Grey Wolf. This is true as much for the Mastiff as the Chihuahua. In fact, such domestication, if genetic and archaeological evidence is to be believed, indicates that humans effectively began cultivating wolves to their use at the latest fifteen thousand years ago, and possibly as far back as thirty thousand B.C.

Studies clearly show that some wolf pups, if reared by humans from the early age of three weeks and younger, are quite easily tamed, and certain experiments have demonstrated that even *adult* wolves can be successfully socialized!

Many scientists are convinced that ancient peoples adopted orphaned wolf cubs and nursed them alongside human infants, and once these early cub adoptees began to breed among themselves, a new legion of disciplined domestic animals resulted. Over generations, of course, they inevitably become more and more dog-like.

The phenomenon is easily believed when comparing the Grey Wolf with today's Alaskan Malamutes, German Shepherds, and Siberian Huskies…but their canine cousins,

Miniature Poodles, Terriers, and other small breeds are hardly what one would call wolf-like…either in appearance or temperament.

The fact is there are easily as many different types of dog lovers on Earth as there are varied canine companions to match up with those fanciers. Indeed, just as Rome itself is said to have been founded by Romulus and Remus, the human twin babes suckled by a she-wolf of ancient lore, the current bond between man and the Grey Wolf's progeny has never been stronger.

That attachment was especially true in the case of Lisbeth Wren and her Boston Terrier…and Peter Ravens knew he was in big trouble when Gigi went missing.

* * *

Ironically, the abduction of the happy little purebred had been facilitated in large measure because of Lisbeth's solicitude regarding her dog's care under the equally attentive veterinarian, Dr. Simeon Forrester. As a physician herself, Lis Wren knew the importance of maintaining an itemized record of any patient's history. And this was especially true in the case of dumb animals; they obviously could not be depended upon to make specific information available of their own accord. Consequently, Gigi's mistress had provided Forrester with every conceivable detail concerning the Terrier's pedigree, diet, medication, and behavior.

Lisbeth's Boston had been one of a healthy litter of five… as had her dame and her grand dame. They, as well as the sires involved, were apparently sound, were still alive, and had all been AKC registered. The environment in which Gigi lived was closely controlled, and frequently sprayed for canine parasites like ticks and fleas. No other animals shared the home, nor were any permitted on the premises. Nonetheless, Gigi had been spayed at seven months as a precaution against the prospect of her straying when coming into season.

The sprightly dog's shots had been meticulously administered, and her diet consisted exclusively of dry Purina dog chow, with not more than one medium-sized dog biscuit permitted per day. Her one-pint water bowl was rinsed and replenished twice daily in summer—once in the afternoon during the rest of the year.

Lis and Peter appeared to be equally fastidious about tending to the animal's emotional and physical needs by walking her religiously for half an hour each day, except in the most inclement weather. Much of that obligation fell to Peter, of course, because of Lisbeth's frequent military deployments overseas and her attendant stateside training sorties. In addition, she was an esteemed Primary Care physician at the nearby Veteran's Administration Medical Center, one of the country's most advanced health care facilities.

Essentially a house dog, Gigi was permitted a full hour's morning exercise period in the fenced backyard of the modest home that Lis and Peter shared in well-kept, residential Plainview, Long Island. The daily regimen took place in early morning—or if that was not feasible, Peter arranged to drop by the house later on to let the dog out for her constitutional romp.

It was on such a day that the canine protective gods seemed to be looking the other way…at least as far as perky little Gigi was concerned.

Bashkim Inasah had arrived at Kennedy International in a driving rainstorm, but now, at nine-thirty a.m., the low-pressure cell had moved east toward Montauk. A freshening breeze accompanied by clearing skies had overtaken western Long Island, and the visitor from Ovosok called his conspirator at the Uniondale Animal Hospital. Simeon Forrester, in turn, telephoned Peter Ravens at the golf course where he worked. *Would Gigi be available to be seen today?*

"Sure, Doc...what's up?"

"A virus going around. She should have a shot. What time can I stop by?"

"I'm gonna let her out for an hour at eleven, then meet somebody for lunch. You need me there?"

"Not at all. I'll stop by."

Chapter 15

Balkan merchants were highly accommodating of men, while regarding women as mere adjuncts.

Ilaz Thaci is a typically stretched out, mile-long village whose quaint, single story houses and shops flank both sides of the north/south highway from Skopje to Jaziref. The charming Café Sandino where Bashkim Inasah had decided to dine on his beloved lamb kebob, lures Madonicans, Albanians, and Ovosoks alike in an eclectic mix of Christians and Muslims, even on a Friday night like this one.

Thus, the appealing *restoran* proved a doubly fortuitous choice now that the obliging American Doctor had accepted Bashkim's proposed half-hour tour of the 'Quilted Mosque'… followed by his dinner offer…after which, of course, the dashing Curator would gladly drive Lis to her new quarters at the home of Frau Henschel.

They were practically neighbors, after all, were they not? Things were working out well, it seemed.

Lisbeth, woefully deficient in her knowledge of Western Balkan food, and wine in particular, accordingly deferred to Bashkim's familiarity with regional fare and suggested that he do the ordering. He, in turn, having determined that like most Americans, Lis "loved" what she called "shish kebob," ordered a double portion of the broiled lamb and peppers dish. As for the wine, he explained that while eighty percent of Madonica's production was of the 'Red' variety, he strongly suggested a bottle of Smederevka. It was a mild white wine, he explained, which would not overpower the delicate flavor of the lamb…or interfere with the sharper seasoning provided by the green peppers.

It was clear to the Colonel that the apparently dignified man into whose arms she had leaped two hours earlier, knew a thing or two about food and drink. She had already witnessed his expertise in the 'kissing' department. That would be enough romance for tonight…and Lis Wren hoped for both their sakes that Bashkim Inasah wouldn't push the issue.

He himself had pointed out the likelihood they would be seeing a lot of each other.

There was no hurry.

Besides…she was starving.

* * *

The young waiter seemed to know Bashkim, though Lisbeth wondered if the youth's attentiveness might not be merely reflective of something she had learned in Orientation this morning…that Balkan merchants were invariably highly accommodating of men, while regarding women as mere adjuncts…temporary guests who, like children, were expected to speak only when spoken to.

The server's brass name tag read 'Teke' and he approached the couple's corner table with a small basket of '*Mekici*'… deep-fried pieces of dough fresh from the oven, powdered and covered with a checkered napkin the way Hanna's biscuits had been at breakfast. Teke bowed to Bashkim, nodded vaguely toward Lisbeth, and placed the wicker container in the middle of the table.

"*Tarator,*" Bashkim said to the neatly dressed waiter, pointing to the hand-written parchment menu. The boy smiled approvingly. He made a penciled note on a twice-folded sheet of paper and returned to the kitchen.

"It is a traditional Madonican soup," said Bashkim. "You must try it. Here at Café Sandino the *Tarator* is said to be the finest in all of Europe." He lifted the cloth cover from the fried bread and passed the basket to Lis. She took two small pieces of the *Mekici*, placed one on her plate, and bit into the other.

"It's sweet," she said, surprised.

"It is made from yogurt, eggs, and flour," he said, "with a touch of olive oil…sweetened with honey." Bashkim helped himself to one of the irregularly shaped morsels.

"What's in the *Tarator,*" Lisbeth asked looking from her corner chair to get a glimpse of what the dozen other diners at Sandino were eating.

"It is a wonderful cold dish," said the enthusiastic man. "Some refer to it as 'Liquid Salad.' The main ingredient, again, like many dishes here in The Balkans, is yogurt, but it is distinguished primarily by thinly sliced cucumber…flavored with walnut, dill, and garlic." Lis looked at him skeptically. "The slightest *touch* of garlic," the Curator said perceptively. He added, "*Tarator* is to Madonica what vichyssoise is to France." He nibbled on his wedge of crisp *Mekici*, then touched his lips with his napkin "…only better! As you Americans say, 'Trust Me.'"

Lisbeth chose the moment to say what had been on her mind since their impromptu embrace on the cobblestoned street at the base of the *Sarena Jemija* minaret.

"I hope you don't consider me…," she twisted her napkin and stared at her hands, "…impulsive."

Bashkim Inasah's smile vanished and was replaced by an almost brotherly expression of reassurance. "There is a great distinction, Lisbeth, between 'Impulse,' and 'Instinct,'" he said. He placed his comforting hand on hers. "What you did when I frightened you tonight was 'Instinctive,' my Dear." The dazzling smile returned and he added, "It was not 'Impulsive.' Not in the least."

"You're very kind."

"I try to be honest…at least, when dealing with beautiful women."

"Tell me," said Lis, biting into her second chunk of golden *Mekici*, "…have you never married?"

"A fair enough question," Bashkim replied. "No…I have never married." He lifted a wedge of the deep-fried bread from the basket, broke it, and placed the larger half on Lisbeth's plate. "Unlike yourself," he added, "I have never entered into a romantic union of any sort…not a serious or lasting one, at least."

Lisbeth fixed him with a steady gaze. She narrowed her eyes in a not-unfriendly manner and evaluated his response, wondering how the impeccably polite man opposite her could possibly know she was in a committed relationship.

But Bashkim Inasah was too perfect a gentleman to warrant being interrogated, or even being questioned in some suspicious, roundabout way. "Unlike myself, you say? But you don't even know me."

Any trace of pretense or innuendo had disappeared from the Curator's tawny face, and he reached into the inner pocket of his well-tailored sport coat. "Please do not be alarmed," he said, his soft brown eyes seeming to plead for understanding. "But I know a good deal more about you than perhaps I have a right to." He removed a business-sized, white envelope from his breast pocket and tapped it softly on the neatly ironed tablecloth. "In fact, Doctor Wren, my associates and I probably know more about your personal life than even the United States Army does."

She sat stark still.

Bashkim Inasah removed a slightly creased photograph from the envelope and held it face forward for her examination. Even by the dim candlelight of Café Sandino, Lis Wren recognized the photo immediately. It was a snapshot of Lisbeth, her mother, and three of her sisters. It had been taken less than seven months prior at, of all places, Machu Picchu…an Incan palace half a world away…a site so remote in the high Andes that even the Spanish Conquistadors had never found it.

Lis scanned the room reflexively, then focused an accusing glare at Inasah.

"Where the hell did you get that?" she demanded quietly… bitterly.

"We have been hoping to meet you for some time," said Bashkim. He passed the group photo to Lisbeth, followed by the envelope. "There is another photograph in there," he said, "…a somewhat newer one."

She leveled him with a withering look and tore the second picture from the number ten envelope. It was her little dog, Gigi.

Chapter 16

Forrester might never get another nickel from the gang that controlled vital organ trafficking.

A polar vortex, or glacial cyclone, is an ongoing huge weather system situated near one of the planet's poles. On Earth these huge vortices are located in the middle and upper atmosphere, and extend even into the stratosphere. The cyclones constantly surround glacial high pressure points in both the Arctic and Antarctic. There, they occupy the wake of polar cold fronts whose life-threatening temperatures rarely have been recorded in temperate zones…but just such a phenomenon was due to dip down through Canada and into the Northeastern United States in the next few days.

These extremely frigid weather systems grow stronger in winter, Doctor Forrester knew, and weaken in the summer, because they rely on the difference in temperature that exists between the equator and the polar caps. It had been an unusually warm spring and summer in the northeastern U.S., and all the meteorological models had indicated the reverse would be true in the Northern Hemisphere this fall and winter.

It was the sort of occurrence that Simeon had experienced only once in his life—and never while practicing Veterinary Medicine. Accordingly, he had installed a state-of-the-art air conditioning system in the animal hospital in May, and it had proven effective throughout a sweltering July and August. But the improved heating plant that would protect his patients (some of them highly cold-sensitive) from the prospect of a polar vortex, was not yet fully functional. In particular, the Doctor was concerned about the four-year-old Boston in cage seventeen. The normally perky animal had seemed a bit lethargic of late. True, no one on the staff knew specifically who the abducted Terrier belonged to…and even Peter Ravens would never have guessed her whereabouts… but the Madonican, Inasah, knew. He, in fact, had proposed the scheme.

That's what bothered Simeon Forrester as he dialed 'Four Seasons Climate Control' from the desk in his office, and waited impatiently for someone to answer. If the new heating ducts designed to raise overnight temperatures in the Uniondale Animal Hospital five degrees were not fitted in place this weekend…and if Lisbeth Wren's darling Gigi became seriously ill as a result…Bashkim Inasah would have "The Doc" at his mercy—Forrester might never get another nickel from the cold blooded gang that controlled vital organ trafficking in The Balkans.

* * *

The photograph from Machu Picchu had surprised Lis Wren, but in actuality it represented no implicit threat to anyone. In fact, Lisbeth recalled when the picture had been taken by their Peruvian tour guide. The five women shown were all healthy adults, apparently quite capable of taking care of themselves, and the normally unflappable Doctor had quickly regretted her somewhat paranoid reaction. She had even submitted the candid shot to the Northport V.A.

Hospital's online magazine, where anyone could have easily copied it.

But the photo of the eighteen-pound Gigi, curled innocently on a rich-woven rug, beneath a plate glass coffee table, a rubber sandal held provocatively between her front paws…that endearing image was another matter altogether. What possible reason could Bashkim have for reproducing a picture of her dog? Especially a photograph taken in the privacy of her own home? There was obviously a message being sent here.

"What's this all about?" said Lis.

"I was asked to give it to you."

She jerked her head to one side and looked at him out of the corner of her eye. "By whom? Why?"

"My associates will explain," said the Curator.

'Teke' the waiter materialized from behind a fringed curtain, a large tray balanced over one shoulder, and he deftly lowered the *Tarator* to the tabletop level.

"I think I'd enjoy my soup more if I knew where you got this picture of my dog." Lis placed Gigi's picture on the table next to her *Tarator* and tapped the face of it expectantly.

Bashkim moved his napkin from the table to his lap. "It is all quite innocent," he said, adding several shakes of black pepper to his shallow bowl. "We in Ovosok and Madonica are a very accommodating people. We like to make our guests feel at home."

"How considerate," said Lis, apparently unconvinced. She floated her own table napkin to her thighs, hiked her chair forward, and dusted the cucumber soup with pepper.

"It is still early," said the broad shouldered man. "If it pleases you, we can meet with my acquaintances in Tavoto after dinner. Be assured they will be happy to answer any and all questions, I assure you."

Lisbeth Wren ostentatiously pushed back the sleeve of her blazer and lifted her shirt cuff. "It's not quite eight. Where in Tavoto are these friends of yours?"

"Why, at the 'Quilted Mosque,' of course," Bashkim smiled. "But bear in mind that they are my colleagues…I never said they are my *friends*."

* * *

Normally Hanna Henschel would not have invited anyone, especially a man, into her little house on the *cul-de-sac* of Ruga Dognal…certainly not after eight o'clock on a Friday night, at any rate. However this man at the door was her benefactor, Captain Eric Mueller. He had arranged for her meeting with the pleasant young Doctor Wren, after all, so the least she could do would be to offer him a cup of tea. And to tell the truth, Hanna relished the opportunity to converse, if only briefly, with still another person who was fluent in her native language.

At the kitchen table, they sipped strong tea and spoke in German.

Mueller nodded toward the staircase. "I assume the Colonel has gone upstairs for the night."

Frau Henschel added a generous spoonful of sugar to her steaming mug. "No…shopping…for souvenirs, I think." The tiny woman pushed the ornate sugar bowl toward Captain Mueller and he declined with a shake of his head.

"Has she gone back to Billingham, then?"

"She does not tell me, and I do not ask," said Hanna. "Would you like some cake? Schnapps?"

"But the Doctor has no transportation…unless she called a taxi," said Mueller. "Or perhaps she took a bus. Do you know?"

"She is a grown woman, Captain," Frau Henschel said flatly, a trace of annoyance in her voice.

Eric Mueller finished half of his tea, stood, and donned his perfectly shaped patrol cap. "There are several souvenir shops in the Enver Hadri section of Jaziref," he said, walking through the modest living room and toward the front door. "I'll pass there on my way back to the Camp." At the door, he slid the security chain free and turned toward Hanna. "When Colonel Wren returns, tell her that I will call on her during the weekend." He opened the door, stepped into the cool night air, and strode toward the curb where his Jeep was parked.

When he reached the end of the short walkway the Henschel woman's shrill voice brought him up short. "You might want to telephone before your next visit," she said in her most officious tone. "It is a courtesy I extend to my guests. You understand."

Without acknowledging, Captain Eric Mueller climbed into the canvas-enclosed vehicle and pulled the small door behind him. As Hanna Henschel closed her blue front door and locked it, the gray-haired Captain made a tight turn in the *cul-de-sac*, drove the length of Ruga Dognal in fifteen seconds, and turned right on Braim Ademi. It was five short blocks to the specialty Enver Hadri shops that surround the University. *Perhaps she walked there,* he thought. Then he cursed inwardly, *Goddammit...I should have asked the Henschel bitch what she was wearing! Never mind...I'll spot her.*

Chapter 17

Tereza Mimona pedaled harder as she turned onto the Radovan Footbridge.

Tereza Mimona had stayed late at Lola Books, busying herself with the myriad duties that are never finished in her line of work. But actually Reza's chief objective in filling her mind with the thousand and one things one could always find to do in a bookstore, was ridding herself of the nagging suspicions regarding Bashi's often mysterious itinerary. More than anything, she hoped against hope for some concrete indication that would prove her misgivings groundless where he was concerned.

When finally she could no longer concentrate on her musty inventory of secondhand hardcovers, Tereza rolled her ancient bicycle from behind the counter that held the cash register, pushed the bike out onto dark Karaorman Road, and locked up Lola Books for the night. She climbed on the dented old bicycle she'd owned for thirty years and rattled south down the sloping street in the direction of the river.

Where *Ulica Goce Delcev* met the winding banks of the Pena, Reza turned west and wobbled along the narrow alley in the direction of the '*Sarena Jemija*.' In a few minutes, she could see that her friend Bashkim's Citroen was not parked in its usual place…he had gone for the weekend. *Heading home to Jaziref,* she concluded…*if in fact he isn't there already.*

Tereza Mimona pedaled harder as she turned onto the wooden Radovan Footbridge. In her round rearview mirror she noted the sudden illumination of the 'Quilted Mosque's' minaret. The lavender glow meant that it must be after nine o'clock—the Muslim equivalent of the Jewish Sabbath had been officially over for hours.

* * *

Bashkim Inasah's silver sedan took on the violet hue that bathed the *Sarena Jemija's* narrow spire, and Lisbeth saw the same color reflected in the Curator's chiseled features as he edged the car toward the base of the minaret. The bluish-purple tint gave his face a funereal aspect, Lis thought, and she knew that her expression must be similar in appearance. She quickly lowered the Citroen's padded sun visor, leaned forward, and slid aside a leather panel that covered a small vanity mirror. If anything, the attractive woman's flawless complexion was enhanced by the indigo cast that now highlighted her Teutonic cheekbones and prominent brow. In particular, her eyes were enriched by the cobalt cast in much the same way that sapphire eye shadow seems to add size and luster to a subject's cerulean pupils.

As always, Bashkim parked the car with the passenger-side wheels on the high stone sidewalk. The move might have been expected by Lisbeth, who had seen the sedan thus positioned earlier, but for whatever reason, she seemed taken by surprise, and slid helplessly to her left…into Bashkim's protective embrace.

Instantly, she turned her face to his, preparing to apologize for the sudden intrusion, but just as swiftly, he pressed his warm mouth to hers. "Shhh," he whispered through parted lips...the faintest taste of garlic traded in their spontaneous kiss.

Lis Wren had been desperately in and out of love a dozen times. Since the age of fourteen she'd developed a fair idea of the sort of trigger that inevitably foretold the onset of that helpless feeling of commitment. But Bashkim Inasah's kiss was not such a signal. He was made for passion, this olive-skinned, mysterious man, and while he might have been easy for many women to love, Lisbeth knew she never could have been numbered among them.

The realization alarmed her more than any of her former overpowering romances had. Perhaps it was her unfamiliarity with the sudden intensity of the episode there in the car. It was one thing to feel yourself falling inexorably in love, but surrendering completely to a total stranger's invitation to a purely sexual interlude, was patently frightening...even for a mature woman of the world like Doctor Lisbeth Wren. This was new to her.

He cupped her breast tenderly with his hand, resisting the impulse to invite her own intimate touch. "I will stop when you tell me to," he breathed in her ear. "If you wish, I will take you to your new residence on the Ruga Dognal...and you need never see me again, if that is what you want." Lis had lowered her eyes and focused them on the hand that caressed her so invitingly. Bashkim tilted her chin upward with a feather touch and awaited her response. "I have never forced myself on a woman," he said, "and I never will."

"I believe you," said Lisbeth, stroking his cheek slowly with the back of her hand. "and I want to...*be*...with you." She kissed the cleft in his chin. "But not just now, Bashkim... and certainly not here. Give me a little time. I think you understand."

Once more their eyes met for several silent seconds in the glow of the floodlit *'Sarena Jemija's'* minaret that towered over them like some phallic sentinel. Then, as lovingly as when he had first fondled her, Bashkim Inasah slid his palm away... and carefully re-buttoned her shirt.

* * *

The Elders of the 'Quilted Mosque' sat smoking Murad cigarettes and drinking Basler Kirshwasser schnapps. Grand Imam Nazmi ben Zullah had ruled that they must thus partake tonight (*praise be to the all-knowing Allah*) in order to assure that the American Doctor would feel *'comfortably at home'* during this initial meeting. The seeming violations of the Holy Koran were sure to be forgiven, the Grand Imam had pointed out, since such indulgences were common among most non-Muslims, and were absolutely necessary when undertaking business ventures that included Western infidels.

Only the Grand Mufti al Nimar had taken issue with the pronouncement of ben Zullah. He, in addition to questioning the excess as *'unnecessarily immoderate,'* further railed against entertaining an undoubtedly unclean woman in their private labyrinthine quarters so close to the *Sarena Jemija's* great overhead prayer room.

"It is not necessary that we touch her," said the Grand Imam, confident that to do so would be to stretch the immensely-loving Allah's tolerance past all endurance, "It is required only that Inasah the Curator win her confidence... and maintain it."

"And if he should succumb to the temptations of her body?" Rhija the young Caliph asked.

Nazmi ben Zullah shrugged and poured himself another cup of Kirshwasser. "Why, then he will be beheaded," the Grand Imam said lightly.

Chapter 18

She could hardly be mistaken for the average Balkan female.

The Enver Hadri shops occupy a five-block strip along Besim Rexhepi, the most cosmopolitan thoroughfare in all of Jaziref. The avenue is the ancient city's equivalent of Rodeo Drive in Beverly Hills, the Champs-Elysees in Paris, or Worth Avenue in Palm Beach. Though to compare the 1000-year-old boulevard to those glitzy monuments to excess would be something of a stretch. Most of the shops in the quaint quarter that forms the northern perimeter of Jaziref University are open-air establishments where transactions usually take place on the sidewalks…amid racks of luxurious gowns and burkas…bangles and veils…turbans and designer blue jeans.

Captain Eric Mueller guided his Jeep slowly in the westbound lane nearest the Besim Rexhepi curb. Here, in the shadow of Ovosok's largest school of higher education, well-heeled pedestrian shoppers were uncharacteristically slow-moving and discriminating, whereas in other parts of the old town, business was conducted at a frenetic pace, often punctuated with haggling and curses.

The uniformed Captain had not undertaken such a patrol since his days as a Military Policeman some thirty years prior, and he had to remind himself that tonight, despite his rank, he held none of the authority that he'd wielded when perambulating the wartime streets of Saigon or the rubbish-strewn alleys of Seoul. Here Eric Mueller was a guest of this tiny Principality where he worked, and he was expected to behave as a visitor should. He wore no armband signifying supremacy over anyone. He carried no threatening sidearm… not even a nightstick.

On fashionable Besim Rexhepi, Jaziref's typical aroma of peppers and boiling cooking oil was replaced by the fragrance of expensive perfume or hazelnut coffee. And of course in this upscale section, at least, no prostitutes stepped brazenly in front of his vehicle, insisting that he stop short, and inviting him to '…*come round corner, Gee-Eye, for fazt fawk—ten euro.*'

Eric Mueller was confident that he would recognize Lisbeth Wren when he saw her, whether in or out of her Army Combat Uniform. Granted, she would certainly stand out in the 'Camo Greens' but at five-foot-ten she could hardly be mistaken for the average Balkan female, no matter what she was wearing. However, when the Captain and his Jeep at last passed the trendy shops 'Sami'… 'Hysen Terpeza'…and finally 'Kuvendi,' Eric still had not spotted the Lieutenant Colonel. Perhaps he would double back to the Braim Ademi highway, turn around, and make another pass.

He flashed his lights and made a U-turn. There were *some* things almost anyone could get away with.

* * *

Where the glow engulfing the 'Quilted Mosque's' pointed minaret faded into the darkness of the surrounding grassland, Bashkim and Lisbeth hurried hand in hand toward the granite *turbe* thirty yards away. From their chosen path on the shadowy edge of the lavender ring of light, they could see the illuminated *Sarena Jemija* quite clearly, but since there were no other lights in the mosque's heavily treed complex along the River Pena, they themselves were practically invisible.

"Where are we going?" Lis asked in a hoarse whisper as they rushed up a modest incline topped by the stone mausoleum.

"Stand here...in the entryway," said the Curator, and he removed a large iron key from his jacket pocket. In seconds the tomb's lone door swung inward, Bashkim eased the Doctor inside, and the heavy door swerved shut with an echoing click. By the radiance of only a small keychain flashlight he made his way toward the pair of marble slabs in the center of the austere mausoleum. Bashkim reached toward the metal ring that extended upward from the sarcophagus on the right, twisted the heavy iron loop...and the pink marble block slid slowly backward. In the space thus revealed, Lisbeth could make out a circular steel ladder that wound down into the gloomy void beneath.

"Follow me," said Bashkim Inasah. "Follow my light."

As the muscular Curator moved nimbly down the ladder's snaking metal rungs, he held the small light source clamped in his teeth, enabling its slender beam to light the way on the gray stones that enveloped the stairway. The wall was never more than two feet from Lisbeth's face: *Not for the claustrophobic*, she thought, and the slender Doctor was thankful both for her slim physique...and her hours of medical school training in cramped, inactive, MRI chambers. *This is like climbing down the inside of a fifteen-foot barrel, for God's sake!* She looked up to see if the mysterious marble slab had moved, but could make out nothing in the inky blackness.

In mere minutes Bashkim stepped from the lowest rung of the ladder and tapped the curving siderail twice with the penlight—a signal that he had reached the bottom of the narrow shaft...and that she should follow him quietly.

Lis Wren took the last long step from the ladder's bottom rung and saw that her partner had shone the light on the irregularly shaped stepping stones at his feet. A narrow corridor, wide enough for only one person at a time, led southeast by Lisbeth's estimate...in the direction of the 'Quilted Mosque.'

The Curator held the light against his thigh...pointed downward...as he began to walk slowly along the flat stones. A throwback, Lis thought, to the relative civility of her mother's recollection, when ushers in theaters guided patrons to their seats in that manner. *But this is no Hollywood film*, Lis said inwardly, *and if we're in a movie house, it's a friggin' strange one!* She squeezed the handbag with her elbow and felt the reassuring bulge of the Beretta.

After they'd stepped-off perhaps forty paces in the level, unlit tunnel, Bashkim stopped, reached behind him, and pressed his palm into Lisbeth's midsection. He turned off the penlight and she grasped the hand that now restrained her.

Bashkim pushed a low, metal door and it opened easily into a sort of anteroom whose dull green lighting revealed walls hung with tapestries. The room contained four U-shaped chairs, two of which were occupied by obviously frightened women. On the cool air of the subterranean chamber Doctor Lisbeth Wines detected the dense, unmistakable odor...of ether.

She spun toward the somber Curator. "What's going on here?" she demanded.

*　*　*

Captain Eric Mueller completed his second drive-by of the fashionable Enver Hadri shops that lined the five-block strip along busy Besim Rexhepi. With Lisbeth nowhere to be seen, he cursed and pointed his Jeep eastward on the Jaziref highway…past the crossroads communities of Bibaj and Sojeve…in the direction of the Camp.

At a gradual curve in the two-lane artery north of Billingham's western extension, Mueller sped south on the access road leading to the giant facility's Main Gate. Once there, he sullenly flashed his ID, and without waiting for the Military Policeman to complete his snappy salute, the Captain flipped him a poor excuse for acknowledgment…and sped down Gen. George S. Patton Drive, tires squealing and smoking, in the direction of the Bachelor Officers' Quarters. The General for whom Billingham's main road was named would have slapped Mueller roundly had he been there to witness the display—if for no other reason than the Captain's abuse of government property.

Truth be told, the manipulative Eric Mueller deserved far more than a gloved hand whipped across his face. Even a lifetime spent in Leavenworth's supermax military prison would be considered a light sentence if his full complicity in Tavoto's ongoing cruel harvest were ever fully known.

He parked behind the BOQ. Christ he was tired! He hadn't slept in forty hours!

Chapter 19

"The Caliph requests that before entering, you button your shirt to the neck."

A muffled chime sounded on the far side of the conference room door, and Bashkim released the braided lavender cord that hung there. At the sound of the dull clang, the two worried women on the other side of the gold curtain whimpered loud enough to be heard by the attentive Lisbeth Wren in the second anteroom. She shook off the Curator's hand, took a firmer hold on her leather bag that held the Beretta, and backed slowly toward the draped alcove.

The Doctor stopped short of the shimmering curtain and listened intently to determine if the young women in Muslim garb on the other side continued to moan…but the keening seemed to have stopped.

The richly embossed door to the Elders' meeting room opened noiselessly, and a lightly bearded Caliph, evidently the lowest in rank among the five *Mullahs*, stood holding it ajar from inside. He nodded to Bashkim and, like the blasé waiter at Café Sandino, seemed at first to take no notice of Lisbeth whatsoever.

But apparently the Caliph had observed the attractive Doctor Wren…and had, in fact, examined her in detail. He leaned toward the Curator and murmured something in a derivative of Farsi, that of course she did not comprehend.

Bashkim turned to Lisbeth and said apologetically, "The Caliph requests that, uh, before entering, you button your shirt to the neck…and he also asks that you, uh, kindly fasten your jacket."

Lis fixed the young cleric with a smug stare and she maintained it as she said to Bashkim, "And you can tell the Caliph to go fuck himself." Whereupon, Doctor Lisbeth Wren brushed past both men, and strode into the conference chamber.

Of the four men seated at the long Olivewood table, Nazmi ben Zullah, the Grand Imam, was the only one who looked directly into the face of the audacious American woman. Lisbeth Wren returned his disapproving gape and dropped brazenly into the chair the Caliph had vacated in order to admit them. She waved her hand impatiently in front of her face and performed a series of exaggerated coughs…a firm message that she found the tobacco smoke intolerable.

Speechless, the young Caliph snatched his clay cup and ashtray from in front of Lisbeth, marched them to the far end of the richly grained table, and flung both into a receptacle half-filled with sand. Ben Zullah gestured for him to take a seat by the door, where Bashkim Inasah was already sitting, and at the Grand Imam's second nod, the other Elders lifted their ashtrays and cups of Kirshwasser, and disposed of them in the trash container as the Caliph had done. Then they returned deferentially to their seats.

As if to demonstrate his rank, Nazmi ben Zullah dropped his own Murad cigarette on the floor beneath his chair, stepped on it ostentatiously, and moved his decorative goblet to the side. He leaned forward on one elbow and fingered the tip of his beard. The other hand was planted firmly on his hip. The Senior Imam studied Lis with his intense, dark eyes, an attempt to intimidate her through the stare-down. But she merely smiled sarcastically in return.

"You are younger than I had been led to believe," said ben Zullah.

Lisbeth was in no mood for small talk. "What interest could you possibly have in my little dog?" she asked icily.

"Surely you are not forty-nine years of age," the Grand Imam persisted.

"If anything happens to anyone in my family…especially my helpless dog, Gigi…I swear to God, Allah, or Jehovah…I *will* kill you!"

"My, my," ben Zullah scoffed. "Such a vile threat from one sworn to protect life and limb."

"I have also sworn with that same oath to honor my special obligation to all human beings," Lis Wren hissed. "I envision that obligation as including the eradication of anything that threatens innocent life." She stood, leaned on the table with clenched fists, and said coolly, "…even if that threat resides in another human being—like you, Imam! Is that clear?"

Ben Zullah sat straight in his chair at the head of the conference table and looked down his hooked nose, evaluating the woman whose services he had already invested nearly half a million dollars to obtain. Incredibly a slight smile overtook his weathered face…and he dismissed the other Elders with a single wave of his hand. When they had left the meeting room through the large, carved door where Bashkim sat apprehensively, the Grand Imam motioned for the Curator to join Lisbeth and him at the long table.

"I find you an excellent candidate for inclusion on my team," he announced, addressing the Doctor.

Lis frowned and glanced at Bashkim, who sat attentively with arms crossed.

"Therefore, in one hour," said Nazmi ben Zullah, "...at midnight—six o'clock New York Time...I will arrange for you to see that your beloved pet is happy and well." He smiled. "Surely you are familiar with 'Skype' technology."

The Grand Imam reached for his ornate drinking cup and filled it with a generous draught of schnapps. His thoughtful abstaining from smoking was a courtesy not lost on Lisbeth. "Meanwhile permit me to outline a manner in which you may demonstrate your admirable dedication to mankind... through a method that probably has never occurred to you."

* * *

Pete Ravens had beaten his partners in today's threesome at Bethpage, so he had no choice but to spring for beers on the clear but chilly November afternoon. It was a sacrosanct part of golf etiquette, after all...I collect a buck from each of you...that means I have to buy Buds all around. In other words, I win a deuce, and I have to lay out six bucks, plus tip—a total of eight. Geez! It was enough to make a guy intentionally miss a seven-inch tap-in. Well...not really! Especially when that last putt meant breaking eighty.

Jonesy and Mark had signaled Angie the bartender for another round, but Pete demurred vehemently. "Nope. Gotta go, boys." He stood, laid a five and three singles on the bar, reached for his iPhone, and took a 'selfie' close-up holding his Bethpage Red Course scorecard with the dark-penciled '79' next to his face. He smiled viciously. "I'll email both of you a copy to put under your pillow."

Golf's a gentleman's game, but it's great to rub it in once in a while, Pete thought as he wheeled out of the big parking lot that served the famed five-course Bethpage golf complex. When he exited the Long Island Expressway fifteen minutes later, the clock on his car's dash read exactly five-thirty. *Past time for Gigi's constitutional*, he said to himself. *Hey, I couldn't help it.* He parked at the curb directly in front of the house. *Never mind. If Lis already called, she figured I was still out walking her. No big deal.*

But when Peter Ravens had lugged his clubs into the garage, and whistled for Gigi in the fenced back yard…Gigi wasn't there!

What the… He entered the house through the back door and whistled from the kitchen. "Come on, Gigi…let's go, Gorgeous."

Nothing.

Pete stood ramrod straight in the middle of the living room. He moved only his eyes, and he weakly repeated the little Boston Terrier's name. There wasn't a sound in the dead-quiet house.

This *was* a big deal.

Chapter 20

"I am a kind and reasonable man, but no more nonsense, please."

Grand Imam Nazmi ben Zullah passed his cup of schnapps to Bashkim and with a flip of his hand motioned for the Curator to dispose of it in the rubbish. Lisbeth picked up the package of Turkish cigarettes and tossed them toward Bashkim as well. "Throw these out, too," she said. Bashkim Inasah looked to ben Zullah for confirmation before picking up the slim box of Murads. The head *Mullah* nodded and Bashkim took both items to the trash.

"I wish to show you something that must remain confidential," said ben Zullah. "My associates and I require your agreement in that regard before we can proceed. Do I have your word?"

The Doctor looked him in the eye and waited for several seconds before answering. "Surely you're aware that I cannot agree to anything that would compromise my position as either a Physician…or a member of the United States Army."

"Understood," said the Grand Imam.

"Two other stipulations," said Lisbeth Wren, convinced that ben Zullah was neither drunk, nor stupid. "I want Curator Inasah to accompany us…and you have to assure me that I'm free to leave at any time."

Nazmi ben Zullah turned to the Curator and said, "Bashkim?"

"I will be pleased to accompany the Grand Imam and the Doctor," the Curator stated. "And of course I shall gladly escort Colonel Wren to her destination if the Grand Imam so wishes."

"Very well then," said ben Zullah. He leaned closer to Lisbeth. "When you have had the opportunity to see more of Madonica…of Ovosok…and indeed, The Balkans in general, you will discover that the people here are plagued with two unfortunate conditions: The first is a regrettably inadequate health care system, and second is the scourge of abject poverty." The Imam gestured toward Bashkim. "As our *Sarena Jemija* Curator knows well, many wealthy Northern Europeans visit our suffering southeastern nations on a regular basis. Some come to visit our Mosques, Cathedrals, and Monasteries. Others journey here to enjoy our superb Balkan cuisine. And many come to acquire our artwork, so rich in its Middle Eastern influence."

Nazmi ben Zullah paused as if hesitant to discuss the next item in his inventory of the area's resources. Then, lowering his voice, he said, "However, there is one cherished prize… perhaps the richest treasure of all…that even the poorest individual citizen of our impoverished villages holds it within his power to provide. In a very real sense, it is the gift of life itself."

The Grand Imam stood, and raising his hands with palms turned upward, he invited Lisbeth and Bashkim to join him.

Lisbeth Wren followed ben Zullah along a corridor that led, it seemed to her, in a westerly direction, though she could no longer be sure. Bashkim trailed close behind. After a dozen or so paces the Grand Imam stopped in front of a metal door, opened it, and motioned for his guests to step inside the dim enclosure. Then he too entered, and quietly closed the door behind him.

The *Mullah* pressed a switch on the wall of the twenty-foot-square room and immediately the small chamber was brightly illuminated by a series of ten long fluorescent light bulbs in dusty fixtures suspended from the ceiling. Two of the tubes flickered annoyingly, a sure sign that they were burning out. Three walls of the room were lined with rusting metal supply cabinets under which wadded paper wrapping lay discarded on a cluttered counter. In the center of the workspace was the key fixture that revealed the room's intended purpose—it was a stainless steel table two-thirds of which was covered by a white cotton sheet. The shroud had seen better days…it bore obvious bloodstains that had been incurred at various times past, and survived a hundred washings. The oldest irregular blots were now a light brownish hue; the newest were darker and some still showed traces of crimson.

Lisbeth thought of the two women in the far anteroom. What was this place, a crude abortion mill? Were those women to be subjected to the perilous indignity of this filthy, makeshift clinic?

In dismay, Nazmi ben Zullah closed three of the wall compartment doors that had been left ajar and he immediately wiped both hands on the sides of his floor-length *Galabiyya*. The *Mullah* then glanced up at the sputtering fluorescent tubes, opened the door, and called, "Rabee!" In seconds, the Caliph rushed into the room, performed *Salaam* with a deep bow, his right palm pressed to his forehead, and he maintained the reverential stance while waiting for instructions from the Grand Imam. Ben Zullah growled something in Farsi to the young *Mullah* and shoved him through the doorway.

"I must apologize for Rabee's poor housekeeping," said Nazmi ben Zullah. "He will be replaced. His successor will arrive from Skopje by morning."

"The two women on this side of the tunnel," said Lisbeth guardedly, "...why are they here?"

Either ben Zullah had not heard the question...or he chose simply to disregard it. "We must return to the conference room," he declared with authority. "Now that you are familiar with our facility, it is necessary that my associates and I become better acquainted with you. Please follow me."

"The women," Doctor Wren insisted. "...have they come to have pregnancies terminated? They don't seem to be here voluntarily."

"Neither assumption is correct," the *Mullah* murmured. "Come. We will talk in more comfortable surroundings."

"And when do I get to see my dog?" said Lis Wren shrilly.

But the Doctor had finally overplayed her hand. The Grand Imam slammed the door to the offensive operating room, and spun toward her. With dark eyes blazing, he tore the handbag from her grasp and pulled the Beretta free. Expertly, ben Zullah flicked a lever that released the magazine in the gun's handle, and the ammunition receptacle slid from its housing. The angry *Mullah* jammed the magazine into the pocket of his flowing *Galabiyya*, and he flung the weapon into the leather bag before hurling the pocketbook with its heavy nine millimeter pistol back at the Lieutenant Colonel...hitting the astonished Lisbeth Wren squarely in the middle of the chest.

"In Madonica we have an expression—'*Svinya edna*'—it means 'Stupid wild pig.' Do not give me reason to call you a '*Svinya edna*.'" The Grand Imam re-opened the door. "As I have already said, you will see your precious dog before midnight...while it still has all four of its legs...unless you insist on abusing my patience," ben Zullah warned. "In that event you will observe a somewhat altered animal—if, in fact, you are permitted to see the little bitch at all."

Lisbeth's hand went to her mouth.

"As for the *zans* in the waiting room, they are here because their unfortunate father was in need of funds. If you must know, each daughter has agreed to donate one kidney to a charitable organ bank operated by the *Sarena Jemija*. For his benevolence Papa is to be paid the generous total of one thousand euros." The Grand Imam smiled compassionately while Lisbeth Wren fumed. "The humane *mard* has received the sum of three hundred already."

Lis turned and looked at Bashkim. *Surely he must be aware of this 'organ bank,'* she thought. However the urbane Curator knew better than to alter his expression one way or the other. He and the Doctor were virtual prisoners in this underground catacomb—at least for the time being—but Bashkim Inasah was confident that ben Zullah would soon release them. After all, the chief cleric held the trump card in Gigi, the Terrier. Months of close observation in America had established beyond any question that the peppy purebred was, of all living things, the closest to Lis Wren's heart. Certainly, she loved her family, her country, the Army…liked and respected her patients…and God knows, she loved Peter unconditionally. But incredibly, it was the threat to little Gigi's welfare that would ultimately compel Lisbeth to agree to the demands soon to be made of her. That, compounded of course, by the evident opportunity to insist on sanitary surgical attention where only the most primitive treatment was now being crudely dispensed. Who could fault her…or any Doctor…for initiating such measures?

"Now, let us return to the conference room," the *Mullah* said with finality. "I am a kind and reasonable man, but no more nonsense, please."

Chapter 21

Reza shuddered only partly from the cold.

At a quarter to twelve, Tereza Mimona was still reading the book prophetically titled, 'We Shall Not Sleep.' *How,* she wondered, *can such unthinkable things be taking place in my innocent little country?* In her bed, her head and shoulders propped up by two large pillows, Reza shuddered only partly from the cold, as she continued to read by the light of a tall table lamp near her right elbow.

> *In one of several trials last year, a court in Ovosok convicted six men of purchasing eighty vital organs (in this case, kidneys) for clients visiting from, Germany, Switzerland, Mexico, and Ireland. During the trial it was revealed that the donors had been paid a generous 5,000 euros per kidney (the average purchase price is said to be in the neighborhood of 3,000)...while the organs were sold to the wealthy recipients for 100,000 euros each.*
>
> *Though witnesses for European Union prosecutors were unable to prove their theory, it is generally concluded that the kidneys in question were harvested in Madonica, refrigerated, and shipped north overnight to Prishta, where they were*

implanted using private facilities disguised as walk-in veterinary clinics.

How clever! Reza Mimona murmured inaudibly. *Who would suspect an animal hospital of illicit activity?*

She turned the page and read on.

The sad fact is that trafficking in vital organs is widely accepted on the international stage, where the practice is expanding daily. In Iran, for example, such commerce is perfectly legal. In China, even spokesmen for the government admit that executed prisoners frequently are operated on for removal of vital organs which are subsequently utilized in transplants.

Only the world's major religions seem adamantly opposed to such abuse of human dignity.

Tereza Mimona thanked Allah for the gift of her Muslim faith, lacking in fervor though it might be. She closed her book, and vowed to cut back on the brandy.

* * *

"Doc, this is Pete Ravens." Simeon Forrester had been expecting the call. He paused for an appropriate few beats.

"Peter! How's our favorite scratch golfer? Have you heard fro…?"

"Doc, I can't find Gigi."

The veterinarian let a four or five-second silence fall. "What?"

"I said, I…can't…find…GIGI! for Christ's sake!"

"She was in the back yard at eleven forty-five," said Forrester calmly. "I gave her a CDV shot…merely precautionary…"

"I'm telling you, Simeon, she's not HERE."

"Well she was prancing around the inside perimeter of the fence when I left, Peter. And I assure you I locked the gate behind me."

"Well I can goddam well assure YOU that dog is not here. I looked everywhere. I even looked under the fuckin' pool cover."

"I imagine you searched inside the house…upstairs, where the other Boston used to sleep?"

Peter Ravens lowered his tone to a menacing growl. "Simeon, if I haven't found that dog before Lis calls tonight or tomorrow my ass is toast. That woman will have me whacked!"

Doc Forrester looked at the wall clock over his desk. It was five minutes to six. *Musad* had arranged the half-minute Skype session for six on the dot, and Simeon needed to prepare the microphone, webcam, and instant messaging setup. He also had to make sure that today's front page of Newsday was prominently positioned on the floor in front of cage seventeen, though the cage number itself had already been obscured with duct tape.

"What you should do," said Forrester, "…is put a cup of dry dog chow in her dish and set it in the middle of the patio where she's bound to see it. You might put her water bowl alongside." It was three minutes to six. "Also leave the patio lights on. And Peter, get a flashlight and check along the base of the fence to see if she might have dug underneath it." Simeon glanced at the clock again…two minutes. "I'll call you in half an hour."

The veterinarian didn't wait for a reply. He grabbed the Friday Newsday from his desk, and took the newspaper along with his laptop and its built-in mic and camera, to Gigi's cage in the most remote section of the kennel. Forrester smoothed the paper on the concrete floor in front of the enclosure's mesh door—the headline read: ISLAND BRACES FOR WEEKEND STORM. He set the computer on a low stool in front of cage seventeen, and turned on the power switch. Almost immediately, a ping sounded. The Boston Terrier cocked its head and emitted a brief inquisitive whine as the screen on the angled monitor was filled with the tear-stained face of Doctor Lisbeth Wren.

The peppy little dog leaped and barked for joy…and just as quickly the computer's display went dark.

"Good girl, Gigi," said Doc Forrester.

He stripped the duct tape from the cage, picked up the copy of Newsday, and with the laptop under his arm, walked back to his office. He had to call Peter Ravens, but first he must see if the over/under for tomorrow's Ohio State-Michigan game was still fifty-one points.

Chapter 22

"First thing I think about in the morning—last thing at night."

Majors Stufkoski, Cockbyrne, and Kelvin had decided to call Lis Wren at Frau Henschel's house early Saturday morning. Maybe by then their body clocks would be sufficiently in sync with the local time to permit them to enjoy a weekend night out on the town. The six-hour jet lag the three Field Grade Doctors were going through had totally upended their sense of routine. They wanted to eat ham and eggs, or Raisin Bran, for instance, when everybody else in Ovosok was devouring lamb stew or couscous for dinner…and six or seven hours later, of course, the situation was reversed. Cocktail hour for the Majors came when local partyers had already imbibed their share of adult beverages, and were interested only in hitting the hay.

"By the time we get accustomed to this shit," said Ophelia, "…it'll be time to go back to The States."

Nan Stufkoski rolled her eyes. "From your lips to God's ears," she said, "…but maybe leave out the 'shit' part."

"Hey, I'm not ready to pack this deployment in yet," said Kelvin. "We haven't seen a single mosque, for example."

"MOSQUE?" Nan and Ophelia said in astonished unison. "We come five thousand miles…and you wanna do *mosques*? Jesus, girl!"

"Just sayin'," chastened Peggy Kelvin offered. "I mean… in ten years there's gonna be two billion Muslims heading for their neighborhood mosque. Don't you ever wonder what the big attraction is in those places?"

"Oh, yeah!" said Nanette Stufkoski. "First thing I think about in the morning—last thing at night." And she repeated her patented eye roll.

"Well," Cockbyrne chimed in, "There's always those Monasteries up in the mountains they told us about in Indoctrination."

"Oh, sure," Nan scoffed, "…they must *really* be thrilling."

"Nanette wants to check out the local version of The Chippendales," Kelvin said, winking at Ophelia.

Stufkoski's eyebrows went way up. "Now yer *talkin*!"

* * *

Colonel Wren had reluctantly taken Bashkim's advice and donned a mantilla for her conference room meeting with the Grand Imam and the *Mullahs*. The Curator had explained that the Muslim clerics would undoubtedly be much more comfortable and forthcoming in their discussion if she followed the ancient protocol. "Surely it's a simple enough concession," said Bashkim, "…if it prevents the mutilation of your innocent and helpless little dog."

On that note, Lisbeth had reacted to the observation immediately and without objection. She promptly withdrew the lace head covering from her large handbag. It was the same black mantilla she had purchased at a Machu Picchu souvenir boutique, and worn during her one and only visit to Vatican

City in September. Lis draped the large, virtually transparent scarf over her head and shoulders, barely obscuring her hair and facial features at all, but if Bashkim Inasah's approving nod was any indication, the action would undoubtedly serve to mollify the sensitivities of the five *Galabiyya*-clad Elders (*Peace be upon them*).

Bashkim and Lisbeth sat in chairs flanking Nazmi ben Zullah. The three of them faced the *Mullahs*, who had taken up their regular positions at the oval table, but seemed not at all sure that they were pleased to be there...or that they really wanted this discussion even to commence. Only the newly dismissed Caliph Rabee was missing...his seat unoccupied...a replacement cleric would fill it by the time the morning *Muezzin* had sounded. It was one of the matters that the remaining trio found disconcerting, and they'd suggested awaiting the new *Mullah's* arrival before continuing.

The stern ben Zullah, however, had no intention of postponing his well-laid plans any further, and he addressed his subordinates in their native Farsi.

"I have spoken candidly with Doctor Wren," ben Zullah said in the clipped and guttural-sounding terms so familiar to the group, the 'Quilted Mosque' Curator included. "She is aware of our good works...and she has agreed to our terms... though as a physician, she understandably requests certain provisos before she can engage in any surgical procedures."

Lisbeth Wren looked at Bashkim quizzically. *What's he saying?* she mouthed.

"Silence!" the Grand Imam screamed in English. "You will speak when spoken to."

One of the Grand Muftis, the tallest of the three Muslim scholars, frowned at Nazmi ben Zullah. He seemed frankly stunned that a mere woman...and an infidel at that...would be able to provoke the Grand Imam into rashness so easily. He glanced from side to side, to determine whether his two peers at the long table had reacted as negatively as he to ben Zullah's sudden outburst.

Their faces were ashen, but it was impossible to tell why. It might have been fear that was written on their blank expressions; then again, the unsuspecting sages, too, could have been astounded by the bullying display for the same reason the tall *Mullah* was—because such intimidation ill-became so great an academic as their vaunted leader.

Bashkim had no choice but to adopt a hopefully neutral visage. True, he had been able to reason with the Grand Imam when dealing with him one-on-one...ben Zullah's permission for Bashkim to sport a clean-shaven chin was proof in itself. But that dispensation had been easily arrived at pursuant to a frank discussion of monetary concerns, and in particular, Bashkim's role as an 'ecumenical' fund-raiser for *Sarena Jemija*. His limited facial hair would make eminent good sense in his dealings with the poorly schooled Christians and the narrow-minded Reformed or Conservative Jews. The issue at hand now, however, involved a round-table dialogue that must result in unanimous agreement among all four Elders convened here in the bowels of the 'Quilted Mosque'...and yes, Doctor Lisbeth Wren's concurrence too would be required.

As Bashkim Inasah knew full well, Nazmi ben Zullah's reputation was at stake...as was the multi-million-euro enterprise he had cultivated since the day, in 1999, when a 12-year-old boy, wide-eyed and terrified, had been brought to him by the youth's cunning uncle.

"For the Doctor's benefit," said the Grand Imam, "... henceforth we will speak in her language." He looked at Colonel Wren with a thin smile that seemed, if not apologetic in nature, then at least intended to placate her. "My colleagues will appreciate your listing the requests that you outlined for me earlier." Ben Zullah nodded benignly. "You may proceed… and slowly, if you please."

Lisbeth Wren looked at Bashkim, as if seeking moral support from the man whose advocacy she was certain she could depend upon. She was tempted to reach for his hand, but such an expression of affection would, she knew, prove counterproductive. She spoke humbly…but clearly…and with an air of authority befitting both her military rank—and her profession.

"Esteemed clerics: More than twenty-five hundred years ago…in a land only a few hundred miles southeast of here…a wise man established many of the rules by which modern Doctors function—his name was Hippocrates." Lis made lingering eye contact, first with the Grand Imam, then with each of the other three *Mullahs* in order. It was clear that her reference to the great Greek physician had riveted the attention of the *Sarena Jemija* Elders.

"You are aware that I am a practicing physician," Lisbeth stated proudly…her chin held high. "Accordingly, I have sworn to obey the code that Hippocrates set forth in Greece a thousand years before the birth of the Prophet Mohammed." As Lis had anticipated, her command of the historical facts involving figures familiar to every Muslim schoolboy, was not lost on the formerly skeptical *Mullahs*. Nazmi ben Zullah was especially pleased with her presentation thus far. Even Bashkim appeared captivated by her words.

"But, honorable clerics, the Code of Hippocrates is not to be trifled with, as you, of all leaders, well know. The good practitioner of clinical medicine and his precepts command respect throughout the entire world. In my own country," she said, "…even on the façade of the United States Supreme

Court…you will find the words, *"…If a physician operate on a man with a bronze lancet and cause that man's death; or open an abscess and destroy the man's eye, they shall cut off his fingers."*

Once more Lisbeth Wren looked from one strict Elder to the next. Not even an eyelash moved on their faces as she surveyed them. The Doctor was talking to these stern men in terms so graphic that the phrases might have been taken from their Holy Koran itself.

"When the Grand Imam told me of the scheduled organ extractions that will be performed here at the Mosque during forthcoming weeks…and the desperate need for a skilled practitioner to assist in these procedures…I was frankly hesitant to become involved."

She paused and glanced toward the door that opened onto the anteroom where the two women waited. Then she looked in the direction of the hallway that led to the filthy operating room. "However, I have come to realize that to turn my back on the existence of the primitive methods employed here… regardless of who might be responsible for them…would be to violate the oath I have sworn to uphold."

Again Lis looked at Bashkim, hoping that somehow he would be understanding of her rationale. What she saw in his dark eyes was an expression of the utmost pride.

"Therefore, Grand Imam ben Zullah and I have come to an agreement: I will lend whatever capabilities I possess, to assure that all patients who enter this facility are provided the finest care available…assuming that my participation remains confidential…and with the understanding that the most sterile conditions are provided."

Lisbeth stood, as if preparing to leave, and addressed her closing remarks to the three *Mullahs*. "The Grand Imam has further pledged that my identity will be held in the strictest confidence by the members of this council...and that should anyone in this room violate that assurance, Nazmi ben Zullah will consider such disobedience a betrayal of his own authority as defined in the Holy Koran itself. Accordingly, the treachery will constitute just cause for the most severe punishment."

The Elders eyed one another furtively. It was clear that they understood the promised castigation would include unspeakable torture and death. The Grand Imam sat ramrod straight, his posture alone affirming the accuracy of the American Doctor's version of their pact.

"Finally," said Colonel Wren, "...lest any of you consider yourselves unfairly put upon by this arrangement...I have made a similar guarantee to your leader...and by extension to this body. To the extent that all men and women operated on under my supervision are treated humanely, I too will keep in strict confidence their reason for being here...or I may expect to suffer similar consequences."

While the *Mullahs* put their heads together and murmured, Lis Wren sought Bashkim's glance and seemed to plead silently for the tall Curator's indulgence.

How can she possibly believe that these ruthless men will live up to their promise? he asked himself. *Isn't she aware that vows mean nothing to committed thieves and extortionists?* Bashkim seemed to be peering into her very soul and saying, *Men like this are not merely members of another religion, Lisbeth—they are sworn advocates of an insidious tradition that tolerates no other culture on Earth.*

Lis read Bashkim Inasah's concern as surely as if he had spelled out his unease in foot-high letters. *Don't worry,* her blue eyes seemed to say. And as if to demonstrate the reason for her confidence, she nudged her large open handbag toward Nazmi ben Zullah's chair with her foot. He reached into his loose-fitting *Galabiyya*…eased Lisbeth's cartridge-filled, nine millimeter magazine from his pocket…and surreptitiously slid the ammunition into the Doctor's deep leather purse.

"We will re-convene following the *Midday Salat*," the Grand Imam announced, dismissing his associates with fluttering fingers. "Thank you, Doctor, for a worthy presentation. I think you will be pleased with the sanitized facilities you are likely to find here by sunset tomorrow." Ben Zullah clapped Bashkim Inasah's broad shoulders with his liver-spotted hands. "See that the Colonel arrives at her new residence promptly," he instructed the Curator. "She undoubtedly wishes to contact her family in America…in all probability to tell them of her gracious and obliging Balkan hosts."

Bashkim flashed the Grand Imam a faux smile and said inwardly, *Well, no matter what the message to her family is, you'll know it…word for word. Unless I'm badly mistaken, the duplicitous Captain Eric Mueller will see to that.*

Chapter 23

*"Are you telling me she asked you to call?
Does she know I am involved?"*

Simeon Forrester's cell phone sounded as he was examining Harold Sickpig's incision. The eight-inch wound was healing nicely following Lisbeth Wren's operation for removal of a renal cyst dangerously close to the posterior vena cava. "You're a lucky fellow," the veterinarian said as he affixed a smaller bandage to the middle of the Choctaw Hog's belly. The dressing that Nurse Amy Longpré had applied following Wednesday morning's surgery had covered the ninety-pound animal's entire abdomen and was fastened securely along its shaved back…and Mr. Sickpig detested it!

Harold was one of perhaps a hundred surviving Choctaws described by the American Livestock Conservancy as 'critically rare' and therefore assigned 'high conservation priority' status by the noted protectionist group. For that reason alone, Simeon's prescient diagnosis and Lis Wren's deft extrication of the tumor had been wholeheartedly welcomed by the black and white pig's owners.

Doctor Forrester applied the last wide strip of adhesive tape to the rare hog's Mercurochrome-painted belly and the phone, having been silent for sixty seconds…rang again.

The veterinarian did not need to look at the digital display to identify the caller. The one-minute delay had done that.

"Yes, *Musad*."

"Forgive me for calling during your dinner hour."

"No worries," said Forrester, mimicking the trendy idiom employed by his young employees. "I trust Doctor Wren was gratified to see her Terrier alive and well."

"Indeed," said Bashkim Inasah. "She has only one misgiving."

"What sort of…misgiving…" Forrester asked nervously.

Bashkim assumed his most reassuring tone. "The Doctor was unable to make out the date on the Skype newspaper image. She wishes to know if indeed the Long Island coast is expecting a storm this weekend, as your Newsday publication claims."

Simeon Forrester was alarmed. "Are you telling me she asked you to make this call? Does she know I am involved?"

"Not at all," said Bashkim. "I simply advised the Doctor I would contact NOAA Weather Service anonymously."

Forrester's response was heated. "For your information, *Musad*, the front has begun to move in from the south already. The Island is expecting two-to-three goddam inches of wind-driven rain by morning. Now leave me alone! The next time you make contact, it had better be to advise me that I am permitted to set Lisbeth Wren's dog free…do you understand? And if you must know, I…" But the connection was broken. Apparently Bashkim's question had been answered to his satisfaction. Nor did the Curator seem at all concerned about any inconvenience he might have caused his jumpy American collaborator.

It was 7:45 PM. All football bets had to be placed with bookies not later than five minutes prior to kickoff…so Simeon Forrester had to act quickly.

As on Long Island, the weather in Columbus was windy, wet, and cold. The Las Vegas book had determined that, on the one hand, the resulting poor footing in Ohio Stadium probably bespoke a non-stop offensive aerial performance by both the OSU Buckeyes, and Michigan's favored Wolverines. Conversely, field goals would be rare in the blustery November conditions that prevailed in the depressingly flat geographic center of Ohio.

Football games, Simeon knew, were traditionally high scoring affairs when the passing game was the key component… just as games that featured a running attack and three-point field goals generally resulted in low scores. It was a good guess, therefore, that barring a last minute injury or some other unforeseen occurrence, fifty-one total points should be about right for tonight's Ohio State-Michigan Big Ten encounter.

But one other factor would be in play during the highly anticipated Friday night contest that perhaps the odds makers in Nevada might have overlooked…the lights.

Ohio Stadium, also known as 'The Horseshoe,' or simply 'The Shoe' because of its shape, was the fourth largest football venue in the country, having once accommodated more than one hundred six thousand souls, but incredibly the stadium contained no permanent lighting! When OSU's Buckeyes were called upon to host night football games, it was necessary for the University to arrange for the temporary installation of huge banks of floodlights. And the upshot was that one never knew whether host or visitor was most likely to benefit from the unseemly arrangement.

At twelve minutes to eight, there was no time to research past Ohio State night time scores—so Simeon Forrester did what any self-respecting diehard gambler would do; he picked up the phone…dialed the number he'd called so often…and flipped a coin.

* * *

At 12:45 AM Ovosok time an exhausted Lisbeth Wren kissed Bashkim lightly on the lips and climbed from the silver Citroen. He remained in the car and watched her while the engine idled and she made her way to Hanna Henschel's front door. Lis unlocked the blue door, then with a fleeting wave of her hand, she entered the house, locked the door behind her, and made her weary way to the staircase.

At the foot of the stairs, Hanna's bedroom door was slightly ajar and Lisbeth heard the woman snoring softly. She elected to leave a dim living room table lamp burning, not knowing whether it was the elderly woman's practice to do so. *I'd never forgive myself*, she thought, *if the tiny Frau Henschel awoke at this hour, expecting to be greeted by a night light, only to find the house in utter darkness.*

Lis tiptoed up the narrow steps and hurried directly to the porcelain bathroom for a visit that was long overdue. She could hardly have excused herself to answer nature's call while subjected to the offensive stares of the vulgar *Mullahs* in their subterranean meeting room. For all she knew, the uncouth elders of the 'Quilted Mosque' had no private facility available for use by mere women. Then what would she have done? She shuddered at the prospect. Thank God for a cast-iron bladder! Doctor Lisbeth Wren said in an earnest prayer of thanksgiving.

In her room opposite the lavatory, and a few steps down the narrow upstairs hall, Lisbeth switched on a milk glass lamp atop a mirrored vanity. Beside the dressing table was an armoire whose lower drawers held her neatly arranged General Issue clothing. For the first time in hours a smile crossed Lis's face when she noted that Hanna had set her precisely folded pajamas next to the lamp where she could not have missed seeing them.

One of the small drawers near the top of the ornate armoire was partially protruding. It was the narrow compartment Lisbeth had selected to contain her nine millimeter Beretta. The Lieutenant Colonel was positive she'd closed the drawer after removing the weapon earlier in the evening, and her smile broadened when she realized that Hanna Henschel must have left the drawer partly open as if to remind her that the gun should be put away properly.

Lis removed the Beretta from her handbag, inserted the magazine, and switched on the safety. She then placed the pistol in the drawer, covered it with a hand towel, and closed the topmost compartment of the highly polished armoire. It was an appropriate place to store the nine millimeter, Lisbeth thought…or any weapon…*after all, that's what 'armoire' means in French*, she grinned.

She sat at the vanity and prepared to brush her hair, but when she looked in the mirror, the smile vanished from Doctor Lisbeth Wren's tired face. "Damn," she said to her image, "You look like hell, Colonel."

* * *

Bashkim Inasah felt that he was facing the most burning moral dilemma since the murder of his parents in 1983. Should he take action?…perhaps even kill the members of the cabal who were forcing their will on the American Doctor?…or should he keep his mouth shut—feign continued cooperation with the cutthroat gang, thereby maintaining a position from which he might more effectively protect her from within?

In the first scenario, it would be necessary to inform Lisbeth Wren of Eric Mueller's role in the vile network that trafficked in the illicit harvesting and sale of vital organs throughout The Balkans. But the U.S. Army was a formidable entity to embroil in such an international scandal—was the newly minted Lieutenant Colonel likely to walk with the Curator down that potentially hazardous path?

On the other hand, to permit Doctor Wren to participate in the contemptible practice she seemed to have endorsed would put her, no matter how noble her intentions, essentially in the same category as the loathsome Captain Mueller. Once involved, it would be impossible for Lisbeth to un-ring that bell…though sooner or later, she might very well be required to do so before an international tribunal.

The Doctor's options were clear: Either she must testify in a matter that would surely disgrace the Army and probably bring an end to her military career…or she could chance being ultimately cleared on humanitarian grounds of engaging in activity forbidden by the very oath she was sworn to. In either case Lisbeth Wren's future had become murky, to say the least.

Bashkim would sleep on the matter—or try to.

But in his heart he knew that the woman with whom he had fallen in love must make the final decision on how best to handle the predicament…the quandary that he, as much as anyone, had created for her. In whatever she decided, Bashkim Inasah would be fully supportive, he vowed. The Curator of *Sarena Jemija* owed Lis Wren that—and much more.

Chapter 24

*She should discuss the matter with Bashkim.
He seemed to know what these people were up to.*

Rarely did Lisbeth Wren awaken later than six in the morning, but on Saturday, November 17th, the beginning of her first weekend in Ovosok, the distinctive cherry and schnapps aroma of Hanna Henschel's *Schwarzwälder Kirschtorte* jolted her from a dream in which her father had baked one of the selfsame Black Forest cakes for her sixteenth birthday.

Lis shot upright in the large feather bed and groped for her wristwatch on the night stand to her left. She read the time in the morning light made dim by the drawn blinds. *Jesus!* she swore inwardly…*it's after nine!*

Lisbeth stepped into a pair of fuzzy slippers she had bought at the PX soon after arrival at Billingham on Thursday…or was it yesterday—she couldn't be sure. She shuffled her way to the bedroom door and eased it open to determine whether the coast to the bathroom was clear. It seemed to be. Hanna had her shortwave radio tuned to a German talk radio station from the sound of things.

Lis left the door ajar and trundled back to the armoire where she retrieved a fresh set of underwear. She removed the chain that held her dog tags and the friendship ring that Pete had given her last year, and dropped it next to her watch on the night table.

Not surprisingly, Hanna had laid out a pair of fresh bath towels. They sat atop a wicker hamper near the foot of the tub, parallel to the porcelain valves flanking an old iron faucet. Lis twisted the hot water tap and immediately the room was filled with the roar and accompanying steam of the cascade. God, how she looked forward to scrubbing the grime of the 'Quilted Mosque's' dismal sub-basement from her otherwise-refreshed body! Lisbeth stripped away her flannel pajamas and stepped cautiously into the half-filled bath. She eased her slender body beneath the surface, slowly at first, careful not to slip in reaction to the nearly-searing water. Finally, submerged to her chin, her head resting on the back of the tub, Lis closed her eyes and wondered exactly when she would see Bashkim.

Slowly but inexorably, the bathwater began to cool. And with the change in temperature, Lisbeth's euphoria was replaced by the recollection that there was much to be done today—not all of it pleasant. Bashkim had promised to call for her at midday. They needed to talk, he'd told her…"… *serious talk*," were the words he used. How fortunate she was, the Lieutenant Colonel thought, to have encountered so considerate an intermediary in this whole, bizarre affair, as was the obviously well-connected Curator of the place that everyone called the *Sarena Jemija*.

And the resourceful career soldier Captain Mueller, Lis mused as she sat at the vanity brushing her hair after her long bath— *now there was a dependable friend if she'd ever seen one!*

Regarding the little Boston Terrier—Lisbeth had seen with her own eyes that the dog was healthy and happy. Had the animal been otherwise, she would have detected it immediately. No one knew Gigi like Lis did—with the possible exception of Peter.

As Lisbeth dressed preparatory to her meeting with Bashkim, a strange combination of guilt and resentment overcame her. She gazed into the mirror, frowned, and asked herself a pair of rhetorical questions: *How come Pete hasn't tried to contact me about Gigi? Is it possible he doesn't know she's missing?*

Perhaps she should discuss the matter further with Bashkim, she concluded. He seemed to know what these people were up to.

* * *

Tereza Mimona's one-room apartment was on the third floor of an affordable, if rickety, stucco building that leaned perilously close to the River Pena. Her only companion was a well-muscled Russian tomcat oddly named Rajah, whose protein-rich diet of mice, small snakes, and the occasional water rat kept the male Kurillian Bobtail nutritionally sound, in good coat, and well exercised.

Most of Reza's time was spent in the store on Karaorman Road, which contained all the rudimentary comforts that a single woman living in Tavoto might reasonably expect. Rajah could stay at home and handle the vermin that the river provided…Reza wanted her espresso…and Courvoisier brandy, of course…along with the usual meat pie and maybe a raspberry tart for supper taken at the bookstore's counter. But most of all she exulted in the company of her beloved books.

Through a single grimy window overlooking the old section of town, Tereza Mimona could make out the tall, pointed minaret of the 'Quilted Mosque' on *Ulica Goce Delcev* just beyond the narrow Radovan Footbridge. Some fifty yards further than that, she could see 'Lola Books' with its lettered show window, and the narrow, cobblestone alley that curled around from Karaorman Road and followed an irregular course along the rear of the bookstore and adjacent stone buildings.

Reza had been awakened by the morning *Muezzin* that issued from *Sarena Jemija* and despite Rajah's disdainful objection she climbed out of bed, cast off her long, loose chemise, and poured a pitcher of cold water into a chipped porcelain washbasin that sat atop a simple wooden commode. Shivering in the November morning chill, Reza dipped a washcloth into the basin and proceeded to scrub her goose-pimpled body from head to toe, bravely singing a song from her childhood, as if the ditty could somehow warm the frigid bath water…as her mother had assured 5-year-old Tereza would be the case. "Just scrub hard, Darling…sing loud…pretend the water is hot…and dry fast—your sisters are waiting for the towel."

Reza had learned it at an early age: Mothers were the most loveable liars!

Now forty, she had been orphaned for thirty years, her mother, father, and sisters brutally murdered by a squad of the same Belgrade assassins that had claimed Bashkim Inasah's innocent parents.

And to think Bashi himself might now be engaged in the sort of criminal behavior he has always detested, she thought. *What could have hardened his heart?*

She dried herself briskly, hung the damp, worn towel on a makeshift clothesline stretched above her bed, and after checking the empty street beneath her window, Reza, as usual, flung the bathwater three stories down to the sidewalk.

Reza dressed in a second-hand aqua wool tunic that she had bought from a traveling merchant. The garment covered her black, flared pants to the knee, making the outfit modest enough to satisfy her somewhat orthodox customers, but sufficiently stylish to place her among the semi-trendy merchants in town. Her printed babushka doubled as a headscarf, though it was a bit too revealing to be considered a true hijab.

Thus attired, Tereza, gathered up her copy of '*We Shall Not Sleep*,' placed it in a woven straw handbag along with her cosmetics and other personal items, and she opened the door of her cluttered room. Immediately Rajah scampered over her open-toed shoes, and down the unpainted wooden staircase, toward the stone wall that formed the north bank of the River Pena.

* * *

Major Nanette Stufkoski was always the first of the Doctors housed in Billingham's SEA Hut 37 to climb out of bed in the morning. According to Ophelia Cockbyrne, it was because Nan was just too nosy to sleep, when God-knows-what might be going on in the men's accommodations across Gen. Hap Arnold Boulevard.

Peggy Kelvin figured Stufkoski had programmed her laptop to wake her up early so she could get an eyeful of the two snappy Bird Colonels who jogged by every morning at 0600 hours. The well-muscled men wore silk shorts so clinging and translucent that, "…they might as well be bare-assed," she'd opined.

Naturally, the observation only served to turn Nan into an even earlier riser. And, had Majors Kelvin and Cockbyrne been presented an opportunity to download the long-lens digital photos from Stufkoski's new Nikon, they'd have discovered just how close their assessments were to the truth.

When it came to categorizing men, Nan the Dentist had maintained, "...some females are 'Ass-women,' some are 'Leg-women,' and some are 'Pec-women.'" Major Stufkoski was all of the above...and a whole lot more.

In their singing, Bessie Smith and Brenda Lee might have promoted the notion that *'A good man is hard to find,'* Nanette always noted, "...but what they should have sung is, '...*a HARD man is GOOD to find!* Now, *that's* more like it!" naughty Nan claimed unequivocally, declaring that her observation was based on twenty-five years of experience. And that quarter century included four, count 'em, FOUR happy marriages—each happier than the one before. Why happier?... because the successive nuptials invariably incorporated an overall harder hubby than the last, she'd explained with a simple shrug.

"Those two Birds aren't as sexy as the Marines we watched doing PT in Afghanistan last year," said Psychiatrist Kelvin to Ophelia Cockbyrne, as they waited in front of SEA Hut 37. They planned to walk with Nanette to the South Mess for breakfast. "Don't get me wrong, they can put their boots under my cot any day, but those Jarheads...they were the real McCoy, girlfriend!"

The Primary Care Physician rolled her eyes and fanned herself with an open hand. "Oh my God," she murmured in breathless agreement. "If the Good Lord ever made anything juicier than that Squad of Beefcake, She kept it for Herself."

"Mmmm," said Peggy. "Those cute little PT shorts oughta' be illegal, you ask me."

"You're the Shrink," Cockbyrne said. "You think it's possible the government would send those rock-solid boy-toys to Kabul just to drive me crazy?" The blushing Major closed her eyes and shuddered in rapturous recollection.

Stufkoski danced down the steps of Hut 37. She flung her arms wide as she approached her colleagues with a soprano 'Ta-Da.' The oft-wed Dentist announced, "Nan's the name—drillin's the game," then she straightened, frowned, and leaned closer to Ophelia. "You feeling okay, Honey?—you look a little flushed."

Chapter 25

At no time had either of them used the words 'dollars'—'money'—'bet'—or 'points'.

Superstitious to a fault, Simeon Forrester would never dream of using anything but his tried and true Kennedy half-dollar for a coin toss. Granted, 'The Doc' was probably just as far behind the eight-ball flipping the fifty-cent piece honoring the nation's 35th president as he was making any of his other bets, but the irrational veterinarian was a gambler through and through…his mind was made up. Sooner or later his pet 1970 Kennedy half…minted in the last year that silver was used in coins for general circulation…would reward him with a bonanza. He knew it. It was destined.

Simeon's bookmaker, the bartender at the Hung Chin Restaurant in Westbury, had answered the phone while the uncirculated coin was still spinning on 'The Doc's' desk. Without preamble, Forrester announced his Client Number and the familiar voice repeated the eight-digit sequence in acknowledgment.

"Ohio State-Michigan…fifty," said the veterinarian. The Kennedy half bobbed and rang to a stop, revealing the Great Seal of the United States—tails! "Under," said Simeon Forrester hastily. He had wagered fifty units—five thousand dollars—that the combined point final for the football game about to start in Columbus would total fewer than fifty-one points.

The Hung Chin bartender gave his frequent customer a four-digit confirmation number. Simeon repeated it...and both men hung up. At no time had either of them used the words 'dollars'—'money'—'bet' or 'points'. There had been no mention of 'payment'—'commission' or 'delivery'. Results of the wager would be satisfied in an apparently legal cash transaction between two friends in unmarked 'units' understood to be represented by hundred-dollar bills. The transaction would take place at the Hung Chin restaurant bar during normal business hours. And even if the Nassau County District Attorney's office had listened-in on Simeon Forrester's seventeen-word conversation, they'd have one hell of a time obtaining a grand jury indictment on such flimsy, non-committal evidence. Besides, one of DA Katy Price's top assistants had been on the take at Hung Chin for years.

With that piece of business taken care of, 'The Doc' removed a bean bag version of a Dalmatian puppy from a Walgreens shopping bag. He smiled and walked toward the door to the noisy kennel. Lisbeth Wren's Boston Terrier had still been off her feed, it seemed to Simeon. *This'll cheer resentful little Gigi up*, he assured himself...and he strode amid the barking, yelping, and whining in the kennel toward Cage Seventeen.

As soon as the four-year-old Terrier saw the black-and-white spotted toy that the approaching vet held in his outstretched hand, she performed a series of incredible vertical leaps. Simeon had obviously been mistaken about Gigi's being physically under the weather—she was probably the healthiest dog in the entire Uniondale Animal Hospital. No eighteen-pound dog Forrester had ever seen could possibly jump four feet straight up if it was ailing. She was just lonesome, as was to be expected.

But while 'The Doc' was relieved by the abducted Boston's exuberant performance, it was clear that Lisbeth's pet must never be permitted to leave the five-foot-high Cage Number Seventeen until *Musad* had authorized such a thing. There was too much at stake. If, for instance, the agile Gigi were ever to make her way...but why worry about the enthusiastic pup's behavior? She'd been housed here overnight frequently, and never yet attempted to escape the premises.

Simeon glanced at his wristwatch. "Jesus—five after eight!" He cocked his head in the direction of the open door to his office. The cheering of a hundred thousand fervent fans emanated from his desk radio. The kickoff!

While Gigi leaped and twisted...jumped and twirled... 'Doc' Forrester fumbled a dozen or more times with the various components of his heavy key ring. Finally, after unsuccessfully attempting to unlock the simple latch that kept the frenetic little Terrier imprisoned, Simeon was able to spring the lock with a brass master key. He opened the wire mesh door just wide enough to squeeze the pliable bean bag into the cage, where he dropped it on the dog's extended paws.

Gigi seized the toy in her mouth, then pranced and pushed at the cage door with her muzzle. Her lunges and pirouettes, however, did little to distract the concerned Doctor Forrester, who listened aghast to the roar that radiated from inside his office. "God damn," he mumbled. "Somebody's already scored...on the opening kick!"

He jammed the keys into his pants pocket and slammed the wire door shut in anger.

Though it didn't lock.

And with a mere twelve seconds gone by in the biggest game of the season, 'The Doc' now had only forty-five points to work with...or else he'd be a loser again.

Forrester rushed back past the long row of pet prisons, ignoring the barking, bleating, yowling protests of his patients. His normal concern for the animals in his care had been replaced by trepidation about what was taking place at Ohio Stadium—a venue he had only heard of—hosting a game he knew little about—played by oversized men he would never meet, or want to meet. But for the next two hours Simeon Forrester's very life revolved only around the proceedings being conducted under the lights in windy, soggy Columbus.

Chapter 26

During that initial week they were electronically incommunicado.

Electronic communication among the new arrivals at Camp Billingham presented something of a problem for the first week of deployment. True, everyone would be given a cell phone, and though it was to be used only in the execution of their duties, that stipulation was easily circumvented. If, for example, one wanted to have a fellow soldier join them for dinner, the arrangement could easily be made in the guise of a planned exchange of job-related information. Anything from the confirming of required participation in on-post events, to asking the scheduled times for attendance at Catholic Mass, obviously an elective activity, would qualify as legitimate use of one's cell.

The phone's range was limited, of course. In every foreign deployment area outside of the United States, outgoing calls on government devices were restricted to a thirty-mile radius from the center of the military installation where one was stationed.

The catch was, these phones were not activated during the deployed soldier's first seven days on post, the Army's assumption being that it was best for this brief period of indoctrination to be completed before personnel began contacting one another, often unnecessarily. Seeking info that would soon be supplied during an orderly briefing was considered a waste of time and resources.

Accordingly, newly deployed troops were usually 'down' during that initial week when they were electronically incommunicado.

As Majors Kelvin, Cockbyrne, and Stufkoski finished their late Saturday breakfast at Billingham's South Mess, they decided to try visiting Lisbeth again at Frau Henschel's house. If the Lieutenant Colonel wasn't available, they could always spend the rest of the day playing tourist. The frequent bus to and from Jaziref was free for military personnel and civilian employees of the camp…and it would be leaving the PX in five minutes.

Coincidentally, Captain Eric Mueller was at the Motor Pool arranging for use of a staff car through the weekend… and he had the same destination in mind.

Had the fervently amorous Nan Stufkoski only known! She'd have packed an additional condom or two in the pocket of her above-the-knee, pleated skirt.

"Shouldn't you…uh…*change* if we're going into town?" asked Peggy Kelvin, who was wearing loose-fitting jeans and a turtleneck shirt.

"Why?" said Nan, looking down at her tanned gams. "Is this skirt too long?"

Ophelia gave Stufkoski a sidelong look. "I was thinking you *might* consider a bra."

* * *

When Bashkim Inasah knocked at Frau Henschel's front door at eleven-thirty, Lis was already waiting for him. Hanna, having noted Lisbeth's impatient demeanor as she sat by the living room window with a second cup of coffee, pretended not to hear the three gentle raps. The diminutive woman continued to fuss in the kitchen, thereby permitting her lodger to answer the summons.

Lis stood immediately, set her ornate cup and saucer on a long table in front of the lace curtain, and smoothed the front of her gray tweed slacks. "*Auf Wiedersehen*," Lis called, and she added in German "Don't wait up for me, Hanna."

"*Wiedersehen*," Frau Henschel sang out…and she snuck a furtive look toward the tall, dark man—clearly a local, from his tawny coloring and the continental cut of his sport coat—who stood smiling on her front step.

Bashkim resisted the urge to kiss the American woman whom he had last seen only a little more than ten hours ago. But as Lisbeth closed the door behind her, he did take her hand, and the affable pair descended the two stone steps with their arms entwined. The tall Curator led Lis Wren solicitously along the narrow walk to the curb where his Citroen was running noiselessly.

Half a block away, not far from the intersection where the Billingham/Jaziref bus had dropped them, Majors Cockbyrne, Stufkoski, and Kelvin seized one another's arms simultaneously and came to an abrupt halt. Obviously absorbed only with each other, Lis and Bashkim climbed hurriedly into the newly washed car.

"My oh my!" Said Peggy Kelvin as the trio watched from the shadow cast by the old stone fountain. "Did you see what I just saw?"

"Colonel Girlfriend don't waste no time, does she?" murmured Cockbyrne in a semi-growl.

"You blame her?" Nan Stufkoski asked rhetorically. "That's the nicest ass I've seen since John Travolta did his 'Dirty Dancin'."

The three Doctors turned their heads as the silver Citroen circled the fountain and sped by.

"Travolta was in 'Saturday Night Fever,'" Kelvin corrected her, as the Doctors watched the sleek automobile turn east where Ruga Dognal met the Civesoru-Jaziref highway.

"Fever, Shmeever…Dancin' Shmancin'" said Nan, "Whadda we do now?"

"Let's see if we can find a joint that sells Gummy Bears," said Peggy.

The other two gaped at the Psychiatrist, shocked. "Gummy Bears?"

"Hey," Major Kelvin shrugged, "…they seem to work for Lis."

* * *

In Old Tavoto, halfway between the 'Quilted Mosque' to the north, and the Arabati Baba Monastery to the south, is the fine rooftop restaurant, Oninnam. From their vantage point near the rail that encircles the outdoor dining area of the famed eatery, Bashkim Inasah and Lisbeth viewed Tavoto's two most magnificent edifices; Lis faced the 500-year-old Teḱe, or monastery, built around the *turbe* of Sersem Ali Baba… Bashkim, the *Sarena Jemija*, where he and the American Doctor would be meeting with Imam Nazmi ben Zullah after the *Evening Salat*. It was three o'clock, and Lis and her new friend had much to discuss in the coming hours. But first, the Curator wanted to put Lisbeth Wren somewhat at ease by familiarizing her with the local surroundings.

"The Arabati is the finest surviving Bektashi monastery in Europe," said the always informative Bashkim. His stylish partner gazed out over the sprawling complex that featured broad lawns, dozens of flower beds, some still dazzling with colorful fall blossoms, and a unique marble fountain oddly housed in a wooden pavilion.

"You said the man buried here is 'Sersem.' What does 'Sersem' mean?"

Bashkim smiled and nodded as if to say, 'Good question.'

"The story goes that Ali Baba, who was an official of the Ottoman Empire, gave up his position in order to live the simple life of a Bektashi monk. The Sultan, 'Suleiman the Magnificent,' was so angered by the departure of one of his favorite aides that he yelled after Ali, whom he saw departing Istanbul, *If you will be a fool, then go.* Sersem, the old Turkish term for *fool*, became Ali Baba's nickname."

"Where do the forty thieves come in?" said Lis breaking a long breadstick and handing half to Bashkim.

"We have the nimble mind of Antoine Galland to thank for that obviously outrageous yarn," said the smiling Curator biting into the sesame covered bread. "Galland was a French archaeologist in the late seventeenth century. He's best known as the first European translator of *One Thousand and One Nights*. Bashkim signaled to the waiter for more tea. "Galland actually added the popular Ali Baba story…which has had a huge influence on gullible Europe's attitude toward the Islamic world."

"'*Open Sesame*,'" said Lisbeth…"Galland's version of the nickname *Sersem*?"

"I've always thought so," said Bashkim. He held up his half-eaten breadstick and plucked off one of the beige seeds, "…though it's widely known that, upon ripening, sesame pods split. When they do, they release the seeds with a pop. It has been suggested that's the root of the phrase."

"Maybe if we dropped by old Sersem Ali Baba's *turbe* over there," Lis nodded toward the manicured monastery grounds, "…we could holler 'open sez me' just to see what happens. You think there's a tunnel under that mausoleum too?"

The smile left Bashkim Inasah's face and he swung his gaze around the largely empty open-air café. Slowly, he placed the uneaten portion of the crisp breadstick on his plate. He looked up searching for Lis Wren's blue eyes that were now shifted downward. He leaned and said across the linen covered table, "Look at me Lisbeth." When reluctantly she did so, the dark-eyed Curator of *Sarena Jemija* said in a benign but commanding tone, "You must never allude to the *turbe* of *Sarena Jemija* again. The consequences could be unspeakably severe."

"It was a joke, Bashkim…a silly American joke…nothing more."

"Then perhaps we can put an end to such witticisms," said Bashkim. "The *Mullahs* with whom you are dealing…with whom *we* are dealing…are consistently obeyed, catered to, and revered. They have great influence, considerable power, and enormous wealth. What these men are totally *lacking* in, however, is basic compassion, the understanding of another's right, and above all—a sense of humor."

Bashkim Inasah withdrew a box of Murad cigarettes from a pocket, but noting the discomfort on the Doctor's face, he hastily returned the tin container with the Egyptian motif to the interior of his sport coat.

"My superiors," said the Curator, "…tolerate no mitigating whatever of their Muslim faith, their rigid customs, or what they regard as their innate male superiority. Even questioning what the *Mullahs* perceive as Islamic tradition is considered *Haram*."

"*Haram?*" Lisbeth questioned softly, cocking her head.

Bashkim's eyes swept Oninnam's rooftop with its dozen or so broad table umbrellas. The couple's muted conversation wouldn't be heard five feet away in the open air, where two strolling Madonican musicians played Turkish instruments…

one, a long-necked lute that he sang along with…the other, an end-blown flute that resembled an oboe and emitted a tinny whine.

"I'm surprised your indoctrination classes didn't inform you more fully," the Curator said. The waiter approached with more hot tea and fresh cups. Bashkim took another breadstick and stopped talking except to thank the aproned man with a slight nod.

"Haram is the most strictly prohibited category of sin," he finally said lightly. "Indeed, Islam teaches that a *haram*, or grossly sinful act, is recorded by an angel on one's left shoulder. But unlike your 'Guardian Angel,' this celestial servant is assigned to mete out the cruelest acts of punishment."

Lisbeth glanced at the left sleeve of her cardigan. "And these *Watchdog* Angels," she said, "…do they ever…?"

"No," said Bashkim Inasah, "…they never leave."

"I like to think my Guardian Angel stays with me forever too," said a meditative Lis Wren. "And I hope that my family and friends have their own loving Angel watching over them." A tear formed in the Doctor's eye and she quickly reached for her dinner napkin and brushed it away from her cheek where it had fallen. "I don't suppose my little dog gets the same kind of security," she whispered pensively. "I would give anything to know that my helpless Gigi was being shielded that way."

Bashkim studied Lisbeth's worried face for a long minute. As she returned his gaze, the Curator purposefully removed his iPhone from the right side pocket of his suede jacket. He dialed a series of fourteen coded letters, spaces, and numbers.

It was nearly ten AM on Long Island when Simeon Forrester answered the phone with a curt, "Yes. What is it?" and he added bluntly, "Hurry. I have business to attend to."

Bashkim spoke slowly, conversationally…as if he were talking directly to the Army Doctor seated across from him. "It is *Musad* speaking," he said. "The Boston Terrier…take her home…immediately!"

Lis sat…wide-eyed…her jaw slack…staring at Bashkim as if in disbelief.

The man she'd considered her friend broke the phone connection with a touch of his forefinger on the tiny keypad, and he dropped the device back into his coat pocket.

"Who was that?" she demanded. "Who has my dog?"

"I'm afraid I can't answer that," said Bashkim Inasah. "At any rate, his identity makes no difference. The animal will be returned to your home on Strawberry Lane before eleven AM New York time—in less than an hour." He smiled and nodded politely, "Unharmed. You have my word."

"You seem to have considerable authority in these matters," Lisbeth said shrilly, a note of skepticism in her voice. "How much discretion do you really have? Can you assure me that…" The Doctor realized that a number of the Oninnam patrons were staring in the direction of their corner table; two or three seemed annoyed by the sudden strident tone of the conversation. She feigned a broad smile and leaned forward on her elbows. "It was good of you to take care of that little problem…" Lisbeth took one of the Curator's hands in both of hers and for the first time she added the endearing term… "*Darling.*"

The neighboring diners seemed reassured that what they'd mistaken for a harsh exchange had actually been an exuberant reaction on the woman's part to some surprise announcement…and the placated clientele returned to their hors d'oeuvres and wine.

"I mean it when I say that," Lis whispered. "And I hope you won't be criticized for…"

Bashkim reached swiftly across the table and held an index finger vertically across Lisbeth's lips. "Leave that to me," he said. "But you can help matters greatly if you'll cooperate… at least *pretend* to cooperate…with our friends." He bobbed his head toward the Shar Mountains—in the direction of the 'Quilted Mosque.' "My superiors will see to your complete safety…and mine…but only as long as they feel they can depend on your silence."

The heavily tanned Curator removed his finger from across Lis Wren's mouth and murmured, "I have a plan. But in order for it to be effective, you must promise me that, for now at least, you will discuss with no one—not your family, your commanders, your confessor—*no one*—what you have seen at *Sarena Jemija*."

"I can promise that," said Lisbeth softly.

"Then I can tell you at the outset that there are those both here and in America who seem to have your best interests at heart…but are in reality false friends." Bashkim broke a breadstick in two. "One of them is Captain Eric Mueller."

Chapter 27

Tereza Mimona frowned. What is Bashkim doing here before ten o'clock in the morning?

Earlier in the day, Reza the bookseller normally would have had to haul her bicycle down the three flights of stairs leading from her fourth floor room to the alley that ultimately connected with the Radovan Footbridge near the *Sarena Jemija*. Last night, however, she'd chained the old bike to one of several iron hitching loops by her apartment building's front door. Dragging the bicycle up the thirty-six steep stairs seemed out of the question since she would also be lugging her large straw bag...and the carrier had no shoulder strap.

The skimpy combination lock could be easily smashed by a determined thief, she knew, but the reality was that Reza Mimona's long-abused bicycle wasn't worth stealing. Besides, Tereza Mimona was not sixteen anymore...and like the old two-wheeler, she also was showing her age. Especially in Tavoto's often biting November humidity. So she'd secured the bike at street level and climbed to her room free of the usual burden.

Since today was Saturday, the busiest day of the week for Lola Books, Reza would have no time to read more of the intriguing volume *We Shall Not Sleep* once the shop had been opened for business. Accordingly, she left the book, her straw bag, and all its contents save for her keys and her cash, hidden under the mattress in her meager apartment. Thus, unencumbered, Tereza virtually skipped down the three dozen steps and out into the morning sunshine where she found the locked bicycle exactly as she'd left it.

Rather than take the direct eastward route to her shop on Karaorman Road, today Reza decided to treat herself to some of the newly picked apples grown in the Ali Baba Monastery's orchard, and sold at the Arabati farm store on Kiri Ristoski. It was unlikely she'd be able to leave Lola Books for lunch—and maybe not even for dinner—so shopping for five or six crisp apples, though it necessitated a few blocks deviation from her normal route to the bookstore, could prove time well invested.

As Reza Mimona pedaled southwest along broad Ilindenska Boulevard, the Monastery's cluster of domed buildings became more distinct, and had it not been for a rude motorist who yelled an obscenity from a dilapidated pickup, she might never have looked angrily over her shoulder...and spotted Bashkim Inasah's gleaming Citroen parked on the east side of the busy thoroughfare.

Forced onto the slightly raised concrete sidewalk on the northern edge of Ristoski where the street intersected with Ilindenska, Tereza swerved, skidded to a halt, and returned the truck driver's hollered insult. That the feisty woman did so, complete with unmistakable sign language, had delighted pedestrians and even drawn blasts of approval from the horns of passing vehicles.

But Tereza had been more interested in what she recognized as Bashkim's sporty sedan. The Curator of the 'Quilted Mosque' had been on her mind constantly since she'd come across the provocative book concerning international irregularities in The Balkans...and the volume had given rise to the bookseller's suspicions about her friend's strange travels abroad. Now, here was Bashi, newly returned from a trip to Canada (his stated reason for which, did not quite carry the ring of truth) and for the first time since Reza had known him, Inasah was spending the weekend…or at least part of it…in Tavoto.

The wood-carved sign over the double doorway in front of which Bashi's car was parked read 'Oninnam.' The emporium was renowned throughout Madonica, and even the elegant advertisement itself, with its impressive craftsmanship and eighteen carat gold leaf, was considered a work of art.

Tereza Mimona frowned. *But what is Bashkim doing here before ten o'clock in the morning? Everyone knows Oninnam doesn't open until two PM.*

At that point, the famed restaurant's door was pushed wide from the inside by a tuxedoed waiter. Bashkim and the man stepped far out onto the sidewalk where the Curator pointed up to the bistro's rooftop dining area. The black-and-white-clad man had visored his eyes with one hand as he peered upward at Bashkim's urging. With his other hand, the waiter pointed to the same table and umbrella that the nattily dressed Inasah was indicating…the intimate corner table by the rail. Bashkim nodded, gave the man a bill that was folded in half, touched the cuff of his jacket revealing his wristwatch, and said something that Tereza could not make out from across the broad boulevard. But clearly the widely traveled Bashi had made a reservation and he seemed to know exactly where he wanted to be seated.

Perhaps he's getting ready to present someone with a gift, thought Reza. *Maybe a nice bookmark.* Was Tereza Mimona jealous? Of *course* she was jealous! Jealous enough to drop by after two o'clock and get a look at the competition? Without a doubt!

* * *

"Mueller?" For a moment Lisbeth Wren was dumbstruck. "But it was the Captain who came to my rescue on Thursday." She frowned and shook her head in tight little bobs as if trying to rid her mind of some unwelcome intrusion that she didn't want to believe. "Eric arranged for me to meet the woman in Jaziref...the widow who owns the house where I'm staying."

Bashkim Inasah partially covered his mouth with one hand and spoke softly into his splayed fingers. "That whole scenario with Frau Henschel has been arranged for some time—months, in fact. It was the *Sarena Jemija* Elders who selected you for deployment here...with my help, I will confess."

Bashkim was palpably contrite. Further, he seemed determined to make a clean breast of his complicity in the illicit business that now involved Lisbeth. "Ben Zullah arranged with his friends in The Pentagon to have you deployed here. Mueller secretly works for the *Mullahs*, and has for years." Then the Curator sprang the revelation whose details even he did not know fully. "What's more, Captain Mueller is not the only Army officer assigned to keep an eye on you...one of the Doctors who accompanied you—as yet I do not know which one—is also in the employ of ben Zullah."

While Lieutenant Colonel Wren stared at Bashkim, more furious than fearful, the tall man with the dark features quietly added, "We are surrounded by enemies, Lisbeth. I could not in good conscience permit another day to go by without alerting you."

"And how do I know you're not part of the scheme too?" she snapped.

"I suppose you have no reason to believe me," Bashkim said ruefully, "...but perhaps you should ask yourself why I would reveal these things to you, when the cost of my doing so is potentially...and literally...my head."

Lis Wren was breathing fast and heavily. She folded her arms impatiently and looked away from her seemingly remorseful companion. The afternoon sun sank closer to the snow-covered peaks of the Shar Range that rimmed the Adriatic Sea. She shuddered and fastened the collar button of her blouse.

"The Major—the one you say the *Mullahs* have got on my case, I think it must be Peggy Kelvin. The Psychiatrist."

"Why her?" said Bashkim.

Lis squinted, and muttered in recollection. "About four hours before we left Fort Bliss; before we got on the bus to the flight line, I wanted to take a picture of the three of them: Cockbyrne, Kelvin, and Stufkoski. Nan and Ophelia were all for it, but Peggy, she flat out refused. She insisted on taking *my* picture with the other two." Lis was genuinely puzzled. "I said, 'okay,'...so Peg took the shot with my phone, and handed it back to me." 'Now *you* get in there,' I told her—but no way! She wouldn't have any part of it. It was weird."

"Perhaps she wasn't looking her best," said Bashkim. "Perfectly normal female reaction if that was the case."

Lisbeth stared pensively toward the lengthening shadows cast by the tallest Shar Mountains. She shook her head. "No, that wasn't the only strange thing Peg did." Lis pinched her lower lip and gazed at Bashkim Inasah. "Looking back, I'm willing to guess that I wasn't out of Peggy Kelvin's sight for a full hour during the whole week we were at Bliss preparing for departure."

"I was advised you'd been assigned a watch dog employed by ben Zullah," said Bashkim, "...specifically an Army Major, but I wasn't told wh...."

"Did you know that Kelvin even went to Mass with me last Sunday?" said Lis.

"No. But that doesn't necessarily mean…"

"Cut the shit, Bashkim…Peggy's a New Hampshire atheist. She makes the Sign of the Cross backwards…genuflects on the wrong knee…and doesn't even know The Lord's Prayer." Lisbeth covered her eyes with trembling fingers. "Now it all makes sense. Unless I miss my guess, the only time Kelvin's ever been inside a church was a week ago."

"I see," said the Curator. "But I suggest you keep your suspicions to yourself."

"And I hope you'll do the same," Lis said gripping his hand.

Bashkim grasped her fingers gently in return. "My people have a saying: *'Information is power…but doubly so when an adversary is unaware that we possess it.'* If we trust one another," he whispered, "…we have a clear advantage over ben Zullah and his gang."

Lis composed herself and nodded.

He signaled for the waiter. The tuxedoed man approached them promptly with a pair of large menus. As local custom apparently dictated, the short fellow handed the bill of fare first to the broad-shouldered man, then to Lisbeth, after which Bashkim waved him politely away.

"Sorry, but I'm not very hungry," said the downcast Doctor.

"I can well understand it," Bashkim said. "However it would doubtless be wise to take some nourishment prior to our meeting with the Grand Imam." He looked at his watch. "We meet with him in an hour. You can be certain that ben Zullah will be on the alert for any signs of inappropriate behavior."

Lisbeth seemed to concur and pointed to the Lamb Stew & Couscous. She was a physician, after all, and she knew the importance of nutrition when one was embarking on a project that called for keen perception…and just as importantly, when the ability to disguise one's nervousness would be crucial.

"Excellent choice," said Bashkim with a smile…and he lifted a finger to summon the diminutive attendant.

Chapter 28

Her customers looked from behind like a pair of whispering nuns.

When Reza Mimona pedaled up to her little shop on Karaorman Road, two Muslim women in burkas stood waiting beside the front door. They looked like perfectly vertical, black-draped statues that contrasted with the irregular gray cobblestones embedded crookedly in the sloping, centuries-old street.

"*La bes*," Tereza murmured, and quickly leaned her bike against the show window behind which was a precisely placed array of new and used books. Some stood upright on their flared covers, some rested on their backs in a neat arc. Two volumes, one printed in Slavic Cyrillic type, the other in Latin Script lay open nearest the window pane, as if inviting passersby representing either of Madonica's two major cultures to sample the exposed excerpts. A small hand-lettered card, bearing the price in euros of each book, was propped against the appropriate work.

Reza unlocked the door and opened it amid the metallic tinkling of the small attached bell. The women, newcomers the proprietor guessed, though in their orthodox Islamic garb it was impossible to know for certain, giggled at the sound of the tinny signal, and the pair bowed graciously as they whisked through the narrow portal in a dark flurry of cotton and silk

"*La bes*," they replied. It was the Arabic term that, like the Hebrew *Shalom*, is an expression of all-around civility...*La bes* meaning literally *No evil*...not a far cry from the Hebrew word for *Peace*.

Lola Books was musty after being tightly closed-up throughout a damp November night, but now the late morning sun had climbed high above Old Tavoto and inexorably begun its warming, drying work. Tereza propped the front door open with a large, round stone reserved for the purpose, and she re-positioned her hastily parked bicycle farther down on the sidewalk...where it wouldn't obscure her store window.

Her near miss with the son-of-a-bitch in the pickup truck on Ilindenska Boulevard had dissuaded her from continuing on to the Monastery for apples. *Never mind*, she said inwardly, *I have a reason to visit the neighborhood of Oninnam this afternoon.* There was a McDonald's on the same block, Reza knew, at the corner of Ilindenska and *Goce Delcev*. It wouldn't take her more than five minutes to ride back there.

"That fucking Casanova Bashkim," she muttered indignantly. "We'll soon see what's so enticing at Oninnam."

She withdrew a number of euro bills from one pocket, and change totaling a few euros from another, and placed the cash in her register. Then she approached her customers, who looked from behind like a pair of whispering nuns. "I see you are readers of Local History," Reza said. "May I recommend Hans Steppan?...'*The Madonican Knot*' is wonderful!"

* * *

A grumbling Simeon Forrester drove north in heavy traffic on the Meadowbrook Parkway, then turned east at the busy Roosevelt Field Mall. He uncharacteristically ran a number of red lights despite the fact that Saturday motorists on Old Country Road gave way only grudgingly at the dead-straight thoroughfare's dozens of major intersections between Garden City and Plainview. In the passenger seat, Lis Wren's fidgety Boston Terrier stood on hind legs, her head protruding from the slightly lowered right window. She seemed to realize that the car was passing familiar landmarks, and with her nose turned into the wind, she keened and inhaled great gulps of air, apparently sensing that her liberation was at hand.

Finally, as the traffic lights at Newbridge Road came into view, the veterinarian tapped his brakes, applied the directional, and much to the intelligent little dog's delight, pulled into the far right lane, where Simeon waited impatiently for the green arrow.

Forrester had kept Gigi captive for two days and he was frankly concerned that Peter might be at home when he led the dog into the back yard on Strawberry Lane. Of course it would be a simple matter to explain that...*the precocious pup had probably wandered off...was picked up by a neighbor in nearby Carle Place...and brought to Simeon's Uniondale Animal Hospital by the Good Samaritan...who* (he'd say) *preferred to remain anonymous.*

But this was an unusually warm Saturday morning in November, Simeon reminded himself. A fervent golfer, it was unlikely that Pete would be at home. And even if he were, Lisbeth's *boy toy* would be so relieved to have Gigi back before the Terrier's mistress was able to initiate phone calls home, that he'd be perfectly willing to forget the whole episode. Why relive the matter? Everything would be resolved. Simeon and

Peter would be off the hook…and no one would be any the wiser.

'The Doc' looked at his watch. If he hurried he could drop off the dog and get the five thousand delivered to the bartender at Hung Chin in Westbury before noon.

Promptness was of the essence in these transactions. When one made as many telephone wagers as Simeon Forrester did, one had a reputation to uphold. The worst eventuality that could befall a regular bettor, Simeon knew, was to be considered a deadbeat. A wife beater—*no problem*…an embezzler—*nobody's business*…but a slow pay?—*that* was an unthinkable stigma for an inveterate gambler to carry.

'Doc' shuddered at the horrendous thought and turned onto Strawberry Lane. *Second house from the corner. No cars in the U-shaped, curb-to-curb driveway. Good!*

The frantic Boston Terrier leaped and whined, bumping her flat snout against the dash, the window, the headrest. When at last the veterinarian pulled into the paved semicircle at number sixty-eight, feverish Gigi could contain herself no longer and she urinated on the leather seat.

But no matter. Doctor Simeon Forrester had witnessed such accidents a thousand times before. All that was important today was that he get the agitated animal safely into her familiar back yard. He removed a medium-sized dog biscuit from his pocket and used it to lure his former prisoner out of the car and toward the gate on the north side of the pretty yellow house. The veterinarian opened the self-closing mechanism and in a flash, the Boston dashed inside and embarked on a non-stop sprint around the interior circumference of the four-foot-high fence.

Simeon exited the yard and the gate automatically closed behind him. If he'd worried about the Terrier attempting to stray, he now cast all such concerns aside. Gigi was lying in the farthest corner of her domain…past the rectangular blue pool…in the shade of her favorite tall tree…her muzzle resting on outstretched front paws…literally *daring* anyone to move her.

'Doc' tossed the four-inch biscuit to the part of the patio where the dog lay panting.

She didn't move a muscle. Gigi was home, and she wasn't going to budge from her spot.

* * *

At three-thirty, during a lull in customer activity, Tereza Mimona snatched three inexpensive paperback novels at random from the counter, hung her 'RETURN IN 20 MINUTES' sign on the door, and hastily locked up Lola Books.

Outside, she hooked her straw bag on the handlebar of her bike and rode bumping over stony Karaorman Road, then across the river via the footbridge, and finally southwest on Ilindenska to the six-story Boro Hotel. At the broad front entrance, she hopped from the bicycle, called out the single word, "Delivery," and offering her most flirtatious smile, she pushed the grimy bike in the direction of the uniformed young doorman.

Reza hurried into the tapestry-hung lobby and raced toward the bank of three elevators, one of which was wide open, the triangle over its door pointed upward. As the old oaken doors began to slide closed, Tereza skipped between them pulling her straw bag containing the slender books behind her… and narrowly yanked it into the paneled car, before the doors could pinch it from her grasp.

An elegantly dressed older couple, obviously visiting from Northern Europe, looked at one another—she huffily, he with lecherous raised eyebrows—and the indignant wife pulled him farther away from the winded young woman. Reza smiled at them self-consciously and pressed number six on the panel of protruding brass buttons. The man attempted to reach toward the array of numbered controls, but the woman squeezed his arm severely and she haughtily reached for button number five, punching it herself.

At the top floor Reza exited the lift. Familiar with Boro's layout, she turned right and proceeded to the end of the corridor. There, a glass door opened onto a sun-drenched balcony that circled the hotel and looked down on the lower buildings across Ilindenska Boulevard...including the chic Oninnam dining area.

Tereza stepped through the doorway and sat in one of three unoccupied lawn chairs. From her straw bag, she produced a small pair of opera glasses and scanned the rooftop restaurant.

By the rail on the perimeter of the eatery's outdoor section, Reza immediately spotted Bashi's wide shoulders and broad back. He was wearing the maroon suede jacket she liked so much. In one hand the handsome *Sarena Jemija* Curator held a broken breadstick that he nibbled from time to time. The fingers of his other hand slid contentedly around the rim of a wine glass. Opposite him sat a young woman who seemed to be about Bashi's age, and though seated, she was obviously tall.

Tereza Mimona leaned forward instinctively. She fine-focused the miniature binoculars on the stylish woman in the comfortable American-cut blazer. She was blond, of course... Bashi was such an easy mark for blonds...and her light complexion indicated that she was probably a *natural* blond.

Like Bashi, his companion nipped occasionally at a long piece of breadstick in her left hand…probably the other half of Bashi's, the hussy…and Reza noted immediately that the slim woman wore no wedding band. As a matter of fact, she wore no jewelry at all—not even earrings—and only a minimal amount of makeup. Tereza searched the neck of the woman's blouse for some sign of a necklace or chain, but at first could see none. Then the blond leaned forward, and Reza detected the unmistakable outline of a pair of dog tags weighing down her shirt from the inside.

"So, my darling Bashkim," Tereza Mimona groused spitefully, "…I see you have chosen to focus your considerable charms on an Army slut." She jammed the opera glasses into her tote bag and got up to leave the balcony. "A new arrival at your neighboring Camp Billingham, now doubt." Reza marched doggedly past the numbered hotel room doors toward the bank of elevators. "How very convenient for both of you."

Chapter 29

Who could stand idly by and see the sobbing women literally butchered?

After the initial wailings of the *Sunset Muezzin*, when the night's first call to prayers had been issued, Nazmi ben Zullah instructed his subordinates to remain in their meeting room on the 'Quilted Mosque's' main level. He, however, descended unseen to the labyrinth via the stairway beneath the curtained *mihrab,* just off the great prayer chamber.

When the last of the faithful multitude with their rolled-up prayer rugs had trudged in through the main portal of *Sarena Jemija*, one of the young apprentice Imams positioned himself by the base of the minaret facing *Ulica Goce Delcev*. It was the signal that Bashkim Inasah and his Army Doctor friend would be able to enter the mosque there and descend to the subterranean maze from inside the building without fear of detection by the praying believers.

The pair left the Citroen parked awkwardly on the dark, narrow street, walked to the base of the tower, and Lisbeth preceded the Curator through the entrance that he normally used, but which she had never seen. She knew full well where they were going, of course, and she breathed a deep sigh of relief with the realization that it would not be necessary to navigate once again the dim and musty passageway leading from the *turbe* to the *Mullahs'* conference room.

As Lisbeth followed Bashkim down the circular metal staircase under the *mihrab*, she noted that this set of steps was much newer and cleaner than the ancient access stairs beneath the distant *turbe*. Obviously, it was a considerably newer installation. *How long*, she speculated, *has this clandestine activity been going on…scant yards beneath the bare feet and bended knees of hordes of semi-prostrate worshipers?* It could not have been long, the Doctor concluded. The business of buying and selling illicitly harvested organs was a relatively new enterprise…at least on a large scale, it was. But Bashkim had told her at Oninnam that the *Mullahs* had been involved in this dangerous and revolting business for a relatively short time—about fourteen *years!*

My God! thought Colonel Lisbeth Wren, *the number of unfortunates who must have died as a result of the unsanitary procedures they'd been subjected to…the accumulated slaughter… it could number in the hundreds!* What truly dedicated Doctor could turn a blind eye to such carnage? Who could stand idly by, for instance, and see those two sobbing women in the nearby anteroom, literally butchered in the Grand Imam ben Zullah's filthy slaughterhouse?

As Lis and Bashkim approached the slightly ajar door to the conference room, where the head *Mullah* sat alone sipping schnapps and incongruously scanning the Koran, the Curator placed a cautionary hand on Lisbeth's shoulder. "Never enter the Grand Imam's chamber unbidden," he mouthed, "…even if the door is open." He glanced over his shoulder and lowered his voice even further. "Ben Zullah has been known to pamper himself with, uh, sexually gratifying activities…deeds that most men who thus indulge themselves, prefer to enjoy in private. You see, the Grand Imam appears to be something of an exhibitionist in that regard. If anything, the public display seems to enhance his, uh, pleasure."

"Perhaps we should have brought Big Ben the latest Muslim edition of Penthouse," joshed Lis Wren, only half kidding. She jerked her head toward the meeting room. "But you can do me a big favor if you'd kindly go in there and tell him to put his little weenie in his *Galabiyya* for the time being…at least 'til after we get a look at the new, improved dump that these assholes call an operating room."

"It would probably be best if we simply disregarded him," said Bashkim Inasah. "He may be a billionaire, but like all wealthy perverts, he's a moral midget when not standing on his wallet."

"Whatever you say," Lis shrugged. She patted her handbag, indicating the Beretta, "…but if that camel jockey tries anything with his dingleberry while we're supposed to be talking business, I'll fix him so he'll never have another impure thought as long as he lives."

"It is wise to be cautious with ben Zullah," Bashkim whispered. "Remember that he is accustomed to having his orders obeyed…promptly, and to the letter. And don't forget, he was able to seize your gun once, and might attempt to do so again."

Lisbeth looked coldly at the narrow opening in the conference room doorway. She was unconcerned that she might detect the *Mullah* engrossed in a flagrantly compromising act. While a former Police Officer on duty in the streets of New York, she had been required to observe downtown vagrants and uptown playboys alike behaving like crazed monkeys in heat. Nobody knew better than Lis Wren that it's almost impossible to shock a New York City cop. As for giving in to ben Zullah's demands for obeisance, both her medical and law enforcement training had taught her that such deference was the very *last* approach one should take when dealing with a morally repugnant bully.

"And he won't grab my weapon, either—that's the kind of oversight that can happen even to the best of us—but when we get away with it once, it never happens again. Believe me."

She pointed to the bulge in her oversized handbag. "The Beretta's not loaded…at least not yet." Lis reached into the side pocket of her blazer. "But I brought two rounds…one for you…" she handed Bashkim a single nine millimeter bullet… "and one for me." Whereupon Lieutenant Colonel Lisbeth Wren deposited the second round snuggly in the center of her bra. "Now hide that bullet in case I need it, and let's go see if Nazmi's replacement for Caliph Rabee has 'sanitized' the facilities down the hall as thoroughly as the jackoff promised."

* * *

"So Whadda we do now?" the scantily clad Major Nanette Stufkoski asked her two comrades. "It's obvious that it never occurred to our erstwhile friend, Colonel Wren, to arrange weekend dates for her three poor Battle Buddies."

"R.H.I.P." said Ophelia. "Rank has its privileges."

"And vibrators do have their limitations…or so I'm told," Peggy Kelvin mumbled.

"Not that you'd *know* or anything!" said Nan dubiously. "That what you're trying to tell us, Honey?"

"Leave the poor girl alone," Ophelia said, her words fairly dripping with sarcasm. "You saw how she nearly broke down and cried when the clerk at the PX told her they were out of batteries last night."

"You made that up!" Kelvin stormed. "They had plenty of batteries."

"At least they did until you bought their entire stock of nine-volts," Stufkoski grinned.

"An Eveready in need...is a friend indeed," Major Cockbyrne offered, settling the matter once and for all with her typically flawless logic.

"I think we oughta take a run down to Tavoto," said Peggy counting a fistful of euros from her fanny-pack. "It's supposed to be the Riviera of The Balkans."

Nan eyed the Psychiatrist's multi-colored stash of bills. "Where the hell'd you get all that loot, Shrink Lady? You been selling batteries on the black market again?"

"Wow!" Ophelia gushed peering over Peg's shoulder, "... business must be good. Most of those bills are twenties and fifties!" She winked at Stufkoski. "I guess we know who's buying dinner."

Chapter 30

Lisbeth walked to the center of the room. This is a miracle, she said inwardly.

When the Grand Imam Nazmi ben Zullah saw Bashkim's shadow on the floor outside the partially open meeting room door, he hastily downed the last of his Kirshwasser and stowed the half-empty schnapps bottle in a cabinet behind his chair. The 'Quilted Mosque' Curator rapped twice on the door and the *Mullah* summoned Inasah and Doctor Wren inside.

Lisbeth looked furtively around the room and, noting that Bashkim remained standing, she too stood behind the chair she'd occupied during her impressive speech the night before.

"I trust you slept well?" asked a slightly slurring ben Zullah, obviously addressing Lisbeth.

She answered with a question of her own. "Where are the women who were in the waiting room yesterday?"

Bashkim shot the Lieutenant Colonel a reproving glance.

The Grand Imam waited several beats before answering, his expression clearly indicating that he found the American's initiation of the topic insulting. Finally, he raised himself from his seat at the head of the olivewood table. "They were sent home to their husbands," he said, and he added, "…but I doubt that they slept well."

"And why is that?" Lisbeth demanded before Bashkim could stop her.

The *Mullah* smirked and he nodded knowingly toward the Curator. "Because by their weeping the whores have brought discredit on themselves, shame on *Sarena Jemija*, and discomfort to the Grand Imam. For these sins they have already been whipped." Ben Zullah strode in the direction of the door leading to the hallway and the primitive operating room. "If not for your concern, Doctor, both '*Svinya edna*' would have been stoned—the appropriate sentence for a pair of 'Stupid wild pigs.'"

The *Mullah* stepped into the corridor and Bashkim followed, leading Lisbeth by the hand. "But as it is, you will see them again…when their wounds have healed somewhat."

Lisbeth Wren had no choice but to hide her revulsion. As she and Bashkim followed Nazmi ben Zullah along the hall that Lis was now sure led in a westerly direction, the Doctor was also certain little would have been done to correct the unsanitary conditions she'd observed in the operating room yesterday. Colonel Wren had, in fact, begun to rehearse mentally the various excuses she might offer for being unable to participate in the Grand Imam's illicit enterprise.

When the trio arrived at the familiar door, the first thing Lisbeth noted was that a lock had been installed immediately below the steel doorknob. If it was there yesterday, Lis certainly hadn't seen it. Was this ben Zullah's notion of renovating a decrepit medical facility that should have been sterile? Adding a *lock*, for God's sake?

The *Mullah* reached into the pocket of his *Galabiyya*, removed a brass key, and inserted it in the lock. He twisted the key clockwise and the action produced a smooth scraping sound followed by a solid click as the deadbolt slid free of the jamb.

As ben Zullah pushed open the door leading into the darkened room, Bashkim stood behind the cleric, his arm circling Lisbeth's waist as if to lend support and prepare her once again for the filthy sight he knew the Doctor found so repugnant. The Imam reached into the dim void and flipped a switch upward.

Immediately Lis Wren recoiled in utter shock.

The newly appointed operating room was instantly bathed in a uniformly illuminating bright, white light that emanated from a series of recessed panels in the powder blue ceiling. Beside each glowing rectangle was a louvered conduit—a series of six ducts in all—and half of them sent a consistent stream of cold, clean air flooding almost imperceptibly throughout the room; the other three were intakes that kept the pure atmosphere circulating noiselessly.

Beneath the light switch next to the door was a white enamel table that contained several pairs of aqua-colored paper booties with elastic tops. These were intended to be donned while standing on a disposable paper mat, thus it was never necessary to contaminate the skid-proof epoxy floor, which was a robin's-egg mirror image of the ceiling, except that it was lightly pebbled.

An eight-foot dressing table bearing long paper smocks, masks, and bonnets occupied much of the OR's south wall, and beside it was a six-foot-long scrub sink that could accommodate two users simultaneously. Centered above the stainless steel sink was a shelf bearing boxed Latex gloves and higher on the wall, the room's only analog clock—white with black numbers, black minute and hour hands, and a red sweep second hand.

All four walls were pure white, and Lisbeth Wren swept them admiringly with her deep blue eyes as she counted a dozen electrical outlets in a raised sill built into the perimeter of the room at waist level.

Lis stepped onto the paper mat and pulled on the booties… then she handed two pairs to Bashkim. He slipped one over each shoe, and he handed a pair to the *Mullah*, who did the same. Wide-eyed, Lisbeth walked to the center of the room and began to examine the state-of-the-art equipment. *This is a miracle*, she said inwardly.

The focal point of everything in the futuristic chamber was, of course, the operating table itself.

Specifically highlighted, in the absence of a patient, was a two-foot square area in the center of the multi-sectional black pad that would eventually support a supine subject. This chosen section was lighted by a pair of moveable concave discs…one above each end of the adjustable Stryker table… and the intensity of the two converging beams that were directed downward from the bowl-shaped mirrors literally defied description. Now the shafts of light made even the dark vinyl cushion glow as if illuminated by a dozen suns, and when the slab was draped in snow-white sheeting, stocked in four high cabinets opposite the sink, the dazzling array would be brighter still.

Lower than the half-hollow dishes, and slightly below the eye level of a six-foot surgeon, were two full-color, two-by-three-foot Visual Display Units, each containing an identical image. Currently the pair of high-definition monitors displayed a standard VDU screen saver showing what Lisbeth recognized as the renal arteries and veins in the vicinity of a left kidney. It was the human equivalent of the area from which Doctor Wren had removed Mr. Sickpig's renal cyst ten days ago. She smiled at the somewhat familiar, though vastly more complex conglomeration of blood vessels, organs and muscles displayed on the screens.

Finally Lisbeth rounded the Stryker table and its arrangement of ivory colored appliances mounted in a maneuverable quartet of shelves counter-balanced overhead. Anchored in the spotless ceiling, the grouping was a deceptively simple-looking collection of aural and visual contrivances that would provide respiratory and cardiac support during anesthesia. The machines included emergency resuscitative devices, patient monitors, and diagnostic tools. Many were combined in multi-functional mechanisms the size of a breadbox…a tribute to the marvel of micro miniaturization.

Doctor Wren, despite her misgivings concerning the despicable Nazmi ben Zullah, could not help but nod at Bashkim in open admiration that such a transformation had been effected so quickly and with such precision. "I would like to meet your anesthesiologist," she said without making eye contact with the *Mullah*. She continued to gaze about the room…studying the millions of dollars-worth of potentially life-saving equipment.

When the Grand Imam failed to answer, Lisbeth looked gravely at him where he stood by the heavy wooden door. Ben Zullah smiled weakly. "I am afraid that is not possible," he droned. "Our Resident in charge of such things chose to return to her native India." He shrugged. "It's said she met with an unfortunate accident on her arrival in Mumbai."

"Be that as it may, Imam, it is necessary for your surgeon to be assisted by a certified…"

"Enough!" cried ben Zullah. "We are not Americans. We are unconcerned with pampering our clients." He opened the door and tore off his paper shoes. "Caliph Rabee's replacement will assist you. You will meet the new Caliph Fahd tomorrow."

The Grand Imam stood waiting impatiently in the doorway, where he leveled Lisbeth Wren with a threatening stare. His body language said that the guests had seen enough. It was now time for everyone to leave the premises. Lis took a more secure hold on her handbag and with the strap over her right shoulder she gave the *Mullah* as much room on her left as she could while hurriedly stepping past him and into the corridor. Still, she could detect the distinctive odor of Kirshwasser schnapps as she brushed by.

The hallway seemed particularly dark compared to the brilliance of the operating room, and as Bashkim turned off the chamber's main light switch, the white-paneled facility too was plunged into darkness. Ben Zullah closed and locked the heavy oaken door, and Lisbeth stood with her back to the passageway's concrete wall…waiting for Bashkim's cue.

The Grand Imam addressed Inasah with a brief, muddled command in Farsi and pointed down the hall toward the circular staircase that led upward to the *mihrab* in the still-crowded mosque. Lisbeth and the Curator were being summarily dismissed, and the Doctor emitted a sigh of relief. "The stairs," said Bashkim, "…the way we came." And knowing better than to touch the woman in the presence of the *Mullah*, he gestured politely with an upturned palm toward the metal steps that were vaguely visible some twenty yards to the west.

Chapter 31

"So, that's where you've taken the minx," Reza growled.

Tereza Mimona left Lola Books early and intentionally pedaled the crusty old bike past the turn she would normally take to go to her apartment. At a quarter past six by her watch the always busy intersection of Kiri Ristoski and Ilindenska was already ablaze with amber streetlights, and the outdoor dining area on the roof of posh Oninnam a few doors toward the river was clearly visible. Even from street level Reza could see that the cozy corner table by the rail…where Bashi had been entertaining the tall American woman so lavishly… had now been vacated.

Well, I'm certainly not going to search the town looking for them, Tereza decided bitterly. *If Curator Bashkim Inasah wishes to lower himself to the level of a common male prostitute, so be it.* She made a U-turn on Ilindenska and headed for the bridge over the River Pena. When she'd arrived within a few yards of the *Ulica Goce Delcev* and the familiar minaret that rose above the 'Quilted Mosque' Reza could hear that the *Muezzin* was electronically announcing to the faithful that it was time for the *Sunset Salat*.

With the three new books in the straw bag that dangled from her handlebars, Tereza swung the bike in a wide arc northwest onto *Goce Delcev,* causing the spokes of her front wheel to chew at the fraying old tote. She cursed her hasty turn in typical Tereza Mimona style, her profanity neutralized slightly by the reverent whining that blasted from the speakers of the minaret.

As soon as the proprietor of Lola Books had crested the slight hill on which *Sarena Jemija* was built, she saw Bashkim's silver Citroen…parked, as always, with two wheels on the sidewalk that skirted the tower.

"So, that's where you've taken the minx," Reza growled, her feral eyes flashing a combination of scorn and discovery. "Do you bed her even during the *Salat?*" She kicked the side of the elegant car as she wheeled past it in the narrow space that remained on the driver's side of *Ulica Goce Delcev.* "There," she said. "I wish it was your balls!"

* * *

Lisbeth and Bashkim sat in his modest office quietly looking at one another…he, wondering about the background of this new *Mullah*, Caliph Fahd…she pondering how anyone could have managed such an incredibly rapid transformation of the Operating Suite a mere fifteen feet below them.

Lis posed her question first. "Do you have any idea how much money is tied up in that room, Bashkim?"

"Money is not an issue for Nazmi ben Zullah," the Curator said lightly.

"The medical equipment alone is easily worth two million dollars."

Bashkim shrugged.

"And the suite itself…my God, the electrical outfitting, the duct work, the plumbing…it must have cost a fortune. That epoxy floor alone is a hundred-thousand-dollar installation."

Once again Bashkim Inasah threw up both hands and let them fall idly on his lap—the gesture said, *chicken feed.*

Lisbeth frowned. "I can't imagine how that system could have been transported here and put in place so quickly? I mean, it's all top-notch equipment: G.E., Stryker, Apple, Biodex...I had no clue some of that stuff was even available outside of New York or Boston."

"What would you say," Bashkim asked, "...if I were to tell you there is a stockpile of stolen medical equipment, not thirty-five miles from here, that would be the envy of Johns Hopkins or Sloane-Kettering hospitals?" He nodded slowly. "And it is all brand new...not even uncrated...some of the devices have never been tested or even seen by your American colleagues."

Doctor Lisbeth Wren sat wide-eyed and unblinking... unable to believe what she was hearing.

"Oh it's true, my Dear. In the fifteen years since ben Zullah's friends, the Somali fishermen, began forcing their way onto commercial ships, these cutthroats have turned East Africa's waters into the most dangerous...and financially productive areas on Earth. There is nothing our oil-rich *Mullahs* cannot have immediately...and for virtually a handful of euros!"

Lis sat spellbound. "Ventilators," said Bashkim, "...infusion pumps, emergency resuscitation equipment...anything can be delivered in a few hours. Of course, MRI and CT Scan equipment might take as long as half-a-day."

"And the people who installed these devices?" she murmured, "Where did they come from? Where are they now?"

The Curator held a finger to his lips, got up to check the lock on his office door, and re-positioned himself beside Lisbeth. They could hear that with the conclusion of the *Sunset Salat*, worshipers by the dozens were departing through the colorful mosque's main entrance on Ilindenska Road. "Most are political prisoners being detained over in Skopje," he said. "Some are employed by firms that design and produce apparatus such as you saw this evening…others are what Americans call 'transfer students' who have been careless enough…at least in the opinion of the clerics…to wander into 'sensitive areas,' let us say. All are highly intelligent and well-trained in their medical specialties. If their assigned work is satisfactory while they are under investigation for suspected 'espionage,' it is likely they will be released in three to five years."

Lisbeth was aghast. "Three to five *years?*"

Again the Curator placed a finger in front of his mouth and nodded toward the door.

"And if they reveal what they've been forced to do?" Lis demanded in a husky voice.

"That has happened only once since I have been Curator of the 'Quilted Mosque,'" Bashkim replied. "It was a female—a student of cardiology named Sorensen. She was permitted to leave…then when ben Zullah was called to account for certain 'crimes' she accused him of, he produced her two associates. They told a team of Danish investigators that the Sorensen woman had fabricated the story—that she had been expelled from Madonica when the mosque's Elders refused her demands for money."

He looked longingly at the decorative tin of cigarettes on his desk, but just as quickly turned away from the Turkish Murads. "Shortly thereafter, the young woman hanged herself…at least, that's what the authorities in Copenhagen concluded." With a wan smile, Bashkim Inasah said, "Helga Sorensen's friends were dispatched by our Grand Imam to attend her funeral…a gesture conveying that neither he nor the people of Tavoto harbor any animosity whatever against the obviously 'unbalanced' student."

"So," said a gravely indignant Doctor Wren, "...that explains why so many professionals in so many different specialties have gotten involved with these people...and never blown the whistle—to do so would be suicide...literally."

"Precisely," the equally resentful Curator answered. He made a steeple of his slender fingers, held them touching the cleft in his chin, and spoke solemnly. "The reach of the Balkan Cabal knows no limits geographically. All members are as well-connected in America and the Orient as they are here in Eastern Europe. Even the notorious Mafia recognizes the scope and cunning of the *Sarena Jemija*-headquartered vital organ traffickers, and bows to them. Why? Because The Mob cannot begin to match Islam in numbers...financing...or for that matter...ruthlessness."

"When you say 'well-connected'...do you mean politically? Surely ben Zullah and his henchmen haven't compromised the United States Congress!"

Bashkim Inasah took Lisbeth's hands in his and said compassionately, "The Congress? My dear Lisbeth, the U.S. Congress represents but *one* arm of your nation's government."

The Lieutenant Colonel shot upright in her chair as if an electric shock had pierced her body. "You mean...you can't be implying..."

Again Bashkim shushed her tenderly. "I am implying nothing. I am stating a fact. Even America's Executive branch has been infiltrated at the highest levels...the same is true for the U.S. Supreme Court."

Lis Wren looked pale and weak...as if she'd had the wind knocked out of her.

"I've already told you," said Bashkim, "...that Eric Mueller is, in effect, a double agent...as is one of the field-grade officers who came here with you. So obviously, ben Zullah's gang has infiltrated the Pentagon as well."

"It's becoming hard to know who can be trusted in this God-forsaken place…and who can't," Lis mumbled. "Does Mueller know which of the Majors is watching me?"

"I don't know that he's even aware one has been assigned," Bashkim said, raising a finger of caution. "And whichever Doctor it is, may not know of Captain Mueller's involvement either. You see," Inasah lowered his voice to a whisper as the faithful on the other side of his office door could be heard exiting the mosque. "…the Grand Imam is a true genius when it comes to keeping his enemies at sword's point…assuring that they are constantly suspicious of one another."

Finally, with the last of the worshippers having departed, the Curator leaned forward and spoke in a normal tone of voice. "For all I know," he stated, "…the *Mullah* could have enlisted you to test my faithfulness to him." He smiled faintly. "It is a chance I have decided to take."

Chapter 32

"Jesus!" Stufkoski blasphemed, glaring at Cockbyrne "I think I'm gonna be sick!"

The bus ride to Skopje from Jaziref was as pleasant as a stand-up, half-hour, bone-jarring journey can be among a horde of sardine-packed, foul-mouthed, hygiene-challenged workmen heading home on a Saturday night.

The three Majors had boarded the rickety vehicle at the corner of Braim and Ahmet in South Jaziref. If they thought for a moment they and the burka-clad women with them would be the beneficiaries of some degree of male chivalry regarding seating, they were in for a first-class, Ovosok-style surprise.

Here, even 5 and 6-year-old boys took male superiority for granted, Stufkoski, Kelvin and Cockbyrne noted. They said nothing, of course, but merely rolled their eyes in disdain. Like their slouching fathers, the young lads were invariably seated in relative comfort, some clutching chickens and dogs on their laps. Their veiled mothers and sisters, however, stood nearby, swaying in a constant battle against the inertia produced by the twists, turns, and sudden stops of the old, free-wheeling bus.

The driver, naturally, had the best seat of all. He sat in a sort of cage, bent over a broad steering wheel, singing his lungs out, and maneuvering the nearly flat wheel with his elbows…as he simultaneously pared an apple with his small pocket knife. Every few seconds he would force open the vent window by his left ear and fling a curled slice of apple skin into the night, permitting dozens of flies, gnats, and moths to invade the crowded transport before he yanked the glass panel tight again.

The American Doctors stood squeezed in the aisle approximately two-thirds of the way to the rear of the lorry. "I think I want to get off this fucker," groused Nan, trying in vain to distance herself a few inches from a scruffy man who was sleeping while being held upright by his equally immobile neighbors.

"Poke him if the snoring bothers you," said Peggy.

"He's kinda cute, if you ask me" Ophelia said sneaking a ninety degree peek at the drooling dozer.

"Jesus, he's *what?*" Stufkoski blasphemed, glaring at Cockbyrne incredulously, "…I think I'm gonna be sick!"

"Well, if I don't eat something pretty soon, I *know* I'm gonna *faint!*" said Ophelia. "There's a great restaurant in Tavoto…Oninnam…it's expensive, according to Sergeant Grayson in Billeting, but," she patted Peg Kelvin's euro-filled pocketbook and smiled a toothy grin, "…the Major here is loaded…aren't *we* Major?"

"And none of that *Dutch Treat* bullshit," said Nanette the Dentist. "Takes all the fun out of it, don't you think, Cockbyrne?" Then, sensing that Kelvin was about to object, she added reassuringly, "I'll buy next time."

"No," said the unfortunately named Ophelia Cockbyrne, "Next time's my treat. We can go to *Restoran VEH-cheh-rah.*"

Nan frowned and said, "*VEH-cheh-rah?* Where's that? I never heard anybody mention any *VEH-cheh-rah* restaurant."

"Hey!" Peggy Kelvin hollered as the grubby fellow, who was asleep on his feet, involuntarily dropped his head to her shoulder. He awoke with a start, jumped backward, and accidentally stepped on Ophelia's toe in the process.

"Ouch!" yelled Major Cockbyrne, at which point, the wide-eyed workman yanked his offending foot away from hers, and he found himself wobbling unsurely on one leg. He reached forward with both hands in an attempt to stay himself, only to grab the braless Stufkoski in what the manual called *an inappropriate manner*.

Peg and Ophelia both took note with alarm and each gave the skinny dude a rap alongside the head.

"Girls! Girls!" Nanette cautioned, seizing them by the wrist. "Easy does it—the poor guy's just trying to take a nap for heaven's sake."

* * *

Captain Eric Mueller smelled a rat. Sure, he knew that easing Doctor Lisbeth Wren into the system here in The Balkans was a touchy and important part of Bashkim Inasah's function. And yes, Mueller was aware that the Curator was trusted implicitly, if not by all the clerics who convened in the 'Quilted Mosque,' then certainly by the Grand Imam, Nazmi ben Zullah himself. In the final analysis, that's all that mattered. Still the Captain had his suspicions.

What nagged at the big career soldier wasn't so much Inasah's apparent affability where Lieutenant Colonel Wren was concerned, after all, that's the impression the native Madonican had been instructed to convey to the American woman whom the *Mullahs* had targeted for participation in their nefarious enterprise. What bothered Eric Mueller was the readiness with which Lisbeth seemed to cozy up to the handsome Curator.

According to Mueller's covert contacts in the Pentagon, Wren was a bright, self-sufficient, ex-cop who had become a Doctor against all the odds, and joined the Army when a handful of terrorists had murdered three thousand of her fellow New Yorkers on a cloudless morning in September, 2001. The woman was known to be a tough, no-nonsense soldier who had climbed to field-grade level faster than anyone in the history of her Unit. Though she lived in suburban Long Island with a retired Policeman and a dog she loved in equal measure, Lisbeth Wren had displayed her independence by stoically, and readily, accepting the hardships that were part of modern military deployment. Accordingly, she had been frequently decorated and looked to be on the fast track to full Colonel status. A genuine success story.

But the romantic spark that Bashkim seemed to ignite in her was the kind of thing that the Captain's surreptitious associates had implied would never be a problem. Even by her own definition Lis Wren was far from what she termed a 'girly girl.' Why then, this ostensible infatuation with a man the Roman Catholic Lisbeth had known for only a few short days…and a renegade Muslim, at that? It didn't add up.

There were enough military vehicles on the roads that linked Prishta, Jaziref, and Tavoto to assure that Eric Mueller's Jeep would attract little attention as it accompanied the eclectic flow of southbound traffic from the Camp Billingham area. Only the occasional prostitute waved in the Captain's direction when the olive drab vehicle with the big white star sped by on Highway 122. But Eric had other things on his mind.

Also, there was little room in Mueller's Jeep for anyone, or anything, apart from him and his cargo. The load consisted exclusively of a dozen five-gallon Jerry Cans…so called because in the 1930s they were designed by Germany (dubbed 'The Jerries') to hold fuel, and occasionally water. Like any number of German inventions, the cans were so efficiently suited to their purpose…easily filled, stacked, and transported…that the modern 'Jerry Can' has maintained the same familiar design to this day, regardless of which nation's military currently carries it in its inventory.

Nine of the rectangular containers occupied the entire back seat of Mueller's sturdy vehicle, and three more were stacked beside him on the floor. Deep diagonal indentations and corresponding ridges in the sides of the pressed-steel cans allowed them to nest effectively, thereby preventing slippage. The cans that Captain Mueller was known to distribute during his trips up and down the Southeast European corridor… from Madonica down to Athens, and north to Bucharest… were stenciled with the international symbol for Drinking Water. It consisted of a white circle with a simple rendering of a white tap inside, and a suggestion of drops of liquid flowing into a rudimentary cup—what could be more innocuous? Additionally, the canisters were all covered with condensation, further indication of the harmless nature of Mueller's cargo.

One glance from a guard at any of several roadway checkpoints throughout the various Balkan States that the Captain traveled produced nothing more than a derisive grunt and a wag of the head: *Take your precious water and move on, Yankee,* they seemed to say.

In reality, however, these sweating 'Jerry Cans' contained insulated blocks of dry ice—frozen carbon dioxide, with a surface temperature of minus 109 degrees Fahrenheit. The ice also had the fine feature of Sublimation…as the blocks broke down they turned directly into gas—carbon dioxide—as opposed to a liquid. The extremely cold temperature and the Sublimation features made the dry ice perfect for refrigeration over long distances.

In today's load of 'Jerry Cans' the dry ice was *all* that the innocent-looking canisters contained, but in a day or two each can would also hold a newly harvested human kidney... and some other unscrupulous career soldier would be making the delivery to a clandestine organ dealer somewhere between Greece and Bulgaria.

Of course, the deliveryman would again be an unprincipled Army officer—and, like Eric Mueller, an imposing one at that. After all, he would be collecting one hundred thousand euros per can, on average. Only a high-ranking representative of America's vaunted military machine would be assigned such a function. Hardly a job for a PFC.

As for the mechanics of taking the altered 'Jerry Cans' apart to load and unload them, the procedure was both clever and uncomplicated. The universal symbol for Drinking Water was actually an externally threaded disc, ten inches in diameter that screwed into an internally threaded gap exactly the same size in the side of the 'Jerry Can'. When screwed tight, the disc was flush with the surface of the can, and the stacking slots and ridges lined up perfectly. There was no reason to think the image was anything more than a stenciled illustration identifying the container's everyday contents.

As the jam-packed Jeep neared Kolkovo, northwest of Skopje, Mueller followed the highway's western extension, first in a broad, sweeping turn to the south. This permitted him to avoid the glare of the setting sun whose rays already reflected off the snow-covered peaks of Valbona Valley National Park in Montenegro...far beyond his destination in Tavoto. In a few minutes the road would turn to the right and take him on a direct path toward the little city itself. By that time, the sun would have descended behind the distant mountaintops, and the remainder of his brief trip to the 'Quilted Mosque' would be uneventful.

The Captain had himself filled the cans with the dry ice. It was supplied to him unquestioningly at the Billingham Quartermaster's Depot for his twice weekly run to the local slaughterhouses south of Jaziref. Once a week he would actually drop off half a dozen canisters to selected butchers there in return for their illegible signatures on blank Army vouchers, which he would then complete himself. Mueller never charged the favored butchers for the frozen carbon dioxide. They assumed the swarthy Captain had seen to the largesse out of the goodness of his heart. And one thing was certain: deliveries of the precious ice were prompt and unfailing. The merchants could virtually set the clock…and therefore their valued out-of-area deliveries…by their dependable provider. Indeed Captain Eric Mueller was a true friend of the working man.

Chapter 33

The most dangerous warning sign yet…he was starting to hear things.

On the ninth green at Muttontown's manicured Golf and Country Club between Oyster Bay and Plainview, Peter Ravens three-putted for the sixth time in an hour. He hadn't done that since grade school for Christ's sake! *This is a goddam waste of time*, he bitched to himself. "That's it for me gentlemen." The scratch golfer slammed the untrustworthy putter into his big red and white Spalding bag, and lugged it in the direction of the clubhouse.

"Aw, come on Pete," club pro A.J. Richard whined. "They'll start dropping on the back side. You always score better coming in than goin' out."

"Not today I won't," Ravens said with a disconsolate shake of his head. "Too much on my mind. Drinks are on me," he called over his shoulder. "Tell Anita to put 'em on my tab." He bypassed the clubhouse door and walked directly to his car. Two veteran caddies shining shoes on the locker room porch could tell from Peter's body language that this was not a good time to make small talk. They bent low over their task and wisely diverted their eyes as Pete Ravens passed, flung the clubs in the back of his Camaro, pulled off his spikes, and drove south on Cedar Swamp Road in his stocking feet.

In the fifteen minutes it took to negotiate the six miles to his yellow house on Strawberry Lane, Peter had imagined…then discounted…a dozen scenarios that might have prompted Lisbeth's Boston Terrier to sally forth from the cozy confines of her back yard in Plainview.

He'd considered the prospect of theft—*hardly a likelihood*, he told himself. Bostons were not what you would call exotic animals…certainly not worth doing time for. Besides, though he never would have shared his opinion with Lis, Gigi, with her squeezed-in snout, bulging eyes, and squat little legs, was far from most people's definition of 'beautiful.'

The dog had been spayed at practically the earliest possible time—*she certainly isn't in season*, he concluded.

And even before Gigi had been sterilized—*the lively Terrier had never been known to stray even as far as the front sidewalk*, he recalled reassuringly. No—she never would have wandered off.

When the process of elimination had left no circumstance surrounding the animal's disappearance that could be termed even somewhat probable, Peter Ravens was forced once again to assume that the four-year-old Boston was either hiding somewhere on the premises…or had been given shelter misguidedly in the house of a bleeding-heart neighbor.

However, Pete was a retired Policeman. And ex-cops were supposed to be good at locating missing individuals (presumably humans and animals alike), were they not? Well, his best efforts notwithstanding, so far the only traceable result of Gigi's loss had been a total devastation of Peter Ravens' fucking golf game.

Impatiently, he pulled into the U-shaped driveway a bit faster than he should have, braked with a squeal and a dip of the hood, and threw the gear shift into 'park.' As he sat wondering how he could explain this whole mess to Lis when she called tomorrow or the next day, the distraction to which he'd been driven now manifested itself in the most dangerous warning sign yet…he was starting to *hear* things. Pete covered his ears with both hands, closed his eyes, and rested his elbows on the Camaro's steering wheel. It didn't help. The sound of Gigi's sharp yip-yipping still rang in his imagination.

Jesus, he thought, *what the hell did I do to deserve this?*

* * *

Like everyone else living in close proximity to the *Sarena Jemija* and its electrified minaret, Tereza Mimona got little sleep until after the day's final *Muezzin*—the Evening Call to Prayer—had been played. The raven-haired woman had long been convinced that the whole idea behind blasting a woeful chant through the peaceful community at this serene time of night was to ensure that none of the faithful within earshot should be permitted the opportunity to engage in pleasures of the flesh.

Not that the interruption would thoroughly deter Reza. On nights when the romantically compulsive bookseller had been known to achieve *Musad*, or 'get lucky' during *Salat*, she'd thought nothing of easing her partner's religious scruples by jamming her fingers into his ears and belting a mezzo-soprano rendition of whatever national anthem he subscribed to… while bouncing in rhythm to the chauvinistic composition. It went without saying that Reza Mimona was well versed in every jingoistic jingle sung throughout all of Europe…and a good part of even the sexually *civilized* world.

But tonight, revenge more than sensuousness was on Reza's mind, and nothing short of Bashkim Inasah's prompt tarring and feathering would satisfy her, though stoning might do.

She threw on her coat, tossed her cat Rajah a woolen sock stuffed with catnip, and flung open the lock on her door. Shifting her battered old bike into a corner on the far side of her dresser, she kissed Rajah on the nose and exited the room, leaving the light burning. She bounded down the three flights of stairs and once on the footpath that lined the south bank of the River Pena, Reza marched east until she found herself within a few yards of the granite *turbe* behind the 'Quilted Mosque.'

Where she came across something totally unexpected.

At first, she'd *heard,* not seen something—the distinctive sound of hollow metal on stone. Then, after lowering herself to the grassy berm, erected centuries before to protect the mausoleum from the often swollen river, she peered over the crest of the embankment. She saw the uniformed man...a Captain...he was carrying two-foot-tall cans from a vehicle only vaguely distinguishable behind a grove if thick Madonican Pines. The rectangular containers were nearly eight inches thick and the officer was carrying one in each hand. *They must be empty*, Reza estimated...*or nearly so*.

When the row of brown cans beside the *turbe* doorway numbered a dozen, the leathery man rubbed his hands, first on the damp grass, then on his khaki pants. He scanned the immediate area, retreated to the waiting Jeep, and eased his way onto Ilindenska Boulevard without benefit of headlights. In a moment he turned off Ilindenska at the corner of *Goce Delcev* and entered the all-night McDonald's.

"Very interesting," said Tereza Mimona in a monotone. She stood and brushed the dew from her hooded jacket. "That man could almost pass for Eric Mueller's brother."

When it came to her customers...at least, those of the opposite sex...Reza didn't miss much, not even in the dark.

Well, there's one sure way to find out, she mused. She circled the 'Quilted Mosque' and strode innocuously into the brightly lit restaurant beneath the golden arches.

The uniformed Captain was seated at a corner table with his back to the roughly thirty patrons who, like fast food customers throughout the U.S., occupied all of the place's one-dozen booths, but only a couple of the smaller tables. On the wall in front of Mueller was one of fifteen three-foot-square, framed photographs. They were arranged attractively on the beige, Sanitas-covered walls, and typified the incongruous meeting of eastern and western decor found in most of Tavoto's American-owned eateries. Predominantly red, yellow, and orange—the standard McDonald's motif—the neon and fluorescent interior of this particular restaurant contrasted with the franchise's collection of vintage pictures…different views of the famed Clifte Amam…the renowned 500-year-old Turkish bath of Skopje.

Depicted in the huge photos were interior views of magnificent waiting and changing rooms. Two large halls that looked to be situated in the central part of the structure were furnished with beautiful, richly ornamented fountains. And some of the smaller rooms revealed white marble urns for collecting bath water, while others had obviously served as ancient saunas.

In America, the host establishment might have been mistaken for a mini-museum or art gallery—here, its historic theme was considered entirely appropriate, even for a public bistro…even one in which could be heard the constant sounds of meat patties sizzling on open grills, and French fries cooking in bubbling oil.

Tereza knew that Eric was watching her approach mirrored in the glass-covered photo before him. She ambled to the back of his chair, smiled as she looked closely at his reflected face, and placed her hand lightly on his broad shoulder. "Captain Mueller, I believe."

"Hello, Tereza." He continued to peer at her reflection in the exquisite photo of the Clifte Amam. "Early for Lola Books to be closed on a Saturday, isn't it?"

Reza Mimona gave Eric's shoulder a squeeze, kissed him on the cheek, and pointed to the empty chair opposite him. "Is that seat available…or must I go home and cry my eyes out?"

A resentful Muslim couple was pretending not to notice the public display of affection on the part of the vulgar female in the heavy tunic and head scarf. It was obvious that she was boldly flirting with the handsome soldier. Disgraceful!

Eric Mueller stood and gestured toward the vacant chair. "Please," he said. "Be my guest." The Captain was careful not to touch the clearly local woman. McDonald's or not, this was Madonica, after all, and a certain degree of decorum was required here when the sexes interacted in public. Even the whores handed their johns business cards containing storefront addresses, and met them in shabby back room facilities.

"Let me get you something to eat," said Eric, still standing. He pointed to the colorful menu high above the counter to his left. "Today's specialty is Beefburger (he stressed the word 'Beef' to distinguish it from 'Ham') and *pommes de terre au Francais*."

"*Bon*," Reza responded, pleased to note that Eric had benefitted from the French/English dictionary she had sold him weeks prior. "*Et une Coke, s'il vous plait*." The Muslim couple gave her another dirty look, and the tall American strode to the counter.

"*Numero trois*," he said holding up three fingers and handing four euros to the clerk. The brown-skinned man poked the cash machine, deposited the bills, and slid three coins from

204

their slots in the register. In seconds another clerk brought a tray containing a paper place mat, a wrapped Beefburger, an open-ended envelope of hot *pommes de terre au Francais*, and an empty cup emblazoned with the script word 'Coke,' the most widely recognized symbol on Earth with the possible exception of Mickey Mouse.

Eric proceeded to the beverage station, dispensed a generous amount of crushed ice into the plasticized cup, and filled it the rest of the way with effervescing Coca-Cola. He stepped to the table and placed the tray in front of Tereza, who acknowledged his gallantry with a firm squeeze of his hand.

The gesture was too much for the Muslim couple at the next table. With an Albanian oath that could be heard across the busy room, the seething man, clad in a dirty *Galabiyya* and torn sandals, shoved his uneaten food aside, spat on the tray, and marched out the side door with his obsequious woman close behind.

Eric Mueller excused himself and strode into the night behind the pair. In seconds, he re-entered the restaurant holding the terrified fellow by the hair. The Captain signaled for a busboy, and a small, aproned lad came running. Eric grabbed his damp cleanup rag, lashed the Muslim man across the face with it, then dropped the cloth onto the tray. He forced the fellow to his knees, muttered something to him in Farsi, and gave the handful of hair a twist. Instantly the man became submissive in the extreme. He picked up the rag, mopped the spittle from the tray, folded the damp cloth, mopped the tray again, then repeated the process a third time.

Satisfied that he had made his point, Mueller pulled the man back to the restaurant door, opened it and flung him into the parking lot where he landed and slid on his face. The man scrambled to his feet wide-eyed and bleeding. He took one look behind him, then ran like a deer down Ilindenska Boulevard. As Eric nodded toward Reza and headed for the men's room to wash his hands, the man in the *Galabiyya* continued to race north until he turned west at the corner of *Ulica Goce Delcev*...and disappeared into the shadows cast by the darkened 'Quilted Mosque.'

* * *

The three Majors' dinner at Oninnam was everything it had been cracked up to be—a great start for a night on the town—but Stufkoski's allergy to curry had ruined her evening. "I'm going back to the camp," she announced glumly, just as a huge platter of baklava and candy-sweet tulumbi was wheeled to the edge of the round table.

"Don't you dare," Ophelia warned. "We can't head back until we've had our espresso fix."

"Take your time," Nanette said, standing. "I'm grabbing a taxi to Billingham. This attack'll be over in an hour or so." She slung her pocketbook over her shoulder. "I owe you one," she said, bending and kissing Peggy Kelvin on the cheek. Ophelia started to rise, but Nanette pressed her firmly back into her chair. "See you at the SEA hut, ladies."

Chapter 34

*He held up the hollow-pointed cartridge.
"I have envisioned a plan."*

As I see it," said Lisbeth, "…it would be a relatively simple matter to report Nazmi ben Zullah to my Commander at Billingham. He would grant me safe passage home, I'm sure—get me the hell out of here while the Army takes up the matter at the highest level."

Bashkim Inasah reached into his pocket. He fingered the nine millimeter round Lis had given him to hold in case she needed it. "You know your people better than I do," he said, apprehension detectable in his dark eyes and in the grim set of his jaw. "My chief concern, however, is that the extent of the Grand Imam's influence might be broader than you think."

The Curator reached for her hand. "In The Balkans, justice is swift and harsh," Bashkim said. "In America, I'm given to believe, application of the law can be a slow process requiring much deliberation." He studied her face and frowned his unease. "The judicial process…even before NATO became involved, and they surely would have to…could take months—and possibly years."

He released Lis's hand, removed the bullet from his pocket, and twirled it in contemplation. "During such a prolonged period—with all the public exposure that you Americans have become so insistent upon—the Army, and even the full United States government, might find it difficult to guarantee your safety." The tall man leaned even closer to the bravely naive Doctor. "Consider that there are now millions of dedicated Muslims in America...Islamic edifices everywhere you look... three hundred mosques in New York City alone. Should ben Zullah issue an order of *Fatwah* upon you, your future would be uncertain at best."

He held up the hollow-pointed cartridge. "I have envisioned a plan that would circumvent such an eventuality."

Lisbeth Wren sat staring at the man she had met just a few days earlier. She silently mulled over the plan that, though unstated, clearly involved the shooting of her antagonist...the wicked and powerful cleric, Nazmi ben Zullah. She nodded toward the nine millimeter bullet that Bashkim Inasah held suggestively between his thumb and index finger. "You would do that for me? Kill him?"

Bashkim answered in a low monotone. "I would do it for both of us."

"What do you mean?" she asked, "...*both* of us?"

He set the brass-encapsulated projectile on the desk, its lethal-looking slug pointed upward. "How long do you think the Grand Imam will permit me to live after he is through with you—after you have added a few million euros to his coffers?"

Lisbeth Wren felt a sudden ache in her chest. She hadn't considered the possibility that others, besides herself and her helpless little dog, might be at risk. But now that she had seen the proof of ben Zullah's unvarnished cunning, it became plain to her that Bashkim had assessed the revolting cleric correctly...he was indeed capable of anything.

"Where would you do it?—and when?"

"In the operating room." The Curator bobbed his head toward the stairway he and Lis had just climbed. "It should be done at the completion of your first extraction."

"My fir..." Lisbeth was shocked. She had not agreed specifically to the *Mullah's* demands and she reminded Bashkim of that.

Again Bashkim raised a cautionary finger and held it to his lips. "Hear me out."

She looked at him testily, deep misgivings distinctly etched on her face.

"Ben Zullah is the most distrusting of men. He requires ocular proof to decide for himself whether his Doctors are to be trusted. In order to observe the results of a surgeon's initial performances first-hand he must, of course, be physically present at the conclusion of the procedure."

Bashkim returned the bullet to his coat pocket and a semi-smile crossed his face. "Ironically, this compulsion on the part of the Grand Imam provides us with the opportunity we need, first to kill him...and then successfully to dispose of his body."

Lis cocked her head and furrowed her brow. "I don't understand...about the body."

The Curator edged closer to a curious Lisbeth Wren. "The medical hacks employed by ben Zullah have produced a mortality rate approaching thirty percent..."

"Wha...?"

Bashkim Inasah nodded his head ruefully. "Those bodies are cremated immediately and the remains scattered over the city." He folded his arms and leaned back in his chair, apparently content with his plan. "After I have killed him, we will place his body in a wooden box in the sub-basement reserved for the unfortunates. Only we will know of the deceased's true identity. It will be a fitting end for Nazmi ben Zullah."

"Where is the crematorium," she whispered.

"In the minaret," said Bashkim. "The ashes are hauled to the top and disposed of on the first windy day."

* * *

In addition to conducting *Salat* throughout the day, and disposing of the cremated remains of the dead from the underground medical facility, the apprentice Imams, Aalil and Aamil, had been trained to handle Nazmi ben Zullah's unique method of doing away with those accomplices he had never trusted—and no longer needed.

In the minaret, basking in the warmth radiating from the ceramic bricks that formed *Sarena Jemija's* rectangular, gas-fueled crematorium, was a flat, screen-covered insect colony that looked for all the world like a miniature, single-story, apartment complex. It could have been a toy train layout, or an architect's model for a retirement condominium such as might be found adjacent to a Florida beachfront or golf course. And the residents of this community were all widows...'Black Widows'...insects that characteristically had killed their mates with one venomous bite—then devoured them. Eventually, all two dozen of the eight-legged assassins would be employed as individual, untraceable merchants of death by the Grand Imam of the *Sarena Jemija*.

The Latrodectus spider...one of thirty-two similar species... and probably the best-known member of the dangerous category, is the appropriately named Black Widow. The poisonous bite of any in the entire Latrodectus genus can be fatal to humans, but the female Black Widow has particularly large venom glands, making her bite an almost certain killer, especially when young and aged victims are involved.

As far as the 'Quilted Mosque's' chief *Mullah* was concerned, he had found his replacement for the Indian Doctor who had tragically been bitten in Mumbai. And accordingly, the elderly Simeon Forrester's number was now up also.

As instructed, Aamil unlocked the clasp that held a six-inch-square hatch closed atop a small unit in the broad tray of nests. This one held the glossiest and fattest Latrodectus, indicating that it was undoubtedly the oldest—and therefore the most venomous.

With his right hand protected by a canvas glove, Aamil lowered a tin Murad cigarette box into the nest, and immediately the jet-black spider scurried several inches to the corner farthest from the intruding container. The young cleric pushed the metal box slowly through a tangled web of silken, but sticky fibers, careful lest he provoke the insect to bite his glove, and thus deplete her of the supply of venom she'd stored.

Withdrawing his gloved hand, Aamil daintily plucked the tin cover from the top of the screen, re-opened the hatch, and eased the Murad lid through the opening. When the cover was inches above the trap he waited patiently for the spider to crawl curiously into the cigarette box…at which point, he slammed the box top home, and the metallic click pronounced the Black Widow captive…the first step on her journey to Uniondale, Long Island—and the otherwise sanitary office of Doctor Simeon Forrester.

The apprentice had performed the routine before. In the Spartan room he shared with Aalil, was a three-by-five-inch index card containing only the name 'S. Forrester, DVM,' and the address of the Uniondale Animal Hospital. When the tin box had been pierced with three holes no larger than the tip if a ballpoint, Aamil, put it in a similarly perforated plain cardboard box, fastened the index card in place with clear packing tape, and wrote 'Fragile' across the face of the small parcel. The cautionary word was spelled the same in both English and French, and its meaning would be recognized by any carriers along its several thousand mile route. He affixed ten euros worth of postage above the address and took the packet to the all-night post office on Boro Vulic Road.

Chapter 35

"When you decide to shoot that bastard...don't miss. Go for his chest."

The worshipers having left the mosque; the doors of *Sarena Jemija* had been locked by Aalil; and the moment that Lisbeth Wren had dreaded most was at hand. She looked at Bashkim grimly and shrugged her shoulders bravely—an unsuccessful attempt to make light of her misgivings about what she knew would be the most difficult charade of her life.

She would have to win the Grand Imam's confidence, if only for an hour or so, and there was just one way to do that...Lis would have to appear willing to perform invasive surgery on another human being. If it seemed she could not—or would not—there was no hope that Bashkim Inasah's intricate plan to rid the world of the evil Nazmi ben Zullah could be implemented.

Lisbeth reached for her bag and produced the Beretta. She handed the unloaded gun to Bashkim handle first. "Do you want the other round?" She pointed to the area above her sternum where the cartridge was hidden in her bra.

"No," he said. "I think you should hold on to it." He removed the magazine from the pistol, slid his single round in place, and slapped the device back inside the handle of the nine millimeter where it belonged. "If anything goes wrong, there's a possibility you can save the situation…but only if you have access to that bullet. All the firearms in the world are useless without ammunition, but even one round can hold a dozen enemies at bay."

He stood, checked to be sure the Beretta's safety was on, and shoved the gun inside his waistband at the small of his back. "Buy as much time as you can," said the Curator confidently, "but don't let ben Zullah think for a moment that you're stalling." He waggled a cautious finger at Lisbeth. "He will not tolerate being toyed with, as you know."

Bashkim took her arm and they walked toward the office door. "And do not be upset if it appears I'm critical of you. I am being as closely scrutinized as you are, don't forget."

"Got it," said Lisbeth. "Just do me one favor. When you decide to shoot that bastard…don't miss him. Go for his chest."

They exited the Curator's Office and walked to the *mihrab*. In mere minutes they had entered the curtained alcove and were descending the circular metal stairway. Once in the labyrinth's main basement corridor they could see Imam Nazmi ben Zullah standing in front of the newly outfitted Operating Room. With him was a diminutive, loosely garbed individual whom they both concluded must be the inept Rabee's replacement, Caliph Fahd. He was already dressed in paper booties, bonnet and scrubs, a surgical mask covered his nose, mouth, and chin…tinted goggles protected his eyes giving them a somewhat menacing aspect.

The Grand Imam opened the wide door and the American Doctor entered the brightly illuminated room, followed by Bashkim, and finally the *Mullah* himself. She stopped next to the scrub sink and the others followed suit.

The smell of ether in the Operating Suite was pervasive, and in the center of the room, strapped to the narrow, padded

Stryker table, a boy apparently in his teens, lay on his side. He was covered by sterile paper blankets and was breathing deeply under the primitive general anesthesia. A gurney had ostensibly been used to deliver the young candidate donor, and having been rolled aside, it now was positioned against the far wall. Caliph Fahd rounded the brightly lighted operating table and its youthful occupant, and took up an observatory position next to the empty, white-draped gurney.

"We will dress and scrub in order," said Lisbeth in an officious tone that indicated she was clearly in command. She pointed at Bashkim, "First you,"…then at ben Zullah, "You next,"…and then she said, "Finally me…and keep out of my way—that means everybody!" Fahd, she'd decided, need not be involved.

As had been the procedure in Lis Wren's simple nephrectomy work with Harold Sickpig and other large animals, Lisbeth knew she would be required to make a ten-inch-long incision on the patient's left side…immediately below his ribcage… and hope that in this instance it would not be necessary to remove the bottom rib altogether. A certain amount of fat, muscle, and tissue would have to be cut into, and temporarily re-positioned in order to access the kidney itself. In the case of the lean young man on the table, Lis was confident, fat would cause little interference, but muscle might be another matter. Otherwise, tonight's surgery would be a relatively straightforward process: The tube…the ureter…carrying urine from the kidney to the bladder must be cut away from the kidney, as must the renal vein, renal artery, and other blood vessels. These would then be promptly clamped and sutured…and the kidney itself removed and placed in a sterile, plastic bag before being consigned to its refrigerated transport container. Finally, the long cut would be closed… in this case with staples…and less than an hour after Lisbeth's initial incision, the donor's antiquated anesthetic would be permitted to wear off.

Lisbeth had dressed and scrubbed much more painstakingly than had the men in the suite. Her thoroughness was intended mostly to kill time—though largely to assure the sterility of her hands and forearms in the event she would have no choice but actually to conduct the surgery.

When she finally slid her slender hands into the Latex surgeon's gloves, Lis Wren strode to the middle of the Operating Room, looked at a small table to her right, and began to take careful inventory of the various marking pens, scalpels, clamps, and other hand-held devices arrayed there atop a white linen cloth.

As she counted, separated, and otherwise repositioned the gleaming tools in the logical order of their use, it occurred to her that Bashkim, standing to her left at the foot of the Stryker table, was looking intently, first at her, then surreptitiously toward ben Zullah, who stood with arms folded next to the patient's head. The Curator's dark eyes shifted from straight toward her…then left in the direction of the Grand Imam… then back at her again…time after time. *He's sending me a message*, Lis thought. Then it dawned on her. *Bashkim wants to get closer to the bastard.*

Lisbeth retreated one step and announced firmly, "You're obstructing my light, both of you." Then, taking a calculated risk she commanded, "If you must stand practically on top of us, stay either between the overhead lamps or outside of them! And for God's sake…back up!"

Bashkim waited until ben Zullah had eased himself a half step backward and to his right…then moved slightly left and a full stride to the rear. He was now within arm's reach of the *Mullah*—and slightly behind him. The American Doctor had read Inasah's intention and reacted perfectly.

Lisbeth muttered a curt, "Thank you," and used a four-inch-square surgical sponge to apply a thin layer of Povidone-Iodine skin prep solution to the side of the patient's abdomen. She measured the mixture's drying time by the sweep second hand on the wall clock next to the door, and when sixty seconds had elapsed, Lisbeth lifted an aluminum tube labeled 'Surgical Marker' from the instrument table. She twisted the cap—the rotation met no resistance whatsoever. *This device has been used already*, she theorized, *probably on a previous patient*.

Rather than risk cross contamination, Lis snapped the plastic marker in two, marched to the table by the door where her handbag was, flung the broken marker pieces into a lidded biohazard container, and retrieved a ballpoint from her purse. She washed the pen at the sink, clipped it to her sterile paper gown, then re-scrubbed her hands and lower arms. "Not ideal, perhaps, but at least I know where this marker's been," she said, glaring in annoyance at the masked Caliph Fahd…whom she assumed had prepared the instrument arrangement.

Chapter 36

"Goddamit, Gigi, do you know how close you came to getting me killed?"

As soon as Peter exited the Camaro he moseyed in his stocking feet, spikes in hand, to the back of the car to remove his clubs. A neighbor driving by honked his horn and the disconsolate Ravens waved back absently. The illusory sound of his lost dog's yapping had mercifully stopped, but now it was replaced by a desolate, whimpering whine that seemed to come from the far side of the back gate. It had never happened before, but it was possible that a dog from elsewhere on the block had somehow gotten itself trapped in the fenced yard.

Pete leaned the big pro bag against the rear fender of the car, shoved his Foot-Joys into the largest side pocket, and idly walked to the five-foot gate behind which the canine moaning had now stopped. He reached over the gate's slightly arched top, intending to depress the latch, and reflexively the agile Peter Ravens yanked his hand away…but not before the leaping Boston Terrier had washed his fingers with a lightning series of familiar licks.

"Jesus Christ," the ex-cop exploded as he peered over the gate and the little dog looked straight up with her round head cocked inquiringly to one side. "Where the hell have you been?" Pete squeezed into the yard, squatted and hugged the by-now frantic animal. "Goddamit, Gigi, do you know how close you came to getting me killed?"

The dog answered the rhetorical question with only one piercing bark followed by a woeful moan. Peter Ravens understood. "She'll be calling tomorrow," he promised, "… and you damn well better be here. Now let's get you something to eat."

* * *

At Oninnam Majors Cockbyrne and Kelvin dawdled over dessert indulging in great slabs of both the familiar baklava, that Ophelia was interested to learn from the waiter originated in Turkey, not Greece…and a surprisingly delicious tulumbi, deep-fried true Madonican pastry soaked in syrup. Like all Americans, both women overindulged in their coffee, and on the third espresso Peggy felt compelled to point out, "I love baklava, but for my money, you can't beat that 'tumbleweed' whatchamacallit."

"Tulumbi," Ophelia corrected, and added, "If the damn stuff wasn't so sticky I'd bring some back for Nan."

"Forget it," said Peggy. "I may be a mere shrink, but I know gastrointestinal distress when I see it. I told her not to order the curried lamb."

"She said she's allergic," said Cockbyrne.

"Bull," Peggy Kelvin replied. "Stufkoski was as light on her feet as a ballerina when she bounced out of here. Didn't look like allergy symptoms to me. The lady had an appointment, if you want my opinion."

"Maybe she's got a date with Sergeant Grayson in Billeting," said Ophelia, raising her eyebrows and grinning wickedly.

"Are you serious?" Major Kelvin huffed, "…one roll in the hay with Nan would kill that little goofball."

"Point well taken," Cockbyrne said. "At any rate, let's get back to the Camp. If Nan's available we can all catch a late movie. I understand they're showing 'Nanette Does Nantucket.'"

"That's about the size of it," said Peggy Kelvin, standing and brushing baklava crumbs from her lap. "You're welcome for dinner, by the way."

* * *

"So what brings you to our thriving metropolis at this hour, Captain?" Reza picked up a thin French fried potato slice with her fingers and dipped it in an inch-high paper cup of bland American ketchup. "Or should I ask?"

"Military secret," said Eric Mueller, plucking two French fries from a red cardboard container…then taking a huge bite of his Cheeseburger. He lifted his paper cup of Coke and studied Tereza Mimona over the rim as he drank. *She's avoiding eye contact*, the brawny Captain thought. *I don't like that. It's not her style.*

Reza gave him a fleeting glance and caught the look of suspicion in his penetrating blue eyes. She bit into her Beefburger to keep from having to make conversation for the moment. Mueller continued to stare-down the self-conscious woman as he methodically chewed the combination of meat, cheddar, onion, and mealy bun.

Finally, Mueller returned his cup to the table and looked out the window. "Where's your bicycle, Reza? I didn't see it outside."

Tereza frowned. "Bicycle?" Then she smiled weakly as if in sudden realization. "Oh, you mean my old bike? I, uh…I left it in the shop," she lied.

"I see," he murmured…and inwardly said, *liar!*

"I never bring it home on Saturdays," she said with fake levity, compounding the falsehood. "Unless it's raining, of course."

"Of course," said an ostensibly agreeable Eric Mueller… who was now thoroughly convinced that Tereza Mimona had seen him deliver the supply of custom-outfitted Jerry Cans to their pick-up point…at the *turbe*…behind the 'Quilted Mosque.'

* * *

As a child, Hanna Breughel had confided in and otherwise trusted only one boy in her young life. Ultimately, she had fallen in love with the intelligent Otto Henschel in their native Germany, and following their elopement, the tiny Hanna had come to adore and depend completely upon the handsome charmer of her childhood…until the midnight call ten years ago, when then Army Lieutenant Eric Mueller had brought the awful news—that Otto Henschel had succumbed to Chronic Kidney Disease in the Camp Billingham hospital.

What should have been a relatively routine kidney transplant, virtually guaranteed under the generous insurance umbrella covering civilian Engineers at one of the world's major military installations, had somehow been mysteriously squandered.

Details of the forfeited opportunity had never been explained to the distraught woman. Nor did she care to have the incident expounded upon. All she knew—or cared to know—was that half of her very soul had been torn from within her. The only thing that was important now was that she live her final, empty years…no matter their number…the way Otto Henschel would have expected her to—with the dignity and grace of the girl he'd loved and married.

Eric Mueller's fateful appearance at Frau Henschel's door on that sultry Ovosok evening in mid-summer had proven to be the first of many visits. Indeed, the German-speaking Lieutenant had interceded with Billeting officials suggesting that they house deployed Teutonic-literate Americans in the home of the lonely woman, who spoke no English. And that noble comforting of Hanna, it was widely assumed, was Mueller's only motivation. It was the least the Army could do.

But nothing could have been farther from the truth.

Though Frau Henschel did not know it, all of the expediently German-speaking military personnel that Eric Mueller had deftly arranged for her to lodge, had been carefully selected for their medical expertise by the cabal which Nazmi ben Zullah headed. And the Grand Imam's clandestine U.S. Army liaison was, of course, the bi-lingual Eric Mueller. Thanks to his cunning, in their off-duty hours ben Zullah's commandeered staff was uniquely free to come and go unsuspected between the little yellow house in Jaziref, and the mysterious *Sarena Jemija* in doughty old Tavoto.

Military deployments for Doctors, Nurses, Medical Technicians and the like, normally average four months or so at Camp Billingham. Accordingly, Captain Mueller had arranged for the accommodation of well over two dozen such specialists in Hanna's Ruga Dognal *cul-de-sac* home in the decade since her husband's death. Furthermore, Hanna Henschel's convenient 'widow' status had been similarly predetermined…when Otto had been allowed to die, alone and unattended in a Billingham psychiatric ward…when it was generally assumed he was being transported under Mueller's watchful eye to a kidney transplant facility in Vienna. It was murder, pure and simple.

Such was the reprehensible nature of the butchers whose '*cruel harvest*' had been so vividly described in Tereza Mimona's volume on illicit organ trafficking in The Balkans.

Chapter 37

The stunned Doctor's hand closed around the handle of the shining lancet.

Lasers are 'scalpels of light,' Lis knew, that are uniquely capable of sealing blood vessels such as renal veins and arteries—the major vessels that, in addition to the ureter, need to be secured during a simple nephrectomy. Unfortunately, Doctor Lisbeth Wren was unskilled in modern laser surgery and its state-of-the-art procedures. Had she been familiar with the technique and experienced in its application…and assuming that she was unalterably committed to operating on the boy who lay unconscious in front of her…*the kidney harvesting procedure would be a far less daunting task*, she theorized.

She removed the ballpoint pen she'd clipped to the high neckline of her surgical gown, and leaned over the youthful patient. Lisbeth held the chrome pen level with her ear and clicked the plunger that protruded from the back of the instrument's barrel. She drew a straight test line on the loose sleeve of her paper gown. It would be a bad time suddenly to discover that the always trusty pen had inexplicably betrayed her…or to find that something else had unexpectedly gone wrong. But the resulting blue-ink line that followed the contour of her wrist was uniformly distinct on the light green gown. And for a minute she breathed easier.

Lisbeth looked at Bashkim as if silently urging him to relieve her of the necessity to continue the procedure. The Curator gave no indication that he intended to do anything of the sort, and a moment of panic overtook her. *What if his courage has failed him*, she thought. *Worse yet…what if he'd never intended to intervene on my behalf?*

The former Police Officer had been trained to recognize when hesitation would render her impotent in the face of the enemy…and she now felt the alarm going off in her gut. If she vacillated for another moment the delay might well result in her own death…in the murder of Bashkim…and most regrettably of all, in the killing of the defenseless young man who lay on his side on the Stryker table…sleeping…possibly never to awaken.

Lis drew a slow, deliberate, ten-inch line from the boy's ribcage to the top of his pelvis. "Where's the Crash Cart?" Lis demanded of Fahd the assistant, knowing full well that none had been ordered. Where, after all, would she take her young patient in the event of a catastrophic turn of events…this *was* the facility of last resort so far as he was concerned. The Caliph, in turn, merely regarded her with an insouciant gaze through the amber-tinted goggles…and ben Zullah slowly twirled his finger, signaling for the impertinent American Doctor to get on with the business at hand.

Bashkim, too, seemed eager to proceed with the surgery and Lis was startled to note that he now folded his arms impatiently as she placed the ballpoint on the tray containing the arrayed surgical tools. *Is the idiot intentionally making access to the Beretta more difficult for himself*, she wondered, *or doesn't he know that my next step involves making the incision itself?* Surely the Curator was aware that once the boy's abdomen had been opened Lisbeth would be in no position to participate in the dispatching of ben Zullah…certainly not until her patient's wound had been stapled at the very least—a process likely to take five minutes or more…twice that if sutured. She shuddered at the image of the chaotic scenario that would ensue were Bashkim to take it upon himself to fire at the Grand Imam while she was engaged in such a delicate procedure.

This is not the meticulous Bashkim Inasah I know, Lis thought resentfully. *What the hell's going on here?*

For the first time since entering the Operating Suite, a nervous Lisbeth Wren's forehead began to glisten with droplets of perspiration despite the sixty-five-degree temperature of the room. She made eye contact with each of the men who stood watching her guardedly…flashed an unmistakable warning glance at Bashkim as she reached toward a long-bladed Number Ten Scalpel…then stopped. On the tray, beside the lancets, was a two-inch stack of gauze pads. Lis gestured toward the sterile swabs, leaned slightly to her left, and summoned Bashkim forward with the single word, "Sponge!"

The Curator reached for a gauze pad, prepared to mop Lisbeth's brow. Simultaneously, a suspicious Caliph Fahd tore off the protective goggles, leaped between Lisbeth and the tall Curator, and screamed, "Don't touch that!"

The stunned American Doctor's hand closed around the handle of the shining lancet, and squeezing it, she backed away from the small intruding figure…whose surgical mask had now slipped down to neck level. Disbelieving, Lisbeth exclaimed the single word, "Nanette!"

* * *

Eric Mueller swept the fast-food restaurant with his cold, blue eyes. The patrons, mostly Albanian like Tereza, seemed determined to avoid the solid man's gaze lest he turn his ire on them too. Those that were gathered in knots of three and four, obviously Muslim as indicated by their loose-fitting *Galabiyya*, knew that it was a sin to leave food uneaten on the table, and they hurriedly jammed condiment-drenched buns and meat patties into their mouths, eager to leave the scene of the beating administered by the American Captain.

"You look uncomfortable," said Mueller to Reza in perfect Madonican. If anyone at the nearby tables heard him, they didn't reveal the fact.

"I seem to have lost my appetite," the bookseller answered in a muted response.

Eric reached across the table, took her half-eaten Beefburger, and consumed it in two great bites…never moving his stare from Tereza's downcast brown eyes.

He reached again, lifted her envelope of French fried potatoes, and spilled them out on the paper placemat in front of him. The Captain dusted the golden *pommes de terre* liberally with salt from a shaker and proceeded to shovel them into his mouth four and five slices at a time.

Watching the officer with the cropped military haircut from beneath her visoring hand, Reza Mimona marveled at the fact that his crisp uniform showed not the slightest sign that the man had been involved in a violent altercation.

He balled the papers from his plastic tray and shoved the compacted sphere into his empty Coca-Cola cup. "Why don't I walk you home?" he said. "You look like you could use some fresh air."

"That won't be necessary Eric," said Reza dismissively, standing and turning toward the door.

Eric Mueller seized her wrist in a vise-like grip that startled the trembling woman. "You heard me!" he said, a false smile on his resolute face. "We can walk along the river."

Reza Mimona slung her pocketbook over her shoulder and peered about the interior of the brightly lit eatery…looking in vain for a familiar face…or any potentially helpful Samaritan to assist her. No one showed the slightest willingness to interfere in what appeared to be an unfortunate, but personal misunderstanding between disgruntled lovers. A few of the diners even snickered at the unfolding scene. "I think she's drunk," one Tavoto dowager huffed judgmentally.

The husky Captain held the door open and, pretending to secure Reza's bag on her slender shoulder, he twisted her arm upward behind her back until the pain made her gasp. With an artfully executed knee delivered to her buttocks, Mueller propelled the grimacing Reza through the exit, and the heavy glass door closed automatically behind them.

"I have to get my bike," Tereza protested, pointing with her free hand in the direction of the footbridge.

"I thought you never bring it home on weekends," said Eric, increasing the upward pressure on her arm and causing her shoulder to ache terribly.

"But it's going to…to rain…tomorrow…" Tereza panted, beginning to sob.

Eric Mueller released her arm, and simultaneously seizing a handful of her hair, he pushed the groaning woman out of the McDonald's parking lot and marched her, stumbling and weeping, toward the dark pathway that bordered the River Pena.

"Shut your mouth," he commanded, heard only by a second busboy taking a smoke break, "…or I'll break your fucking jaw."

"But what have I done to you?" the terrified woman pleaded, her straining neck pulled back in an unforgiving arch. "I thought we were friends."

"Then perhaps this will disabuse you of that notion," said Mueller...whereupon he snapped one of the cervical vertebrae immediately below Reza's shivering skull.

Tereza Mimona's head flopped like a rag doll's as he hoisted her over the waist-high wall of the narrow footbridge and heaved her into the swollen river. When the current had swept her corpse east of the Ilindenska Overpass and out of sight beyond the white water of the Lenin Rapids, the Captain walked casually back to his Jeep...then he drove in the direction of Skopje...and north toward the Jaziref-Billingham road.

Chapter 38

"I'll take it up with Captain Mueller, my Dear."
And she turned out the light.

The industrious widow Henschel had never had trouble sleeping. Usually exhausted from long stretches of housecleaning in the early hours, washing and ironing at midday, baking in the evening, and quilting after dinner, Hanna was usually asleep five minutes after she'd locked the doors, pulled the shades, and conducted her nightly conversation with Otto.

But lately Otto had seemed disturbed by the way things were going in and around his tiny wife's house by the fountain on dead-end Ruga Dognal. Though Hanna had assured her husband's quiet, handsome ghost that nothing was amiss, Otto had exercised his protective instincts and rebuffed her protests. *'I want you to keep the doors locked, Hann,'* he'd insisted night after night recently. *'Trust no one...not the Muslims...not the Americans...no one.'*

"Not even my new American friend, the Doctor," Hanna had asked aloud in her native German, gazing lovingly at Otto's sepia-tinted picture by her bed.

'Not even her, Dear Hann. Often those who seem most innocent can accidentally betray you.'

"My poor darling," she'd smiled and said. "You worry so unduly."

'It's all I can do from here,' Otto said in quiet frustration. *'There are limits on this side of the grave...as you will see one day.'*

She picked up the wood-framed picture, kissed it, and returned it to the lace doily she'd crocheted after the funeral.

"I'll take it up with Captain Mueller, my Dear." And she turned out the light. The nocturnal conversations had become as normal and as regular to Hanna as was her morning cup of tea, and she would probably have forfeited life itself rather than forego either one.

* * *

Once on the outskirts of Jaziref, Eric Mueller was tempted to stop at Frau Henschel's house, if only to establish a quasi-alibi for his late night whereabouts on what had turned out for him...and particularly for the unfortunate Reza Mimona...to be an eventful evening indeed. On reflection, however, the murderous Captain had decided on a cover story that would be more likely to win him the support of Billingham's Military Police unit currently on duty at the main gate.

At the intersection of the Jaziref/Billingham highway and the road north to Prishta, Mueller pulled his Jeep into a ramshackle twenty-four-hour cigarette store. He sounded his horn to awaken the grubby merchant who sat on a high stool behind a cracked, half-raised window...sleeping. At the shrill sound of the horn, the disheveled shopkeeper's bearded chin flew up from his chest, and his dark eyes grew round at the sight of the beige colored fifty-euro note that Mueller waved.

"Murad," the Captain demanded, pointing and holding up four fingers—"Four."

The vendor quickly reached into a rack that held five rows of Murad cigarette tins, extracted four of the metal containers, and hastily dropped them into a crumpled paper bag that was seeing its third or fourth incarnation. He extended the sack with one hand and simultaneously snatched at the fifty-euro bill with the other. Mueller released the note only after he'd peered into the bag and counted the decorative containers. The man patted the pockets of his shirt helplessly, then his trousers, then he shrugged as if he could not come up with the twelve euros change for the 'fifty.'

It was routine procedure with off-post purchases and Mueller waved and smiled knowingly at the squalid man, confident that the generous twelve-euro tip he was leaving would assure the fellow's agreement if the Captain ever needed to have him swear the transaction had taken place between 9:00 and 9:30. It was now 10:45.

Eric Mueller sped eastward to Camp Billingham, and pulled up to the north gate, where a Military Policeman recognized him and saluted.

"Had to run out for my Turkish smokes," said the Captain returning the salute…and he tossed one of the sealed Murad cans to the Corporal, who had no choice but to grab it in mid-air. "Figured you'd want a pack."

"Hey, thanks Cap'n," the young NCO said, slipping the Murads into the shoulder pocket of his camo blouse. "Sure 'preciate it."

Eric Mueller winked at the MP and returned the second salute. "Just keep it to yourself, Jackson," said the Captain. "Don't want the Brass thinking anybody on duty 'round here is accepting contraband…do we?"

"Uh…no, Sir!" muttered a suddenly nervous Corporal Jackson, his eyes darting left and right.

"And for the record," Mueller added with a smile, "…anybody wants to know, I came through at 9:30…or thereabout."

"Yes, Sir," said an officious Jackson, snapping to attention. "Nine-thirty, Sir…give or take."

* * *

Like grassy waterfronts everywhere, the banks of the River Pena provide an attractive nighttime trysting place for youthful lovers. And amorous pairs of the more outgoing young Tavoto residents still dot the open, green slopes on both sides of the bubbling rapids in chilly November. They are the modest romantic adventurers. The more intensely passionate couples exercise their ardent pursuits under a dozen old stone bridges where damp, dark walkways render the opportunists all but invisible as they conduct their mercurial activities mostly unseen and usually unheard.

Where the Pena leaves Tavoto proper, preparatory to beginning its due eastward surge toward Skopje, there is one final bridge that separates the Old Sector of town from its ancient surrounding farmland. It was in the gloom of this moss-covered hideaway…the hollow arch beneath the Vidoe Bato Bridge…that Valentina and Teodor lay holding one another in a blissful embrace, their bare feet ankle-deep in the onrushing river.

When, swept onshore by the swift current, murdered Reza Mimona's wide-open mouth encircled two of Valentina's tingling toes, the normally modest 16-year-old emitted a screech of such intensity that Teodor concluded he surely must have outdone himself performance-wise. Accordingly the Romeo pressed his flushed face deeper into Valentina's neck, hoping for more pyrotechnics…but the once-vocal object of lusty Teodor's desire was quiet and immobile for the first time in their marathon lovemaking…the pretty girl had fainted.

At first, Teodor was afraid to move, or even touch the unconscious girl, and he tenderly released her from his amorous grasp. *What had he done?* the boy wondered in near-panic. He stood slowly, never taking his eyes from Valentina, as he inspected the girl, beginning with her tangled blond tresses.

The hair that covered her forehead was damp and dark from the pair's recent energetic escapade…but even in the darkness he could tell that the honey-colored curls were not bloodied. "Thank God," he breathed in the most earnest prayer of his young life. Her eyes were closed, and her relaxed features showed no sign of distress. Her breathing seemed regular, if the rising and falling of her small, firm breasts was any indication.

Teodor removed a blue and white striped handkerchief from his back pocket and stepped toward the river's edge where he squatted to dampen it, hoping that cold water taken from the swift-moving Pena would revive the stricken girl when applied as a compress to her brow. He plunged the bandana into the current that bubbled over Valentina's bare feet, and in doing so, he brushed aside a thin stream of waving debris that obscured his friend's submerged toes.

But the debris was Tereza Mimona's hair, and when the river's course that swept it downstream had been interrupted by Teodor's kerchief, the strands settled temporarily, forming a thin layer barely covering her staring eyes and gaping mouth.

Now it was the young boy's turn to scream…and he did so involuntarily as he stumbled back from the horrible apparition…and fell into the protecting arms of Valentina, who was now awake, and standing.

The blue and white handkerchief floated lazily on the River Pena's eastward route, as did Reza's wide-eyed corpse, having been freed from its blockage the minute Valentina instinctively yanked her right foot from between the bookseller's teeth.

Valentina pointed toward the woman's rapidly fading image, now obscured in the middle of the murky river. "Do you think she's dead?" she asked Teodor.

Chapter 39

The penetration of the trapezius was minimal, and the Doctor knew it instinctively.

"Imam!" Nanette Stufkoski yelled, flinging herself between Nazmi ben Zullah and Bashkim Inasah. The *Mullah* backed slowly toward the Operating Suite's only doorway, and the Curator swung his left forearm across Major Stufkoski's exposed face. She dropped to the floor in a green-robed heap, stunned but not unconscious.

Bashkim reached for the opening where his surgical gown was tied in the back, but in the few seconds it took for him to place his hand on the Beretta's knurled grip and draw the pistol from his belt, ben Zullah had reached the heavy door, pulled it open, and exited the room in an antiseptic flurry of paper clothing. And he'd taken Lisbeth's handbag.

Bashkim dashed around the table and toward the oaken door…where he heard a distinct clacking sound as, from the outside, the Grand Imam inserted his key in the lock and swiftly turned it.

Nanette Stufkoski shook off most of her temporary unsteadiness. Holding onto the operating table, she climbed to her feet coughing on the blood she'd inhaled from her fractured nose and severely bitten tongue.

Having placed the scalpels and other surgical tools in the order she wanted them, Lisbeth Wren was able to reach for the longest lancet on the utensil table and take a firm grip on it without ever taking her eyes off of Nanette's bleeding face. The Dentist had a similar idea and now she too went for a scalpel, slamming her Latex-covered hand on the table and the nearest knife.

Having been rebuffed by the locked door, Bashkim spun quickly around, and seeing the incipient encounter, he drew a bead on Stufkoski's chest with the nine millimeter. "Drop the knife!" he commanded, holding the gun in both hands. Lisbeth reacted reflexively, leaning low over the Stryker Table to remove herself from the trajectory of the nine millimeter slug.

Then Major Stufkoski jammed the scalpel into Lisbeth's vulnerable back.

Lisbeth grimaced from the pain of the thrust as the point of the metal device skidded off her left shoulder blade and into the muscle between her scapula and spine. But the penetration of the lower trapezius was minimal, and the Doctor knew it instinctively. She quickly glanced upward at a large, angled mirror that had been pre-positioned over the still sleeping patient, who lay oblivious to the chaos erupting all around him. Immediately Lisbeth Wren recognized her shining chrome ballpoint that slid from her stinging back, landed with a ringing clang on the skid-proof floor, and clattered spinning in Bashkim's direction.

Nanette, realizing that she had grabbed the makeshift surgical marker in her haste to seize a weapon, reached again toward the array of surgical knives. But Lisbeth, with only the minor abrasion of her upper back to divert her...and her fist still tightly closed on the number ten scalpel...now held the clear advantage, and she drove the razor-sharp blade into the back of Stufkoski's hand as it groped for a second weapon on the surgical tray.

"Son-of-a-bitch!" the Major screamed. She pulled her hand away in a reflexive action that tore an inch-long gash where the titanium blade had sliced through to the middle of her palm.

Lisbeth pulled the scalpel free, and with her other hand, intentionally knocked the tray of surgical devices flying out of reach in a spray of silver-tinted projectiles...as Nanette Stufkoski fell to her knees...wide-eyed and weeping uncharacteristically...watching her own serum blood bubble through the clenched fingers of her useless hand.

Bashkim Inasah sped to the gasping woman's side of the Stryker table, tore the paper bonnet from her head, and pressed the muzzle of the Beretta into her ear.

"Don't shoot her," Lisbeth Wren yelled.

But the Curator slowly, deliberately, squeezed the trigger of the nine millimeter, ultimately firing the cartridge and sending a teacup-sized section of Major Stufkoski's skull, and much of her cerebral cortex, flying against the far wall...while her hair burned and the odor of cordite filled the formerly sterile room.

"Jesus!" the slender Doctor gasped.

"Give me that other round," Bashkim ordered, holding out his rock-steady hand. "I need it to blow the lock on the door. It's our only way out of here."

As if in a slow-motion dream, Lisbeth stared unbelieving at the smoldering hair atop the grotesque corpse of the woman she had considered her friend and associate...then she lifted her horrified gaze to the stern face of Bashkim Inasah. The impassive Curator merely stood with his open hand extended. "The other bullet," he repeated.

There was no longer any need to maintain a sterile environment, the American Doctor knew. She shook the loose surgical scrub from her trembling shoulders and let the pastel garment fall to the floor. She then inserted two fingers of her right hand between the third and fourth buttons of her shirt and into the shallow cleavage of her chest. Lis Wren withdrew the nine millimeter round from her bra and placed it on the operating table beside the anesthetized boy. She had no intention of risking contact with the man whom she had just seen commit cold-blooded murder. "There," Lisbeth said, indicating the hollow-nosed bullet, "…perhaps you plan to kill me too."

She stared at the tall man who had so recently held her in his embrace, and she touched her breast slightly above and to the left of her sternum. "All I ask is that you shoot me here…in the heart." With her other hand Lisbeth pointed to Stufkoski without looking at the pitiful mess on the floor. "Please don't send me out of the world looking like that."

* * *

Nazmi ben Zullah had taken possession of the *mihrab* near Bashkim's office and he now sat behind the alcove's concealing curtain, an AK-47 across his tunic-covered legs. Regardless of whoever would emerge first from the circular stairway shaft that connected the now-vacant *Sarena Jemija* to the secret sub-basement, the Grand Imam would have to wait until all three of his dupes had revealed themselves, before he could open fire with the Soviet-made rifle.

The *Mullah* would not kill, or even seriously injure the American Colonel, of course. She was his "meal ticket," as Captain Mueller was fond of saying. But the other two with her in the Operating Suite were now expendable. When all three had come through the portal, ben Zullah would incapacitate the blond woman…and kill the other two. Unlike Lisbeth Wren, whose value to him obviously remained paramount, Inasah and Stufkoski were becoming bothersome, the Grand Imam felt. And he now wanted them out of the way.

The first gunshot that resonated throughout the subterranean labyrinth and now echoed along the walls of the empty 'Painted Mosque,' took even the unflappable ben Zullah by surprise.

With the Curator and the two American women locked in the Suite, somehow one of them must have gained access to a weapon. It could not have been the Major—the *Mullah* himself had searched her person thoroughly and without incident earlier in the evening. As for the Colonel, had she been in possession of a weapon upon her arrival with Bashkim Inasah, it must have been in her large handbag—the stylishly dressed woman could not possibly have concealed the Beretta beneath her form-fitting civilian clothing. And the *Sarena Jemija* Curator would certainly never have risked beheading by displaying blatant disobedience for his Islamic master's long-held decree concerning firearms. Ben Zullah dumped the pocketbook's contents on the floor. There was no gun.

But there was no mistaking the boom that had thundered from below. A pistol *had* been discharged…and Nazmi ben Zullah jacked a round from the AK-47's forward-arcing banana clip into the rifle's chamber. He then placed the gun gingerly on the stone floor, lay prone on his stomach, and turned his head until one ear was pressed solidly against the granite base of the gossamer-draped *mihrab*. He would hear anyone climbing the stairway into the dead-silent mosque… and he would be ready.

Chapter 40

"When I came out, guess who was leaving Nan's billet."

When the jitney carrying Cockbyrne and Kelvin dropped the two Majors near their SEA Hut just short of midnight, the women could see as they stepped from the bus that fully half of the two-story building's apartment rooms were still illuminated. It was Saturday night, after all, and while Camp Billingham was known for its variety of creature comforts, the place was still a military installation; it wasn't a jail by any means, but you wouldn't call 'The Big B' a country club, either. Even high-ranking officers can take only so much midnight chow…movies that are carefully chosen to bolster morale…and long walks with stray dogs adopted, neutered, and inoculated by the Camp Veterinarian. The alternative, when one's computer hasn't yet been enabled, is to sit in your room, write letters in longhand, and listen to muted soft rock melt the night away.

"I think we should have come back with her," said Ophelia.

"Hey," Major Kelvin objected indignantly, "…she's the one who insisted, remember? Nan's a big girl. Besides you know as well as I do, she had something a whole lot different in mind than coming back to an empty billet."

Cockbyrne was unconvinced. "All the more reason to see that she at least got back to Jaziref okay."

The two walked on the otherwise empty sidewalk in the direction of SEA Hut 37's main entrance. "That's us," Peggy Kelvin said, nodding toward the two darkened windows on the second floor, adjacent to the corner casement...which was glowing behind partly closed Venetian blinds. "And isn't that end room Nan's?"

"No," said Cockbyrne guardedly, "Her room's the corner one alright...but on the other side of the hall."

"Well, I guess you won't be satisfied until we barge in and wake her up," Peggy said, rolling her eyes petulantly. "But let's get a move on—I need the john." They turned into the SEA Hut entryway and climbed the stairs...Kelvin taking them two at a time.

The two Doctors entered the second floor corridor and immediately Peggy headed for the lavatory. "I'll meet you at Nan's room in a minute," she said, and hurried into the bathroom.

When the Psychiatrist emerged from the john rubbing her hands to disperse residual moisture from the washing, she was surprised to see Ophelia standing there looking around like a nervous sentry. "Is she tucked in?" Major Kelvin asked, a mischievous grin on her face.

"So to speak," murmured Ophelia Cockbyrne. "I stopped at my room to take an Advil. When I came out, guess who was leaving Nan's billet."

Peggy's eyes were suddenly round and inquiring. "Who?" she whispered. "No...don't tell me." She snapped her fingers. "Lieutenant Forbes!"

Major Cockbyrne shook her head slowly, provocatively, from side to side.

"Well who?" Peggy demanded breathlessly.

"Captain Mueller," Ophelia purred, "...and you know what else?...he's got a key!"

* * *

"Why would you even think such a thing?" Bashkim Inasah said to the young American Colonel. "When have I given you the slightest reason to distrust me?"

Lis narrowed her eyes. "You summarily blow a helpless woman's head practically from her shoulders...and you want an explanation as to how I can possibly *distrust* you?"

Bashkim slid the Beretta's safety down a half-inch, thereby covering the distinctive red dot above the grip. The scarlet spot had indicated the gun was ready to fire, but now Lisbeth saw that the marker was hidden, meaning the pistol was secured. Still, she was clearly shaken and uneasy—and Bashkim knew it.

"Major Stufkoski was the worst kind of fiend," he said. "She would never have rested until you had served your purpose... and been executed."

"But why?" said Lisbeth, finally managing to look directly at the ghastly corpse. "She was so full of life. Flirtatious?... sure...but I can't believe Nan was intrinsically evil. There had to be some medical explanation." The confused and pallid Doctor looked up into Bashkim's somber face. "Could she have been drugged...hypnotized?"

The Curator held Lisbeth's shoulders in his outstretched hands. "*When devils will their blackest sins put on, they do suggest at first with heavenly shows.*" He released her and covered Nanette's upper body with one of the blankets from the Stryker table. "A wise man said that—his name was William Shakespeare." Bashkim took Lisbeth by the arm, and releasing the Beretta's safety, he walked her to the door that ben Zullah had locked.

The Curator told Lisbeth to stand behind him.

He aimed the nine millimeter at the wooden door's two-inch-square area between the knob and the jamb. Lis buried her face in the small of Bashkim's back. The lone round in the pistol's chamber represented their one opportunity for escape. As he had done with Major Stufkoski, he pressed the muzzle of the gun against its intended target…and without flinching squeezed the trigger. The Beretta rang out in an explosion of wood, fire, and lead…and when the smoke from the blast had dissipated, the spherical, stainless steel handle from the operating room door lay dented and discolored on the epoxied floor.

If the Albanian Curator and the American Doctor held any hope of escaping the clutches of Nazmi ben Zullah and his minions, they would now have to maneuver the corridor beneath the 'Quilted Mosque' undetected, and climb to freedom armed only by their wits.

Laboriously, Bashkim pried open the heavy door that hung warped and awkward on its hinges. He pushed Lisbeth through the narrow space between the shattered panel and the Operating Suite wall, and she added her one-hundred fifty pounds to his wedging bulk. Between them they managed to spread the gap sufficiently to free him too.

Once they were both standing in the smoky subterranean hallway, Lisbeth instinctively turned toward the stairway that led up to the *mihrab*—the alcove near the Curator's office—the entryway from which they'd descended an hour hence. But Bashkim seized her wrist before she could take a step.

"No!" he cautioned in a hoarse whisper. "This way—the mausoleum."

Chapter 41

"I would have to reveal the falsehood to Father Methodius in Confession"

Teodor had wanted to see Valentina home and swear her to silence concerning their grisly experience under the Vidoe Bato Bridge. She, however, insisted that it would be impossible for her to manage even one minute's sleep unless and until they had at least reported the incident. It would not be necessary to give investigators a detailed account of their interlude, she maintained. "We can say that we were watching for fishes," the naïve young woman suggested.

"Looking for Carp at midnight in the shadows of the Vidoe Bato?" asked Teodor incredulously. "How stupid do you think the Tavoto Police are?"

"My father fishes at night," Valentina offered meekly, and with a weak shrug.

The boy knew there was no arguing with the headstrong girl, and in fact the truth of the matter was that Teodor, too, would be relieved once the authorities had been notified concerning the unidentified woman's obviously drowned corpse.

"We will say that I was showing you the place where I used to catch Ohrid Trout," said Teodor, "…but let me do the talking."

"And if they ask me what…"

"Never mind what they ask you," Teodor barked. "Tell them only that going to the bridge was my idea…and my idea alone. You understand?"

"But that would be a lie," Valentina protested. "I would then have to reveal the falsehood to Father Methodius in Confession, would I not?"

The youthful suitor was becoming totally confused, and for a fleeting moment he thought that perhaps he should simply deny knowledge of anything his unsophisticated sweetheart might say. But that would solve nothing, he knew. There would still be Valentina's short-tempered father to deal with… and though detectives might be enjoined from administering corporal punishment to young Teodor for initiating the late-night dalliance, the irascible Kiril Milevski would be under no such constraint.

The pair began to walk to Tavoto's Policiska Stanica not far from the *Sarena Jemija*. It was a long distance on foot, but unlike ingenuous Valentina Milevski, the reluctant Teodor was in no great hurry to get there.

* * *

The solid rock from which the warren beneath the 'Quilted Mosque' was carved, formed an ideal conductor of the blasting noise that emanated from Lisbeth's Beretta. With little or no porosity to dissipate its vibration, the tremor traveled outward from the walls of the Operating Suite as if millions of tightly packed dominoes had picked up the pulse of an abutting neighbor and passed it along instantly and undiluted throughout the formerly soundless *Sarena Jemija*.

In the veiled *mihrab* scant yards above the boom's origin, the reclining Nazmi ben Zullah, the side of his head depressed tightly against the granite floor, now took the full, unexpected jolt of the ear-splitting report along the bones and cartilage of his skull. He recoiled from the explosive assault, his hearing reduced to a ringing cacophony, his vision a mass of irregular, flashing white lights as if his shocked system had been suddenly deprived of essential glucose.

For several minutes the Grand Imam staggered about the compact alcove, able to hear only the screaming echo of the gunshot. Bereft of any vision save for the blinding light, a man whose every sensory perception seemed to have betrayed him, the *Mullah* dropped to his knees, cursed the day when he had arranged for the deployment of Colonel Lisbeth Wren to Ovosok and ultimately Tavoto…and vowed revenge on the American Doctor.

When finally the passage of time had restored ben Zullah's senses somewhat, he lifted the AK-47 from the floor and tore down the curtain that separated him from the stairway door. He adjusted the gun to 'full automatic' and sat against the wall, eagerly waiting to dispatch the first person that Allah would send walking through the narrow exit from the labyrinth.

* * *

By the time the perplexed *Mullah* concluded that his intended prey must be lying in wait for him in the basement complex, Bashkim and Lisbeth had made their way westward along the main basement corridor, climbed the metal steps that led to the *turbe*, and entered the mausoleum by moving the counterbalanced pink marble headstone from underneath.

The load of Jerry Cans, arranged outside the door that was inscribed with the names of the mosque's founding sisters, extended above the sill of the tomb's front window and Bashkim noticed them immediately. He ordered Lis to lie prone alongside the sarcophagus while he used his penlight to scan the marble room. The Curator then let himself outside the multi-sided *turbe* using his iron key to unlock the heavy stone door. Leaving his penlight lying activated on the threshold of the mausoleum as a diversion, he slowly circled the tomb and its nearby gardens. His feet were still covered by the paper boots donned in the Operating Suite. In one hand he held the useless Beretta as a ruse, pretending that he was prepared to fire the empty weapon.

Finally, determining that he and the Doctor were alone among the *Sarena Jemija's* dark, grassy mounds and barely distinguishable flowering shrubs, Bashkim Inasah returned to the *turbe*, leaned through the black void of the open entranceway, and chirped a pre-determined signal for Lisbeth to join him. She was already standing behind the stout, inward-opening door not two feet from him.

"I have to get the hell out of here," she whispered. "I don't want to see this place again for as long as I live."

"Let's go," said Bashkim, speaking in clipped monosyllables. "We'll walk on the edge of that tree line." He pointed to a grove of Junipers with twisted trunks. "Hold on to the back of my belt if you can't see. When I turn south," he said, "… you must run to that footbridge." As they walked he swept his finger to the east indicating the narrow span that was vaguely visible above the swift-flowing rapids.

"I thought we were going to your car," Lisbeth stammered. "I just want to get out of here the fastest way possible."

"Then do as I say," the no-nonsense Curator demanded. "Ben Zullah's snipers will be positioned in the minaret in a matter of minutes. No doubt he has Aalil and Aamil watching the car by now. But I can handle them." Bashkim pulled Lis closer to the concealing cover of the hardy evergreens that bordered the River Pena. "From here we have to take separate routes. Make your way to the Lola Bookstore on Karaorman Road. I have an acquaintance there who will help you. Her name is Tereza."

The tall man reached into the breast pocket of his jacket and produced one of the bookmarks he had purchased from his friend the bookseller. "Show her this," he said, pressing the colorful cloth strip into Lisbeth's hand. "Reza will know where you got it."

Lis Wren looked wistfully at the bookmark with its intricate embroidery. It was precisely the sort of souvenir she'd had in mind for her friends and family at home. She could not help but think of how much had transpired between Bashkim Inasah and herself in the short time since they had initially met at the airport. Apparently this dear man had responded immediately to the very first request she'd made of him...and to think that only moments ago she'd virtually assumed him guilty of the most hideous intent. She threw her arms about Bashkim's waist and buried her face in his chest.

"None of that," he said, peeling away her clinging hands and turning her toward the rippling current of the Pena. "Now run," he said. "The little bridge. And don't look back!"

Calling upon her Policeman's training, Lis burst from the cover provided by the prickly Junipers, ran a zigzag pattern down a grassy incline toward the river, and clambered over a low stone wall that circled the grounds of the 'Quilted Mosque.' She veered to her right along a gravel pathway and in mere seconds details of the green-painted footbridge came into view. With a final dash, Lisbeth sped across the wooden overpass and collapsed exhausted on the Pena's slippery northern bank.

*Lola Bookstore...Karaorman Road...Tereza...*the winded Doctor recited under her halting breath—then she heard three rifle shots. They rang in quick succession from high on the *Sarena Jemija's* ancient minaret…after that, nothing.

Lisbeth Wren squeezed the richly adorned Byzantine bookmark in her sweating palm, and prayed to God that her gentle friend Bashkim was still alive.

Chapter 42

"The girl is Mayor Milevski's goddam daughter!" the Sergeant snapped.

It took Valentina and Teodor a little more than an hour to walk to the Policiska Stanica on Marshal Tito Boulevard. When they finally arrived at the municipal building that housed all of Tavoto's civic branches of government, only three uniformed officers remained to man the dreary complex reserved for the Police. Two of the men, both Sergeants… yawning and seemingly disinterested…listened nonetheless to the frightened youngsters. Simultaneously, the third officer, a Patrolman in shirtsleeves, typed with two fingers on a prehistoric Olympia typewriter most of whose black letters had been largely worn from the German machine's lime-green keys.

After a sanitized account of Tina's physical brush with the dead woman's corpse had been confirmed by Teo's description of what he'd seen, one of the Sergeants stood, brusquely beckoned to the youths, and led them to a patrol car parked at the corner of Marshal Tito and winding Karaorman Road.

"My parents will be waiting up for me," said the girl.

"Mine as well," echoed Teodor.

"My father is Kiril Milevski," Valentina added.

The Sergeant merely grunted and held open the back door of the dusty cruiser so that both kids could climb in. Then he drove to the Vidoe Bato Bridge.

Once at the river's edge, and with the patrol car's headlights illuminating the rapids downstream from the sighting, Valentina and Teodor pointed out the exact spot where they'd last seen the corpse as it drifted toward the rocky section of the River Pena. The Sergeant ordered them to remain in the white vehicle adorned with the triangular blue shield, and he walked toward the rapids, adding the ray from his long flashlight to the beacon shining from the sealed-beam recesses of the squad car's front fenders.

After what seemed to the youngsters an eternity, the Sergeant returned to the vehicle which had been running all the while. Without a word or glance directed to the apprehensive occupants of the backseat, he reached into the car, plucked a microphone from the dash, and with his elbows propped on the car's low roof, he requested a van from the Coroner's office in the rear of the building. "It's Reza," the Policeman said matter-of-factly. "She's wedged between the rocks just east of the Vidoe Bato." He glanced at Tina and Teodor who had heard him, and who now clutched one another fretfully. An unintelligible transmission squawked on the radio. "Yes. Tell them I will be here with my lights on. But first I'm taking the boy and girl home."

There was another scratchy communication.

"Because the girl is Mayor Milevski's goddam daughter!" the annoyed Sergeant snapped. "*That's* why!"

Within seconds Sergeant Pandev and Patrolman Ivanoff sprang into action.

"Get over to Lola Books and watch for anything suspicious," the Sergeant ordered.

Ivanoff stopped his faltering typing in mid-sentence and grabbed his civilian jacket from the back of the chair. "Don't go to Karaorman…go to the alley next to Ivo Ribar," said Pandev. "You can see inside from there. And you will not be noticed. Identify yourself and detain anyone who even looks into the side window. Understood?"

The patrolman withdrew three pairs of handcuffs from a locker and hooked them to his belt as the Sergeant dialed a landline number. "Will you send someone to assist me when the homicide squad comes?"

"Why?" the Sergeant asked irritably. "Do you anticipate a large gathering?"

"Not necessaril…"

"This is a drowning, Iosif, not an uprising."

"Just warn whoever comes that I'll be in back…tell them not to shoot me, for God's sake."

Sergeant Spiro Pandev slowly blinked away his impatience with the rookie. "I'll try to remember that," he said, a patronizing faux smile crossing his thin lips.

The sleepy voice in the telephone receiver croaked, "Alo," in Pandev's ear. And young Iosif Ivanoff set out on foot for the cobblestone lane behind Tereza Mimona's little bookstore.

* * *

Lisbeth Wren hadn't the vaguest idea who Tereza Mimona was, where Lola Books was, or for that matter where Karaorman Road might be. Furthermore, she doubted seriously whether it would be a good idea to inquire as to the whereabouts of the store at this ungodly hour. It was nearly one in the morning, after all, and Old Tavoto…at least the part of it that she could see from her vantage point on the bank of the Pena…was closed up tight.

Even in the relative safety of American cities like New York—where Lis knew her way around as well as anyone—it was never a good idea to present one's self as a vulnerable woman alone on the street after midnight. But here her dilemma was compounded. Unfamiliarity with the language, customs, and locale were all issues she'd be forced to deal with in her attempt to meet up with Bashkim Inasah. Thus, her prospects of a successful rendezvous with the Curator, or of finding this Tereza woman before daybreak, seemed hopeless. And she would be exposing herself to unspeakable consequences if she elected to spend the night like a common vagrant here on the shore of a meandering river.

But perhaps there was one safe haven available to Lisbeth.

Considering the area's relatively modest Catholic population, Tavoto, though a largely Muslim city, boasts an inordinate number of Byzantine churches. Most of these Shrines are ornate Eastern Rite edifices, she'd learned during indoctrination at Billingham, and as with the country's hundreds of mosques, they are renowned for their history of hospitality and sanctuary. *What was the name of that holy ruin built on the periphery of Tavoto in 1822? An unusual name. Was it 'Saintly Mother of God?' Yes. That was it… 'Saint Holy Mother of God.'*

Like most sacred sites throughout The Balkans, the 'Mother of God' ruin bore a subtitle. These explanatory captions helped visitors to identify the nature and history of a given tourist attraction, facilitating attendance and therefore bolstering monetary donations. In the case of 'Saint Holy Mother of God,' the added description 'Fortress Queen of the Source' was intended to inform the curious as to the original function and physical location of the place: In this instance, protector of the natural spring that gives birth to the River Pena.

Peggy Kelvin had noted that the military manual issued them at Billingham gave the reliquary the French subtitle, *Notre Dame de L'eau*—translated, 'Our Lady of the Waters.' Furthermore, the place was categorized '*Sanctuaire.*' Surely, Lis thought, a religious site listed as a 'Sanctuary' would afford her safe accommodation...at least until morning.

She began to trudge upstream...careful to follow the footpath that hugged the Pena's steepening north bank. Was she placing undue trust in the righteousness of still another so-called holy place? History had proven time and again that duplicity was generously spread among the world's great religions. Islam had no monopoly on treachery.

Lisbeth Wren felt she had no choice but to follow the River Pena to its source at the Byzantine Shrine. At least she would be putting distance between herself and the dreaded *Sarena Jemija*.

* * *

As usual Mayor Kiril Milevski was still reviewing reports from a dozen or more Tavoto municipal agencies when Valentina unlocked the front door, entered, and sheepishly mumbled, "Papa?"

"In here, Tina," the stout man called from his study. "It's late. Your mother was worried."

"There is a man," the girl said standing just inside the open front door. "He wishes to speak with you."

"A man? What man?" Milevski rounded his desk and strode to the entrance hall. He saw the Sergeant standing on the modest porch and noted the white squad car parked in front, its lights on, its motor running.

"Naumov," said the Mayor, recognizing the Policeman. Milevski's suspenders had been dangling casually at his sides and he now pulled them over his shoulders. "Is there trouble?"

Sergeant Stefan Naumov gave a bowing salute. "The children," he said, "…they were good enough to report a drowning near the Vidoe Bato Bridge. Your daughter's friend is in the car. I am taking him home. We regret detaining them at this hour. They took me to the scene. I have identified the victim."

Kiril Milevski looked at Valentina, relief clearly etched in his tired, blue eyes. "And Teo…he is alright?"

"They are both fine, Mr. Mayor. Understandably upset, but physically well. Again, Honorable Milevski, my apologies for such a late intrusion."

Milevski turned, snapped his fingers at his daughter, and pointed to the top of the stairs. His bathrobed wife stood there waiting, her arms crossed, her eyes wide and inquiring. Valentina dashed up the steps and disappeared around a corner in her whispering mother's embrace.

"You say you have identified the victim," said the Mayor. "Is it one of our Tavoto residents, Sergeant?"

"I'm afraid so," said Sergeant Naumov.

"Who?"

"The deceased is…Tereza Mimona," the Sergeant said deferentially…referring to Mayor Kiril Milevski's former mistress.

The rotund man yanked a cardigan sweater from a hat rack in the hall and quickly donned it. He called a goodbye to his wife, who was seated on Valentina's bed listening to the girl's account of the traumatic incident. "I will be back in an hour," the Mayor said, "Don't wait for me. Go to bed." And he left with Sergeant Naumov.

"This woman," said Olivia Milevski, frowning and peering down at the street as the Police Cruiser pulled away from the curb, "…I don't suppose you recognized her."

Tina avoided eye contact with her mother and slipped into a pink and white chemise. "I think she used to be a friend of Papa's," the girl said. "The Policeman said her name is Reza."

Chapter 43

A slight bubbling sound seemed to be radiating from beneath the stone path.

Lisbeth was undecided. She wasn't sure whether she should resent the moonless night in the eastern foothills of the Shar Mountains, or be thankful that the darkness permitted her to make her way unseen toward the high plateau that she knew was home to 'Saint Holy Mother of God.'

But what of the feral beasts that roamed the region? she thought. Their sense of smell and superior vision exceeded that of humans by a factor of one thousand. This was their natural habitat…not hers.

An animal lover from early childhood, Lis had seized the opportunity to study the fauna of Ovosok and nearby Madonica as soon as she had gotten word of her deployment to Camp Billingham. During that time she had learned that three distinct species of wild animals abound in the Balkan Peninsula year-round…Brown Bears, Eurasian Wolves, and the stealthy Iberian Lynx.

A novice might have concluded that the abundance of these distinctly different classes of predator would make nocturnal foot travel particularly hazardous in the heavily wooded Shar range…particularly at night. But Lisbeth Wren knew full well that the doglike Bear and Eurasian Wolf are far less likely to attack a human than the other way around. The same could *not* be said for the Lynx…a true carnivore that, when mature, eats approximately four pounds of meat a day!

For all the Bear's half-ton bulk, and the Wolf's canine cunning, it was the speedy, agile Lynx that Lis Wren feared most. Thankfully, the feline bore a singular marked disadvantage as a hunter—its reflecting eyes were known to give the five-foot marauders away, even in the virtual absence of ambient light.

Lisbeth was aware that she was near the fortress Shrine built astride the source of the River Pena even before she had seen the stone stronghold itself. A slight bubbling sound seemed to be radiating from beneath the crushed stone path that she had been climbing at a steady pace for nearly an hour. By her reckoning, she must have ascended a good two hundred feet from the narrow footbridge near the 'Quilted Mosque,'—her point of embarkation—but there was no way of gauging that for certain. The gloomy landscape of Old Tavoto that had been dimly visible over her right shoulder in the early going, now had given way to rolling countryside, and Lisbeth could only conclude that she had semi-circled the broad plateau which housed the Byzantine ruin and its murky vestiges.

Some twenty or thirty minutes prior, Lis had partially stumbled on a four-foot Walnut branch and now used it as a walking stick. She waved the crooked bough extended in her right hand much as a blind person uses a cane, and she held her left arm straight out from her side feeling for solid contact that would tell her she'd arrived at the rocky fortress dedicated to the Mother of Jesus.

When her fluttering fingers touched the cold wall of the Shrine, Lisbeth stopped walking and brought the Walnut limb around to her left, probing the air, until finally, with a thud, it poked the stone battlement of the fortress church. In a 'blind-man's-bluff' manner she read the surface of the façade with her palm, while taking a shorter grip on the stout stick in the event she would need to use it as a defensive weapon.

Before proceeding, the exhausted Doctor made a three-hundred-sixty-degree visual sweep of her near-black surroundings. If her progress were being tracked by one of the big cats almost sure to prowl this upland terrain, the animal's glowing, yellow eyes would surely have betrayed it. Lis saw nothing. She was alone amid the fitted limestone boulders that had stood overlooking old Tavoto for hundreds of years.

She felt her way along what she'd correctly guessed was the western perimeter of 'Saint Holy Mother of God'—the wall that faced the upper foothills of the Shar Range. Here the gurgling of the Pena as it gushed from its mountain spring was more pronounced than at any time during Lisbeth's journey...and now she was aware of an intense thirst.

Her prodding fingers found an end to the jagged surface, but the Walnut limb she wielded had penetrated another space a few feet ahead. *A doorway?* she wondered, and crouching, she felt for some sort of threshold where the opening met the gravel path on which she stood. But below the gap was a continuation of the church's close-fitting stone exterior. She'd located a window!

The aperture was waist-high at its low point. It measured some eighteen inches wide—the length of Lis's arm from elbow to finger tips, and probing with the wooden branch established that the casement was slightly deeper than it was wide. Four feet up from sill level, where a modern transom would have been, was an arch whose matching, tapered stones flared from the space's interior and defined its semicircular top in a graceful curve. Lisbeth could feel that the span consisted of an identical number of fitted boulders on each side of the topmost keystone…each contributing to, and exacting support from, its neighbor.

With her head thrust into the void, still clinging to her length of solid Walnut, the tall woman could see nothing. She listened intently to the sound of splashing water and its echoed splattering told her the source must be in this room… or very close by. In any event, Lisbeth Wren was now at the mercy of two obsessions…she needed water…and then she would have to lie down. The matter of her dehydration must take precedence, the Doctor knew, and pushing her trusty wooden staff ahead, she slithered through the window…only to tumble into a shallow granite basin the size of a double bed.

She had located the source of the Pena, and in the bargain had assured that the water would augment her fading strength. That the resourceful woman must now spend the night in a dismal fortress, soaked to the skin, teeth chattering… was, though unfortunate, a preferable alternative to many predicaments that might have befallen her in this Balkan hellhole, she knew.

Lis drank great gulps of the sweet spring water, retrieved the Walnut club that floated in the cold pool beside her, and crawled to the corner nearest the window. There she wedged herself into the rocky V, knees tucked under her chin, the heavy stick held in both hands protectively across her shins.

Soon she fell asleep to the soothing ripples of the life-giving river…the same tributary where Tavoto's longtime Mayor Kiril Milevski now watched as two of his Policemen pried the body of Reza Mimona from the rocks near the Vidoe Bato Bridge.

Chapter 44

Damned if he was going to lose sleep over the death of a slut like Reza.

At two in the morning, Captain Eric Mueller was sleeping like a baby. He'd intentionally beaten the living shit out of the young Muslim in the McDonald's parking lot because he knew the display would intimidate the other patrons and staff who had seen him in the fast food restaurant with Tereza Mimona. The sociopath had quickly realized that Reza was wise to his nocturnal delivery of the customized Jerry Cans and dry ice to the nearby mausoleum. Obviously it was necessary to do away with her, and if, after the discovery of her body, there was one sure way to keep witnesses from coming forward to identify him as the man who'd left the eatery with the proprietor of Lola Books, his savage attack on the lightly bearded youth in the soiled *Galabiyya* would serve that purpose.

There was an economic deterrent in play, too.

Though the local officials might claim to decry the presence of American military personnel in their villages, towns, and cities, they readily welcomed the almighty U.S. dollar. Indeed, officers like Eric Mueller injected more money into regional coffers in a month than the beaten Islamist in the parking lot would contribute to the Balkan economy in a year.

With the added precautions Captain Mueller had taken establishing the times of day he supposedly had been observed back here in Ovosok, there was virtually no cause for concern...and Eric would be damned if he was going to lose sleep over the death of a slut like Reza. Her passing would go unnoticed...and she herself unsung.

Except, possibly, by Mayor Kiril Milevski, who had claimed to be conducting a meeting of the Tavoto Planning Commission earlier tonight...when in reality he was keeping a rendezvous with Taska Babunski. Who, at seventeen years of age, was a classmate of his only daughter, Tina.

* * *

Both apprentice Imams knelt on the round catwalk near the top of the *Sarena Jemija's* distinctive minaret...both continued to train their Tokarev rifles on the light green, unmoving mound they'd shot at from their high vantage points...with apparent success.

"I will go and make sure he is dead," said Aalil, looking up from his weapon.

"Do," Aamil said, continuing to peer through his own ten-power scope at the motionless form covered by a mint-colored *Galabiyya* of the type they had never seen before. "But use your knife," the young cleric added, passing his flattened hand in a sweeping slash in front of his throat. "The Grand Imam orders 'limited gunshots'"

Aalil slung the semi-automatic on his shoulder. He then began the long descent from the lofty perch lined with loudspeakers and lavender-tinted floodlights, both of which had been turned off hours earlier.

When he could no longer hear his departing colleague's footfall on the granite steps, Aamil rested his rifle against the low railing, sat back, and in the solitude of the moonless night he lit a cigarette stolen from the Curator's office.

Still covered by the disposable paper robe from the Operating Room, Bashkim Inasah lay stark still, faintly breathing, his black hair covered by the sterile bonnet. He had survived the three errant shots fired from the minaret…the young Imams were not experienced marksmen, after all. But Bashkim was also sure that had he continued his dash toward the Citroen, the likelihood of his being shot, even if not fatally, would have increased exponentially with every stride. *Better to lure the enemy into close proximity*, he decided…*take my chances mano a mano.*

The darkness is my friend tonight, the Curator said inwardly, and through eyes reduced to mere slits, he focused on the rail that circled the 'Quilted Mosque's' minaret just beneath its pointed spire.

It was then that Bashkim saw the flare of Aamil's match, and the puff of white cigarette smoke that hung visible on the quiet air until the match had been waved dead. *A great indiscretion*, he thought…*and perhaps your last, my imprudent friend.*

In a few minutes the huddling Bashkim saw the shadowy figure of the second apprentice emerge warily from the door at the base of the tower.

The youth's weapon was slung.

Good!

The faintest glint of a knife blade in the vague starlight.

Even better!

Imperceptibly Bashkim slipped first one arm, then the other, from the wide sleeves of the disposable surgical gown. He reached behind him…and the young Imam continued his approach as if stalking an injured animal.

Bashkim found the knotted ribbon that held the long paper robe in place…and he stealthily pulled it free.

The boy was within a dozen paces now, the hem of his *Galabiyya* brushing the grass as he approached the prone Curator on the south side of the *turbe*.

Surreptitiously, Bashkim grabbed a handful of the antiseptic gown. With the apprentice whom he now recognized as Aalil only an arm's length away, the much taller Bashkim suddenly stood…freezing the alarmed Imam's progress…and he flung the pastel robe over the youth's helplessly flailing arm.

Now the heavy Tokarev rifle became an impediment to Bashkim's would-be assailant as with every thrust of the six-inch knife the gun swung crazily across Aalil's back destroying his sense of balance and causing his sandals to become entangled in the long, restricting *Galabiyya*.

The Curator, now with the upper hand, had no intention of killing the boy, though the reverse was not the case. However the contest that was playing out on the rolling grounds of the *Sarena Jemija's* lush garden was one of sheer survival. With Aamil positioned on the catwalk of the minaret, he would quickly see that his partner faced a losing battle…if he hadn't come to that obvious conclusion already.

Bashkim kicked his adversary solidly in the groin, eliciting a scream from Aalil, who dropped the knife and clutched his aching privates with both hands. Immediately Aamil leaped to his feet and flung his cigarette over the railing that defined the minaret's high balcony. He seized his rifle, raised the scope to eye level, and through it, searched the grassy field where he now realized his cohort was in distress.

Bashkim had no time for careful calculation. The only available shield between himself and the sniper in the tower was the boy who now lay writhing at his feet. Grabbing the suspended Tokarev in a two-handed grip, he lifted the youngster from the turf that way and swung him toward the tall spire, confident that firing from the catwalk would ensue. Right away, a shot rang out. The round entered Aalil's neck just below the thyroid cartilage and tore through the top of his spine, killing the apprentice Imam instantly…and virtually drenching the stooping Curator in a cascade of arterial blood.

A second bullet clanged and caromed from one of the rocks that lined a nearby garden path. Apparently the first shot had been a lucky one. Bashkim pressed the quick release clasp that held the Russian-made rifle across dead Aalil's blood-soaked back. The gun fell loose immediately and the Curator wiped the scope free of the sticky crimson that coated it.

Luckily, the young Imam's blood had not covered the lens of the rifle's ten-power scope, and now Bashkim lay prone on the grass, the Tokarev's muzzle aimed upward toward the balcony of the minaret, its forestock supported by the boy's motionless chest. The scarlet-bathed Bashkim took careful aim at the indistinct figure that he knew must be Aamil. Because of his opponent's command of the high ground, the Curator would be at a disadvantage in an all-out fusillade of flying lead. Bashkim hoped for a one-shot gunfight, therefore…and he slowly squeezed the slippery trigger.

Chapter 45

*What have you discovered?" Milevski said.
"Discovered?" said Stefan Naumov.
"What did you just write?"*

At first, it was speculated that Reza Mimona, like her favorite British writer Virginia Woolf, might have been a suicide. But though in 1941, at age 59, novelist Woolf had filled the pockets of her overcoat with stones and walked into the River Ouse in Sussex, nothing about Tereza's death gave authorities reason to suspect that the bookseller had emulated her idol and taken her own life.

No one could have been more relieved than Mayor Kiril Milevski to hear the Tavoto Coroner make that preliminary on-site announcement. Had his former mistress killed herself, he thought, she would probably have left a suicide note. And had that been the case, such a record might well have documented details of their illicit affair…and surely brought about his political undoing.

Tavoto was not Washington D.C., after all. In America, Milevski had read in the papers, sexual depravity was both rampant and generally accepted. In the U.S. Capitol even the most revered public figures seemed to consider lascivious conduct nothing more than mere dalliances. For God's sake, the very impeachment of the philandering president for 'Moral Misconduct' had been treated as an international joke! Not a stoning offense…nothing deserving of a whipping…a silly little rendezvous that didn't even warrant a fine!

As he sat in Sergeant Naumov's squad car watching Reza's once beautiful body loaded into the Coroner's Mercedes ambulance, Mayor Milevski shuddered to think what his fate might be in this staid Balkan town were the particulars of his steamy encounters with Reza Mimona somehow made public.

As the rear doors of the long black van were slammed shut he breathed a pronounced sigh of relief…and secretly wondered if perhaps the Americans didn't have the right idea. Live, and let live.

But if not a suicide, then what *did* lead to Tereza Mimona's ultimately becoming trapped among the River Pena's rocks east of the Vidoe Bato?

Sergeant Naumov climbed into the white cruiser, nodded to the Mayor, and turned the key in the ignition. But before shifting the car into 'drive' he removed a small notepad from his shirt pocket and scribbled three or four words. He returned the pad to its usual place, clipped the pen to his lapel, and backed away from the bank of the river, making a three-point turn.

"What have you discovered?" Milevski said attempting to sound casual about the inquiry.

"Discovered?" said Stefan Naumov.

"What did you just write?"

Without commenting the Sergeant removed the pad from his pocket and handed it sideways to the stocky official. The Mayor turned on the car's overhead light and read Naumov's entry: '*Coroner says neck broken.*'

Kiril Milevski felt sick to his stomach. How many times had he flippantly warned Reza…*try that again, and I'll break your neck…do you want your neck broken?…you deserve a broken neck!* Had anyone ever heard him issue the juvenile threat that could now conceivably involve him in a potential murder?

"It's possible the woman…"

Sergeant Naumov jerked his head to the right and stared at the Mayor in disbelief. Had Milevski really referred to Tereza Mimona as *The Woman*? Every Tavoto adult including Olivia Milevski (and most children over the age of ten) had known that the coquettish bookseller and His Honor the Mayor had once 'kept company' at the very least. Indeed, Kiril Milevski had frequently pressed Naumov, Pandev, and their two dozen fellow officers into service as an unofficial 'private Security entourage' when he and Reza needed to be transported to one trysting place or another as if on *Official Business*. And now the corpulent Romeo was calling his former longtime girlfriend *The Woman*?

The Sergeant raised one eyebrow and reached to his right with beckoning fingers. Naumov's skepticism was not lost on Milevski, who hesitantly placed the notebook in the Policeman's open palm…whereupon Sergeant Naumov slid the pad back into his shirt pocket.

"Home, Mr. Mayor?" the Sergeant asked coolly…with strained respect.

"No," said Milevski, "…the Morgue."

* * *

Lisbeth Wren dreamed that she was in Holy Rosary School in New York's westernmost borough of Staten Island. At nine years of age, she was clearly tiring, and her tiny right arm was beginning to ache from printing the same seven words on the green chalkboard…over and over…

I will... never do harm to anyone.

I will... never do harm to anyone.

...over and over...

I will... never do harm to anyone.

With eighty-eight of her assigned one hundred lines completed, the yellow-chalked words from the Hippocratic Oath were beginning to run downhill.

Sister Mary Monica stood with her arms folded, her hands tucked within the flowing sleeves of her wrinkle-free, ankle-length habit, her ears, neck, and brow covered by a snow white coif. The whole business was secured by a white linen bandeau, and atop that, was pinned the nun's veil that formed a black crown and draped down her back...ending at her undefined waist. Understandably it had been assumed (mostly by the impudent boys in Lisbeth's fourth grade class) that nuns had no ears...a hypothesis the straight-A Lisbeth Wren found illogical at best, and in her reverential mind, possibly bordering on blasphemy. As for the rumor that the Good Sisters shaved their heads—*well,* that's *a distinct possibility*, Lisbeth seemed to think, even if her friend, fifth-grader Jackson Kamp, had assured her it was absolute nonsense.

In the dream the nun had ordered Lisbeth's chalkboard penance after the blond 9-year-old had secretly absconded with the class mascot—an adopted Toy Poodle-Boston Terrier mix—and taken it home for the weekend. Needless to say, the misappropriation had sent the convent into a fanciful whirlwind of tearful rummaging until the revengeful Peter Ravens had finally tattled on Lisbeth (to the Police, if you can believe it). It was her punishment for denying the 10-year-old Lothario's demand for a kiss during Friday afternoon recess.

All the key components of Doctor Lisbeth Wren's young life were included in the whimsical montage that constituted her dream...though the elements were strangely out of whack: Lis *had* indeed been presented with a six-month-old Poodle...but for her *tenth* birthday...though she'd expressed her preference for a *Boston Terrier*...which she wouldn't receive (from her husband *Peter*, actually) until they'd both retired from the Police Department. As for the *kiss*—it was *Lisbeth* who had initiated the request...and the intended *kissee* was the straight laced *Jackson Kamp*. Furthermore, envious Mary Monica Delaney (a *playground proctor*, not a nun at all) had been witness to the proposal...and quickly conveyed the sordid details to *Mother Superior*...who, in point of fact, hadn't worn the old-fashioned, *black habit* in years. Such are the vagaries of fact-based dreams.

Lisbeth awakened in the same seated fetal configuration she'd assumed when falling asleep hours earlier...the only difference now was that she had released one handhold on the Walnut walking stick. The stone walls that met in a V in the corner of the empty room still supported her hips and hunched shoulders, preventing her from tumbling sideways. Her heels had found a foot-long groove in the floor and she had used it as a horseman might employ stirrups to steady her hunkered body. Her dominant right hand still gripped the trusty Walnut branch protectively...if only lightly.

Lis was aware that forty percent of all people are known to sleep regularly in the defensive fetal position...and more than half of those, women...still, she was surprised that she'd been able to sleep so soundly in what most would consider an uncomfortable, if naturally protective posture. *It must be the water*, she concluded, *constantly soothing and bubbling under the fitted slate floor.*

In the ambient pre-dawn light that now enabled the supple Doctor to gauge her surroundings accurately for the first time, Lis lifted her head a few inches from her knees. Having completed only that minimal movement, she shifted her narrowed eyes from far left to far right and back again, looking for anything threatening…especially the yellow orbs that would reveal the hypnotic stare of a hungry lynx.

She was the only living creature in the stone chamber.

Lisbeth straightened her stiffened back, releasing the knees that her arms had held pressed under her chin for hours. She groaned…not from discomfort, but more out of relief that, for the time being at least, the incipient dawn and 'Saint Holy Mother of God' were pronouncing her safe…safe and in their keeping.

"Pen…Watch…Apple," she said aloud, reciting the key words she required her elderly patients to repeat in order to establish their mental acuity…and thereby assessing her own.

Then Lisbeth crawled to the shallow granite cistern and drank again of the clear, cold water.

When she had stripped away her still-damp clothing and spread all but her flat civilian shoes on the deep window ledge to catch the dawn and dry, the trim woman, her well-toned physique the product of Army discipline as well as personal pride, decided to investigate the adjacent room that had formerly been only a dull shadow on the far side of a constricted portico.

With the smooth stick in hand, her low-heeled shoes protecting against the pitted floor, Lis Wren thrust her Walnut probe through the archway to test for spider webs or other nests of insects. The branch came back free of any filmy residue. *This doorway's been in recent use*, she thought.

With that, the Doctor was overcome with a realization that brought her up short and sent her running back toward the clothing arrayed on the windowsill. "My God," she said aloud, struggling into her clinging underwear, "It's Sunday—and this *is* a Christian Shrine!"

In her near-panic brought on by consciousness that early-morning worshipers might be filing into 'Saint Holy Mother of God' at any moment, Lisbeth tripped on the waistband of her panties and hopped around the fortress room on one foot, trying desperately to insert the other into the resisting lingerie without the unwelcome prospect of putting her bare buttocks on the rocky ledge, or the rough slate floor.

Finally, her underwear was in place and if still damp, Lis rationalized, at least it was rinsed. She berated herself nonetheless. How could she have failed to calculate that the sacred ruins were likely to attract locals as well as tourists on this of all days…was she beginning to forget the significance of the Christian Sabbath?

"Pen…Watch…Apple," said Lisbeth in a loud, irritated voice.

"Pen…Watch…Apple," Bashkim Inasah's voice echoed from the gloomy doorway…and he held out the embossed bookmark the Doctor had placed near the fork in the steep path from the footbridge.

Chapter 46

And last night there was no moon to speak of…only an insignificant sliver.

As always, Hanna Henschel was up with the birds and on this cool morning she was concerned that Colonel Wren, wherever she was, might have been ill-prepared for the chilly overnight weather. Lisbeth had only a flimsy jacket when she left with the tall man in the Citroen yesterday, Hanna recalled. She checked the outdoor thermometer through the front window and saw that it read sixty-two degrees on the Fahrenheit scale. *Perhaps I am unduly worried* the tiny woman said inwardly. *Sixty degrees is hardly productive of hypothermia.*

At any rate, she figured, *this Lisbeth is a Medical Doctor… and a smart one, it seems to me.* Hanna pulled the chain that wound the cuckoo clock. *If she doesn't know how to prevent the body's temperature from dropping below normal metabolism levels, well…who does?*

Frau Henschel ran three inches of tap water into the kettle and placed it on a back burner of the stove. The cuckoo clock in the living room popped, beeped…and a little wooden bird emerged and chirped six times…then the expandable arm retreated, pulling the carved songster back inside its brightly painted alpine house.

Hanna sat waiting for the teakettle to begin whistling... and in short order, of course, it did so...at first with a low-register hum, then ever higher in pitch, until at last the aproned housekeeper picked up the screaming kettle and poured a good ten ounces of boiling water into her blue and white porcelain teapot.

While waiting for her green tea to steep, it was Hanna's practice to listen to the six o'clock morning news on the radio, a habit that served a dual purpose: The program supplied her with useful weather information (she preferred to hang her wash on the clothesline during these brisk fall days, for instance—but only if the forecast promised sun)...and the precise voices of the Albanian language station's announcers were useful in acquainting the German-speaking woman with certain commonly-used words and phrases in the local vernacular—the *time of day*—the Albanian words for *rain, snow, sun*—traffic-related terms that translated to *heavy, light, slow-moving*, and *accident*—the day's schedule of classical music listing the familiar names of *Mozart, Handel,* and above all, *Wagner.*

Thus it was that on this Sunday morning in Jaziref, Frau Henschel interrupted her regimen, replaced her steaming teacup in its saucer, and turned up the volume on her kitchen radio. She could swear the newscaster had said something to the effect that a woman had been found in the River Pena... near Tavoto...Police were involved, she thought she heard.

The American Doctor seemed to have an unusually keen interest in Tavoto and its sights, Hanna recalled, and with the swift logic of a concerned mother (as she'd come to envision herself in Lisbeth's case) she wished she'd warned the Colonel about the poor footing on many of the bridges over the Pena.

Also, some of those damn guard rails are too low to prevent stumbling accidents.

And last night there was no moon to speak of…only an insignificant sliver near the horizon.
And wouldn't the Doctor have told me if…?

On and on a litany associated with imaginary misfortune continued…until finally, convinced that something *fuchtbar* must have happened, the concerned woman abandoned her beloved green tea, poured it in the sink, and went to the living room to sit and worry. If there had been an *unfall*, surely Captain Mueller would know—and he would come to tell her.

Hanna parted the curtain a few inches and gazed fretfully at the curb near the water fountain. It was where the Captain parked his vehicle whenever he stopped in…but Frau Henschel prayed to God that Eric Mueller would have no reason to come by today.

* * *

Peggy Kelvin and Ophelia Cockbyrne were both Protestants. They didn't know what kind, they just knew they weren't Catholic…they were *not* Jewish, thank you… and they certainly were neither Muslim nor Buddhist. By the process of elimination, unless they were atheists they had to be Protestant.

Peggy was aware also, though Ophelia had some misgivings about it, that anybody could go into a Catholic church, no questions asked, any time they wanted, and probably even partake of the Bread and Wine they gave out during Mass.

"Gedouddahere," said Ophelia, climbing back into bed and balancing the container of coffee Peggy had brought, on the tent formed by her knees.

"No lie," the Psychiatrist said. "I won't go into detail, but one of the other shrinks back at Fort Bliss told me you don't have to be a Cardinal…or even a Priest, to be pope."

"I'll believe that one when I see it, Sister." Cockbyrne sipped the hot coffee and groaned her appreciation. "Next you're gonna tell me some *Black* could get the top job, right?"

"Could."

"A *gay* Black?"

"Might."

"A gay Black *Episcopalian*?"

"Not impossible."

"A gay Black Episcopalian *woman*?"

Kelvin looked at Major Cockbyrne, blinked her eyes ever so slowly, and studied her manicure. "Now you're being ridiculous, Honey."

Ophelia jumped out of bed, coffee in hand, made a bee line for the john, and closed the door behind her. "So what time do we have to be there?" Her voice was muffled as she mumbled through a mouthful of foaming toothpaste.

Peggy glanced at her watch, "Fifteen minutes."

The bathroom door flew open and the astonished Major stood there wrapped in a white bath towel embossed with the inscription 'US ARMY, her toothbrush held at chin level, Crest Fluoride coursing from the corners of her gaping lips. "Fifteen…you gotta be shitting me!"

"No problem if we're late," said a reassuring Peggy Kelvin. "Everybody'll figure we're a couple of real Romans…I heard they're always late for church."

Ophelia disappeared behind the john door once again. The shower drummed on the walls of the enclosed stall inside. "After all this crap, Lis better damn well be there," she bellowed.

"Of course she'll be there," Peggy called back. "Where else would she be on Sunday morning?"

* * *

As for the Tavoto Coroner, Viktor Yanev, he hadn't seen the inside of a church since his First Communion sixty years ago in Zagreb, the multi-cultural capital of Croatia where he was born. At exactly five feet tall, Viktor was frequently referred to as a *peuce*, or 'midget'; the derogatory term for Dwarf. But the fact is the dapper little man had technically avoided Dwarfism by two full inches.

Nonetheless, Viktor found it necessary to stand on a six-inch-high footstool when conducting his postmortems, and that's what he was doing at five o'clock Sunday morning in Tavoto's so-called Autopsy Suite behind the Police station.

Assisting the diminutive Coroner in the rear of the municipal building was his niece Jovana, a Nurse Practitioner. She was the only candidate who had come forward when Viktor had announced his forthcoming retirement and put out the call for a replacement.

In front of Viktor and Jovana, on a stainless steel table, was the bloated body of Tereza Mimona. The unpleasant business of dissecting, rinsing, weighing, and otherwise examining Reza's pallid remains was made all the more distasteful by the fact that both Viktor and his niece had known the popular bookseller personally for nearly two decades.

Still, there was work to be done here: The Coroner didn't like the discoloration in the area of Reza's clean-shaven lower rear skull...or the fact that no foreign fluid could be detected in the lungs.

With Jovana holding the subject's head Viktor made two longitudinal incisions, one on each side of the cervical spine, and pulled the woman's flesh aside in a pair of bands that looked like thick strips of bacon.

"Note the pronounced misalignment and angle of the neck in relation to the skull," said the Coroner, moving his face to within eight inches of Reza's exposed nape. "This is a hallmark of someone who has sustained a traumatic atlas subluxation."

"Your conclusion?" said Yanev's niece, holding the corpse's head by the hair while spraying rinse water on the ivory-colored vertebrae.

Viktor seemed ambivalent. He nodded at Jovana indicating that she could now lower Tereza Mimona's head to the steel surface. She did so, and the ashen woman on the table stared upward through startled, unseeing eyes that were large and dilated.

"Let's turn her over," the little man said. "That alarmed look is telling me we're likely to find a clean fracture."

Jovana and her uncle wrestled Tereza onto her slippery belly.

"Mmmm. There!" the Coroner announced. "Someone or something broke poor Reza's neck." He pointed to a semi-bald area on the matted skull, "...and tore out a handful of her hair in the process."

"An assault, Uncle Viktor?" the nurse murmured.

"That is for others to determine," said Yanev, as he climbed down from the footstool and began stripping away his Latex gloves. "We will report only what the cadaver has told us: Death by sudden traumatic fracture of the cervical spine. Lungs free of water. Drowning was not a factor here."

Chapter 47

They sank together to the floor of the fortress Shrine.

After a long moment of wide-eyed disbelief, Lisbeth dropped her still-damp shirt and tweed trousers onto the stone floor by the window, and running to Bashkim Inasah, she hurled herself into his encircling arms. "You're alive," she whispered in the tall man's ear, relief and gratitude fairly choking the words as they erupted as if directly from her thankful heart.

"I love you, *Habeeb Qalbi*," Bashkim breathed for the first time in his life…and they sank together to the floor of the fortress Shrine, impervious to its harsh surface, or the rivulets of icy water that overflowed from the smooth granite cistern.

"What does it mean…*Habeeb Qalbi*…Lisbeth murmured, smothering the Muslim Curator with a world of hungry kisses. "Say it…tell me."

"It translates to the fondest words a lover can imagine," said Bashkim. And he pulled her even closer to his heaving chest.

* * *

Viktor and Jovana Yanev, Kiril Milevski, and Sergeant Naumov sat in the uncomfortable Policiska Stanica on

Marshal Tito Boulevard. The Coroner, a longtime friend of Mayor Milevski, was orally deciphering the handwritten autopsy notes that his niece had not yet had a chance to transcribe. She had been sewing back together Tereza Mimona's chopped, sliced and otherwise torn asunder body parts, and had just now finished that reconstructive phase of the analytic procedure.

Stefan Naumov had been creating his own version of Yanev's report in his unique hieroglyphics as the conversation progressed, and currently seemed absorbed in a diagram he'd drawn as an adjunct to the actual medical report. It showed the approximate course of the River Pena all the way from its entry into Western Tavoto, to the rapids east of the Vidoe Bato Bridge…the shallows where Reza's body had been trapped by the rocks.

Of particular interest to the Police Officer was the portion of the river nearest to Tereza's apartment…the poorly illuminated section consisting of the Radovan Footbridge, the Ilindenska Overpass, and the murky Lenin Rapids. Along that three-block stretch of the Pena, there was only one place where adults congregated in the evening hours between nine and eleven o'clock (the time span during which Tereza had died, according to Viktor's calculations). It was the all-night McDonald's restaurant adjacent to the *Sarena Jemija.* Sergeant Naumov knew it was probably out of the question that any of the eatery's customers from the previous evening would be immediately available for questioning, but he contented himself with the conclusion that the McDonald's staff, not the clientele, would be more likely to turn up a witness who could place the Mimona woman at the restaurant…if indeed she had been there during the time in question…or for that matter, at any time on Saturday night at all.

"She was not one for publicizing herself," grunted the Policeman. "We have searched the victim's apartment as well as her place of business. I need a picture, but it seems there is no photograph of her to be found." He looked knowingly at Mayor Milevski. "Unless the municipal offices would have reason to keep such a thing on file."

"Did you contact the Bureau of Commerce?" the Mayor asked coldly.

"At four o'clock on Sunday morning?" Naumov responded with equal indifference.

"Mmmm. Of course," Kiril Milevski muttered. "I will have someone search the Lola Books tax records."

"Ah. Lola Books," said the Sergeant. "Then you are familiar with the occupation of the deceased."

"What do you mean, '*familiar*,'" snapped the Mayor, as the Coroner eyed the two men, puzzled. "Of course I am *aware* of Lola Books! My family has patronized Miss Mimona's business for years."

Yanev had assumed that Milevski and Reza had at least known each other (and, as it was rumored, much more). Be that as it may, the familiarity Sergeant Naumov had implied surely would not constitute an unheard of situation. Indeed, half the town's population knew the gregarious bookseller… and practically *everyone* knew the city's chief elected official! After all, was it not part of the Mayor's function to act as liaison between Tavotons and their local merchants? So why was the popular Mayor distancing himself from Tereza Mimona so insistently? *None of my business*, thought a dog-tired Viktor Yanev. *He has his reasons*.

Which is exactly what Sergeant Naumov was thinking. And for the first time, the Policeman found himself wondering where Tavoto's defensive and lecherous Mayor had been between nine and eleven last night…the hours preceding Valentina and Teo's grisly discovery.

"I am going for breakfast," Naumov said. "I will be back." And he set out on foot for the red-and-yellow fast-food restaurant near the 'Quilted Mosque.'

* * *

Sergeant Stefan Naumov ordered an American-style breakfast…apple juice, scrambled eggs, hash brown potatoes, bacon (fried on a separate grill in deference to Muslim clientele), two large buttered biscuits, and an enormous container of black coffee. Had he been in uniform, the McDonald's management was authorized to give Stefan (and any other Tavoto 'cop'—a term that was discouraged) a fifty percent discount. As it was, Naumov ponied up the full seven euros, paid the young counter clerk, and proceeded to the condiment station. There he loaded up on salt and pepper and a zesty garlic and horseradish mixture, the Madonican equivalent of America's ridiculously bland sauce known as 'ketchup.' He weaved his way among the dozen or so mostly older 'sunrise' customers and out of habit took a seat at a corner table…where he could see both glass doors leading in and out of the establishment.

Revealing just enough of his shoulder holster to assure his request would be acted upon forthwith, the Sergeant summoned the busboy and asked him to send the Manager. The gaping Muslim lad backed slowly from Naumov's table, mesmerized by the sight of the distinctive Jericho nine millimeter pistol near the man's armpit. When he was a few yards away, he spun around quickly and ran to the door that led to the open kitchen. In minutes the worried looking

Supervisor approached the Policeman and asked if there was a problem.

Once again Stefan flashed the weapon, and motioned for the lightly bearded man to sit down.

After apologetically lifting up the cleaning rag that the retreating boy had dropped on the chair, the Manager sat and crossed his legs in an attempt to appear unconcerned.

By this time the kitchen staff was abuzz with speculation sparked by the Albanian busboy's whispered disclosure that the boss was about to be arrested and thrown in jail for life—if not shot on the spot. Over their shoulders, the workers furtively watched their supervisor in the black bow tie, as each one's hands continued to fly in the uninterrupted performance of their assigned tasks.

Sergeant Naumov dove into the spice-covered breakfast and, through a mouthful of potatoes, casually asked the black-and-white-clad man if he was a resident of Tavoto.

"Yes. It is a requirement of the company."

How long had he lived here, Naumov inquired idly, shifting his attention to one of the well-buttered biscuits and biting off nearly a third of it.

"Two years—almost three."

When he had washed down the golden crusted *mekika* with steaming coffee, the Policeman smiled politely and asked if in the past two-and-a-half years the Manager had gotten to know any of the other merchants in the immediate area.

"Yes. Many are customers…regulars."

The sergeant put down his plastic fork. "Do you happen to know, Reza the Bookseller…from Karaorman Road…Lola Books?"

"Yes. She was here last night. With a friend. An American. A soldier."

Stefan Naumov gazed into the Manager's dark eyes, impressed with the promptness and certainty of the response. He nodded pensively and wiped crumbs from his lips with a paper napkin. "Perhaps you would be good enough to accompany me to my...er...*office*," he said, folding over the lapel of his jacket and exposing a silver badge. "And please... speak to no one but me. You understand?"

Chapter 48

Tereza Mimona would be opening her shop on Karaorman Road. She would hide them.

The dawn had broken an hour earlier, and now the morning sun streamed through two of 'Saint Holy Mother of God's' low, arched windows, and into the ancient sanctuary. The day's first light warmed Lisbeth and Bashkim, and cast their coupled shadow across the slate floor toward the western rock wall of the fortress room where they lay, spent and clinging to one another.

The American Doctor could not shift her gaze from the Curator's dark, penetrating eyes. She seemed hypnotized by them…by him…by this unlikely place…where true love seemed to have burst along her veins for the first time in her life. She moved a few wet strands of jet black hair from her lover's brow and kissed the damp spot where the curl had been. "Will it always be like this…for us…say it will."

He drew her even closer and returned her kiss. "Yes," he said. "Always."

"And we will never quarrel…never tire of one another…never lie?" Lis pressed her ear to Bashkim's chest and listened for his response. "Tell me."

"Never," he murmured, demolishing with that single word, the vow he'd made in this holy place where their love had so recently been born.

"I believe you," Lisbeth said…and Bashkim Inasah wished with all his aching heart he had not heard her.

He turned his head and brushed away a tear. "We have to leave now," the tall man said almost inaudibly, standing and lifting Lisbeth to her feet.

That part, at least, was true. It was time for them to go. Soon, he knew, Tereza Mimona would be opening her cluttered little shop on Karaorman Road. She would hide them until an hour-long flight across the Adriatic to Naples could be arranged.

"But on Sunday?" Lisbeth protested, dressing hurriedly in clothes that were finally dry.

"Reza is not governed by Christian rules," said Bashkim, and he added, "Why don't you drink some water…we have a long walk."

* * *

Eric Mueller had requisitioned a staff car for the remainder of the weekend, and at ten AM he pulled the olive drab vehicle into the Ruga Dognal *cul-de-sac* and parked next to the stone fountain. Hanna Henschel was still sitting in her living room hoping that her new boarder would make an appearance. When she saw the unfamiliar military automobile, her heart leaped in expectation, and the petite woman's first inclination was to rush into the kitchen and boil water for tea.

As soon as she had gotten to her feet, however, Hanna's spirits sank. Captain Mueller had exited the American sedan… and he was striding up Frau Henschel's front walk, looking over first one shoulder, then the other.

Initially, Hanna had thought it a good idea to disregard the Captain's knock. Perhaps he would go away…leave her alone. Upon reflection, though, she feared that he might be bringing some word about Lisbeth. Good news or bad, the diminutive woman could hardly forego the opportunity to hear what the insufferable man in the Class B uniform had to say. He knocked on the door three times brusquely. Hanna hesitated for a five-second interval, walked to the door, and threw the lock bolt…just as the doorknob began to turn under Mueller's impatient twisting.

Frau Henschel stood unsmiling in the open doorway, head held high, chin thrust forward, waiting for the officer to speak.

"Is she awake yet?" the Captain demanded.

Hanna blinked her indignation and made a non-committal shrug.

"Tell Doctor Wren Eric Mueller is waiting," the Captain ordered, as if instructing some PFC to run an errand.

"This is not a barracks," said Hanna Henschel, emboldened by her awareness that Lisbeth must not be in harm's way…as far as Mueller knew, anyway. "And I am not your Orderly."

The Captain's ruddy face reddened even more and he fixed the landlady with a vicious stare. He removed a business card from his shirt pocket and scribbled what appeared to be a phone number on the reverse. "Give it to her," he said. "I'll be back this afternoon."

Hanna closed the door solidly and re-locked it.

Almost immediately there was a high-pitched squealing of tires on the cobblestone street, and it caused the woman to wince and turtle her head between her shoulders. She walked to the kitchen, placed the calling card on the table next to a teacup that Lisbeth had admired, and filled the dented old kettle anew. *At least the people at Camp Billingham must be satisfied that Lt. Colonel Wren was safe…otherwise how could Mueller think she was at home in her bed?*

Still, Frau Henschel pondered, placing the teakettle on the stove, *it's time someone investigated that man—he might be dangerous!*

* * *

Grand Imam Nazmi ben Zullah had ordered the young Caliph Rhija, to see to the prompt cremation of the bodies of Aalil and Aamil. Though Sharia, or Islamic religious law, calls for *burial* of a dead body, and specifically forbids cremation, these formalities meant little to ben Zullah where his youthful apprentice clerics were concerned. They had been foolish enough to allow Bashkim Inasah and his whore to slip through their fingers…accordingly they would be denied a place in paradise for eternity. It was only fitting.

And Rhija knew better than to disobey…or he might suffer the same disgrace…possibly even without benefit of having died before being consigned to the fire…the forbidding oven installed in the stone base of the minaret.

When Eric Mueller arrived at the private entrance to the 'Quilted Mosque' he knew right away that a cremation must have been conducted recently. The late morning air was thick with drifting residue, a sure indication that the disposal of incinerated remains was underway. Also, two of the mosque's elders were peering down sheepishly from the lone balcony high on the pointed tower.

The Captain drew a finger along the hood of the Curator's car as he passed the dusty Citroen on *Ulica Goce Delcev*. He rubbed his thumb and forefinger together and felt the grit. *I wonder who it is. Maybe Inasah himself,* he speculated, not without a degree satisfaction.

The door to the mosque was unlocked, as ben Zullah had told Mueller on the phone it would be, and the impatient officer entered, shoes in hand. It would soon be time for *Salat*, and the faithful were already making their way to *Sarena*

Jemija, waving the airborne ashes from before their faces as they congregated.

The Grand Imam was waiting in the *mihrab* and he escorted the Captain to the labyrinth. In the Operating Suite, Major Stufkoski's body lay where it had fallen. The chill temperature had prevented the corpse from showing significant signs of external deterioration. The young patient had awoken and been moved to the anteroom next door.

Mueller squatted and examined the woman's massive cranial wound. "Who's the assassin?" he asked casually.

"Only Inasah and the Doctor were with her when I left," ben Zullah murmured.

Captain Mueller frowned and slowly stood. "Where are they now?"

"Escaped," said the *Mullah*. "Almost certainly through the *turbe*."

Eric Mueller pointed to the dead Doctor. "You must get rid of her, Imam. And quickly. This is not good."

"After the Evening *Salat*," ben Zullah said. "Rhija will arrange it."

"As for the Curator and Doctor Wren…it is imperative that we find them, my friend."

Nazmi ben Zullah nodded, opened the door, and followed the brawny Captain into the corridor. "I have ordered a search party," he said. "But be advised, Inasah knows the area as well as any man alive."

"Then," said Mueller, "…we have to make sure that he isn't alive much longer."

Chapter 49

'In Islam, if a man takes a new wife...it is unnecessary to replace the first one's picture?'

When they had moved halfway down the easternmost slope of the Shar Range, the hill on which the Kale, or 'Fortress Shrine' was built, Bashkim suddenly brought Lisbeth up short and pointed toward a rotting wooden lean-to some yards off the steep path. "We will rest there until the *Muezzin* sounds at noon," he said. "Ben Zullah's men will already be looking for us...but they will stop for *Midday Salat*. We'll make our final descent while they are at prayer."

"Do we really have to hide in that hovel?" Lis asked with alarm. She shivered. "Looks like it's crawling with dangerous... God-knows-what."

The Curator took her by the hand and together they strode through waist-high grass toward the ramshackle hut. "Appearances can be deceiving," he said. "Madonica is a crossroads for hundreds of species of migratory birds. In an open field like this, insects and small vermin don't have a chance...especially in November."

After they had secured a back-to-back spot inside the shed...one that gave them a combined wide-ranging view of the oblique terrain above Old Tavoto...Lisbeth was pleased to note that her fears regarding poisonous creatures seemed to be unfounded. However, she voiced another concern that had been on her mind since they'd left the Shrine. "What chance do we really have of evading the *Mullah's* searchers in broad daylight? I haven't seen another American woman since I came to this town."

"I will take care of that," Bashkim declared reassuringly over his shoulder.

"How?"

"There is a saying in Middle Eastern countries," he answered. *"'In Islam, if a man takes a new wife…it is unnecessary to replace the first one's picture?'"*

Lisbeth frowned…confused. Then the adage's implication dawned on her. It was a fact, she had to agree, that from the age of ten or so all Muslim females looked pretty much the same.

"How sentimental!" she said. Then, visualizing herself disguised, she admitted, "Actually though, I've always wanted to try on one of those hijab doohickeys."

The tall man laughed for the first time in days. "No 'hijab doohickey,' for you my Dear—you need a burka! It is the most concealing of all Islamic veils. The burka covers both the body *and* the face. Through its mesh screen your lovely blue eyes will be all but invisible."

"I suppose it goes without saying you'll be able to find one."

"Mmmm…I have been known to purchase such a gift on occasion," Bashkim Inasah replied…greatly understating the generosity for which the handsome Curator was legendary among the shrouded women of Tavoto…and beyond.

* * *

At Tavoto Police Headquarters on Marshal Tito Boulevard, Sergeant Naumov sat at one side of the larger of two desks. Across from him was the chatty McDonald's Manager in his white shirt and black bow tie.

At the smaller desk Iosif Ivanoff's clerical function had been assumed by Sergeant Spiro Pandev, an even slower typist than the inept Patrolman.

After establishing the time (about ten o'clock) when the American soldier and the bookseller had left the restaurant, Naumov embarked on a line of questioning that, though hearsay would not be admitted by a trial Judge, he hoped would justify his temporarily detaining the Army soldier…a procedure which was his right under Madonican law.

"Did the American soldier and the Mimona woman seem friendly?"

The Manager shrugged and said he had no reason to believe otherwise.

"Well…did they smile at one another?"

The supervisor seemed to recall that they had—briefly.

"Only briefly?"

The man in the bow tie grinned weakly, and added that there are different kinds of smiles…some more genuine than others.

"And the soldier's 'smile' was less than enthusiastic…is that what you mean?"

"She seemed happier than the soldier—at first," said the Manager.

Sergeant Naumov leaned forward on his elbows. The action seemed to imply that *now* he felt he was getting somewhere!

"Did you hear their conversation, *Gospodin* Bogdani?" It was the first time the Sergeant had called Halil Bogdani by name, using the formal word for 'Mister.'

"No," said the Manager, "…but the busboy did."

"And…"

"He told me Reza called him *Eric*."

Sergeant Pandev stopped his laborious typing and said, "Spell, please."

Bogdani threw up his hands, nonplussed. "How do I know the way Americans spell?"

"Write E-R-I-C," Naumov growled. "What's the fucking difference?"

"Ah. That's another thing," said the Manager. "My busboy told me the soldier said to Reza, 'I'll break your fucking jaw.'"

Sergeant Naumov sat back in his chair and regarded the man in the black bow tie for a disbelieving ten seconds. "Did it not occur to you to bring that to the attention of the Police, Halil?"

The man shrugged again. "I thought it is just something Americans say. As you know, they are always joking."

Naumov was not amused. He snapped his fingers and flicked them impatiently, instructing Spiro Pandev to give him the barely legible typed document. He scanned it with disgust and passed it to the McDonald's Manager. "Sign this, Halil…then write the name of your busboy…and the address where he can be found."

When Bogdani had complied, the Sergeant returned the signed deposition to Pandev. In the manner of Police investigators the world over, he said to the manager, "You are not to discuss this matter with anyone, Halil. Nor will you leave town until I say you may. Understood? Dismissed."

Halil Bogdani departed Headquarters and immediately Naumov located the busboy's address on a large wall map in the office. The Sergeant jabbed his index finger onto a small, red-circled section of the chart. "Just as I feared," he muttered.

"What's the trouble," said Pandev, who was now attempting without success to replace a frayed ribbon in the old Olympia typewriter.

"I knew it as soon as I saw his name. The kid lives in the Vlach compound adjacent to the orphanage. He's a goddam Bosniak!"

"Then no Judge in Tavoto will accept his testimony," Spiro Pandev grunted, returning to the task that seemed thoroughly to mystify him.

"And Kiril Milevski would have all of our jobs for infuriating his friends at Camp Billingham," Stefan Naumov said ruefully. He went to the coat rack, seized his hat and a seldom-used raincoat, and prepared to leave the building. "I am going to the bookstore," he announced. "Don't tell Ivanoff I'm coming. Let's see how alert our Patrolman friend is."

"Just be careful," Pandev called as the Sergeant pulled the door closed. "I promised young Iosif no one would shoot him."

More likely to be the other way around with that little shit, a skeptical Sergeant Naumov thought…and he began to trudge along empty Marshal Tito Boulevard…toward Karaorman Road.

Chapter 50

*"If ben Zullah comes within a mile of me…
I'll castrate the son-of-a-bitch."*

The sound that arose from the dozens of mosques in Old Tavoto, and reverberated around the hill where Bashkim and Lisbeth sat dozing, was not unlike that of a large orchestra whose muted components test the pitch of their instruments prior to performing a major musical work. Some of the holy sites were miles from one another, others mere short city blocks apart. A few neighborhoods in the oldest parts of town counted more than a single mosque within their ancient boundaries. But the collective wailing of the *Muezzin* proclaimed the same age-old summons…it was time for the faithful to gather, either in their mosque, their homes, even on the side of the road, and kneel facing Mecca.

Fortunately for the Curator and the American Doctor, Mecca is located on the Arabian Peninsula, southeast of Tavoto, approximately 40 miles inland from the Red sea. Thus, by religious decree, the members of ben Zullah's posse would be facing away from Bashkim and Lisbeth during the *Salat*…and for the most part, with their foreheads on the ground to boot. It was a factor that Bashkim Inasah had counted on from the moment they'd left 'Saint Holy Mother of God.'

From the village stretched out at the foot of the fortress hill, the chant of the *Muezzin* began to wane, and Bashkim nudged Lisbeth. She had slept less than three hours overnight in the ruins of the Catholic shrine, and now, having napped a mere fifteen minutes, she stirred reluctantly.

"We leave in two minutes," said the Curator. "When they have begun *Salat*." He stood and extended his hand.

"What time is it?"

Bashkim gave her a condescending look.

"Dumb question," she said, standing and flexing stiffened muscles. "How long will they be praying?"

"Each prayer lasts between five and ten minutes," he said. "It will give us time to reach that growth of Horsetail Ferns down to our left. See them? Once we're buried in that, the Grand Imam himself would practically have to step on us to realize we're there."

"If ben Zullah ever comes within a mile of me again, he'll find out where I am alright…I'll castrate the son-of-a-bitch."

"Here we go," said Bashkim. "Stay on the path. If you slip, keep on rolling. I'll stop you."

If anything, the descent, Lis felt, was more difficult than her late night climb up the steep hill. In the first place, daylight had added a new dimension to her attempt at evading would-be abductors. Now she had to pay attention not only to the pathway immediately in front of her, but also to the entire sun-bathed vista that dropped away before her. Frequently she found herself holding her breath while negotiating each new twist and turn in the trail, and the increased demand on her concentration was tiring in the extreme.

But that was largely psychological. There was also a physical necessity associated with descending that made her current activity a tricky proposition indeed. In proceeding uphill, one knew that a minor slip…or even an outright tumble...was likely merely to bring a hiker to his knees. On the downhill, however, the same misstep could send you careening downward at an ever-increasing rate until it might be impossible to recover your footing. Lisbeth had heard experienced mountaineers describe the phenomenon, and she now understood what she'd formerly considered doubtful—that descent was the hardest part of hiking.

Lis Wren harkened back to her experience in the spring—when she had climbed to Machu Picchu with her family—why hadn't she experienced the sensation then, she wondered? The answer, of course, was that the Andes trip involved a controlled trek...directed by an experienced guide...with a dozen adults tied to one another by a stout rope. And though the thin atmosphere made breathing difficult at times, there was virtually no chance of accidentally lurching to one's death, either while approaching or departing the ancient Aztec city.

Bashkim was well ahead of her, perhaps twenty yards distant, and he stood there strong and confident...watching and waiting...arms akimbo...scant yards from the growth of Horsetail Ferns that was their temporary destination. They would hide there, he had said, until the next *Salat* at three o'clock, when once again the face of every Muslim would be turned toward Mecca...the birthplace of Muhammad...the holy city where non-Muslims are forbidden entry.

"Quickly," the Curator said, taking Lisbeth's hand and leading her into the knee-high growth of greenery. They knelt and peered down the hill through the ferns. The beginning of vague movement was detectable near the city's dozens of mosques as the faithful began to empty into the streets. *Midday Salat* was clearly over. "We wait here," said Bashkim. "If they take the path up to the Shrine and pass us, you'll follow me...we run straight down to the river. If they don't approach, we'll make our dash for the footbridge during the next *Salat*. But stay low in either event." He paused, a sudden look of alarm in his dark eyes. "You *do* know how to swim!"

"Like a fish," Lisbeth replied.

Bashkim tugged on her arm, pulling her under the mantle that the low greens provided. "Good," he said.

* * *

At the conclusion of Camp Billingham's ten o'clock Mass the Catholic Chaplain blessed his modest flock, making the Sign of the Cross over them from behind the altar. "The Mass is ended…go in peace," he said, and with his two altar boys—a Corporal and a Captain—he walked into the adjoining small Sacristy to de-vest and store the cruets, chalice, and paten for use at the twelve noon service.

Doctors Peggy Kelvin and Ophelia Cockbyrne had been seated in the rearmost pew where they enjoyed a bird's-eye view of the chapel. Now standing, as the keyboard 'organist' played the recessional hymn '*Be Not Afraid*,' they looked at each other perplexed.

"Well," said Major Cockbyrne, "…that was interesting. Any other bright ideas, Doc?"

"There's only one other place she could be," said Kelvin. "I noticed a church about three blocks from that house where she's staying. I think it said Saint Bulimia on the front."

"Saint *what*? Bulimia? Come on!"

"Something like that. Let's head into town. Maybe it was Balsamic."

"Know what I think?" Ophelia said. "I think you're trying to drive me crazy. Then you can have one more nutjob patient to justify your existence in this shithole."

"Tell you what—I'll pay for lunch," said Peggy the Psychiatrist. "Come on."

"Well," purred Ophelia Cockbyrne, "…since you put it *that* way."

* * *

Sergeant Naumov turned the corner onto Karaorman Road and immediately noticed that there were at least half a dozen customers in front of Lola Books, apparently waiting for the place to open. He himself had never patronized Reza Mimona's little store on Sunday. As a matter of fact, he'd been inside the shop only once…a year ago…to buy his wife a specific gardening book he'd been unable to find anywhere else.

Patrolman Ivanoff was nowhere to be seen.

Naumov walked to the end of the block and turned left at the Ivo Ribar Alley. Iosif Ivanoff was seated precariously on an overturned trash can that had been emptied by the municipal pick-up the previous afternoon. He was smoking a cigarette.

Even in the dead of winter, the robust Stefan Naumov never wore a topcoat. Thus, clad as he now was in a black raincoat, the Sergeant represented an unrecognizable figure for the rookie Patrolman. "Ivanoff!" Naumov called from forty feet away.

Iosif looked up, startled. He quickly leaped from the garbage pail, dropped the Turkish Murad, and failed in his hasty attempt to step on the rolling cigarette.

The Sergeant frowned. No one had suggested that smoking while on stakeout was forbidden. *In fact,* thought Naumov, *it might provide good cover for a solitary figure pacing a back alley as if killing time.* Perhaps the young policeman was somewhat embarrassed, the Sergeant concluded…because it was well known in Headquarters that Iosif Ivanoff did not smoke.

"I didn't know you used these things," Stefan Naumov said, bending and picking up the two-inch butt.

"I don't," said Iosif lamely, jamming his hands in his pants pockets.

"Of course," Sergeant Naumov said agreeably. Then he held up the still glowing half cigarette as if to ask, *So what's this?*

"A friend…he gave it to me." Ivanoff smiled.

"Of course." Naumov repeated, staring at the Patrolman in the checked sport coat…waiting…unblinking.

"Not a friend," Iosif corrected himself. He turned the trash can right side up and dusted the seat of his trousers. "An acquaintance…a soldier…from the Camp…near Jaziref. I've never even seen him before."

"I don't suppose this *acquaintance*…this *soldier*…spoke to you," said Naumov, as if he'd just asked a silly question.

"Nah," Ivanoff replied in the same light vein. "He didn't even know I'm a cop."

"Until when?" asked Sergeant Naumov. Then, without waiting for an answer, he turned on his heel and growled, "Never mind, you imbecile. Come with me…we're going to McDonald's for lunch."

* * *

Chapter 51

The Captain had tried dialing ben Zullah. He wasn't answering. Something must have come up.

Eric Mueller had not been surprised to encounter the naïve Iosif Ivanoff after he left his meeting with ben Zullah. As soon as he'd seen him staking out the store, he knew intuitively that Reza's body had been recovered downstream…and had been identified. Furthermore, the police must have at least *conjectured* that she'd been murdered. Why else would they be plainly watching to see if a plausible suspect would show up at her place of business?

Perhaps he shouldn't have shown his face, the Captain thought, but in the absence of any other way to learn the *status quo* in the middle of a sleepy Balkan weekend, Mueller felt he had no choice but to risk the back-alley snooping. Better to know as much as the authorities did, even if it meant he'd have to invent a far-fetched excuse for being at Lola Books at noon on a Sunday. His erstwhile associate, the *Mullah*, had told him nothing, if in fact ben Zullah himself knew of the Police activity.

Also among Mueller's concerns was the situation with the goddam Jerry Cans. They should have been taken down to the underground storage area last night, but a slow cruise in the staff car past the 'Quilted Mosque' and the adjacent *turbe* when departing his meeting with the Grand Imam showed that, for whatever reason, the distinctive containers were still neatly stacked against the wall of the mausoleum.

The wary Captain had tried dialing ben Zullah's private number right away…before the *Midday Salat*, but he wasn't answering. Something new must have come up, and the likelihood of an increased police presence here in the old part of town, where speculation spread like wildfire, would only exacerbate matters. One thing was certain: Eric Mueller dare not even think of entering the American fast food emporium adjacent to the *Sarena Jemija*. Though when you thought it through, there wasn't one chance in a thousand the same crew that was on duty last night would be working today.

But happenstance is not necessarily governed by the laws of probability. Indeed, the verbose little Manager who now sat at a corner table with Sergeant Naumov and Patrolman Ivanoff represented a classic example of the fact. Halil would have been home sleeping hours ago had his wife not called to say that her mother had "dropped in to visit" on her way back to Skopje…occasioning his volunteering to work a double shift just to avoid laying eyes on the old bag.

"Describe your soldier friend for Mr. Bogdani," the Sergeant instructed Ivanoff.

The Patrolman was about to take a large bite of his Beefburger, but stopped. He squinted in recollection. "He was tall," said Iosif, and he returned to his sandwich.

Naumov glared at his rookie police officer in abject disgust. "And…?"

"He had short hair."

"What color," prompted Naumov, slamming the table. "Color! Color! Color!"

The Manager in the bow tie looked around the room at his startled patrons, apology etched in his face.

"Light hair," Ivanoff stammered…"The color of old corn silk. And cut short, as I said. Also, tall as a horse."

"That's him," the nodding Manager said quickly, eager to get the Officers out of his restaurant. "That is Reza's friend."

Naumov stood and snatched the Beefburger from the Patrolman's hand. "Come," he barked, "You can finish this later."

* * *

It was a little after noon when Bashkim Inasah nudged Lisbeth to wake her. She had fallen asleep in the shade provided by the Horsetail Ferns and now merely groused incoherently under the prodding, before rolling over on her stomach.

The Curator had noticed a group of six men, each wearing a knee length tunic and led by a modestly bearded fellow in a long, black *Galabiyya*. Bashkim had first seen the party crossing the footbridge near the *Sarena Jemija*…they now were unmistakably making their way up the rugged path that Lisbeth had climbed in the dead of night some fourteen hours earlier.

Even at a distance of a quarter mile, Inasah was confident he recognized the group's leader as ben Zullah's underling Caliph Rhija, one of the Elders.

There could be no question about the party's destination. The trail led directly to the 'Saint Holy Mother of God' fortress. There were no other buildings on either side of the solitary pathway. Bashkim placed his hand gently over the American Doctor's slightly parted lips and elbowed her again.

Alarmed more by his silencing hand than the elbow that poked her ribs, Lis seized Bashkim's wrist and tried to pull his hand from her mouth.

"Shhh," he cautioned. "They're coming."

Lisbeth looked down the hill in the direction Bashkim had indicated with a jerk of his head. There they were—a contingent of obviously Muslim men. Most of them were quite young, if the length of their meager beards was any indication...and they moved easily up the irregular path, their eyes seldom focused on the rutted dirt at their feet.

How the hell can these guys negotiate such uneven, rocky, terrain without damaging or even soiling those loose, ankle-length clothes? she wondered. Last night she'd covered the same stretch of ground in sturdy tweed pants, and torn the cuffs of her trousers to shreds in the process. As for footwear, the Muslims had on simple, open-toed sandals with thin leather soles, the only other protection provided by a wide canvas strap over the instep. Lis, by the same token, wore durable flat shoes...and had still turned both ankles several times during the overnight trek to the fortress.

She consoled herself with the reminder that her journey over the unfamiliar landscape had been conducted in pitch black conditions, while these climbers were ascending the hill with the benefit of broad daylight. Still, she knew full well that—give the Devil his due—what to Westerners were the forbidding footpaths of Madonica, for these people, were the equivalent of smooth, inviting sidewalks.

The midday breeze rippled the concealing ferns and Lisbeth Wren wished she were wearing her camouflaged Army Combat Uniform. Had that been the case, and given the benefit of a full magazine in her sidearm (still sadly empty and tucked in Bashkim's belt), she could have picked-off her pursuers in an explosion of cordite and a hail of bullets that, though it might not have killed the shadowy party to a man…would certainly have roundly disabled it.

But that was wishful thinking. At the Curator's command she crouched lower and waited for the shrouded posse to pass. When they'd climbed nearer the ruins of 'Saint Holy Mother of God,' Bashkim would give the signal. She would then crawl with him toward the closest bend in the trail, and once there, they would sprint together downhill and plunge into the swift-flowing river. They wouldn't wait for the *Afternoon Salat*.

* * *

The last member of ben Zullah's search party had reached the Shrine and disappeared through the arched eastern entrance into the void formed by the surrounding ruins. Bashkim squeezed Lisbeth's forearm. "Now," he whispered. "Follow me."

The broad-shouldered man burst from the concealing ferns and crawled on hands and knees through an adjacent field of high grass. Behind him, Lis kept pace, relieved that they were finally putting distance between themselves and the young Muslims. When they reached the stony path, they saw that it immediately veered south, then quickly north, forming a chicane. Bashkim jumped to his feet and exploded along the trail, pumping his muscular arms like pistons and following the twisting route this way and that with every bit of speed at his command.

Lis was in close pursuit, her long legs eating up three or four feet of the sloping hillside with each determined stride.

In what seemed like seconds, but in reality was slightly more than three minutes, the rutted pathway broadened somewhat and plateaued out…and a hundred yards ahead the familiar footbridge came into view. Bashkim made a cautious glance over his shoulder, though he had no doubt that the Doctor would be close behind. He was breathing hard...she heard him panting and wheezing.

Fucking cigarettes, Lisbeth said inwardly and scornfully. A man of his intellect should know better!

As they drew ever nearer to the north bank of the River Pena, Lisbeth became more apprehensive, and soon her pace decreased somewhat, as if her running feet had a mind of their own. She hadn't overstated her aquatic ability. She'd been a champion swimmer since high school. Still, she hoped an alternative to the Curator's chosen escape route would present itself. There had to be a less dangerous way.

But her wish died as quickly as it had formed. A rifle shot sounded from somewhere and Lisbeth winced reflexively, though she kept on running. Then, not ten yards in front of her, Bashkim Inasah hurled himself in a long, graceful arc over the riverbank's retaining wall.

Now there was no time to seek a different course of action...*no choice...the wall...now*...Lis Wren didn't have the opportunity to skip a single step. She filled her lungs with the cold mountain air...and launched her body, smooth and committed, down toward the swirling torrent.

Chapter 52

A dozen .30 caliber rounds raised miniature geysers near her feet.

Sergeant Naumov, after searching Lola Books for anything unusual, had in lieu of posting a Patrolman outside the front entrance of Tereza's store, placed a simple sign in the show window that said TEMPORARILY CLOSED. The notice did not contain the answers to any questions regarding the reason for the closing...or when the store might be expected to re-open.

Naumov had dispatched three armed and uniformed men to the footbridge where he was convinced Reza Mimona had been killed...almost assuredly by the flaxen-gray-haired American soldier who had been snooping around the Ivo Ribar alley. It was one of the policemen posted at the bridge who had fired a single AK-47 round into the air when he saw the man and woman running suspiciously toward the River Pena. But the shot had clearly failed to deter the pair, who'd leaped into the water fully clothed.

As the current swept Lisbeth and Bashkim swiftly downstream toward the footbridge, the eager cop switched his assault rifle to full-automatic mode and trained it on the helpless Curator. He'd followed the flailing man with the rifle's muzzle and been prepared to fire...when inevitably the low stone wall on the span where the three armed men stood obstructed his view. Speedily, the officer turned his attention to the second suspicious swimmer...a woman who seemed to be dressed in American clothes...and who was expertly stroking the water a few yards behind the man.

Intent on shooting the second swimmer before she too passed under the bridge, the officer fired in haste and the water behind Lisbeth splashed violently as a dozen .30 caliber rounds raised miniature geysers in a straight line near her feet.

Alarmed, Lisbeth took in an immense lungful of air and called upon her PD survival training to dive for the rocky bottom of the river. As she watched rows of high-caliber rounds wobbling down from the surface in front of her, and to the side where the gunman was positioned, she was seized by a moment of panic. *What if she were forced to rise for air before reaching the protection of the bridge?* Lisbeth made a silent vow that she would drown before exposing herself to what she recognized as assault weapon fire.

She also redoubled the speed and force of her underwater breaststroke, and amid the tumbling bullets, each of which trailed a tiny stream of bubbles, she finally saw the distinct shadow of the footbridge outlined on the riverbed perhaps fifteen feet distant.

Sitting exhausted on the narrow shoreline in the shade of the arched overpass, a winded Bashkim Inasah scanned the cascading water for a glimpse of the woman who had told him she swam "*...like a fish.*" If that were the case, he wondered, where was she? Careful not to reveal himself to the armed men less than ten feet above him, the Curator dared not call Lisbeth's name, nor could he venture back upstream in search of her without inviting certain death. Instead, he waded waist deep into the river and slammed the surface of the water with his flattened palm, hoping that the Doctor would recognize the unnatural disturbance as a signal that he was waiting.

As soon as Lisbeth's slender form slid smoothly into the protected waters beneath the old span, her endurance gave out. With her last ounce of strength, she kicked against the rocky bottom of the river and thrust herself straight upward. In seconds, her head broke the surface of the River Pena…her blue eyes wide in desperation…her nostrils flared and mouth agape…in anticipation of finally sucking in the open air.

The three gunmen had run to the downstream side of the bridge and opened fire blindly on the churning water, certain that one or both of their targets would be emerging from beneath at any second. As Lis collapsed on the shaded safety of the rock-strewn bank, Bashkim tore off his shirt and flung it to the center of the river where the current was strongest. The instant that the slightly submerged garment sailed from under the span and into the sunlit section of the stream, all three AK-47s roared simultaneously in a non-stop fusillade that filled the air with the odor of gunpowder…and tore the undulating shirt to shreds.

At that moment a squad car driven by Naumov and bearing Mayor Milevski screeched to a halt near the wooden entrance to the footbridge. "What's going on here?" the Sergeant demanded, as the three over-ardent policemen slung their weapons and saluted.

"We have shot the perpetrators, Sir," said the officer who seemed to be in charge. "There were two of them." He pointed east. "The river has taken them."

"Good," Mayor Milevski interjected with an abrupt nod. "They will be retrieved at the rapids beyond the Vidor Bato Bridge. The same as that woman they obviously murdered."

Again—'that woman,' Naumov snorted.

"Take me to the Vidor Bato," Kiril Milevski ordered. "Good work, men." He opened the car door and climbed inside. "Hurry, Naumov. Why are you dreaming?"

* * *

Saint Bislimi church was locked up tight. An almost indecipherable, hand lettered sign stuck in one of a number of shattered stained glass windows said it all. '*Closed Due To Vandalism,*' or words to that effect.

A few blocks away, Hanna opened the door to the two American women. It was half-past one, and the petite Frau Henschel was preparing her third pot of Sunday tea. Ophelia had told Peggy Kelvin they were wasting their time. It was ridiculous to think that Lisbeth was still in bed...she was known to be among the earliest of early risers...still Kelvin insisted on exhausting every avenue in looking for her. The Psychiatrist was frankly and openly, worried.

Unable to speak a word of English, Hanna could only gesture toward the steaming kettle on the stove in offering the Doctors a cup of tea. A simple shake of the head on their part, accompanied by a smile, similarly was sign language enough to spell out their graceful but definite *No, thank you.*

Determining if Lis was still in her room, should be a piece of cake, Ophelia assumed. "Lis?" she said, emphasizing for Frau Henschel's benefit that she was asking a question.

The German woman frowned. "*Leees? Vas ist Leees?*"

Peggy elbowed Ophelia to one side. "Lisbeth," she corrected Ophelia pleasantly. "Lisbeth Wren."

"*Ach,*" said Hanna. "*Lisbeth.*" Then she added, "*Ja...wo ist sie?*"

"What did she say?" Cockbyrne asked eagerly. She looked toward the stairs. "Is she here?"

310

The smile had vanished from Major Kelvin's face. She shook her head slowly. "Unh-unh," she murmured. "I don't think Mrs. Henschel knows where she is, either."

"Well, we oughta' stop dickin' around," Ophelia Cockbyrne announced. "I say we get somebody down here to translate for us. Do we know where Eric Mueller is?"

"*Nein!*" a terrified Hanna Henschel erupted, wringing her apron at the mention of the Captain's name, and shaking her head from side to side. "*Ihn nicht, Mueller…ihn nicht!*"

"Jesus," said Peggy, "…guess we know where our crew-cut friend stands, don't we?"

"You said it!" Ophelia mumbled. "Even I understand *'not that asshole'*…no matter what language I hear it in."

"*Ich glaube, sie ging nach Tavoto,*" said the diminutive woman meekly, as if in apology for her outburst. Then she wagged her finger. "*Aber nicht mit Mueller…nicht mit ihm.*"

"Guess she went to Tavoto," said Major Cockbyrne offering the no-brainer and shrugging.

"See that," Peggy said, "…you know more German than you thought."

"But she definitely *did not* go with Mueller," Ophelia added proudly.

"No kidding," said Kelvin, "You're a walkin' German dictionary, girl! Come on…we're catchin' the bus to Tavoto."

* * *

Eric Mueller had never been one to fear risk. The man's flamboyant self-reliance, combined with the clout of his Army status, had always stood him in good stead, and the Captain doubted it was going to fail him now. Accordingly, he decided to proceed with the brazen act he'd been considering since the morning after killing Reza Mimona. This afternoon, in broad daylight, he would personally remove the traceable, and potentially incriminating Jerry Cans stacked in front of the *turbe*...then he would bring them to Omar the butcher in Jaziref.

Unlike the 'Quilted Mosque' itself, the mausoleum, though considered a revered site, was not deemed a consecrated place...to deliver goods to the sturdy little building, or to remove any commodities mistakenly transported there, could hardly be termed an offense punishable under Islamic Law. In fact, Mueller's comings and goings in the manicured area surrounding the *Sarena Jemija* were common occurrences that few even took note of.

Mueller knew that the hours between the midday and afternoon *Salat* would be the best time to load the Jerry Cans into the staff car he'd requisitioned. He'd drive the official vehicle adorned with the big, white star right up to the side of the *turbe* and load it as if he were performing a service authorized by the Elders. He would act with determination and dispatch, clearly implying that he was not to be interrupted. No one in Old Tavoto would think for a moment that a mature American soldier with two shining bars on his collar was up to no good...no one, that is, except the Grand Imam himself. And he was hiding in the sanctuary of the famed mosque.

After stopping beside the highway on the outskirts of southeast Tavoto, and checking the sedan's trunk to be sure it was empty, the Captain maneuvered the car onto Ilindenska Boulevard and sped in the direction of the River Pena.

* * *

Majors Kelvin and Cockbyrne stepped off of the reeking bus in Skopje for the second time in as many days. "I'm starting to feel like a friggin commuter again," said Ophelia, the General Practitioner from Quincy, Massachusetts. "I thought I'd left that sweet smell of success stateside."

"Geez, the odors are as bad as the rush-hour Metro between Owings Mills and Johns Hopkins." Baltimore native Peggy Kelvin wrinkled her nose. A precocious one-year-old slung in a South European version of a papoose noted the puckered expression and mimicked it perfectly, earning a shake from her veiled mother.

"Did you bring your popcorn with you?" said Cockbyrne.

"I did this time," Peggy answered patting her zippered pocketbook. "You?"

"You betcha," Ophelia smiled. "And an extra magazine."

'*Popcorn*' was the code word used in public for 'sidearm.' And '*magazine*' was not necessarily something to read. They disembarked from the odiferous bus and Kelvin immediately stuck two fingers in her mouth and whistled for the nearest cab. The child in the sling, who was right behind, tried again to copy Peggy's action…this time without success.

Two taxis vied with each other in a race to pick up the prized fare the American women represented. Amid the drivers' curses and flailing gestures the dusty sedans screeched to a halt not two feet from the pair, their tires on the driver's side scraping the curb in front of the crowded terminal.

"Now, now, boys—don't fight," said Ophelia…and she muttered to Peggy in an aside, "I think the guy in front's cuter. Besides he got here first."

"You're starting to sound like Nan Stufkoski," Peggy chided, hopping into the backseat.

Ophelia followed her in the car and slammed the door. She patted the handsome young driver on the shoulder. "Tavoto," she said, and added, "My friend here is buying lunch."

Major Kelvin rolled her eyes and called to the cabbie, "I don't suppose there's a McDonald's in Tavoto, is there?"

"Okay," the eager driver answered, "McDonald's. Fifteen minutes. Okay."

Between them, Peggy and Ophelia had ninety-six euros, two model 92FS Berettas, and three magazines containing a total of fifty-six rounds of ammunition. Now all they had to do was assure themselves their friend Lisbeth was safe and sound…which they were virtually positive was the case.

Chapter 53

Naumov dropped the dripping rag at Milevski's feet. "I would have expected different clothing."

Stefan Naumov ordered his rifle detail to proceed to headquarters and await his return there. The three patrolmen were not to discharge their assault weapons unless attacked with deadly force by an armed adversary. Was that clear?

"Come," said Mayor Milevski, loud enough to be heard by Bashkim and Lisbeth in the shadows under the footbridge. "We must identify the killers before anyone has had an opportunity to search the bodies."

Having thrown his white shirt into the swirling river as a decoy, the Curator, in a sleeveless undershirt, clung with Lisbeth to the moss-covered arc formed by the inner surface of the narrow span and listened intently.

"Will there not be other conspirators to deal with?" one of the three riflemen asked, a tone of disappointment evident in his question. Bashkim Inasah held his breath and covered the Doctor's mouth with one hand.

"No, you idiot," Naumov roared. "Now proceed to the Municipal Building and stay there until I relieve you. Any man who disobeys will be directing traffic on Tito Boulevard in the morning."

The Sergeant activated his emergency lights and siren, made a quick turn off Ilindenska onto Lenin Road, and followed the thoroughfare due east. Once clear of urban traffic, he sped southeast, until eventually the road narrowed to two lanes and the squad car was speeding unimpeded through larger and larger farms…toward Skopje.

When he spotted the familiar scene where the Coroner's people had recovered Tereza's body from the rapids, Naumov killed the red and blue lights as well as the siren and coasted to a silent halt on the southern bank of the bubbling Pena. And for the first time the already skeptical law enforcement official was forced to concede that he had been outwitted.

Where his own men had given him reason to believe he would find two bodies snagged by the protruding rocks, Stefan Naumov found only a man's white shirt. There was nothing else. No trousers, coat, or undergarments…and most depressingly…no bodies.

"Where are they?" moaned Kiril Milevski, who stood perplexed at the river's edge.

As if he hadn't heard the baffled little degenerate, Sergeant Naumov strode into the white water kicked up by hundreds of centuries-old rocks, and pulled the tattered remains of Bashkim Inasah's bullet riddled shirt from a jagged limb where it was impaled.

"Here," he grunted. "Here's your perpetrator." Naumov dropped the dripping rag at Mayor Milevski's feet. "But I would have expected him to be wearing different clothing altogether."

* * *

Bashkim was fairly certain that ben Zullah had mounted more than one search party in pursuit of them. The question was: How many...and where were they deployed? The Curator's house in Jaziref was surely under surveillance, and if it wasn't already, the dead-end street where Frau Henschel lived soon would be staked out too. Infiltrating Camp Billingham with Muslim operatives was out of the question for the Grand Imam, despite the *Mullah's* sphere of influence, but Bashkim didn't want to seek refuge there anyway. Explaining his involvement in the organ trafficking scheme would undoubtedly necessitate weeks...and even months...of de-briefing with U.S. Army Intelligence. He was not prepared to undergo that kind of interrogation...not just yet.

There seemed little reason to think ben Zullah would have gone to the attention-getting extreme of setting up road blocks on the north/south highway between Madonica and Ovosok, so if he and the American Doctor could only get to Lola Books, a mere five or six blocks from their current hiding spot, Reza would supply them with disguises, and they could take the train to Prishta. From there it would be a short flight to notoriously lax Naples—a city where practically anything could be arranged for a modest price.

Before setting out for Tereza Mimona's shop on Karaorman Road, Bashkim explained to Lisbeth exactly what his strategy was. Only two aspects of the plan disturbed her. One: What if she were convicted of Desertion? Under the Uniform Code of Military Justice, the Doctor could be committed to the Regional Correctional Facility in San Diego for the rest of her natural life. And secondly: Her gun had been used to kill Nan Stufkoski. That would take one hell of a lot of explaining, at best. The Army did not look kindly on soldiers, of any rank, who couldn't retain possession of their weapons.

"If we don't get out of here soon," Bashkim said, "... everything else becomes academic. Ben Zullah will kill us both…you in a particularly brutal manner…because you are a woman. As for this," he reached and pulled the Beretta from beneath his belt at the small of his back, "…I will dispose of the gun when we no longer need it. You will not know where or when I have jettisoned it. If necessary, a polygraph will vindicate you." The Curator replaced the empty gun near his spine and covered it with the hem of his sleeveless undergarment. "Now we have to go. Let your hair fall over your eyes."

* * *

When Eric Mueller approached the *Goce Delcev* he could clearly see that Bashkim Inasah's silver automobile was parked in the spot that it normally occupied on weekdays if the Curator was in his *Sarena Jemija* office. There was no police presence in close proximity to the vehicle…no crime scene tape…no apparent damage to the Citroen. But neither had the Captain expected to find any of those things. Ben Zullah probably had a sniper stationed in the balcony of the minaret…prepared to fire in the unlikely event that Inasah foolishly attempted to retrieve his car.

An aggressive gunman, however, was of little concern to Mueller. The last thing the Grand Imam would want would be the attention of the United States Army investigating the wounding or killing of one of their officers on a Muslim holy site. Accordingly, as Captain Eric Mueller turned his staff car casually onto the grounds of the 'Quilted Mosque,' and steered it toward the granite *turbe* and its array of stacked Jerry Cans, he waved nonchalantly in the direction of the high crow's nest.

Amazingly, one of ben Zullah's Mufti henchmen responded by lifting an AK-47 in salute, the loose sleeve of his *Galabiyya* flapping in the Sunday afternoon breeze.

In less than five minutes Mueller had loaded the containers of frozen carbon monoxide into the trunk of the staff car, and after another insouciant wave toward the minaret, he eased the sedan onto *Ulica Goce Delcev*. The grinning Captain then turned left at McDonald's, and drove along Ilindenska until the wide roadway met Marshal Tito Boulevard. There, he proceeded west in the general direction of Omar Hamidi's meat market.

In a corner booth by the fast food restaurant's glass front door, Ophelia Cockbyrne nearly dropped her Big Mac. "Look. Look." She pointed frantically to the northbound lane of Ilindenska Boulevard. "It's Mueller!"

Peggy Kelvin craned her neck and just about caught the staff car's vanishing tail lights. "Was Nan in the car…could you tell?"

"I don't think he had anybody with him," said Ophelia, "…unless she was lying in his lap."

Kelvin fanned herself with her napkin. "And I wouldn't put that past our Dentist friend for a second," she said, cramming the three-inch-thick burger into her mouth.

Chapter 54

It was going to be a spectacular explosion.

Eric Mueller drove north on the two-lane highway at a leisurely pace. There was no hurry. If Nazmi ben Zullah's men had not disposed of Inasah and the Lieutenant Colonel by sunset, he would hunt them down and kill them himself. *But better*, he thought, *to have members of the Muslim cabal do the job.* Not that the Captain found murder particularly offensive...it just seemed preferable to have the clerics directly involved as much as possible. *Keep them off-balance, so to speak.*

Had Mueller himself paid more attention to the images in his rearview mirrors, he might have noticed a black S-Class Mercedes-Benz with heavily tinted windows trailing his staff car at a fifteen-vehicle interval. The $200,000 dollar sedan was chauffeured by one of ben Zullah's assistants, and the Grand Imam himself sat alone in the backseat.

In addition to operating the Mercedes, the driver had, even before the *Dawn Salat*, planted explosive charges in six of the twelve Jerry Cans that now filled Eric Mueller's trunk to capacity. The *Mullah* had soon learned of the Mimona woman's murder, and just as quickly concluded that Mueller must be the perpetrator. Thus, he was confident the American Captain would come back to see if the implicating containers had been hidden...and if not, he would personally remove them. What choice did Mueller have? The cans were U.S. government property...and easily traceable to him. If local authorities were to find them, he would surely be placed at the general scene of a major crime...and Nazmi ben Zullah would have his cadre of informants testify against the soldier.

"You are certain no one observed you?" ben Zullah asked his driver lightly, as he watched the flat, barren fields glide by on both sides of the big car.

"Only the lookout in the minaret, Grand Imam."

"And you eliminated him?"

"Yes, Grand Imam."

"How?"

"The crematorium, Grand Imam. During *Salat*."

Ben Zullah lit a cigarette. "I hope you prayed for him."

It was not a question. The driver smiled but did not respond.

Nazmi ben Zullah idly fingered the cell phone that would trigger the half-dozen detonators in Mueller's trunk. Each of the bombs consisted of three-pound balls of malleable Semtex and all six were rigged to explode simultaneously when their electronic igniters were fired. It was going to be a spectacular explosion...and both the Grand Imam and his lackey were eager to see where the Captain was headed. Obviously, the Mullah could have pressed the 'Send' button and demolished the olive drab vehicle up ahead at any time. But if Mueller was leading them to Lisbeth Wren and her duplicitous lover Inasah, ben Zullah might well experience the divine gratification of having three primary objectives vaporized in one devastating blast. That prospect made the wait worthwhile.

* * *

Most Christians in old Tavoto rose early on Sundays, walked to Mass or Protestant services with their families, and returned to their homes before *Midday Salat*—at a little before noon. Then the Muslims were on the move, as they were again at about three o'clock…when fervent Christians of every persuasion were sitting down to an early dinner. The less devout of all inclinations cheered-on the home soccer team at sold-out Cabo Taceckh Stadium in the town's northwest sector.

Bashkim Inasah knew that on Sunday afternoon, during the hour between four and five, the part of Tavoto that extended from the River Pena on the southwest, to semi-circular Tito Boulevard on the north and east, was what Americans would have called a Ghost Town. Indeed, he had asked Reza time and again why she opened Lola Books on Sunday at all, since business was practically non-existent for a good part of the day.

"It's when I entertain my secret admirers," Tereza had always responded, though in truth, apart from a notorious year-long fling with Mayor Kiril Milevski, the perky Ms. Mimona was as chaste as any middle-aged woman in town. Though admittedly not of her own volition.

Lisbeth was stiff from her two-hour-long spell sitting in a cramped position under the low arch of the footbridge. "Another minute and my back's gonna damn well break," she whispered, kneading her kidneys with her fists. "Nobody's crossed this bridge in a fucking hour."

Bashkim, too, was eager to set out for the bookstore, if for no other reason than to get into some warm, dry clothes that he would have Reza obtain for them. He was certain that no one was atop the bridge, still, he wanted to make sure. From the water's edge, he picked up a smooth rock the size of a softball and in the manner of his idol Ben Bonhurst, he flung it as far upstream as he could. The twelve-pound rock flew some fifteen yards and landed in the middle of the river with a loud splash. He stood stark still…knee-deep in water… listening. Hearing nothing overhead, he repeated the action, hurling another large stone downstream. When again there was no reaction, he was sure that they were alone. He took Lisbeth by the hand and led her from their shelter, up onto the footbridge. From there, they walked arm-in-arm, heads lowered, in the direction of Karaorman Road.

The few Tavotons who passed them promptly assumed the disheveled man and woman were unkempt partyers making their way home from an all-night binge of drinking and God knows what else. Most crossed the street to avoid proximity to them; the rest also gave the scruffy couple a wide berth.

When the Lola Books show window came into view on the north side of Karaorman Road Lisbeth gave Bashkim's biceps a squeeze.

"Not yet," he muttered, sensing that she wanted to cross the cobblestone street and walk diagonally toward the store's front door. Instead he took a firmer hold on her elbow and they ambled past the bookstore. At the corner of murky Ivo Ribar Alley, they turned left and hastened down the crooked lane, finally stopping at the narrow back door and accompanying window on which was painted the one word, 'Books.'

There was no one else in the alley. Bashkim told Lisbeth to watch the corner from which they'd come while he peered inside Reza's obviously empty store. She crossed the lane and slipped into a dark recess between two small shops that were also closed. From the narrow vantage point Lis focused on Karaorman Road. Bashkim tried the door handle. It wouldn't budge. He visored his eyes with both hands and, with his nose pressed against the window pane, the frustrated Curator scanned the counter, the fully stocked bookshelves, the table at which he and Reza had sat sipping espresso scant days ago. Everything was in shadow...and as still as death.

"Wait here," Bashkim called to Lisbeth in a stage whisper. He ran to the corner, looked both ways furtively, and sauntered to the shop's front door. There was a cardboard sign that he had never seen before. It was wedged into the waist-high corner of the show window: TEMPORARILY CLOSED. Out of habit when viewing such unfamiliar objects, the Curator squatted and read a small notation in the corner of the machine-printed notice. It read: *Policiska Tavoto*.

Either she's been arrested, thought Bashkim...or...but he did not want to consider the alternative.

He hurried to the alley, turned the corner, and called to Lisbeth. "Come. I know a store where we can get some clothes. They accept even soaking wet euros, if you have enough of them." He gestured impatiently. "Come quickly."

Chapter 55

He left them waiting until the last diehard fan had left the stadium at 8:00.

Sergeant Stefan Naumov was furious. Certain that a blond US Army Captain known as Eric was the man he was looking for, he had withdrawn his inept observers from the Lola bookstore and the Radovan footbridge. He'd asked for assistance from the Ovosok authorities in establishing checkpoints at the border crossings shared by the adjacent Principalities, and in the weekend absence of his Chief of Police, the veteran officer had requested advance protocol information from Skopje concerning the detaining of American military personnel where matters involving capital crimes were involved.

As if the incompetence of his own men were not enough to drive him to distraction, Naumov had been denied even a modicum of cooperation from officials in Ovosok, who claimed they needed a current 8 by 10 color photograph of the person under suspicion before they could act. Furthermore, those in the Madonica Capitol had declared that all such vague requests for information involving arrest decorum were filled only on weekdays between 10:00 AM and 4:00 PM... except on Fridays when the *Office of Protocol* closed at noon.

There was little that Naumov could do to punish the fools in Ovosok or Skopje for their unwillingness to exercise even the most basic elements of effective law enforcement, but he knew how to reprimand his own charges for their stupidity: As the acting Chief, Naumov had ordered everyone into Headquarters for a meeting at 3:30 PM (when the capacity crowd at Cabo Taceckh was just settling in to watch the crucial Sunday soccer ritual) and he left them waiting in the dank Municipal Center until the last diehard fan had left the stadium at 8:00.

The upshot, of course, was that Bashkim Inasah and Lisbeth Wren had been fortuitously freed to pursue their escape scenario relatively undeterred by Naumov's grumbling cadre of bitter constables.

* * *

"Do you have a particular color in mind for your, uh, wife's garment?" sneered the clearly disapproving proprietor at Al Mujalfafa Clothiers. Lisbeth disregarded the man and continued to examine the hanging *abaya-niqab* ensembles, evaluating one after the other on the store's revolving rack. The *abaya* (or cloak) seemed to interest her more so than the straightforward *niqab,* which was the separate face covering worn by most Tavoton women over the age of twenty-five.

Bashkim leveled the rude fellow with a long, cold stare. "Gray," he responded sharply. "Your finest quality!" He slapped three soggy hundred-euro notes on the counter. "And matching Najdi sandals." The seller gaped at the money and his demeanor changed instantly.

"Yes, *Gospodine*. Right away, *Gospodine*." He rushed to the clothes rack, elbowed Lisbeth aside as if she were some intruder, and selected the most expensive two-piece outfit in what he estimated to be her appropriate length and shoulder size. He laid the pair of loose garments across the counter with a flourish, careful not to disturb the money.

All business, he snapped his fingers and called out something in Farsi to a young clerk who had been standing, arms folded, by the door. The now-solicitous merchant turned his smiling face toward Bashkim. "Hamad is bringing the shoes. Large, I believe. Will there be anything else, *Gospodine*? He peered suggestively at his customer's discolored undershirt. "We have excellent…"

"Sandals," said the Curator. "For me. And a wool shirt. Also gray. My wife will use your dressing room."

"Indeed," said the proprietor, taking the florid shoes from his clerk, handing them to Bashkim, and issuing the youth another series of commands. The young assistant hurried off again, and the man locked the front door as was the practice at Al Mujalfafa whenever a female client on the premises was indisposed. Lisbeth picked up the clothing, took the shoes from Bashkim, and made her way into the changing room that was fronted by a floor-to-ceiling mirror.

"Your wife has complete privacy," said the merchant. "Hamad and I will leave the room if you prefer."

"Not necessary," said Bashkim, and eager young Hamad returned with sandals and a dark, zippered shirt, both of which Bashkim inspected and donned with satisfaction.

"The price is exactly three hundred euros, *Gospodine*," the man announced, as if the figure had by some miracle matched the money on the counter precisely. He jammed the notes into his pocket and admired the tall man from different angles. "An excellent fit, the *thobe*. Very nice, indeed."

Lisbeth emerged from the dressing room and studied her image in the mirror before turning to Bashkim for approval. He had been prepared for a shock, but to his utter astonishment,

Lis Wren looked absolutely radiant...though not a square inch of her body was visible. Even the misogynist proprietor and his youthful clerk were stunned, and they could not help but take stock of the Doctor's slender form, inspecting her from head to toe. The floor-length *abaya,* intended to conceal the contours of her body, had produced just the opposite effect. Her charms, though only vaguely suggested beneath the full-flowing robe, had transformed Lisbeth into a wonderfully mysterious and appealing figure...a thoroughly intriguing vision of feminine loveliness.

Lisbeth sensed that Bashkim was taken aback. From behind the soft folds of the *niqab* that covered her face except for a narrow eye screen, Lisbeth asked in her deep, concerned voice, "Is something wrong, *Habeeb Qalbi?*"

Bashkim required a moment to compose himself. "No," said the flushed Curator, unlocking the establishment's door and preparing to open it for the newly attired Doctor. "No, everything is fine."

Before leaving, he turned to the shop proprietor. "Kindly dispose of my wife's damaged shoes. They are inside. Here, take mine too." Then he added, "Tell me. Your neighbor on Karaorman Road...Tereza Mimona...did she open her bookstore today?"

The man stopped smoothing out his new trio of hundred-euro bills. He looked at Bashkim...then at his clerk...puzzled. "Apparently you have not heard," said Mujalfafa, the clothier. "There has been a most unfortunate accident."

* * *

In the backseat of his black Mercedes-Benz, Nazmi ben Zullah answered his American-made cell phone with a curt, "*As-salam alaykom.*" He listened attentively, holding the device to his ear with one hand, idly rolling a burning cigarette between brown-stained fingers with the other.

"What is the possibility you are mistaken?" the Grand Imam asked casually...and waited.

At last, he nodded. "I see. And the woman?"

Ben Zullah continued to listen intently, then bobbed his head again. "I am coming. Stay there. Tell no one."

The smug *Mullah* extinguished his Turkish cigarette, mashing it on the plush carpet of the big car with his foot. "Reduce your speed somewhat," he instructed the driver, who promptly slowed from seventy to sixty miles per hour. Ben Zullah dialed a seven-digit number on the iPhone. When the distance between the Mercedes and Mueller's Army Staff car was approximately five hundred yards, he pressed the 'Send' button...and the duplicitous Eric Mueller was instantly incinerated in a hail of glass, metal shards, and burning fuel and rubber.

"Praise be to Allah," said ben Zullah. "It seems the Captain's journey is finished."

The driver slowed even further and looked expectantly into the rearview mirror.

"Back to Tavoto," the *Mullah* commanded. "I am told we have found what was lost."

Chapter 56

The voice of the woman wearing a skirt and carrying a purse, boomed over the throng.

A tour bus filled with French students and their proctors unloaded its animated cargo directly in front of the Tavoto McDonald's, then proceeded to the far section of the parking lot reserved for commercial vehicles. The visitors were bound for the distinctive old mosque only a block away, but the local guide had advised against entering the holy building until the *Afternoon Salat* was over.

The surprise addition of forty hungry pre-teens sent Halil Bogdani and his staff into such a frenzy of cutting open frozen packets of meat, submerging *pommes de terre* in bubbling oil, and slathering condiments on pre-sliced buns, that the bow-tied manager nearly wished he'd gone home at the conclusion of his overnight shift…even if it meant facing his mother-in-law.

"I think we ordered just in time," Ophelia said, as every seat in the restaurant was quickly filled, and the room resonated with shrill, insistent Gallic phrases that contrasted with the muted Madonican monosyllables that had floated on the air just moments before.

Groups of six denim-clad youngsters crammed into booths intended to hold four, and the seven monitors, mostly mothers in their thirties, wisely insisted that everyone be served the same selection—a *'Numero Quatre'*—Big Mac, medium Coke, and large Fries.

"No substitutions; no special orders. Trade if you must."

The stern voice of the senior adult, the only woman wearing a skirt and carrying a purse, boomed over the frenetic throng, "*Huit a la fois dans la salle de bains!—quatre Mesdames, quatre Messieurs.*"

With that, four of the boys and the same number of girls made a mad dash to their respective bathrooms.

"What did she say?" Peggy inquired.

Ophelia smiled wickedly. "She said, 'If you had any designs on the john, you'd better have one strong bladder, Toots.'"

Major Cockbyrne craned her neck to see what was on the brochure that the sextet in the adjoining booth was chatting over so excitedly. In large, multi-colored letters on the flyer's cover were two French words. "Isn't that the place you said you were dying to see?" Ophelia said. The pamphlet's title read *Mosquee Couette*. "If my high school French serves me, I think it means 'Quilted Mosque.'"

"That must be the place right around the corner," said Kelvin. "Come to think of it, it does look a bit like those patchwork bedspreads my grandmother used to make."

Two of the younger proctors, holding trays and looking helpless, approached the table shared by the casually-clad Doctors. "*Puissions-nous nous asseoir avec vou?*" one said.

"Sure," Major Cockbyrne answered, shifting to her left, and Kelvin moved right.

"You are Americans," said the taller of the two French women.

"I am," Ophelia smiled…but Peggy's from Baltimore."

"Ah!" the tall woman said, "…my Great Uncle Franklin ran a chicken farm in Maryland." Both women unwrapped their hefty Big Macs and bit into them. "He began after he suddenly left college at nineteen…very *tete dure*." She rapped the side of her head with her knuckles. "But today, even in Paris, our Perdue name is known."

"Oh…*that* Frank Perdue," said Kelvin.

"It takes a tough man to make a tender chicken," Ophelia announced, chewing on her last McNugget.

"Are you here to see *Mosquee Couette?*" asked the shorter monitor, who also spoke perfect English.

"I could take it or leave it," Peggy smiled, "…but my theologian friend here insists—and she paid for lunch, so we'll probably be joining you." She reached a welcoming hand across the table, then to her right. "I'm Peg Kelvin, by the way…and this is your uncle's former neighbor, Ophelia Cockbyrne."

* * *

Lisbeth and Bashkim had walked the short distance back to Lola Books with considerably more confidence now that the American Doctor was disguised.

Seeing no one lurking in the area of the Ivo Ribar Alley, the Curator had pried the rear door's simple lock, they'd entered the quiet store, then closed the door and wedged it shut with a low but heavy bookcase. In a shallow storage area covered by an unobtrusive, beige curtain, the exhausted pair decided to rest unseen behind a half-filled packing crate, knowing that they undoubtedly would sleep, and realizing just as surely that even the wailing of the *Afternoon Salat* in an hour or so would fail to awaken them.

It had already been a long and hectic day since dawn at 'Saint Holy Mother of God,' and outbound flights from

Prishta, fifty miles away, would end at sunset and not resume until daybreak.

The harrowing descent from the Shrine and their near-miss at the River Pena had robbed them of their strength. They needed to restore depleted energy, Lisbeth knew, and Bashkim suggested they partake of Reza's coffee and brandy, along with some leftover homemade muffins.

Hardly the equal of Hanna's breakfast, Lis thought dolefully, *but welcome and nourishing nonetheless.* First, however, they must rest.

They hugged one another against the chill of the unheated bookstore and in minutes both were sleeping like dog-tired children.

* * *

The tour guide, who was also the bus driver, stood in the middle of the *Sarena Jemija"* and spoke in French. "More than 30,000 eggs were used to prepare the paint and glaze that went into the elaborate decorations you see here." The class comedian let out a cackling noise that evoked guffaws from the boys, giggles from the girls, and earned a reproving glare from the woman in the skirt. "A major difference between this building and other Muslim mosques is that the site on which you are standing is not covered by the typical exterior dome, as is the case with most religious edifices of the early Ottoman Empire."

The guide, now encircled by the fifty or so children, chaperons, and Majors Kelvin and Cockbyrne, pointed to the ceiling without looking upward. "From your viewing standpoint, however, it seems that the roof of the 'Quilted Mosque' is indeed domed."

Everyone looked straight upward simultaneously. Indeed, the ceiling was painted with a series of concentric rings whose lines and decorative figures were pronounced in the exterior arcs, but dwindled in breadth, prominence, and spacing as they approached the middle of the array. The overall effect was that the whole roof appeared to be a hollow space…a vaulted cupola…a dome.

"This has been done intentionally," the guide said. "The distinguishing feature of this particular mosque is not its architectural conformation, but rather, its painted decorations." Now everyone was gazing upward, studying the almost hypnotic spheres. "In addition to the geometric and floral ornamentation…" The uniformed man droned on non-stop for another five minutes until the eyes of even the proctors began to glaze over. That's when the head chaperon scanned the faces of her fidgety charges and, having made an instinctive head count, suddenly bellowed, "Where are Jeannine and Henri?"

From the *mihrab* alcove, whose torn curtain still lay in one corner where Nazmi ben Zullah had shoved it, the two 12-year-olds emerged sheepishly, Jeannine blushing severely, Henri with fists rammed into his pockets in an unsuccessful attempt to hide the bulge in his pants. The girl was carrying a big leather pocketbook they'd found. The oversized Coach handbag was Lisbeth's, and both Doctors Cockbyrne and Kelvin recognized it immediately.

Chapter 57

The woman slid the inscribed flyer under the door of the locked bookstore.

At the conclusion of their visit, the French students and their chaperons, the adults having exchanged addresses, left their new American friends in the *Sarena Jemija*. The Doctors had decided to stay there and await the return of Colonel Wren. Surely Lisbeth would not have left her handbag behind if she'd planned to be gone for any significant period of time. The purse contained her photo ID, cash, family pictures, and of course the hundred-and-one essentials that regularly litter any woman's pocketbook.

In the farthest reaches of the McDonald's parking lot, the driver, having ushered the restless children onto the bus, climbed into his seat, pulled a long, hinged handle that closed the accordion door, and prepared to turn the key in the ignition. But before he could do so, the man was quickly approached from behind by one of the young monitors who ran up the aisle waving her 'Quilted Mosque' pamphlet.

She also held an accompanying leaflet listing 'Points of Interest in Tavoto.' One of them was marked with an asterisk and bore the italicized notation, *Open Sundays*. It was Lola Books…and the chaperon, pointing to a star on her map, wanted to know if it would be convenient to stop there.

The driver seemed skeptical—it was close to five o'clock, nearly his quitting time. Furthermore Madonica Travel Service was reporting on his pocket radio that traffic on the Ovosok highway was being diverted due to some sort of accident, and roads accessing the thoroughfare had been closed to all but law enforcement and military vehicles.

"We won't be long," the woman pleaded in French. "I'm sure the place is nearby, is it not?"

The man took the brochure, frowned impatiently as he recognized the Karaorman Road address, and sighed heavily. "Five minutes," he said with finality...and handed the leaflet back to the woman. She smiled her appreciation in the big rearview mirror and sat in the adjacent front seat, next to the older monitor in the pleated skirt.

The bus left the restaurant parking lot, crossed the lightly travelled Ilindenska Bridge, and in no time was parked on the worn cobblestones of Karaorman Road in front of Lola Books. "*Cinq minutes*," the guide reminded the chaperon with the pamphlets, who danced down the steps of the bus... only to find the bookstore closed. Disappointed, but not discouraged, the young woman seized a felt-tipped pen from her purse and scrawled a message in French on the face of the 'Quilted Mosque' brochure:

*J'ai besoin de deux livres pour les amis Americains—
une, en ce qui concerne 'Quincy', une, 'Baltimore.'
Je serai de retour demain.'
Merci!*

The woman slid the inscribed flyer under the door of the locked bookstore and hurried back to the idling bus. "Thank you," she said to the driver in French. She resumed her seat and told the senior chaperon what she had done.

"*Bon*," the woman said with a single, approving nod...and the chauffeur aimed the bus in the direction of the nearest access road connecting with the Ovosok highway. But like Reza Mimona's little bookstore, all northbound roads were already closed until further notice. There had been mention of a bomb.

* * *

Karaorman Road, and even more so, Ivo Ribar Alley, were in twilight when Bashkim stirred. Trying not to disturb Lisbeth, he stood, parted the beige curtain slightly, and peered into the shop from the stockroom.

All, save the dusk that marked incipient sunset, was as it had been. He and the Doctor were alone.

The Curator hurried about the business of preparing the shop for their overnight accommodation while he could still see what he was doing. Attending to activities that must be conducted in the darker rear section of the cluttered store was his first priority. He propped open the door of a tiny lavatory, utilizing a heavy volume of *Shakespeare's Complete Works* to do so...he used a *Roget's Thesaurus* to do the same with a narrow floor-to-ceiling cupboard door...and he hurriedly filled the espresso pot on the shop's lone round table, using coffee from an envelope dispenser and water from the bathroom sink. He then plugged the pot's electrical cord in a wall outlet as he had done during previous visits. Finally, he removed three large oatmeal muffins and two espresso cups from the cupboard and placed them on the same table that held the coffee maker.

Reza's store was well-supplied with matches on a shelf in the bathroom, a pile of split logs beside her Franklin stove, and a flashlight near the brass cash register...but using any of those items was out of the question. Though there was a bitter chill in the old building, and stacks of books and shipping cartons made moving about in the dark difficult, Bashkim and Lisbeth dared not risk lighting a fire or using any form of illumination to facilitate walking around. Smoke from the shop's rickety chimney, or even a telltale glint of light seen by anyone passing the Lola Books show window, could instantly reveal the presence of the hiding pair and jeopardize tomorrow's planned escape to Italy.

After using the facility himself, Bashkim pulled the overhead toilet-chain, washed his hands and face by the last gray vestiges of the sinking sun, and walked to the room's one vaguely illuminated area…the part of the shop by the front door, where the dull glow from a distant lamppost filtered through the store window…and revealed the inscribed *Sarena Jemija* brochure lying on the floor.

Fluent in four languages, the Curator held the pamphlet angled toward the window and read the message neatly written there in French.

"What's that?" Lisbeth's voice behind him was husky with sleep, and he turned to see her standing in the new *abaya,* hugging herself, and shivering noticeably. She had removed the *niqab* face covering and presumably it was on the floor where they had slept in the constricted closet.

Bashkim quickly doffed his new wool shirt and draped the heavy garment over the tall Doctor's shoulders. She thanked him with a kiss. The coffee was beginning to percolate and Lis turned in the direction of the bubbling sound. Still marveling at the grace with which she wore the burka, Bashkim led her to one of two chairs at the round table, then fetched Reza's precious bottle of Courvoisier from inside the counter by the cash register.

Lis was already biting ravenously into one of the oversized, still-moist muffins. Neither she nor the Curator had eaten anything all day. Bashkim filled their cups with steaming coffee and added a touch of brandy to his own. "What was that leaflet you were reading?" Lisbeth said, one hand holding the baked confection to her mouth, the other cupped under her chin to catch every wayward crumb.

"It's just an order for two books," said Bashkim dismissively. "Someone…a Frenchman…a woman from the looks of the handwriting…is looking for gifts for her American friends." He bit into the muffin and spoke somberly through the mouthful. "Poor Reza. I doubt she could have filled the request at any rate."

"Why is that?" said Lisbeth.

"The person wants one book about Quincy," the Curator said indifferently, "…and another one about Baltimore." He scanned the dozens and dozens of shelves now cloaked in darkness and said. "This is Tavoto, not New York. I doubt that Lola Books carries volumes dealing with either of those cities, celebrated though they may be."

Had there been any light in the bookstore at all, Bashkim Inasah would have seen that his friend blanched markedly. "May I see that pamphlet?" she said pensively, "…the one you were holding."

Bashkim Inasah slid the brochure across the table and Lisbeth could tell only that it was a visitor's guide to the *Sarena Jemija*. But even in the relative darkness that now shrouded the interior of the store…although Colonel Wren knew no French…and with only Bashkim's recent recollection to go by…the Doctor knew that this simple leaflet, and the four words, 'American Friends,' 'Quincy,' and 'Baltimore,' could lead to only one logical conclusion: Intentionally or

339

otherwise, Lisbeth's associates, Majors Cockbyrne and Kelvin, of Quincy and Baltimore respectively, had sent a message that was delivered while she was sleeping—and they might well be waiting for an answer...possibly inside the 'Quilted Mosque.'

Lisbeth reached across the table and found her friend's hand. "Will it be safe if we attend the *Evening Salat* at the mosque tonight?" she asked a startled Bashkim Inasah. "I think some of my associates are waiting there."

A long silence fell over the pair that had become lovers. Obviously neither of them was a devout Muslim, and it was common knowledge that the penalty for feigning devotion to Allah during *Salat* was *beheading*, if you were lucky enough to be dispatched quickly...*stoning* if you were less fortunate.

"Why not let me go and find your friends?" the Curator said. "I will give you money and meet you at the airport in Prishta."

Lisbeth tightened her grip on his fingers. "No. When I was waiting for you in 'Saint Holy Mother of God' I was convinced you had been killed. It was the worst night of my life. I wanted to die, myself, and I never want to experience that feeling again as long as I live."

"Think about it, *Habeeb Qalbi*," said Bashkim, rubbing the Doctor's hands to warm them. "There are two hours before the *Muezzin* calls. Consider the consequences. That is all I ask."

She looked at him as if he were a child that she adored, but found incorrigible. "But you're asking the impossible, *Habeeb*. Thinking about being away from you when you might need my help is a worse fate than anything that could possibly happen to me."

He studied her earnest face, barely visible in the unlit shop. "Get some rest," he said. "I will observe the street from here. You will sleep more peacefully knowing I am awake and watching."

"Wrong again," she said with a smile. "I rest better when we're in one another's arms." And she drew him toward the curtain that formed the back wall. "Come on, we'll be able to hear the *Muezzin* from inside the storage area. Trust me."

Chapter 58

No exceptions. Violators could be...and in some circumstances were...shot!

Nazmi ben Zullah and his hapless driver had no choice but to pull over to the side of the Tavoto/Skopje municipal highway when directed to do so. Sergeant Stefan Naumov's contingent was the only active delegation of Tavoto policemen not assigned to 'keeping the peace' in the seventeen various soccer stadiums that dotted the landscape in Madonica... and had it not been for the Acting Chief's disciplinary order, even they would have been cheering themselves hoarse along with their football-addicted neighbors. As it was, the formerly disgruntled officers now found themselves endowed with more unquestioned authority than at any other time in their brief careers.

Immediately upon hearing the ear-splitting blast a mile south of the border that separates tiny Madonica from Ovosok, Naumov knew he was dealing with a bomb. He had learned to identify such explosions during the conflict that accompanied the volatile breakup of old Yugoslavia into Principalities.

There was one firm set of procedures to be followed in these violent situations: First, and most important: All non-emergency vehicular traffic was halted, and motorists were confined to their conveyances...even pedestrians were promptly sent or brought directly to their homes, schools, or churches.

Second: Quasi-responsible parties (sanitation workers, park attendants, and military personnel home on leave or visiting) were subject to being deputized at the discretion of law enforcement authorities.

And third: Anyone resisting Police, Fire, or EMS agencies was liable to summary arrest.

There would be no exceptions. 'Zero Tolerance' the Americans called such an arrangement.

Violators could be…and in some circumstances were… shot!

Naumov himself had flagged down Grand Imam ben Zullah's Mercedes on the Skopje highway. It was less than five minutes after the fireball that killed Eric Mueller had lit up the sunset sky over Tavoto, and burning residue from the blast pockmarked the roof of the black limousine. It was clear that the Muslim clerics had been in close proximity to the detonation…and so far they were the only potential witnesses the Sergeant had.

"Kindly remain here," he said. "A few questions, please. Give me a moment." The Sergeant turned to leave.

"*Svinya edna!*" the *Mullah* hissed—"*Stupid wild pig.*"

Stefan Naumov heard the muttered remark…and though it was issued in Farsi, he understood it, too. Through the open driver's side window he glared at the sullen cleric in the plush rear seat. "What did you call me, Imam?"

Wisely, ben Zullah looked off to his right and did not answer.

"Stay with this vehicle," Naumov instructed one of the members of his entourage. "I will return in some minutes… then we will see who is a stupid wild pig."

* * *

With Aamil and Aalil dead of their gunshot wounds... most of the other *Sarena Jemija* clerics searching for Lisbeth and Bashkim amid the ruins of 'Saint Holy Mother of God'...and ben Zullah being detained with his driver near the scene of the explosion that killed Captain Mueller... only three relatively inexperienced *Mullahs* remained in the 'Quilted Mosque' as night fell. One cleric, the sniper in the minaret, had fallen asleep but was awakened by the detonation on the Tavoto/Ovosok highway...another was preparing to conduct the *Evening Salat*...and the third was readying the underground Operating Suite for the Grand Imam's late night inspection.

Doctors Peggy Kelvin and Ophelia Cockbyrne, too, had heard the explosion east of town and concluded that it was a bomb blast similar to the IEDs, the Improvised Explosive Devices, they'd had to deal with during previous deployments in Iraq and Afghanistan. The Majors had planned to await Lisbeth's return inside the 'Painted Mosque,' but they abandoned their bench beneath an ornate *Pulpito* when the building quickly filled with sweaty, frightened Muslims, many of whom eyed the American women with open suspicion.

As an alternate plan, Cockbyrne and Kelvin strolled the *Sarena Jemija* gardens, keeping well clear of the mosque itself, lest it be targeted for destruction by some rival religious faction, but staying close enough to keep an eye on the main entrance. They also watched for any activity in the vicinity of Bashkim Inasah's silver Citroen, parked askew on the *Ulica Goce Delcev*, another indication that Doctor Wren could not be far away.

The rifleman in the balcony drew a bead on first one of the immodestly dressed American women, then the other. *They must be new recruits for the Grand Imam*, he reasoned. And he went back to sleep, hugging his rifle and thanking Allah for the great gift of wisdom.

In front of the *turbe*, on the Meditation Bench where they were seated, the Majors listened as the call to prayer wafted from the minaret. The recorded evening chant was programmed to play somewhat more softly than the summonses piped from the speakers during the day. The effect throughout the old section of Tavoto was not unpleasant, and even the sniper in the circular balcony high on the tower slept through the wailing intonation.

Kelvin and Cockbyrne were watching and waiting as believers began to drift toward the 'Quilted Mosque,' when Ophelia suddenly grasped Peggy Kelvin's forearm. "Don't look now," the GP whispered, "...but isn't that the big guy we saw with Lisbeth yesterday...the one who drives that French car?"

The Psychiatrist looked toward the mosque's main entrance where a boy was issuing plastic bags in which the faithful would carry their shoes during the upcoming *Evening Salat*. Major Kelvin squinted and leaned forward in concentration. "Jesus, it looks like him," she murmured. "But if it is, our girl Lisbeth's just been jilted."

"Jilted?...you mean as in ditched? Why?"

"Jilted, as in 'dropped,' 'walked out on,' 'left in the lurch,' 'see ya later.' What other kind of jilting is there?" Peggy bobbed her head in the direction of the *Sarena Jemija* entranceway. "Check out the tall job in the gray burka. That sure as hell ain't Romeo's mother!"

"Ohmygod!" said Cockbyrne, turning and lowering her head, "...it looks like he recognizes us. Maybe he saw us in front of the Henschel woman's house. Oh-oh, I think they're coming our way."

Major Kelvin sat more erect and braced herself. "Let me handle this." She reached in her handbag and released the hidden Beretta's safety. "If anything's happened to Lisbeth, this guy's gonna be one sorry Casanova."

Chapter 59

The dust dispersed amid the red, blue, and amber glimmers cast by the emergency light.

Sergeant Naumov had sent his team ahead to make sure that vehicular traffic to and from the area of the explosion had been halted. Only pregnant women, children under the age of six, and the elderly were to be taken to their destinations by Madonican Army conveyances. The camouflaged trucks and weapons carriers were already lined up along the highway west of Skopje for that purpose.

When Naumov returned to ben Zullah's limousine parked beside the road leading to Marshal Tito Boulevard, the lone Deputy that Naumov had retained parked the staff car at an angle in front of the Mercedes and activated the multi-colored light bar on the roof. He and the Sergeant then departed their sedan and walked in the gloom toward the black Mercedes-Benz.

When the Acting Chief reached the big car and signaled for the driver to turn down his window, ben Zullah's man did so with a smile. The Deputy standing some ten feet behind the Sergeant was, as instructed, watching for any oncoming vehicles that might approach from either direction. Accordingly, he did not see the driver in the flowing *Galabiyya* pull Naumov's head inside the car, swiftly raise the window severely compressing the Sergeant's trachea, and summarily jam a stiletto through his eye and far into his brain...killing the gallant Stefan Naumov instantly.

Ben Zullah's driver quickly started the Mercedes, and with the Sergeant's corpse hanging from the side of the car by his neck, jammed the transmission into 'drive.' The black limousine screeched from the shoulder of the road and sped directly toward the unbelieving patrolman. He fired a burst from his AK-47 and simultaneously dove to his right, toward the side of the road, and landed on his face in a gravel drainage ditch. Five rounds had torn diagonally through the car's dark-tinted windshield and three of them ripped into the Muslim driver's face, neck, and chest. The action might have saved Naumov's young Deputy, but the cleric he had shot bounced heavily off of the leather seat and onto the steering wheel, his sandaled foot caught in the hem of his *Galabiyya*, where it stayed wedged on the accelerator. With its horn blaring and its big rear wheels throwing dirt and rocks in their wake, the Mercedes flew into the shallow ditch where the helpless officer lay screaming. The five thousand pound automobile landed fully on the prone man's torso.

The lives of the three dead men had ended in a matter of seconds. And as the dust dispersed in the twilight, amid the alternate red, blue, and amber glimmers cast by the police car's emergency light bar, Nazmi ben Zullah crawled from the rear door of the hissing vehicle, limped to the idling staff car, and drove unimpeded in the direction of *Sarena Jemija*,... where there was still work to be done.

* * *

Bashkim had been surprised by a sharpshooter in the minaret balcony once too often to suit him. He therefore directed Lisbeth to follow him at a twelve-foot distance, as he approached the American women with one eye peeled for any movement from the tower. The arrangement would not be suspect if a sentry were watching from above. Muslim women were frequently required to walk behind their husbands, fathers, and even sons. When he reached the bench where the distrustful Majors sat watching the couple's approach, Bashkim slowly raised a finger of caution vertically across his lips, and to Lisbeth's surprise, he turned left and soon disappeared inside the mausoleum.

Still unrecognized by her associates, Lis motioned for them to follow her, and she too walked to the *turbe*, where she waited for them by the open door.

By now both Kelvin and Cockbyrne had a firm grip on the weapons in their handbags, and with Peggy scanning the area to their right, and Ophelia checking the shadows on the left, they soon positioned themselves flush against either side of the entrance to the crypt.

Where Lisbeth, standing deep in the darkness of the granite portal, slowly slid the *niqab* from her face.

Ophelia Cockbyrne thought her eyes must be deceiving her, and Kelvin's gun hand went limp. Both women shakily engaged their Beretta's safeties. "Holy crap!" the Psychiatrist whispered to Lis. "Promise me you won't pull that on anybody with a weak heart, girlfriend." She fanned her face with her hand.

Ophelia dropped the gun into her pocketbook and held Lis Wren at arm's length by the shoulders. "Geez, Colonel, have I got my dates screwed up or wasn't Halloween three weeks ago?" The three women embraced and Bashkim gently but busily ushered them into the unlighted mausoleum. He then closed the *turbe* door and locked it with his large iron key.

"This is my friend Bashkim," said Lis. "It's a long story. But you can trust him."

The Curator nodded while continuing to scan the interior of the crypt. "Are you armed?" he asked, and he produced Lisbeth's sidearm from under the belt at the small of his back.

"We're out of ammo," Lis said, releasing the empty magazine from the handle of her pistol and passing it to Major Kelvin. "Divvy up whatever we've got among the three of us."

"I'll go you one better," said Ophelia. She rummaged in the large handbag "Here's a full magazine compliments of the Quartermaster at Fort Bliss." She tossed the jet-black container to Lisbeth.

"This is heavy."

"High capacity—thirty rounds," said Major Cockbyrne. "I don't need it...everybody knows I never miss."

Lisbeth shoved the magazine into the gun's handle and extended the considerably heavier weapon to Bashkim. The Curator, in turn, returned it to the belt at his back. As he continued to grope behind the marble slabs that formed the top of the tomb, Inasah felt a cardboard box that had not been there the last time he and the American Doctor had descended into the subterranean corridor.

Peggy Kelvin produced her keychain with its tiny light.

In seconds Bashkim had identified a partial two-cubic-foot container of plastic-wrapped Semtex, disposable cell phones, and pre-wired detonators...and he knew intuitively what had caused the blast east of town.

Before he could turn off Major Kelvin's penlight, a single shot from an AK-47 rang out and its M43 projectile careened off of the *turbe's* bulletproof east window. He hurriedly filled his pockets from the cardboard box...then swung away the slab that covered the hidden passageway leading to *Sarena Jemija's* prayer room. "Quickly," he said. "Follow me."

Chapter 60

Bashkim appeared in the mihrab and finally vanished through the low door.

When they had made their way through the underground tunnel that led from the *turbe*, past the empty Conference Room and Operating Suite, and the circular ladder that rose to the *mihrab*, the Majors had become virtually dumbstruck. As a General Practitioner, Cockbyrne knew without asking what the labyrinth had been constructed for, but Psychiatrist Peggy Kelvin was full of questions. This, however, was neither the place nor the time for them. Only escape mattered to Inasah and the American women, though in his heart of hearts, not even Bashkim was confident that a successful getaway was likely.

For one thing: *When would the search party return from 'Saint Holy Mother of God?'* Surely they would come directly to *Sarena Jemija* to report to the Grand Imam their failure to locate Doctor Wren, unpleasant though that prospect may be.

And equally important: *Where was ben Zullah?* Bashkim had hoped to encounter him in the clerics' Meeting Room, but not another soul was to be seen in the subterranean maze.

Still, without a plan, all would surely be lost…so the Curator had devised a fundamental strategy.

In the confusion that preceded the *Evening Salat*, Lisbeth, armed with Kelvin's Beretta, would emerge first from the tunnel into the *mihrab* alcove. There, dressed as she was to blend-in with the Muslim faithful, she would act as a lookout while Ophelia and Peggy took Bashkim's key and admitted themselves to his office, where all four, hopefully, would eventually meet.

Phase two involved Bashkim's exit from the prayer room via the door at the base of the minaret, as Lis assumed a kneeling position to the rear of the gathered worshippers, where she would not be seen by the men in front of her facing Mecca. The Curator, detonator in hand, would affix his pocketful of Semtex to the base of the minaret and return to the central room taking up a position in the rear phalanx of the men and boys…as near to Lisbeth as possible.

Finally, when the *Salat* was ended, he would trigger the explosive charge. The blast would have a dual effect: It would eliminate the sniper…and the resulting chaos would provide cover for Bashkim and the three women…who would make their escape in the Citroen on narrow *Goce Delcev*.

A barefoot young Imam took his place in front of the kneeling believers.

As the throng lowered their foreheads to the *Sarena Jemija* floor, Lisbeth, Peggy, and Ophelia emerged from the tunnel entrance hidden in the *mihrab* alcove. Lisbeth in her burka, clutching her sandals, proceeded to the rear of the devotees' ranks. The Majors scurried to the Curator's office, where they admitted themselves with his key and locked the door.

Seconds later, Bashkim too, appeared in the *mihrab*, wound his way among the shadows cast on the wall by a dozen decorative *pulpito*, and finally vanished through the low door that led to the minaret.

He returned in minutes. While Lisbeth watched through the screen of her *niqab*, he waited for the next lowering of faces to floor-level, then jerked his head toward the office where Kelvin and Cockbyrne waited. The Colonel rose and inconspicuously followed the rear wall...the one farthest from Mecca...to the partly opened door where Bashkim stood holding a plain cell phone. "It's our only way out," he said. "...but first we must wait until the worshippers have gone." He tucked the phone into the pocket of his new wool shirt. "Stand over there and watch," he said, pointing. "Come back and knock twice as soon as the last of them has left."

* * *

Lisbeth feigned an attempt to re-position the filmy curtain that ben Zullah had torn from the *mihrab* in his earlier pique. A final handful of devotees worked their way toward the arched front exit. Only one dirty pilgrim in a soiled *Galabiyya* remained kneeling in prayer in the leftmost corner of the 'Quilted Mosque.'

After the disguised Doctor Wren had fidgeted with the gossamer drapery to no avail, she folded the curtain into a compact square and tossed it beside the copies of the Koran piled in the alcove. The unkempt man stood laboriously and hobbled to the Taharah font, where he washed his forehead and dried his hands and face on the sleeve of his robe.

As the man went about the ritual cleansing, Lisbeth impatiently piled the copies of the Holy Koran in neat stacks, waiting expectantly for the man to leave. But he had resumed his kneeling...and seemed to have fallen asleep.

Or perhaps he was ill—he had appeared disoriented when performing Taharah.

The Colonel's first inclination was to approach the disheveled man and somehow determine if he was feverish. If she were to help him to his feet, that brief contact in itself might be enough to permit a primitive diagnosis. She sidled in his direction, bent over the scruffy fellow, and eased her hand into his damp armpit to awaken him.

With the swiftness of a cobra, Nazmi ben Zullah seized Lisbeth Wren in what her Police trainers had described as a 'choke hold.' She recognized it as a law enforcement officer's maneuver of last resort, the frequently fatal move that involves holding someone helpless by wedging an arm around their neck…with sufficient pressure on the throat to make breathing difficult…perhaps impossible.

Lisbeth was unable to summon enough air to scream…or even to cough. She grabbed the Grand Imam's forearm and elbow, frantically raking them with her modest fingernails, but the action served only to increase the absolute dominance that the *Mullah* had over her. Had she been standing, her substantial height might have given her enough leverage to throw the older man over her back, she thought. But ben Zullah had cleverly brought the Doctor's buttocks to the floor the instant that he'd collared her…and he squatted there, with Lisbeth powerless in his tortuous grip, as she saw bright, white pinwheels before her eyes…the prelude to lost consciousness.

With ferocity that belied his modest size, the Grand Imam shook Lisbeth's increasingly flushed head with sudden, jarring bursts of power until, to the *Mullah's* amazement, the violent thrusts dislodged Peggy Kelvin's nine millimeter weapon from the trouser waistband beneath Lisbeth's burka. The gun tumbled free, slid across the floor, and slammed against the base of Bashkim's door.

Determined to grab the automatic, but unwilling to release his killing stranglehold on Lisbeth's neck, ben Zullah dragged the weakened Doctor to the Curator's office with one powerful arm. Once there, he snatched up the weapon, disengaged the safety, and pressed the muzzle of the pistol to the side of Lis Wren's sweating head.

With two final spurts of energy, the wiry Doctor stretched her feet forward and kicked on the door twice. In response, Bashkim, his Beretta extended, thrust open the door…and seeing Lisbeth's predicament, instantly stiffened.

Ben Zullah backed up, withdrawing toward the front of the prayer room—slowly retreating in the direction of Mecca. Lisbeth was now limp, immobile. Thankfully, the unconscious Colonel Wren would never feel a killing shot. And as soon as the Grand Imam had squeezed the trigger, Bashkim would no longer have any reason to hesitate…he would fire as many rounds as necessary into the grinning face of the cleric. It would be the end of ben Zullah…but the victory would be won at such a devastating cost, it would amount to a heartrending defeat.

The roar of the nine millimeter discharge resonated throughout the practically empty *Sarena Jemija*, and Doctor Lisbeth Wren fell to the rich Persian carpet.

Frozen where he stood, the Curator could only stare and gasp…the hollow-nosed bullet that entered Nazmi ben Zullah's left eye tore off the back of his head, showering the forward wall of the 'Quilted Mosque' in a cascade of blood, bone, and cranial matter.

"I told you I never miss," said a scornful Major Cockbyrne from behind Bashkim Inasah. She continued to hold the smoking Beretta…level…rock solid…both hands fully extended. But there was clearly no need for a second shot. "Somebody help me revive the Colonel," Ophelia finally said, "…then I suggest we get the hell out of here."

"The *turbe*," Bashkim shouted, opening the tunnel door and holding it. The two Majors half-carried Lisbeth Wren into the dark void and down the metal stairway. The Curator dialed the detonator phone…transmitted the signal…and quickly pulled the iron door shut.

EPILOGUE

The straightforward escape from *Sarena Jemija* went as Bashkim had planned, and after a two-day de-briefing at Camp Billingham, Lieutenant Colonel Lisbeth Wren, Major Cockbyrne, and Major Kelvin were sent home. In Washington, the women underwent another weeklong interrogation in The Pentagon before being assigned to administrative duty stateside. If any censure of Balkan civilian officials was issued by the US State Department, NATO, or the United Nations, it was done in secret.

Before Lisbeth could return to her home in Plainview, Long Island, the elderly Doctor Simeon Forrester died of complications from a Black Widow spider bite, suffered when he opened a mysterious package said to have been sent from either Spain or Portugal.

Bashkim Inasah, after a brief working vacation in France, was named Curator of St. George's famed Greek Orthodox Church in Jordan. The appointment, a most prestigious one, was secretly facilitated by the CIA.

Peter Ravens fulfilled a lifelong dream when he became 'Low Amateur' in the 2011 US Open Golf Tournament. In congratulations, Lisbeth bought him a French Bulldog, actually intended to keep little 'Gigi' company. She named the dog 'Pedro.'

Hanna Henschel returned to her native Germany, where she teaches cooking at a school for young Roman Catholic nuns. She has been, at long last, accepted by both her family and Otto's.

Amy Longpré, Mayor Milevski, and the soldiers at Camp Billingham, being unfamiliar with clandestine organ trafficking in The Balkans and beyond, continue to go about their lives as if nothing particularly unusual had ever taken place in November of 2010. It is commonly known, however, that illicit commerce in human organs still thrives in Eastern Europe.